Gerald Hanley was born in 1916 and when he was nineteen went out to East Africa to run a ranch. During the war he served in Africa and Burma in the 11th East African Division, attaining the rank of major, and then served as a war correspondent. His first novel, *THE CONSUL AT SUNSET*, was begun on a return trip from India where he later returned for four years to research the background for his classic account of the end of Empire in the sub-continent – *THE JOURNEY HOMEWARD*. Among his other books are *GILLI-GAN'S LAST ELEPHANT* and *WARRIORS AND STRANGERS*.

Gerald Hanley lives in Co. Wicklow, Eire.

Gerald Hanley

NOBLE DESCENTS

Abacus edition published in 1983 by
Sphere Books Ltd
30–32 Gray's Inn Road, London WC1X 8JL

First published in Great Britain by
Hamish Hamilton Ltd 1982

Reproduced, printed and bound in Great Britain by
Hazell Watson & Viney Ltd, Aylesbury, Bucks

For Kate Carney
Mo ghrada go daingean tú

'Do not attempt to do us any more good.
Your good has done us too much harm already.'
—*Muhammad Abduh*

CHAPTER 1

In the valley of Induspur, one of the smallest of the Indian states, curious things began to occur among the few Europeans left there after the end of British rule. For instance, the day after the declaration of Indian Independence Colonel Bingham ('after all nobody's ever really *known* him. Don't forget that') appeared in Indian dress ('yes! And in the *Club*, my dear'). Mrs Tone had driven wildly round the valley with the news.

Not only had nobody 'really *known*' Colonel Bingham but he had been the model of retired British colonelhood, until the day when that tall, commanding, straight-backed figure with the close-cropped grey hair, so familiar in sports jacket and khaki drill slacks, strolled into the Indus Club in Indian dress ('cool as a cucumber, my dear, or perhaps the right word would be *insulting* — yes, I know, don't say it, a cucumber cannot be insulting, but you *know what I mean*'). Mrs Tone could easily become confused when even more excited than usual.

There was nothing exotic about the colonel's Indian dress, nothing silly or overdone. Rather it was sensible, cool, comfortable, and as he said himself, long overdue.

'That was the beginning of it all, of all the ghastly things that followed in the valley,' Mrs Tone would write to her sister, 'now that this whole frightful business is over,' long after Colonel Bingham's shocking departure from the known and steady ways of a true sahib. Certainly the colonel's amazing act could be seen as a symbol of the changes that were to come in the valley, the 'beginning of everything' as seen by Mrs Tone, but it really had nothing to do with what happened in the nineteen fifties.

Yet something might be said for Mrs Tone's theory, for a couple of years after Bingham's silent declaration of sartorial freedom and comfort, Major Brett-Turner ('Always rather insecure, I mean *socially*, you know what I mean —') did an

1

even stranger thing. He left his wife and moved into an empty bungalow on Buggers' Ridge at the end of the valley ('Deserted now by that awful trio, thank God,' Mrs Tone wrote to her sister, referring to three retired military homosexuals who had gone with Independence). He not only moved house but pinned a paper on the faded, torn, baize notice-board of the club which caused Mrs Tone to drive about the valley with the news for days, in an ecstasy of angry and joyful self-righteousness, as if she knew that the major's notice was specially for her.

The major, a small, nervous man in his early forties, still suffering from the effects of three years endured as a prisoner of the Japanese, must have spent a lot of time achieving the final draft of his paper.

It was headed 'Declaration of Independence', and began, 'To All Whom it will most certainly concern, bearing in mind the fascination which the private lives of people living in this Whispering Gallery Mark II have for two or three particular people I need not name, and to short-circuit all coming *bazaar-gup* and gossip, and in fact to stir things up a bit and give a fillip to public gossip in general, I wish to announce that the long-suffering lady who has been my wife, and I, have at last agreed on an amicable separation for my adultery not as yet committed, and, it is to be hoped, which will stay uncommitted, providing that the necessary Strength of Will, Sense of What is Right and Proper, etc, can be maintained, and I am therefore moving house. Further details will be announced from time to time. The likelihood that there is another lady in my life may be therefore safely entertained, though no definite structure should be built on this fact until further notice. That I should add "My wife also has another man in her life" would, as we all know, be bloody silly, and quite unnecessary considering the gossip about that side of it that the two or three people already referred to have manufactured over the years. All Whom it will most certainly concern will know who I mean, of course. Bulletins will be issued from time to time, and another Declaration can be expected as and when "things" come to a final agreement between myself and "the other woman". Signed, Walter Brett-Turner, Maj. (ret.).'

Even the usually reserved Colonel Bingham gave voice about this shocking public statement ('On the very notice-board

2

of the club for the whole world to read, my dear'). He turned to the man beside him and said, 'Letter from an escaped P.O.W., wouldn't you say?' The others around him, staring at the notice-board in shock, turned their heads to look at him. None of them had ever really understood the enigmatic Bingham who could say such puzzling things, and always straight-faced. They watched him, in his long white cotton *kurta*, an Indian shirt reaching almost to his knees, and his wide loose white cotton *salwar* which flopped about his sandalled feet, as he walked into the bar. Then they broke into chatter about this new and exciting scandal which had such enormous possibilities, such promise of a long drama to come.

Whispering Gallery Mark II, as Brett-Turner had called Induspur valley in his Declaration, like the old British hill-stations, had always made and lived on scandal. An 'independent' state within British India, it had never been a true hill-station, but its rulers had welcomed the British as well as the money they brought, and the Maharajahs had allowed them to rent land and build houses there. Two battalions of the state forces had served in the old Indian army and the Induspur club had never been confined to white membership. Even so only four Indians, all ex-officers, had applied for and been accepted for membership after Indian Independence, because the state was so old and hidebound in its own traditions and caste system that no Induspuri gentleman had wished to have membership of the club, not feeling the need for it. The four Indian members, nostalgic like all soldiers for the company of their own kind, now lived in a sort of mid-air with the departure of British rule, and felt even closer these days to their fellow British club members.

The club was small and consisted of the bar, dining room, library, lounge, and a couple of office buildings. Its tennis court had a good lawn, at this height, but as so many British had departed with Indian Independence the club seemed a lonely and somewhat deserted place these days.

As he reached the bar Bingham smiled to himself, thinking of the noise there would have been in the bar in the old days if they had just read Wally's statement out there. He ordered a *burra peg* and then hoisted himself up onto the high bar stool and leaned on the highly polished brass skin of the bar. As the barman, a Kashmiri Pandit called Janki Nath, poured his whiskey Bingham watched the half-dozen people at the notice-board in the hall slowly break up and drift off in twos in various directions in order to discuss this astonishing notice they had just read. Scandal always had to be tested and worked over first in twos, attitudes and opinions felt for and defined, until a general attitude was safely and carefully discovered, usually in order to discover the one who was going to stand against the stream. There was always an eccentric opinion to be found, though in a matter of sexual scandal such as this promised so hopefully to be, it would be the firmer of the women who would in the end induce the others, men and women alike, to adopt a correct public attitude to the scandal, no matter what they might feel privately. And it was going to be difficult, Bingham considered as he raised his glass, because he doubted if even Mrs Tone knew who 'the other woman' was in this case, the woman hinted at in Brett-Turner's amusing little bombshell out there in the hall.

'I'd say that bit of paper out there is the start of Wally's cure, wouldn't you?' said a voice. It was the man to whom he had addressed his remark at the notice-board. Bingham nodded, thoughtful now as he ordered another *burra peg*.

'M'm.' Bingham looked into the man's shrewd little grey eyes. He was not a fellow he would have bothered to have much to do with in other circumstances, but up here with so few of them left you could not be choosy about a companion for a drink these days. Not that Bingham had ever been very gregarious. 'He had a bad time with the Japs,' Bingham went on. 'But coming back and discovering that Meg — etcetera, hit him very hard.' Bingham usually used etcetera if matters of this kind came up for discussion, for everyone was sure to quote everyone else, and he liked to think of himself being reported as having said that somebody or other had committed or had been known to have been involved in etcetera.

Meg Brett-Turner, it was said, had had a strange, wild, completely out-of-character love affair with an American towards the end of the war, in which he was said to have been killed. It, the love affair, had happened in the years of the usual uncertainty which relatives of those captured by the Japanese had had to endure. There were no notifications from the Japanese world of 'killed in action', 'missing', 'prisoner of war'; nothing.

'I thought they were taking it well, didn't you?' Bingham's

4

companion said, ordering another two *burra pegs*. 'Though why the hell she had to tell Wally at all beats me.'

'Come, come!' said Bingham. 'She *had* to be first with the news — in this bloody whispering gallery — one of the women here would have done it otherwise — she was honest about it. Otherwise she would have been "found out" by Wally. Poor Meg.'

'Yes, true. What's he mean, by the way, by Whispering Gallery Mark II. What's Mark I?'

'Mark I,' said Bingham, 'was Kashmir. Now *there* was a real snake-pit in the old days. You couldn't scratch your behind there but it was reported not only all over the countryside but down in Delhi as well.'

He wanted to go. He was well into a long article about the use of *Abjad* in the Arabic inscriptions left by fifteenth and sixteenth century Moghul architects on their buildings, while winding into it a great deal of interesting military lore, for *Backwoods*, a magazine printed in America and owned by an obviously eccentric Irish-American millionaire called Francis X. Condy. The magazine specialized in military history and, unusually for an Irish-American, Condy seemed to be fascinated by the British Empire. He was also, it seemed, very interested in Bingham himself, annoyingly so, for Bingham had received a letter from him a month ago expressing great pleasure about his article entitled 'Asvamedha', a very learned piece about the Hindu horse-sacrifice which he had laced with much obscure and little-known information about the Indo-European horse culture in antiquity. And Condy had gone on to write, 'I was pleased to discover you are an Irishman, like so many thousands of other soldiers of the British army since the time they no longer had to serve in the Irish Brigades of Spain and France in order to hold a commission.'

Except for two or three other Irishmen, and *they* had had to discover it by accident, or guess, or inference, or close questioning, nobody in India knew Bingham was an Irishman. So Condy had been doing some research on him. Prickled by the thought of this, Bingham had sat down and acknowledged Condy's letter and congratulations, and had added, yes, he was an Irishman, though not really what one might call a 'professional'.

He was not listening to the man sitting on the next stool but, an old hand when bored or with thoughts racing on another subject, he nodded in the right places as if by instinct, even his eyes on the other's while his mind was now writing the final paragraph of the article which so absorbed him.

As they finished their drinks, he suddenly realized why he tolerated and even quite liked the man talking at his side. Not only was he obviously a well read man — previous conversations in the club had revealed this characteristic, most unusual up here — but he had spent his professional life in South India, another world, as it had always been in history, and he was not stained by all the old lore of British north Indian gossip about marriages and adulteries, regimental scandals and whatnot. After two years or retirement in Induspur all the man knew of British private folklore here was hearsay, all well sieved, glossed and imprimatured by the final editor of such material, Mrs Tone. Little did he know, for instance, that Mrs Tone had been in correspondence with an old friend in Madras about his life down there. Tone himself, who edited all his wife's letters unknown to her, had told Bingham — an unwilling listener this, and Bingham was the only other person beside her husband who knew that it had been Mrs Tone who had convulsed the valley four years before with a series of ingenious poison-pen letters.

CHAPTER 2

As he walked back to his bungalow Bingham was remembering with amusement, though rueful, that time which was still know as 'the poison-pen period'. It was after the fifth or sixth poison-pen letter that he had suddenly remembered Mrs Tone had received the first one. He was the first she had shown it to. He had refused to read it.

They were in the club library. Mrs Tone was an intelligent and attractive woman of about fifty with a soft velvet voice, and took great but careful pains to try and make friends with Bingham. He too took pains with her whenever she approached him, but in an effort to stay aloof, non-committal, and to withdraw and escape as quickly as he could. But he was trapped that time, right in the middle of one of his pleasures, choosing the week's reading from the well stocked club library. Bingham was in charge of the club library finances so he had the pleasure of choosing and buying all new books from Delhi and Bombay.

'I'm sorry, Mrs Tone,' he said pleasantly, angered, as she continued to press the letter on him, 'I don't read other people's letters. After all – there's a whole library here.' He waved his hands at the bookshelves.

'Oh, you won't be reading other people's letters, Colonel,' she said. 'This is an *anonymous* letter.' He was interested at once and withdrew, crossing the room to another wall of books, calling as he went, 'How intriguing for you, Mrs Tone.'

'But it's very worrying, Colonel,' she said, following him. 'Don't you understand? It's a poison-pen letter. It actually calls me "a scheming, dangerous woman who will soon enough receive her just deserts".' Bingham had now climbed the tall ladder and was pretending to study the top shelf of books, and Mrs Tone relentlessly read the whole of the letter to him.

It had not occurred to him then that she could possibly be

the writer of the letter, and, his neck hair tingling as he listened to the first anonymous letter he had ever encountered, he turned and watched her below him as she read it to him. For the first time he realized how sinister an anonymous letter could be — 'You think you're beautiful, the cynosure of every man's eye,' she was reading, 'but it won't be long until you're a hag. I await that day, you bitch, and remember that I'm watching you ageing daily. You've broken the hearts of many men and you'll pay for that some day —'

'I don't want to hear any more of it, Mrs Tone, do you hear me?' he said in a loud commanding voice, and she stopped and looked up at him, hurt in her eyes.

'What should I do about it?' she asked, waving the letter. 'There'll be more, you can be sure of that. It cannot be allowed.'

She was right there, he supposed, but he said dismissively, 'Why ask me? You've got a husband. Ask *him*.' Tears had appeared in her eyes.

A marvellous performance, he reflected now as he turned into the bazaar and lit a cigarette. He was making so many dollars with his writings, on top of his pension, that he went over to the Pagji Liquordrome and ordered a case of the best whiskey in the store. While old Pagji poured him a whiskey on the house, as usual, he wondered again if he should not break camp and leave this bloody valley, something he wondered every day, while the other part of his mind fingered the memory of when he had received his anonymous letter. He laughed when he thought of how he had dealt with it, pitilessly yes, but it had had to be done. A guess, true, but he had been right. He had typed it, and being the old Intelligence hand he was, had come into this very liquor store and asked old Pagji if he could type a note on his archaic machine. Certainly, Sahib.

'Dear Mrs Tone,' he had typed, having waited of course until another two or three victims had received *their* anonymous letters, so she would not connect his reply with him, 'many thanks for your most interesting anonymous letter and its various enlightening remarks on my shortcomings in general. In this climate we are all liable to various diseases, physical and mental, and suffer from strains of all kinds from time to time. Now, if you continue to write these painful and wounding letters to people somebody is going to have the courage to go to the state police and complain. There will be an investigation and you will certainly be caught. You must think about what this will do to you and your husband, for the police, not wishing to embarrass the small British community here, will demand that you leave the state. You must not allow things to reach that pass. You need a holiday, a break from this valley. Take it now. A couple of months in Delhi now the cold weather is here will do you the world of good, and see a doctor there who will prescribe some of these new wonder pills which will help to dispel the anxieties which are causing you to write these wicked letters. Nobody but this writer knows you are writing these letters, be assured, and your secret, I promise, will never be revealed. But you must see a doctor, and soon. Sincerely.'

Within forty-eight hours Mrs Tone had left for Delhi.

'Have you car with you, Colonel Sahib?'

'Er—no,' Bingham said, suddenly aware of where he was. 'Just send it up to the bungalow,' he said, smiling at the old man. 'And thanks for the drink.'

'Great pleasure, Colonel Sahib.'

He strode out of the bazaar and onto the road now called Sardar Patel Marg. Patel, the iron man who had wrapped up the princely states so swiftly after the British had handed over, each state having nervously watched Hyderabad in its useless but understandable effort to stay aloof as a separate kingdom. It had all worked out quite happily once Patel had acted. Those museums of India's ancient past were now part of the new state of India.

A couple of days after Mrs Tone had scuttled off to Delhi in obedience to his advice her husband waylaid him as he was riding up to the palace for an evening with his old friend, the Maharajah. They were not far from the club and because Tone's request — 'Have you a moment, Bingham? I need your advice' — had urgency in it he had dismounted and accepted a cigarette from Tone. It was part of Bingham's unwanted role to be consulted by people, to be trusted, asked for advice — 'It's well known you stay out of all this bloody gossip here, Bingham' — or — 'I can't tell this to anyone, Bingham, but I know I can trust you.' It was the payment for staying aloof; being part of the crowd when it was there, yes, but always aloof, always alone, no matter who he was with.

'What is it, Tone? Anything I can do?' Christ, there he

went, asking for it again. Would he ever learn? No, probably never. But he was a little nervous. Mrs Tone was capable of just about anything when it came to indiscretion, and she might have shown Tone the anonymous letter he had written her. An anonymous letter was a hell of a thing to get, even when you knew who had written it. It was as if an adder, a *krait*, had crawled out of the envelope into your hand. It must certainly have shaken her, he thought, though in the most salutary way. So before Tone could respond to his question Bingham said, 'Listen, Tone. What I'm going to tell you must stay absolutely secret, do you understand? If you breathe one word, especially to your wife, about what I'm going to say I'm quite liable to break your bloody neck. Do you hear?'

He smiled as he said the last words. He could not abide this garrulous, opinionated, boring, disappointed, unhappy pest who could clear the club bar in three seconds flat just by appearing. So there was a certain amount of pleasure had in that smiling threat he had uttered about this very serious matter.

'What are you talking about, Bingham?'

Tone's indignation irritated Bingham. Tone was good at indignation, even his politics were based on indignation. Living with this little pest, not mad enough to be locked up, he certainly helped to bring out the worst in his wife. In fact when most annoyed by Mrs Tone, Bingham had only to remember her husband almost to forgive. Almost, for she was as great a pest as her spouse.

'Have I had an anonymous letter?' Bingham snapped. 'Yes, Tone, I have. And you haven't, have you, and we both know why. Right?'

Tone's sunburned, freckled hand started to shake as he lifted his cigarette to his thin lips, his eyes averted now.

'Yes, I was going to ask you that,' he said, voice slightly tremulous. 'So you've guessed. Has anyone else guessed? Do they know?'

He had a red-brown face and light blue, vacant, drinker's eyes. His greying yellow hair was thinning on top. A neatly built, nervous man, like a straining whippet, unequal to the task of marriage in a bungalow in this silent valley in the sun, so different from army life with its thousand calling distractions. Mrs Tone had slowly hammered him down with her superior intelligence, once they were retired. He was her hobby, her pastime now, for she had little else that interested her, except the lives of other people, and that was not enough. She should have left this querulous bore long ago, but because she had not done so he was going to pay, and Bingham guessed she was intelligent enough to know all that.

Once he was assured nobody else, as far as Bingham knew, had guessed his wife was the writer of the anonymous letters, Tone sighed with relief and invited Bingham to have a drink with him. Bingham, ignoring the invitation, said, 'See to it that she gets some of these pills they're handing out these days. I've read they're pretty good. But don't ignore it. Those anonymous letters are signals and you'd better take notice.'

Tone took notice all right, Bingham reflected as he sat down in a cane armchair on the long verandah of his bunga-low and his old servant, Hafizullah, appeared. 'The usual, Colonel Sahib?' Bingham smiled at him and nodded, then lay back while Hafizullah slipped his sandals off in one practised, deft movement. Ageing now, Hafizullah had wandered far and wide with Bingham, had seen many dangers with him, and kept many secrets, as Bingham kept many of Hafizul-lah's. They were far more than master and servant. They were like brothers, and Hafizullah, for years, had prayed that Bing-ham would *accept* the light he knew Bingham had already seen, and do what must be done, become a Muslim. This was never discussed.

Tone took notice by taking over his wife's outgoing mail, which was considerable. It was very typical of Tone to do that, because it was obsessional and involved complicated and ingenious behaviour, and gave Tone what he most needed, the feeling of being in charge, and of having won the struggle with his wife, though unfortunately she could not know of this.

'I don't want to hear anything more about it, thanks,' Bing-ham had called out, waving Tone away, when the other, who was wearing an almost demonic grin, came up behind him in the bar some days later and said, 'I've got it all taped. I've taken over my wife's outgoing mail.' Bingham left the bar and Tone had followed him, and Bingham had had to listen, appalled by the joy, the chuckling and the slightly horrific intimacy this confidence of Tone's implied. He knew now that he had become Tone's friend, in Tone's eyes, because of this secret they now shared.

'Thank you, Hafizullah.' He took the whiskey from the silver tray (Teheran, 1942) which Hafizullah placed on the ancient brass Banarsi table beside his armchair. Hafizullah glided off and the blue dusk began to dissolve into cool darkness.

Tone was actually steaming his wife's letters open — she used her own typewriter, she had to because Tone all but lived at his own typewriter — and if he thought it necessary would type a complete new letter, with all objectionable material removed, then sign it with her name, seal it in its envelope, and hand it to the postal clerk with whom he had come to an arrangement, payment by the month.

It worried Bingham when Tone went on to say, 'And by God you'd be surprised what's in some of her letters. She's quite quite bonkers, you know. There's no doubt about it. Listen to this, for instance —'

He had refused to listen further and had walked off. Tone was now inside his life. He remembered the strange scene when the visitor from Delhi had come into the club bar (a visitor could receive temporary membership these days) and had been trapped by Tone.

Tone was writing his life and had been threatening to give it to Bingham for comments for years.

The visitor from Delhi was a film–scriptwriter, an Englishman who introduced himself to Tone as Roger Croon. He told Tone he was travelling in India while researching a film subject — 'Writing's not *enough* . Pastures new and so on.'

'I'm a writer myself,' Tone replied. 'I'm three-quarter way through a book that's going to shake Britain when it comes out.'

'Really?'

'Yes. Really. It took me a long time to find my — er — '

'*Métier, genre* , line ?' suggested the visitor, who, it seemed then to Bingham at the other end of the bar, might be the companion Tone had never had, for he had Tone's instant readiness for chat, self-revelation, the same lapel-grabbing intensity, though far more intelligent than Tone. But a chancer, definitely, for when Tone said, 'Métier — that's the word. French literature and all that, *Madame Bovary*. Read it?', Croon became languid, world–weary, and nodded, saying, 'Yes, thank you. An over-rated writer. All this crap about

12

getting exhausted after writing fifteen words in one day, and then cutting out three, and getting morning sickness after writing about Madame Bovary having it.'

'Proust?'

Croon seemed offended that a retired officer could go on like this about French writing. He overdid his puzzled stare into Tone's eyes.

'Didn't you say you'd been in the army or something — captain, isn't it?'

'Major,' Tone said sharply. 'Why? You mean the one about the colonel saying, "Yes, I did read a book once." Don't believe it. I've read more books than anybody in this bloody country. Just answer the question.'

'Which question?'

'Proust. Have you *read* him?' Tone's voice was edged with anger.

It was quite possible, Bingham reflected, that Croon admired Proust, but now the visitor leaned forward, sliding his elbow along the bar, and said, 'Listen. Get off the bandwagon, Major. You *don't* have to have read Proust, understand? For every ten people who go on about Proust only one has read him, stayed the course, managed to make it, reached quarter way.'

Bingham noticed that the others in the bar, those sitting at tables, had ceased talking, and were watching and listening. One of them winked at Bingham. *Could, would,* Tone be taken down by this formidable looking stranger? Croon was a tall, broad-shouldered man of about forty, and it was already known and being widely discussed that under 'Profession' in the Visitors' Book at 'The Kipling Arms', the local hotel, he had written 'Playboy'. So it looked very promising.

One thing about Tone, thought Bingham; over the years of practice in boring people, quarrelling with them, proving things in this bar at terrible length, especially when mistaken, which was often, and short-tempered though he was, Tone *had* learned to try and control himself. And he was trying now, as he said, in a meaningfully lowered, patient voice, and spacing the words as though talking to a wayward child, 'I — have — read — Proust, sir, again and again, not just once — '

He was going over the top again, Bingham knew.

Croon clicked his fingers for the barman as though he had

13

been a member for years. Nobody would mind that if he could only take Tone down, now, in public. Croon gave his order and then glanced at Tone.

'In French, of course,' he said lightly, eyebrows raised.

Yes, thought Bingham, Tone is going to go over the top.

'In French,' said Tone. 'I do realize, of course, that army officers are not supposed to read books, and that to have read them in French as well is highly offensive. Nevertheless, it has to be put up with, sir, this shock you are obviously receiving —'

Croon began to ask questions in French, but Tone was ready for this. He waved his hand wearily and said, 'Let's not be childish now, sir — ' and Croon lit a cigarette as Tone continued, 'You haven't answered the question, sir. Have you *read* Proust?' Croon examined his cigarette and then regarded Tone, a chilly light in his eyes.

'I did Proust when I was at the Sorbonne, Major, since you insist on making this a schoolboy examination. I *have* recovered from the experience, however. So you are a *writer,* as you put it — '

'As I *put* it?' Tone interrupted, rather admirably icily, Bingham considered, for by now Tone should really have lost his temper — though it was early and he had had only a couple of drinks — 'I am *writing a book,* sir.'

'Would you like a drink?' Croon was cool again, in charge, for now anyway. Tone's grand manner appeared at once.

'I never allow non-members to buy me drinks in my club, sir,' said Tone. 'But that doesn't mean I can't offer *you* one. So have this one on me.' Tone had used this ploy for years with visitors, buying drink after drink for the trapped stranger, the captive audience, for the visitor could not, once he had realized what kind of hands he was in, easily escape.

'Thank you, ' Croon said. 'A large Scotch, please. Do tell me about your book. What's it about?'

'I told you. It's my life.'

As Hafizullah hummed to himself in the dining room as he laid the table, Bingham on the verandah poured himself another Scotch. That was how Croon had come into the life of this valley and really got things going, he reflected, all because he had asked to see the manuscript of Tone's book. Bingham had never weakened about that business, for each

14

time Tone had asked him to look at the manuscript he had said, 'I never read *anything* , Tone, until it is finished. Finish it, and if I have the time I'll give it a read.' Nothing — *nothing* would induce him even to *pretend* to read that manuscript, because of what might be in it. He wanted nothing to do with the thing. Nothing.

'Colonel Sahib, *tayar hai!*' Hafizullah had glided in and stood to brief attention, and Bingham rose and went in to eat a chicken Husseini. Hafizullah had propped the book Bingham was reading up against the heavy water-jug, as always, and as always, open at the right page.

CHAPTER 3

The ripples from the rock thrown by Darwin, into the stagnant pool of so many old and uneasy religious certainties, were still slowly spreading into Asia even when Chandra Gupta was seventeen. The uneasiness they caused had had to filter through Arabic, Farsi, Hindi, and on into Burmese, Chinese, Japanese, yet it was still only the few among the hundreds of millions who experienced the bewildering collision in these many languages.

For the English-speakers, and those aspiring to learn it, mere specks in the Eastern oceans of linguistic traditionalists, Darwin was often still only a word connected with great emotional disturbance in the West. In the ancient world of Hinduism, to which Chandra Gupta belonged by birth and tradition, Darwin was merely one more foreign commentator to be gradually melted down into the simmering compost of forty or fifty centuries. But Chandra Gupta, and growing numbers like him, was now only a Hindu by name. He no longer knew what he was religiously, but he was feverish spiritually, and kept his temperature high by almost nonstop reading of all he could find, about what was obviously a million-year-old, and still unsolved, mystery of mysteries.

Would he have been like this, he wondered, if he had stayed a traditional Indian, been educated only in India, in Indian things, in Indian languages? In the countries and languages of the winners, England, France and Italy, he had learned to look at the world, at history, at man, as if through a microscope, to find the bacillus, diagnose the disease of existence, and if possible, come to terms with what could only be its meaninglessness. But even now, drifting towards middle age, he could not come to these terms.

It always pleased him to read that some leader of a sect in Europe, America, Asia, Africa, had collected hundreds of frightened but acceptant believers on some mountain or other where they awaited the end of the world, which would be on

Tuesday. On Wednesday there were no complaints, no recriminations, merely preparations for the next period of expectancy. This kind of thing had been going on since the beginning, since the first drawn breath, and would go on until the sun died — well, no, possibly, if not probably, sooner now — would go on until the brilliant chimps in uniform at last pressed the buttons and gave everybody eternal rest. It pleased him to know that there were always going to be hundreds of millions of innocent, ignorant, reverent people, the dumb masses so infuriating to the reasonable intellectuals, the soul-engineers, the sociologists who had worked out all the behaviour-patterns. He had come to fear and hate these intellectuals with their blueprints of a perfectly administered prison-life for the masses, but he kept it to himself, shocked by its insistent presence in his thoughts, and puzzled by the sense of relief it gave him.

His quiet obsession about Darwin and his theories had lasted well, and had become a sort of private inner hobby, and was discussed only with his friend, Bingham, sometimes for the sake of the laughter they both enjoyed after arguments or serious considerations. 'Natural Selection' might be defined as a gang of monkeys testing samples from a row of various whiskies, Japanese, American, Indian, Scotch — eventually and inevitably they would select, and stay with, the Scotch. 'And *then*,' Bingham had replied, 'you can put them down at the typewriters and *know* one of them will come up with *Hamlet*.' 'Eventually,' the Maharajah had responded with some gravity, 'though might not *Macbeth* come first? The Scotch —'

Alone, he would sometimes think about how he was living uneasily in this huge museum called India and how he was now an artefact in it, having inherited the *gaddi* and become Maharajah just as the British were hastening to leave. He was already out of date when, in nineteen forty-six, he became Maharajah of a state just big enough to give him that title, instead of Rajah.

While literate in four European languages he had specialized in Persian. The war found him in Italy and came as a nuisance, so absorbed was he in collaboration with his friend Ugo, Barone di Castiglioncello, and with Concetta, the Baron's daughter, on a long work about mediaeval Persian mysticism. He married Concetta and lived with her and the

17

ageing Baron in Rome, until visited by a colonel of the German army with a suggestion that he work for the Middle East and Indian services of the German radio in Berlin. They left for Milan almost immediately and then made their way into the mountains where they settled warily in an isolated house belonging to the Baron's brother. The work on the book continued, but with the fall of Mussolini and the increasing pressure of the German occupation, he joined a band of partisans. He was thirty-three and planned to spend his life in Italy, a land he considered the most civilized of all he had known. His son, Joti Parshad, was born while Chandra Gupta and a group of partisans were trying to make contact with an Indian infantry division over a hundred miles to the south east. It was not until nineteen forty-five that he learned of his elder brother's death in action in North Africa three years before, and that it would therefore be he who would become Maharajah of Induspur. The Medaglia d'Argento he had received from the Italians, for his service with the partisans, meant much more to him than the news that he would become Maharajah on his father's death, which followed in nineteen forty-six.

Returning to an India he had not seen for nearly ten years, he was shaken by the speed with which the British were preparing to leave, after nearly two hundred dreaming years broken only by the odd nightmare — the disaster of 1840 in Afghanistan, the Indian uprising in 1857, Gandhi's decision to free India after the first world war, and far from the scene but most decisive of all, the Japanese victory at Singapore in nineteen forty-two.

He made his way up India from Delhi slowly (despite anxious calls from the palace in the hills to hurry), staying in obscure Dak bungalows in which he wrote long letters to his wife in Italy. 'In the cities,' he wrote to her, 'an almost desperate waiting for independence, while out here in the hills it is like India a thousand years ago – peaceful, friendly, hopeful, no hurry. How long will I be Maharajah, and why? I'm told that the British Counsellor for the Princes, even for as petty a Prince as myself, has burned a few tons of documents which recorded all our sins in the past, as well as the sins the British committed with, for, and against us. My family haven't been very sinful since the eighteenth century but I'm glad the record of that time has gone up in smoke with the rest —'

He went through the ceremonies for the death of his father, and for his own enthronement, ruler now of a small obscure state, one of nearly six hundred scattered across the great hot dusty body of India, and then waited for the arrival of his wife and son. But death, which seemed to be trying to reshape his life, went on with its arrangements, this time erasing his dearest kin. On their way through Egypt to Ismailia — for he had agreed Concetta should shake off the war by a leisurely sea trip to India — they had died with hundreds of others in a cholera outbreak, and he knew they must have died within twenty-four hours of infection, shrunken, emptied of every fluid, relieved to depart from their own black, foaming stench. How much more sense just then the black goddess of death, Kali with her lolling red tongue, made for him, compared with all the other chummy bearded Daddygods in the sky of the Jewish-Christian-Muslim book-thumpers. For about a silent, stunned month the great, slow, turning Hindu wheel of inevitability claimed him, and seemed to comfort him. It seemed true that the puny, unnecessary human being was at the mercy of unknowable forces against which it was useless and contemptible to complain. People held his hand and murmured things to him. He attended a party for some departing British, determined to break with all customs of mourning, just as a month before he had scattered all the hangers-on and retainers of his father's day. A thin nineteenth-century type missionary had condoled with him, and then said, 'They will be waiting for you in heaven, always remember that.' It was the kind of ridiculous statement, he knew, that was both impossible and unkind to question, let alone attempt to refute. It was the informed statement of a theologically informed member of the board of directors, and a reminder about his uninformed, heathen, immortal soul, as well as the kindly guess and hope he would have preferred it to be. For this missionary was leaving after a lifetime of preaching among swarming dark souls whose destination had been set a million years ago, though they had willingly put an icon of Jesus beside that of Krishna in their huts. He had gripped the missionary's hand, thanked him for his kind reminder, and passed on to a conversation about the only truly new topic in centuries, the atomic bomb and the great black pit it had opened up in the mind of the world. Before this appalling product of scientific curiosity his own recent disaster seemed to diminish, but not for long.

He started driving aimlessly across country, stopping in villages where he sat and quietly demanded truthful answers to his questions about food, wages, taxes, hopes, illness. In some of the villages the people hardly knew the British had been, let alone were going. In general, the little state was very productive agriculturally, and the newly discovered coal deposits promised riches some day. In general, the people of the countryside seemed contented. Farming and soldiering were still their honourable professions, as they had been since the first Rajputs had descended from the sun. Those who knew that some kind of enormous changes were taking place somewhere 'out there' only wished to be reassured that they could still be soldiers. The old retired soldiers, once they realized who was visiting them, rushed back into their huts and put on their medals, on their old tunics, then returned. They all spoke to him in the same voice as the people visiting the palace had used since the news of his catastrophe, especially because of the death of his son. The voice was a low, slightly hesitant one exactly right for the showing of sympathy, understanding, shared sorrow. Always in the background the women and girls squatted in a row, silent, their eyes soft, fixed on him, as if ready to wail their grief for him if he raised his finger in signal for it. His terrible affliction was never mentioned, but the hushed tone of voice said all in condolence for him.

Then he would drive off at random again. His exhausted mind felt at times as if about to blossom into blinding light, of vision, revelation, incredible understanding, and driving fast he felt as if he were speeding away from the horizon of his mind, on the edge of which the threatening light was trembling, like a dawning.

Once he stopped the car and waited, waited for the light to rise and flood him, but no, nothing; and nodding, as if in tired acceptance, he drove on. At the same time another self studied all this, watched over it and considered his state, assessed the enigma of sorrow and pain, and now useless affection and love, and considered with him the bafflement of his obsession, the possibility that there might be a meaning in existence, his own existence for a start.

Sometimes during these quiet, frantic drives he made plans, hundreds of them, one of which was that he go back to Italy and join the aged Barone in the work which had used up the old man's long life, but which he knew was never to be finished, but always altered and rewritten, for once it was finished so would be the Barone's life. Only now he saw how he had once threatened the old man's lifelong game with scholarship, by working hard, urging him on, trying actually to finish the book. For the first time he understood how so many human beings did this, lived their lives uselessly and happily, the rich man pretending to himself his determination to explain to the world, once and for all, the meaning of Persian mysticism, or a working man drunk in a bar explaining once more why 'they' would not let him better himself. And the scientists, the physicists. How he had once admired them as the world's elite, the only true international community, above race, pettiness, bigotry, slaving in their laboratories to help the human race, exchanging their papers and discoveries, and anxious to expunge ignorance and evil, especially war, from the earth. Bastards. All they had come up with, finally, each racing against the other for the prize and the international fame, was this hellish thunderbolt, and they had put this into the hands of the apes who *had* actually come up with Hamlet after many tries. He could imagine some burned, dying, fully irradiated survivor surveying deserts of ashes and corpses and trying to remember the 'Alas, poor Yorick' speech — preferably a physicist who had failed to get the Nobel Prize for coming up with the 'clean bomb'. Yes, after all a clean bomb free of radiation effects would mean they could have a real world war, a clean holocaust killing of a few hundred million useless mouths, and still have a non-poisoned world in which to get on with the problem about Marxism's engagement to capitalism, maybe get the marriage done with at last.

A year after India's independence, Bingham, retired now, delighted him by accepting his offer of a house and coming to live in the state. Together they went to oversee what was probably going to be the last symbolic baptism of the state's main river, the Godevi, which the ridiculous, but stubbornly

21

lasting legend maintained had been the true objective of Alexander the Great.

Bingham loved this legend and had always wanted to see the ceremony, keeping a straight face, as straight as the Maharajah's, when he said, 'Possibly the earliest version of the cargo-cult,' a subject which fascinated them both. In the South Pacific from which the armies of Americans and Australians had so recently withdrawn with the end of the war, the natives were building wooden aircraft on jungle clearings, and watching the sky, imploring that the shower of goodies, canned beef, cigarettes, booze, would rain down from heaven again.

The half-dozen remaining British in the state were invited to the ceremony. A big blue and yellow striped *shamiana* was set up, a sort of beautiful enormous tent-roof on poles, and there were drinks, *tanduri*, cold ham and chicken, and the unbelievably out-of-tune brass band occasionally played *Zakmi Dil* or *Colonel Bogey*.

The ceremony took place in a stony clearing at the edge of the wide river rumbling and surging down, cold from the Himalayas. It was the 'cold weather', which meant it was only as hot as, say, Spain, and at the river's edge the Brahmins were gravely busy while the crowds of country folk sat on the rocks and watched with religious respect.

'Hard to believe, Tim, that we're living in a madhouse of a world, isn't it?' said the Maharajah. It was all so peaceful, colourful, timeless, the India of a past which would be the future too, as if unaware of the restless, invisible bacillus now loose.

Bingham nodded sombrely. 'Yes,' he said. 'I do sometimes wish I was illiterate, and deaf, though not often I'm afraid.'

'That's old Pandit Durga Parshad over there. Remember him?' Bingham looked across at the Pandits in whispered conference by the river. 'Oh yes,' he said, grinning. 'The thinker.' They laughed. They were remembering the time when the old half-blind Pandit had asked Bingham if he knew of a good optician in Delhi. He had worn out his reading glasses and needed new ones, glasses that would last, not like the pair he had worn out. He was convinced that it was the glasses themselves which had aged and worn out, not his eyes. When Bingham had explained that it was a man's eyes which slowly wore out, not the reading glasses, the old Brahmin had been shocked by Bingham's ignorance. 'The same eyes that can see into a man's soul, Colonel Sahib,' he had told Bingham, 'as mine have been able to do ever since I put on the sacred thread, can still wear out any pair of glasses, even at my age. It has nothing to do with the eyes beyond the power of those eyes. I simply want a better quality of glass in the next pair, that's all, glass that can stand up to the strain which these eyes of mine will put on them. Is that so hard to understand?'

As things turned out this was to be the last time this ceremony of the river-marriage could be performed, for they were now cut off from the distant Indus river by the new frontier of Pakistan, and by the war for Kashmir.

The ceremony involved the bringing of a sealed jar of water from the Indus river, and a party consisting of two Brahmins and two Rajputs, men of the ancient warrior-caste, conveyed the jar from the Indus across the Punjab. The journey had to be done on foot and took weeks. The story was that this ceremony had been performed for the first time as a magical effort to lure Alexander the Great onward to the territory which, after the first river-marriage, became known as Induspur. Whether Alexander, on his arrival at Induspur, was to be made an ally, or destroyed in battle, had become a subject for argument, but he never came. His exhausted and dispirited soldiers had mutinied, it was said, near the actual Indus river, and thus the great expected marriage of Greek and Brahmin learning never took place. But his name was still revered and many of the tribes among the Afghans and the Afridis, and others in Central Asia, were still proud to name their children Sikander after him.

A loud cheer went up as the Indus water was poured from the jar into the river, and one of the old Brahmins spoke to the river and reminded her once more of the sacred task she had so nearly performed, the bringing of the Greeks, over two thousand years before.

'Godevi,' the old man told the river. 'Accept these tears again from your mighty sister-river, in the name of learning.'

'It does make you think, Tim,' said the Maharajah, as they watched the conch-shells being blown at the end of the ceremony; 'time means nothing. Just imagine how alive the memory of Alexander still is. What a hero. I wonder if I'd like to have lived then.'

23

'I wonder.'

They both laughed as they left the ceremonial area, the Maharajah saying, 'Yes. Tricky if you had appendicitis, say.'

'Or pneumonia,' said Bingham. 'No penicillin then.'

'Very twentieth-century types, aren't we? Comfort, good health, determination to live forever and so on, those are the things that matter to the world these days.'

'Yes,' Bingham agreed. 'It takes a lot to beat a good iced Scotch and soda under a fan. Alexander and his boys never had that.'

Then they had talked about whether the Maharajah should join the *Ganatantra Parishad* which they had heard was being discussed by one or two of the princes, an organization which would discuss their problems with the new government.

'I expect it'll come to nothing in the end,' said the Maharajah, 'and anyway how long do I intend to go on playing this charade? The British needed us, the princes, for the chessboard they worked on — fair enough. We balanced things. But not now. So I'm very restless.'

He had grinned at Bingham. 'I'm like yourself, Tim. Out of date. No, I don't think I'll be long acting out my unexpected role of Maharajah.'

'You mean you miss Italy, Chan?'

'Oh, yes. I miss Italy, quite often. But it's not about returning to Italy I'm talking. I'm not quite sure what it is, I think it's about identification with India. I mean I feel uprooted and not just from Italy and all that meant, but uprooted from India too. That's much more important — or it seems to be. A strange thing happened when the British left. I felt like an actor among other actors, onstage, but the director of the play had gone, and the play was over. I know my lines, my role, but there's no longer an audience. I need a new play —' He hesitated. 'But no audience.'

That was the first time Bingham had heard his friend speak of his unease, his sense of displacement, his wish to 'step backwards' into India, as he had put it later. He had no interest in playing the Maharajah, and left as much as possible of administrative affairs, such as they were in the little state, in the hands of the *Diwan* and his council.

Bingham himself was restless after a life of service. His mind, he found more and more, flinched from doing what most of the others like himself had done, packing up and going 'home'. Home? he would think, now where would that be? The fifty-acre farm in the west of Ireland which the tenacious striving of his mother's family had finally wrested from the débâcle of the Irish land struggle? It was thirty-three years since the misery of his final look around that scene of his boyhood and youth. As one of the hundred thousand Irish volunteers he had gone to fight for 'little Belgium'; he had come back as a special kind of stranger to find that his elder brother was away with one of the 'flying columns' in the murderous struggle with British forces. It was an Ireland in convulsion and a country in which ex-British soldiers like himself, who had marched away to cheers and drums to the troopship at the North Wall in nineteen fourteen, were an embarrassing reminder of quite another world, one which was crumbling in gunfire, the last stage of a struggle lasting centuries. He had felt himself to be a betrayer, and betrayed as well — he had never been able to decide which. He had gone to the war believing that England was at last going to give Home Rule to Ireland, when the war was won, but the men of the secret Irish Republican Brotherhood had proclaimed the Irish Republic in nineteen sixteen, and idealistic volunteers and believers like himself had, so to speak, been disinvented, been made somehow invisible. Even his ageing mother, already 'heart-scalded', as she had put it, by his failure to go through with her dream that he should be a priest, had treated him as this special kind of anomalous stranger. He had taken the wrong road in nineteen fourteen, but who could have known that then? With others like himself he had discussed this curious conspiracy of enforced strangerhood they felt themselves to be in. Some joined the struggle against the British, others faded quietly into civilian life and seldom or never spoke of the trenches or their wasted war years. Then Bingham, after much covert effort, had met his brother. The wall between them, the gunman on the run and the returned British soldier, could not, he found, be taken down. In the back of the pub, one of those used by the leader Michael Collins as a meeting place, he had talked, and then quarrelled, with his brother, now head of the family following their father's death.

His brother had ignored his proffered right hand, ominously, saying, 'I gave you enough hints before you went away with the British army, didn't I? But no, with all your marvellous education you knew better than peasants like myself. Well, now you see it. They're burning Ireland down again, but this time we'll go on shooting until the bastards go home and leave us to ourselves. So you were wounded, and they won the war. For what? This "fellow Celt", as Mister Lloyd George likes to call himself, seems to have the answer to that. Squeeze Germany until the pips squeak, after hanging the bloody Kaiser. And he's let thousands of his drunks loose over here and we're shooting them as fast as we can. So what are you doing back here? Looking for a hero's welcome, is it? I broke my back at the plough to get you educated into the priesthood, isn't that right? And you ran away at the last minute —' Then they had quarrelled.

For years his spirit had cowered whenever he let himself think over that scene among the black pints and the cigarette smoke of the jumpy, watchful bar-crowd in that Dublin pub. Alienated, bitter, he had put on again the garb of the outcast. He had accepted the regular commission he had been offered, had a few last deperate drinks with demobilized friends who had survived the shambles of Gallipoli with him, and sailed for India, a captain and a displaced person.

He thought of that time when, drinking with the Maharajah in the club after the river-ceremony, they said goodbye to a few retired British officials who were leaving for 'home'.

'Home,' the Maharajah said, when the British had left the club, 'I wonder, is there any such place really?'

Bingham was thinking of the last night he had spent at 'home', with the continuous scream of the Atlantic storm in the blackness outside the farmhouse, thinking over the farewell words he would say to his mother in the morning. To have one of her sons a priest, or even a doctor, had been the reason she had given to her life, and he had destroyed it. Even now the assault of anger, pity, love and hatred could rock him if he ever let himself handle memories of that time.

'Home is in the head, I should think,' Bingham had replied. 'Wherever your head is, your home's inside it. Mine is anyway.'

What was he going to do with his life? Do like the others had always done, or tried to do, write his memoirs about what he thought India was, had been, would be?

He and the Maharajah took a kind of refuge in each other's sense of displacement, something Bingham had hardly ever

26

given voice to in his life before. They got into a habit which amused them, of discussing the world as a kind of theatre with themselves as puzzled actors, he Bingham having lost his director, and the Maharajah an amateur European at heart trying to become a serious Indian while temporarily occupying the role of a petty prince in a completely new kind of India.

At times Bingham would toy with a fantasy in which he would live in a small house in Dublin, say in Ballsbridge, where he would quietly drink and read until age, sickness, and death started to take him over. Completely anonymous, a relic of the first world war and of a long adventure in a mighty but dying cultural attack called empire, he could fall off a bar stool one night in a Dublin pub and they could throw his shell into any hole available.

The Brett-Turners joined them for a drink at the bar and the Maharajah, very capable at such politenesses, prodded Wally Brett-Turner into his favourite role, that of the embittered middle-class British ex-officer watching his country from afar as it declined in the dirty hands of this new working-class revenge called the Labour Party.

His beautiful black-haired wife, Megan, would watch her husband with not too secretly amused eyes as Wally, lacking only a monocle, became the stage Englishman and barked querulously about the betrayal of Churchill by the ungrateful working class he had led to victory, using expressions like 'quite *monstrous*' and 'absolutely *atrocious*.' He had been three years a prisoner of the Japanese army, and his marriage was falling apart. When he and Megan had gone home for another quarrel, Bingham and the Maharajah stayed on drinking, the Maharajah praising Megan, her looks, her intelligence, the waste of her on Wally with his already out-of-date posture of political indignation.

Gradually, the Maharajah's obsession with Darwin and his theory of evolution emerged again over the fifth whiskey, and he and Bingham would make one more attempt to clarify it for each other.

Neither could accept the brilliant theory, neither was able to believe fully that there was not some unimaginable but enormous mind behind the increasing mystery of the universe in which the world was merely a speck, a tiny revolving football inhabited by puzzled temporary lodgers like themselves.

27

Their defence in this so often discussed dilemma was wry fun, solemn travesty while edging about the perimeters of the gigantic enigma they never tired of discussing. Each felt that the other was the only person they had ever met with whom each could exchange aloud long half-suppressed exploratory statements of their spiritual bewilderment, about the mystery so awesome it demanded a certain levity. For Bingham this search had begun in a tiny country church in Ireland just after his tenth birthday, when a priest 'on the mission' to reawaken sunken souls, had thundered marvellously about hell. The ten-year-old boy had come away shattered, aware that there could be no such place, knowing for certain that he could never be content on this treadmill of sin and punishment erected by a million fevered theologians since the death of Christ. It was his first secret, a terrible secret he could share with nobody. But he had soldiered on silently, willing himself to believe, and had reached the very edge of his mother's goal, priesthood, until the warning came in his head and he ran for cover, and for a reappraisal which had never stopped.

'All right,' said the Maharajah as they lifted another whis-key and silently toasted the eternity they knew they were living in for a while, 'let's put it this way. There's this — well, this duck. Yes, let's make it the duck this time. For fifty million years it has carefully placed its foot on the mud at the edge of the lake, thinking, "I've got to be sent back to the drawing board, that's obvious. I need webbed feet to live the kind of life my genes are telling me to live." And after fifty million years, presto, the webbed feet start forming, and you have a properly equipped duck. Correct?'

'Very good. Yes,' said Bingham.

'But *why*? Forget the webbed feet bit for a moment. Why the duck at all? Why ducks? So that we can have roast duck with orange sauce? I can't believe that. The question is — why the duck anyway?'

Why anything else come to that, thought Bingham once again. There had to be a reason for all this chain of seeds and life repeating itself endlessly, or did he think that only because he possessed a thing called a mind, and being tiny, being human, he had to discover a reason for it all? But why? Why could he not just accept the mystery and live it, or once more try and force himself to faith, to a belief and an obedience as a kind of reverence for that mystery? But a sentry stood guard

28

in his head, barring the way to a solution by acceptance and faith. He sometimes thought it was a curse on him, this inability to shake off his pursuer, his spirit which seemed to be forever whispering a demand for surrender, and for solace. So they laughed about it and went on exchanging clues, to no end it seemed except entertainment and a sense of temporary relief.

That they were both at a loose end in life, both displaced persons as it were, helped to cement their friendship. Once, when both were somewhat fuddled with whiskey, the Maharajah had said, in ironic sadness, 'I am a lost member of the age-old Indo-European warrior-caste. I dream in Italian, sometimes with my wife's ghost, sometimes with Darwin among the ducks. It is not enough. I must come to a decision, but about what? To be or not to be — that is the answer.' They had laughed about this and then the Maharajah said, 'And you, Tim? What state are you in, never mind the Scotch we've drunk? Define your present state.'

'I? Well let's see now. Yes. I am an escaped member of a farrow of a very ancient sow who will now never devour me.' He did not elaborate further on this Joyceian version of mother Ireland, but went on to add, perhaps with a real sadness, 'I regret to say.' He felt it would be too banal to go on and say it aloud, but to himself he repeated a saying from the tumbled Celtic shadows he had grown up in: 'Long life to you, the woman of your choice, and death in Ireland.' Somewhere, he thought, there is a room, a place where I will die. I wonder where it is, where it will be? But he was thinking of a woman in Delhi whom he had no doubt was thinking of him. He had had a letter from her that morning. It had said ' . . . in your last letter you sound again as if you are trying to become older than you actually are. This subtle ploy will have no effect on my feelings for you. I repeat, I am here, waiting for you to call me.'

They drank on, about Darwin again, about the wonder he had defined, laughing louder as they voiced absurdities dredged up from much reading, and in Bingham's case, from experiences in primitive places. The Australian tribe which had never, in millions of years, made the connection between sexual intercourse and the magical pregnancy. An African cannibal tribe known to Bingham when civilization was reaching it only thirty-odd years ago, which flayed its victims whole and used the skins as water-carriers. The European tribes which daily read their instant astrological charts. Another tribe which had decided to end the Jewish problem and had built a whole enormous fire-machine quite recently and tended it with incantations, at the same time solving the problem of the rocket which would carry their unsleeping minds into outer space. And their favourite tribal leader of all, Stalin, Light of the World according to all Soviet journals and newspapers, who had dragged the Russian people for thirty years through all kinds of suffering and humiliation, and who was cheered as their saviour by his people who were building one more utopia, and who were set upon giving this hellish paradise to the rest of the human race.

Thus they silenced themselves, finished their drinks and went their ways again, the Maharajah to the palace 'to learn a little more of my role' and Bingham to his house where his old servant, Hafizullah, would be hoping for another chat about the *Hadith*, the traditions of the Prophet Muhammad, a subject dear to them both.

CHAPTER 4

As he opened the letter a cheque fluttered out onto his desk and Bingham picked it up, read it, then stared at it. Two thousand dollars. An American bank. Condy. *Two* thousand dollars?

When he finished reading Condy's short letter he did not know what to feel. Pleasure in the, for him, large sum of dollars. Suspicion followed when he read the particular sentence again — 'Your stuff is so good, so unusual that I feel honored to have been discovered by you, and I *must* keep you with me. Therefore I enclose two thousand dollars as payment for your last brilliant piece.' But the next sentence read, 'I have done some research into your life and career, and into the place you live, Induspur. The lousy pensions you fellows receive after a life of service to the greatest empire that ever was prompts me to wish to help in any way I can. Regard it as an investment in the mind of a writer I greatly admire and whose . . . '

Research! He did not wish to be researched. Yet he noticed the buried spark of vanity beginning to glow. Then he laughed when he read again the line, 'honored to have been discovered by you'. His liking for this unknown American was already balancing out his anger about being researched. Should he not now regard himself as a writer and therefore researchable, no matter how annoying that was, rather than the slightly maniacally private person he had made himself, who did not wish to be discovered, known, questioned, researched by others? No matter how he thought it out he still felt disturbed.

As the kind of writer he was he simply wished to throw articles out into the world so that those interested in such things could read, and take pleasure, in all he knew, and he knew he knew a lot. But when he saw that cheque lying there he knew that the realist, Condy, knew all about him. He needed money.

He got into the battered jeep left him by General 'Shagger' Reevy, turned it towards the town and eased it over the rocky sand leading from his house. It had been one of hundreds of thousands spewed all over the world from America for World War II, and this one was part of a batch made for the Russians. Instead of passing through Persia for the Russian front it had been diverted with a thousand others for the Burma campaign. The instruction plate in Russian was still on the khaki steel dashboard. Old Shagger had bounced and slithered it through Burma to Rangoon, and then up to Taunggyi. Not only had Shagger left him the jeep but two spare engines and a case of spare parts as well. Seldom allowing his sentimentality to be displayed, Bingham had relented when a young Indian officer of the new Independent Indian army had driven this jeep up to his door. He was pleased to see that the smartness of the great old Indian army was still there in the young subaltern, who came to attention, saluted, held out a letter to him, and said,

'Sir! General Reevy died last week. My orders were to deliver his jeep to you and this letter.'

It was a short note and he looked at it now. He had framed it, sentimental, relenting, in tough cellophane and had it screwed down to the left side of the dashboard. It read, 'Dear old Bingo, the call has come and I'm off to that great laundry in the sky. *Dry* cleaning up there, I expect. Still – I enjoyed the short holiday tour down here. Now, *this is an order,* Bingo – finish that book we worked on. Hoist a Scotch for me now and again. Enjoy the jeep. *Khuda Hafiz.* Shagger.'

An Indian army truck had rolled up and parked behind the young Indian subaltern, and while a couple of *Jawans* in work fatigues unloaded the two jeep engines and the case of spares he took the young subaltern in for a whiskey.

Shagger's unexpected death, he found, as he handed the subaltern his whiskey, had stirred his sense of the futility of effort, friendship, life; and reinforced what he felt and fought continually, that being here was just a procession of meals, breathing, sex, reading, drinking and laughing, and then the nightly rehearsal for death, the practice for the longest performance of all, eight hours' sleep, a third of life, mumbling in stumbling surrealistic visions called dreams.

He was cheerful with the subaltern though, and surprised again to find that he himself had become a kind of legend,

Bingo Bingham, knower of languages, tribes, far wildernesses, secret scholar, skulking uncommittable Muslim. That subaltern had talked to him as if he, Bingham, knew his own legend and was pleased about it. So he did what he always did when people began to probe him, question him, he guided the questioner onto everybody's favourite subject, once you get them started, himself. They moved on to the partition of India. The subaltern seemed to accept the partition as inevitable, but his eyes fired up when it came to the partition of the old Indian army. *That,* he told Bingham, was the worst of it. Great divisions and regiments torn apart, Muslims to Pakistan and Hindus and others to India. His own division with which he had served during the last days in Burma; he had fought in the Kashmir war against the Pakistan army, and on patrol at night the officers of both armies found themselves shouting, 'Anybody there from 19 Div?' Or 20 Div, or 4th, 5th, 7th, Div after Div, and when the voices excitedly cried, 'Yes', they shouted greetings and moved away from each other, unable to kill each other across that new and as yet unacceptable gulf which had made them foreigners to each other. Bingham nodded understandingly, watching the shift from pride to hurt to amusement at remembered good times in the young officer's black eyes.

'Yes,' Bingham said. 'It was a very special kind of world that only those *of* it can understand. I expect it was the same with the Roman armies, the Persians too. In a way childish, but what's wrong with being a happy child with other happy children?' They had laughed and finished the whiskey standing up, lifting their glasses as Bingham said, 'To the other children, the good friends dead and alive.'

He shook his head as he drove into the little town, remembering that moment, wry now as he recalled his incurable sentimentality, because he was moved and it disturbed him. Age? What else? Bloody idiot! He ought to get rid of Shagger's jeep. Every time he saw it or drove it he found himself remebering long nights full of talk and laughter, in Lahore, Rawalpindi, Peshawar, or on the roof of Moti Mahal's in Old Delhi. Or the long sweeping mountain ranges of Central Asia.

As he was walking into the bank someone was calling him — 'Hey, Colonel! Colonel!'

It was the fellow who had been taking Tone down in the

33

club bar, Croon, inviting him to lunch at his hotel.

Croon was dressed like an American, orange-flowered Hawaiian shirt open to reveal the white tee-shirt, blue slacks and, the only non-American thing in the get-up, a pair of suede, army-type brothel-creepers on his feet. Dark glasses too, and the new fetish, the Parker 51 fountain-pen clipped into the breast pocket of the shirt. Croon seemed British, but American too, a new type he had noticed increasing lately. Like the new seekers after instant-light, packaged-painless-Hinduism, beginning to appear in India, and all from the West, and by God they could be a bloody bore when they started to beat the breast and intone the dirge for the West which was *so* materialistic . . . . He always found himself laughing when he thought of it, this Western pilgrim dirge in the most materialistic land on earth, spiritual India where the struggle to stay alive went on for millions twenty-five hours every day. And the Gurus grinning.

He switched off this inner dialogue as he took Croon's proffered hand and shook it. It was a hand that surprised him, its palm as hard and tough as a labourer's.

'I'm delighted to bump into you, Colonel,' Croon was saying. 'This character, Tone —'

'Ah yes,' Bingham said, walking faster as if to get away from the subject. 'Tone.' Then, evasive, preparing the way for non-involvement of any kind he added, 'Never have much to do with him. I'm a bit of a loner as they call it these days, you know. There's hardly anybody in this valley I really *know* any more.' Then, brightly, 'Enjoying Induspur? Staying long?' But Croon was not to be side-tracked. The subject was going to be Tone.

'I'm a bit mystified, actually,' Croon said as they entered the grounds of the old Victorian wooden building now allowing people to believe that Kipling used to stay there 'in the old days'. Once it had been called Jackman's but recently had been re-named The Kipling Arms, and there was a great deal of kitschy pseudo-Kiplingana scattered about the walls and in tatty glass cases. ' I mean, *is* Tone a bit cracked, would you say? I ask *you* this, Colonel, because the word around here is that you never gossip. Neither do I, but I would appreciate your opinion of Tone.'

They sat down at a marble-topped ironwork table in the lounge, an old-time *punkah* stretching across the ceiling above them. At least that's genuine, Bingham thought as he gazed round at the new Victorian furniture.

'I haven't been in here for a while,' he said. 'They've messed it around a little. What's that over there?' He pointed at a big glass case screwed to the wall, and Croon politely got up and went over to examine it, bending to peer and read the notice inside the case.

'It's a man's Victorian suit with starched shirt and one of those high collars you see in old photographs,' Croon called back over his shoulder; then, reading, 'It says, "type of suit worn by Kipling when he stayed here in the cold weather . . ."'

'Christ! I'm sorry, Croon, that's enough. Good of you . . .' Bingham was shifting uncomfortably in his chair, an expression of asperity or distaste on his face as Croon, grinning, sat down with him.

Bingham tried again. 'Well, tell me, are you enjoying your holiday? Don't be put off, by the way' — he was going to say, 'if you find most of us up here a little scatty', but that opened the way for the Tone area, so he went on — 'if you find things just a bit primitive. Once you're used to it you can get very fond of Induspur. Now take fishing . . . .' But Croon was not to be put off.

'I need to know about Tone because of what happened last night,' he said. So Bingham lay back in the chair as the waiter arrived, resigned, but resolved to make Croon do the talking. They ordered cold beers.

'When was Somerset Maugham up here, Colonel?'

Bingham turned his head and looked into Croon's dark glasses, and — what a sensitive chap — Croon took the glasses off at once, as if he knew the older man did not like staring into dark glasses. Full marks, Croon. Hmm! *Very* interesting. Have to go carefully with this fellow.

'Somerset Maugham? Oh, of course.' He had remembered. Another fantasy of Tone's, one of so many which he had repeated so many times they had become true, for Tone. If Tone met a visiting journalist or writer, 'scribbler-chappies' as he liked to call them, he pretended to become very cagey, evasive, then told about why he was always careful with scribbler-chappies these days, ever since Somerset Maugham had put him into one of his books. Of course, Bingham reflected, now that Tone was writing his own book, which

35

was 'going to shake Britain', he was a scribbler-chappy himself. Bingham was laughing out loud, unaware of it, as he considered the gigantic ego of Tone, his fantasies, his sad, terrible inconsequentiality which kept him alive.

Watching Bingham laughing, Croon was smiling. 'So he *is* crazy, Colonel. Right?'

'I'm not laughing at Tone, really, I assure you,' Bingham lied. 'I was thinking of some of the funny things Maugham said about the British out here in the East.'

'And was Tone one of them?'

'I'm sure I don't know. Why, is it important?'

'He's got it into his head that I'm going to write about him, like Maugham, but at the same time he hands me his manuscript to read. He's writing his life and I practically begged him not to drive back from the club to his house, last night, to get the manuscript for me. But nothing would stop him so he went off and got it.'

Bingham wanted to warn Croon not to have anything to do with Tone's affairs, but decided that it was going to be Croon's business. Stay out. Stay right out.

They had gone on drinking until nearly midnight, Tone and himself, Croon continued, the only people left in the club except the barman, 'I *thought*,' added Croon mysteriously, and against his will Bingham was becoming interested now.

There was something very likeable about Croon, but there was something else there that he could not focus on — was it a hint of shiftiness in the watchful, keen, piercing grey eyes, or was it a permanently lurking sense of fun, of the ridiculous?

'When he had driven off to get his manuscript I had another drink and the barman went off for something to eat.' Croon paused while Bingham signalled for two more beers. 'Then this woman appeared. I'm bloody sure she'd been there all the time, listening to us —'

Bingham was nodding, sighing, murmuring, 'Mrs Tone, who else?'

'You know the curtain, that heavy plush curtain opposite the bar —'

'Yes, leads onto the little verandah, go on.'

'She came from behind that. I tell you I nearly fell off the bar-stool, because she never made a sound. Just appeared in front of me, smiling. Quite a beautiful woman. Do you know what she said?'

Irritated with himself for listening to this further chapter in the long saga of the Tones Bingham suggested, 'Anyone for tennis?'

Croon did not laugh. 'She said, "Be careful, Mister Croon. Do not become involved. Major Tone is as mad as a March hare, you know, although you mightn't think so. There'll be trouble, I warn you, if you get involved. That's all I wanted to say. Good night."

'She left the bar just as the barman was coming back in. I asked the barman who she was and I couldn't believe it when he said, "Tone Memsahib". Then he turned his head away and I saw he was laughing. Now which of them is mad, or —'

'Both of them,' Bingham said. There was no way out. He had to warn Croon. 'It's no madness, really, not as we think of it. I know I'm a little scatty myself, for instance. Everybody who's spent some years in India, Europeans anyway, is slightly unhinged. Indians only become crazy during the hot weather in the cities. It's the climate. Once it used to kill us off like flies. Now it just sends us a little off our rockers.' He paused and they took down long swigs of the cold Solan beer. 'But the Tones are rather a special case. You must never quote me. Understood? That's part of the madness up here, gossip. My Christ, Croon, it's caused such things to happen here in my experience, once even a murder, so keep your counsel and always be careful. Now the Tones. *He* is definitely on the edge of his cliff, and could easily jump off — if *she* doesn't push him first, that is.' He stopped at Croon's shout of laughter. He was going too far, saying too much. It was what made people laugh that they could not resist repeating. 'I'm serious,' he said. 'It's actually quite a delicate situation, those two —'

'Well, listen to this, Colonel, if you need bearing out. He came back with the manuscript. Jesus, it's as big as the Domesday Book, and he's only three-quarter way through it. He's been at it ten years —'

'Five actually,' said Bingham. 'Tone always doubles or trebles everything. He started it when he finally decided to give up writing letters to the London *Times*. He's got a file, you know, of the letters, hundreds of them. He's been writing letters to *The Times* since before the war, and never had a single one printed. He's very bitter about it too. Was actually threatening to sue *The Times* over it, something about malicious discrimination.'

'That's insanity, Colonel. There's no other word for it. Anyway — I took the manuscript home and got into bed and I was going through it, reading here an there, for about and hour or so, I'd say, when I heard this noise coming up the stairs. It was Tone. This is two o'clock this morning. The night clerk wouldn't let him see me, said it was too late and I was asleep, and they were fighting their way up the stairs. The whole hotel was awake and I can tell you I got some strange looks at breakfast.'

'Lunch is being served, sir.' The waiter left them.

'Go on,' said Bingham. He was laughing, unable to stop, because of the bewildered expression on Croon's face as he told the story of his entanglement with Tone.

'The bugger burst into my room, I'm telling you, Colonel, his wife's right. Tone *is* bloody crazy. He stood there panting, then said, "Manuscript. Wife." Then he came over and started to wrap the manuscript up in the brown paper he'd given it to me in. He told me that his wife had given him an ultimatum. That he get back the manuscript immediately or she would pack and leave him — *right there and then* at two in the morning.'

'That may be one of the best things that's ever happened to you, Croon,' said Bingham. 'I'm very glad to hear about it, I mean that he's taken the manuscript back. I would guess that if that thing was ever printed one of two things would happen. Either Tone would be put in the nearest loony bin, or it'd start snowing writs, suits for libel, all over Induspur and a few other places too. Shall we go in?'

CHAPTER 5

On his way up from poverty Croon had learned not to listen too closely to his conscience, but it was troubled now.

Trying to relax in his hotel room with a bottle of highland malt he had found himself pacing the room instead. He guessed he must have paced three or more miles, he felt so tired. He sat down again in the old-fashioned Bombay Fornicator and lifted his long legs, laid them on the extendable arms of the chair and lay back. He picked up his whiskey glass from where it rested in the special hole made for it in another extension from the right arm of the chair.

By God, those old sahibs had thought of everything when it came to comfort out here. It had taken him some time to work out the simple but ingenious workings of this splendid chair, and he had had to ask the old room servant in the end.

'Is for fornicating, Sahib, while is resting back as well. Sahib is lying back while womans on top — you see making arms of chair long — *now* '— the old man swung out the arm extensions on which his legs would rest — 'then while fornicating continue sahib can reach for glass of drink in hole here. Sahib not getting tired. Womans do work and is preventing Sahib going sweaty with tired. Sahibs calling Bombay Fornicator.'

What a country. Total realism. No smug nonsense or any two-faced bullshit about the so-called facts of life. It worried him, though.

A lot of things in India worried him, but he liked what he was beginning to feel of it, a museum of a land, vast, blinded by sunlight and almost mindless with age. Conquerors of all kinds had poured in for thousands of years, Aryans, Persians, Arabs, Mongols, British, and all had been melted down into the ancient simmering Hindu soup, except the British, who had swum determinedly to stay afloat, had won, and had then been skimmed off, saved in time by Mr Attlee.

Because in Delhi a couple of weeks ago he had come unex-

39

pectedly into his hotel room and found the assistant manager reading his diary, he now wrote it daily in French. Having experienced, in trains and planes, the surprising Indian passion for interrogation of strangers, about all things, marital status, number of children, plans for marriage if still unmarried, profession, income, future hopes, pension, diet, state of health, state of urinary and defecatory systems, frequency of wet dreams, star under which born, religious state, belief or lack of it in life after death, and so on, he had not been too surprised when the assistant manager had handed him his diary with the remark, 'You are having interesting life, sir, and many of it to come. Thank you.'

He read the last entry in his diary: 'Definitely must tell Bingham why I am here. Cable and say so first. Awaiting reply.'

He had been right and F.X., with his exaggerated respect for what he had come to think of as Bingham's 'obvious wish for non-involvement except for his writings, and even those are under a nom-de-plume', had been wrong. 'Just do your recce for the projected movie,' F.X. said, 'and if you think we can make the movie there then I'll write to Bingham and ask him if he'd like to work on it, as an adviser or what have you.'

Croon knew he ought to have gone straight to Bingham and introduced himself, said, 'I'm working for F.X. Condy and he sends you his good wishes. I'm here on a reconnaissance for a film of a story which happened here a couple of hundred years ago, and to see if we can shoot it here as well.'

Now, having deferred to F.X.'s overdone qualms about Bingham's privacy — 'anyway, I'm scared he'll run away and I'll get no more of his stuff for *Backwoods*' — he now felt embarrassed, having enjoyed Bingham's company and, in a way, lied to him by his silence.

That morning he had cabled Condy. '*Getting to know Al Zindik stop unavoidable stop must repeat must come clean with him too embarrassing otherwise stop I know he will cooperate stop he is as good as you thought Croon.*'

'When I got his first article,' F.X. had told Croon, 'I was fascinated. I could hardly wait to print it. And I wondered who the hell was Al —*Albert* Zindik? A Czech, an Austrian?' Condy, with his usual fever for being immediately informed, had, through an Arab scholar in New York, discovered that

Al Zindik could mean Freethinker, Unbeliever, and was informed that Al was also El, more familiar to Westerners than Al, and both were only approximations for the Arab sound anyway. Having met Bingham, Croon now knew that there was nothing boringly declamatory about that choice of nom-de-plume. More likely Bingham intended it to reflect a position of uncertainty. He was too cultivated a man to *announce* himself as an unbeliever, unlike that nutcase Tone, who had already hammered his, Croon's, mind with one of the longest denials of the existence of God he had ever heard. When he mentioned this to Bingham the colonel had shaken his head and said, 'Oh, dear dear. We'd all hoped he'd convinced himself at last, because he hasn't orated on that subject for some time now.'

Thinking painfully about his having given in to F.X. and not gone straight to Bingham on his arrival in Induspur, he found himself pacing again and, almost unaware of why, he sat down at the writing table and started a letter to his mother. She was, he had come to understand long ago, the only person alive he could truly be himself with, perhaps because as she had once put it, 'We're both displaced persons, so we understand each other – insofar as that 's possible, of course.' She was very good with riders like that, qualifications which dispelled any hint of possessiveness, or too much knowledge of him, or any threat of ownership, as if she knew well his dread of being owned by anybody, or of ever owning anybody.

No sooner had he begun the letter — 'Dear Mother' — than he put down his pen, lit a cigarette, poured a whiskey, then added soda, and wondered again was it 'healthy' that he, a thirty-eight-year-old man, should still need to write long letters, which he could write to nobody else, to his mother? Not only need to do this but enjoy it as well, feel solaced by having done so, as if the writing of the letter clarified for him what needed clarifying. Was the fact that they had gone through a great deal together enough to explain it? Was some kind of fixation involved, or was such a thought merely one more illustration of how truly modern a man he was, doubting, fearing, interpreting, suspecting all motives as each motive was 'discovered', in other words was he one more victim of the temptation to play psychological games? As he swirled the whiskey in his glass he resented again what he thought of as modern man's loss of thoughtless innocence, but then he laughed as he remembered Condy's view of the matter: 'God-dam it, despite Freud a sausage or a banana is still something to eat, for me. But how long is it going to stay that way? When am I going to start seeing those new Viennese facts?'

His mother, though, was still the best friend he had, which meant someone he could exchange almost any thought with — almost; who had had no plans for him which he had wrecked and could therefore be blamed for, that curse of so many parent-child relationships.

It had begun, he considered, their friendship, when at seventeen he said to her, 'Mother, I can*not* believe. I don't mean *will* not, just cannot. My mind will not accept it any more.'

It had had to be said to her, a devout woman who assumed he had as little difficulty as she did about religion. Yes, that surely was the day their friendship had started, when she had said, 'Well, don't *try*, and don't worry about it. You've got a life before you, and you'll become aware eventually that you're at least involved in an enormous mystery. That'll do to start with.' Then, and it still seemed incredible to him, he had discovered that she was what she called 'a lapsed Marxist'. From that time on long dialogues had continued between them, as now, when he picked up the pen and wrote, 'Just now I found myself wondering if I have a "mother fixation", I mean because you are the only person I could ever write long letters to, pondering aloud in them. Having decided that if I do have a "mother fixation", then I like it, and will continue to live with it, here is my latest news. First — the "scar-tissue" now amounts to eighty thousand dollars, according to my last bank statement, and F.X., that financial wizard, has agreed to invest some of it for me.'

Scar-tissue was his name, used only with her, for the dollars he was so set upon collecting, the covering for the wounds, as he saw it, they had suffered in the struggle with poverty.

'You've got to leave the rathole soon,' he continued, 'and I need to know if you have thought it over and come to a decision. Stop being afraid. I am making a lot of money and it will continue.'

He drank some whiskey. He could hear drums far off in the town — like the background to an old movie, he thought, and drank some more whiskey.

He wanted to uproot his mother. Was she pleased with his

42

plan, or was she pretending to be, and was he right to press her continually to make the move? Was she too old for the thing called 'a fresh start'? She was only sixty, but she had been a long time in that trap, and courageous though he knew her to be, fear could easily have taken her over. His own hatred of the British slum-culture they had both endured, and his still smouldering resentment of the system which had lived off it for so long, should not blind him to any fears she might feel, or that she might have lost her nerve now the choice was there for her.

He sipped some more whiskey slowly, savouring the aroma of the malt, and let his mind browse for a while. He thought again of the day, he was about eleven, when his mother had said after they had had tea one afternoon, 'Let's learn French together, or Italian. Which would you like?' French. It must have been then when learning began to be a pleasure. They had learned Italian together too. Fairly basic stuff, yes, but the door had been opened. He had never been frightened of learning after that.

He was thirty before, like a lightening flash, he had at last understood the quiet tenacity, the extraordinary hope, with which she had clung to her theory, her belief that her husband, his father, was still alive somewhere, in an asylum for mad soldiers in Germany.

That was the day when he, as an officer of the Allied Control Commission in a prairie of ruined buildings which had been a German city, had had an old woman come into his office. Through the interpreter he learned that she wanted information about a certain German private soldier who was 'somewhere in England'. In an asylum. She knew he had been blown up by a shell in France. She had tried again and again for news of him. Please help. Thinking it was about one more German soldier of the millions killed and wounded in the war just over — this was June 1945 — he had asked the usual questions, name, rank, unit, number, and then discovered that the soldier was her husband, killed 'so they keep trying to tell me ' in France in 1917. Forty-seven years of quiet certainty. And she was not mad. This very same strange belief of his mother's about his father, who had been killed on the Somme in 1916, had caused him at times to wonder about his mother's sanity. Yet he knew no one more sane. It was a most tremendous revelation of the peculiar strength and staying power of the female spirit, about love and how it could be felt by a woman, and which a man was quite incapable of.

He had mentioned the story of the old German woman to a colonel who had served on the Western Front right through the first world war. 'Yes,' he had said. 'She's got a point, you know. There's another side to it too. I don't think anybody's ever heard a dying soldier on any battlefield since time began calling out, "Daddy! Daddy! *Always* Mummy, Mama, Mutter, Mother.' And then, Englishly embarrassed by what he had just heard himself say, the colonel had added, 'Of course if one *did* hear a chap dying and calling out, "Daddy, Daddy!" it could be rather worrying, wouldn't you say? I mean it *would* be rather *odd.*'

Even now, Croon reflected, his mother still believed his father was in some soldier's asylum somewhere in Germany, and he had almost come to believe it himself.

As he wrote the words, 'I'm still not quite sure what I'm doing here in India,' he realized that writing the letter was an attempt to find out. 'I feel half-hearted about the project, a film based on a story that happened here in the eighteenth century. It wasn't my idea to do this film. It was F.X.'s idea. Since he "took up India as a subject" he must have read a thousand books. He's never been here but he gave me a book which told me a little of the story that happened here in Induspur towards the end of the eighteenth century, so I'm here looking over the ground. So far — nearly a week here — I've found enough material for a TV subject which could be called "Screwballs at Twilight", or maybe "Rearguard of the Raj". Europeans certainly become eccentric here, though I can see already, after two weeks in India, that nobody in this country can stay normal. There's no real past here, because the past is actually the present, being lived daily. It's a little scary to sit in a train with an elderly Indian who speaks excellent English and be told, quite casually, that if I read the old Indian epics I will see that in ancient India they were using aircraft, and finished up with the atom bomb, which was used in an ancient battle at a place called Kurukshetra near Delhi. They also had television, because, this interesting stranger in the train pointed out to me, it tells in the epic how an old man many days' march away from the battle described the battle in detail as it was being fought. "Then it's quite likely," I said to this fellow, "that the archaeologists will eventually dig up an old bronze television set." He was in no doubt about it. I was fascinated. It was all so normal and ordinary. Then I asked him why the newspapers here liked to scream about the American imperialists with their terror weapon, the atomic bomb, when it was actually an ancient Indian invention and was used thousands of years ago in the most spiritual land on earth. He said, "Those are only low-class, uneducated people who say that kind of thing. But everything that can be thought has been thought here in India. Everything." Certainly, though, this must be the most ancient and continuous civilization on earth. I love it already.

'The film script I wrote last year opened the way for me, and joining F.X.'s company was the best stroke of luck I've ever had. But I'm a bit nervous about this present project in India. This country makes you feel you ought to know all about it before you write a single line about it. But an old timer here said a good thing to me the other night. He said, "Nobody knows, or can ever know, India, no matter how many years he lives here. Only Europeans claim to *know* India. You never hear an Indian claiming to know India. And the average European sees far more of India than most Indians, but he doesn't *know* India. There's too much to know, too many Indias and too many languages and too many religions. Maybe that's why the Indians invented the theory of rebirth. They *have* to keep coming back for another life, then maybe they'll know India some day.

'Enough on that subject. Now, have you made your mind up about the move? I've found the perfect house, not far from New York, in the country and near a beautiful little town —'

He put down his pen. Had he any real right to press her further about what he called 'the move'? He looked into his mother's face now, her thick hair still black, but grey and white streaked, seeing the pale skin of her narrow face with its high cheekbones, and the cool steadiness of her large grey eyes. It seemed impossible that behind such a face could be thoughts about finding a man who had died nearly forty years ago, and again he saw the face of the German widow as she talked across the gulf of the second world war about similar certainties. Nothing mad about such thoughts, he had realized suddenly, when the German woman's quiet certainty had helped him understand for the first time how much more like each other women of all nationalities were, compared

45

with men. Or so it seemed, which called for another whiskey.

'I'm here for the money,' he thought, 'not for the story of the movie we plan to make.' There was a lot of spare American money left over in India from a movie never made, which Condy and his partner were going to use, and already there had been the first signs of the peculiar unreality which was part of the film world. Condy's partner, when told of the plan for the Indian film, had said, 'So — the cast is an Indian woman, an English guy, a Frenchman and an Irishman. Well, one of them's got to be an American, and a star, if we're going to sell this movie.'

'But there could hardly be an American in an isolated little kingdom like Induspur in 1790, Ted,' Croon had protested.

'That's what movies are all about, kid,' Ted Koltz had told him. 'About how an American came to *be* there in 1790. He's not supposed to be there, see, but he's there. How come? Write it and tell it all.'

Croon was already halfway to convincing himself that there could have been an American officer in Induspur in 1790, which was how he knew he was here for the money and not for the film. He had heard himself saying to Condy, 'The fact is, of course, that an American ship could have run aground on the coast of Northern India, and —'

'One of the three survivors,' Condy went on, 'happens to be an American marine captain, who makes his way – maybe captured by one of those wandering criminal tribes who take him up country — he lands up in Induspur and joins the other officers under the Maharajah and helps train the army.' Condy was laughing as he finished, adding, 'You have my sympathy, kid, but go out to India and have a look and kick it around.'

At two in the morning, a few hours after that talk with Condy, Ted Koltz telephoned him and said, 'That idea you've come up with — the American marine captain — F.X. just told me — great! Get your ass over to Induspur and write it, kid. Maybe we start with the storm as the wreckage of the ship breaks up on the rocks and this captain of marines is hurled ashore — the other two survivors die pretty fast — in fact he's bending over them and we see they've had it – so it's just this captain, naked except for —'

Koltz was a small, thin, urgent man in his sixties, who liked to act, and acted out all parts discussed or written, and could

46

bring tears to his own eyes, and carefully hidden embarrassment to his attentive colleagues, during these script conferences when he acted out his version.

Croon's personal target was one million dollars in the bank. And then? Another million dollars. The first million was to be spending money, the second million for investment and taxes.

Only now, as he thought of Ted Koltz and the coming film invasion of this ancient little backwater Indian state, could Croon at last see why he was so hesitant about approaching the Maharajah and doing all the things research for the film required him to do.

The state was an antique. He had sensed that already. It lived in a silence of centuries, and he was planning the end of that golden silence in this room of a hotel devoted to a Kipling who never was, who had never been here. Yet Kipling *had* been here, now, for the story was believed, especially by the hotel owners who had invented it. He had already mentioned in a letter to a friend in America: 'The hotel is old and they say Kipling used to stay here in the old days.' *They say*. Of course.

So why worry too much about making a film here when the thin edge of the fiction-wedge was already stuck fast in Induspur's long dreaming afternoon? There would be a shower of dollar bills, contracts, bit parts, extras, a river of Coke, and the fierce excitement the people would get from living a foreigner's fiction on film about an alleged set of facts from their own history. The place would never be the same afterwards. The silence would fall again, yes, but it would be a disturbed, restless silence.

'I feel quite paternal,' he was writing to his mother after these thoughts; 'fondly imperial, I should say, when I consider that we will probably ruin this place by making a film here.'

CHAPTER 6

Some months after the sudden death of his wife and son, months spent in a state of numbness, a sort of complete emotional sedation, the Maharajah left the palace, telling his *Diwan* that he was going to Delhi for a couple of weeks. Instead he drove north for nearly a hundred miles to a remote village where he left his car. He told the villagers that he was an engineer from Delhi on pilgrimage to Kamalamukhi, a famous shrine sixty miles further north. Pleased to hear this, they fed him and told him they would look after his car.

He took an army pack containing a spare shirt and a few other necessities, and for the next few days climbed rocky hills, descended into deep gorges and passed through silent forests, until far ahead he could see the temple of Kamalamukhi high on its conical hill against the cloudless sky. Then he walked until he came to the forest below the hill of Kamalamukhi where he came on a forest scout with whom he shared tea as they squatted over a fire in the forest clearing.

'Tell me,' the Maharajah said, 'is *Kamalamukhi ki Baba* still living in his retreat?'

'He is,' said the old forest scout. 'I take fruit to him sometimes. Last time he said to me, "Why are you good to me when I give you nothing?" ' The old man laughed as he accepted a cigarette from the stranger.

'And what did you say?'

'I said the truth. I said, "Because you never lie to us. You have no visions. You have attained no wisdom. You have not performed, nor have you seen, any miracles. Over the years we ask you, and never once have you been tempted to tell us just one lie to please us, even though we are disappointed in you." '

'So you like him for that? People are pleased with him for that?'

The old man squinted at the Maharajah through his cigarette smoke as if suddenly realizing that this stranger was a simpleton.

'An honest man?' he asked. 'A *saddhu* who came here in retreat to seek wisdom and sanctity thirty years ago and who has found nothing, and tells us so when we ask for news of his discoveries, and he knows we await that news all these years? And he will not satisfy us even with one lie, just one time? And you wonder that we like him? When he went to the last *Kumbh Mela* between the sacred rivers to meet the swarms of holy men from all over India, most of them liars, cheats, vultures and parasites, even there at that sacred place he found nothing.' The old man shook his head ruefully. 'That's what he told us when he came back. Nothing, Well, I can tell you, there was a row here when he said that, again. People lost their tempers with him. You know how it is, *huzoor*. People want results, especially after all those years of self-denial and solitude of his. After all, he is our man now. He is there *for us*. He represents our wish for holiness, for goodness, for a final understanding of what all this daily living we have to do is all about. Isn't that right? We are simple, ignorant men and he is learned, but even so we have not had one single example of spiritual enlightenment of any kind from him in all these years. Now, it is obvious he is holy, that he is good, that he is learned, but that is not enough.'

'But he is truthful.'

Bitterly, the old man nodded. 'Yes, I'm afraid so. We like him for that. It is against our will, of course, as you will understand yourself, liking him for that, for nothing in fact, but that is the effect that he has on us all. It's not right, but we have to accept it. So, if you're going to him for wisdom or enlightenment you won't get it. All you'll get is the truth.'

The old man broke into a choking cackle of laughter.

The Maharajah reached the cave of *Kamalamukhi ki Baba* in the early evening. He kicked off his shoes, knelt down, made *pranam*, his hands pressed together, then looked across the red, smoking coals of the cooking fire into the calm face of the grey-bearded *saddhu* squatting opposite him. They spoke in the Prakrit dialect of the hills.

'I remember you,' the *saddhu* told him. 'You were the

young kinglet back from education in England and Italy. We talked of evolution. Are you still ruling somewhere down there?'

'For a while longer, I think,' said the Maharajah. 'The wheel has turned and people are falling off. So I cling there, for a while longer, possibly.'

The *saddhu* nodded. 'And if you fall off will you be unhappy?' he asked. 'Will you fight to stay on the wheel, or are you thinking of getting off it in your own time?'

'You seem fairly happy here in your cave, *Saddhuji*? You've been off the wheel yourself a long time now. Do you still speak English or have you forgotten it?'

'I remember it well,' the *saddhu* replied in English, smiling. 'Make some tea for us. I have never had tea from the hands of a king. What brings you here?'

'Whatever it was it's gone now. The walking here did it. I feel refreshed, better.'

'The water is over there in that jar. So — you have not come to me for advice, help, prayer.' He smiled. 'A king hanging on to the wheel would need a political Brahmin adviser, not a *saddhu*. But I'm glad you came. Stay with me the night and talk.'

As they drank their tea they spoke about the Maharajah's permanent, obsessive preoccupation, the mystery of being here — 'or rather the pity about seeing it as such,' said the Maharajah playfully. 'I would have preferred to be the type who never thought of such things. You may not agree with me, *Saddhuji*, but it *is* possible to live a whole life, and enjoy it, without being bothered by such thoughts. Many live that way.'

The *saddhu* nodded. 'Yes,' he said. 'I know. You are right. I've achieved it.'

The Maharajah looked up from pouring the tea, and showed his surprise. 'You have?'

'Once I'd made the decision I never looked back,' said the *saddhu*. 'Thank you.' He took the mug of tea and sipped at it.

'What decision was that?'

'To waste my life. To decide to do nothing with it, or with the body, or the mind. To give it the very minimum of food to keep it breathing, and to breathe. I'm still not totally harmless, though as close now as I can get to it. At first when I came here thirty years ago I used to go to the nearest town

50

every few weeks, to mingle with the crowd, to see if I still mattered, as I had thought of it once. But I only mattered because I was there, with other people, and I knew that as soon as I went I would cease to matter again. It seemed pointless, that experiment, after a while. So I stopped it. Since then I have been steady with my decision and have followed it. I have wasted my life just as I had decided to do it. I have learned nothing, even from watching the beetles and insects, the birds and the animals. Nothing, I am glad to say.'

'No visions? No trances?'

'Trances, yes. They're easy. I can hypnotize myself at any moment. I can enter trance without any trouble. But no visions. Just the trance. I must be the most fortunate of men. Do you understand? I have lost all doubts, all hope, all aspiration, all thirst for spiritual enlightenment, as I once thought of it. That took time, and much waste of it. I can hardly wait for death. Perhaps *that* will be the one vision I shall have. Yet — in this new time we are living in — it will be evident, even to the babe in the woman's arms — soon, that all is changed, forever —'

'The bomb? Are you talking about the annihilation-bomb, the atom-bomb?'

The *saddhu* was nodding, smiling. 'Yes. Those scientists were quicker than the old sages thought. After all this is the *Kali Yug* we live in, the age of iron and destruction, the age of evil and chaos, and it was supposed to last a few thousand more years — but it can end, this age and all the ages to come, for man, that is — at any single moment now. And it seems to have produced a new kind of European, this bomb. I have had three of them here during the last year. They're not like they were, these Europeans. They don't want to lecture about sanitation and other Indian problems. No. They're rather pitiful. They ask me for spiritual advice, for help, for a solution to the problem they have built — built for all of us.'

'And what did you tell them?'

The *saddhu* frowned. He was silent for a while. The Maharajah poured more tea into his mug and waited.

'I found there was enough evil still in me to rise up and speak, I am afraid.' He was silent again, evidently recalling things he now regretted. 'I told them to tell their scientists to get on with the important work, that is to make what I believe they call the "clean bomb", a bomb, apparently, which annihilates but does not poison the world with radiation. I told them to prevent the final war until they have invented that clean bomb, and then to have their war, a war to annihilation. A war that will make all Europe, all the West into a desert. And then we can all be at peace for another few thousand years, Asiatics, Africans, all who have not taken part in the insanity of building this annihilation-weapon, and who do not in any way deserve to share the doom they have been trying to put together since before Alexander the Great reached those mountains across the plain, and then turned back to Greece.'

'What did they say to that?'

'They were contemptible. They agreed with me. They said they deserved to disappear, that their culture was dead and should be annihilated. They had come to India to find spiritual truth. I told them I had none to give them. They refused to believe me. They became angry then. They told me I was too proud to reveal my secrets. They were dressed in saffron cloaks and had begging bowls. They seemed to me like a sign of the end of the world. There will be signs, I expect, and they may have been one of them.'

They talked late into the night. sitting in the mouth of the cave in blazing starlight, the red embers of the fire smouldering between their feet, the *saddhu* expanding his thoughts on the secrets of the thoroughly wasted life.

He had understood, he said, when quite young, that as the purpose of life was the purpose given to it by every individual, which was usually to eat and breathe, perhaps make one or two great statements, write one or two books, derive a theory and prove it, or build an atomic bomb, purposelessness could be pursued as its own purpose. And he had done that. His only spiritual act, while in this steady and devoted waste of his life, was of the right kind, he felt, because it was accidental and it had been continuous — he had lived without harming anybody.

He knew he had disappointed the local people scattered in the few villages among these hills and forests, who had given him grain and fruit to live on, in that he had been able to produce no magic, no wondrous signs, no messages, so that he had no threat, no aura, no sanctity. The *saddhu* fell alseep first. The Maharajah dozed, then heard the *saddhu* speaking in his sleep. He listened, entranced.

'Darwin Sahib,' the *saddhu* was calling softly in *Prakrit*. 'You are there again. Ah, you are there again. Stealer of my innocence, and my hope, of my journey now lost forever. Had you only kept silence, hidden your visions from us all, men would still pray. Do you not think so?' The *saddhu* began to snore.

He woke the Maharajah again later with his mumblings, these again about the loss of belief, hope, faith, and the happiness this loss had given him. Once again Darwin was mentioned, and this time given a title of honour – Darwin Bahadur, breaker of ancient delusions. This time the Maharajah was amused, though it was a compassionate amusement he felt, but for him it seemed an occult happening that the thinker who had for so long dogged his inner journeys with doubt, Darwin, should disturb the dreams of this *saddhu*, and that he, awake, should hear it.

At dawn he was awake and watched the *saddhu* standing in the river below the cave, and praying. Strange that this emptied, faithless, honest and likeable *saddhu* should continue that ancient Hindu ritual and recite the oldest prayer on earth. It was all too strange ever to be understood, what men did, tried to do, failed to do, in these never-to-be-solved and never-to-be discarded areas of personal and spiritual anxiety. And there was nothing mechanical about the way the *saddhu* said his prayer, more a statement to the rising sun he now faced from where he stood in the racing waters of the river. Water and sun, the life-givers in one, saluted with this prayer for hundreds of centuries. Watching the *saddhu*, intent, knowing the words of the short prayer of the *Gayatri*, he said them himself.

'*Om, bhur-bhuvar svar* — we think about your lovable magnificence, O sun — now, stir our thoughts.' It was reverence anyway, even said by the unbeliever, the faithless, the Maharajah thought, and there could never be enough reverence for such things as the certainty of sunrise, the next drawing in of breath, itself a celebration.

As he shouldered his pack the *saddhu* squatting in the mouth of his cave said, 'There is something unsaid between us, and it is in your head awaiting permission to emerge.' He smiled and stirred the embers of the fire, his deep calm eyes on those of his guest.

It was true. All morning he had been tempted to say to the

saddhu, 'I have discovered one thing from you, that we both owe a painful, an unwanted, debt to Darwin Sahib.' But he could not bring himself to say that he had overheard his troubled dreams. Yet the longing to sit down and discuss this permanent and fascinating topic was very strong, especially now that it had been invited.

'I will come again, *Saddhuji*,' he said, and made *pranam*, bowing. Tantalized, conscious of the link between them now, the two men smiled and the Maharajah swung away down the track.

Throughout the long journey back to where he had left his car, at the two sleeping-places where he sat and watched the stars before sleeping, the Maharajah tussled with the strange experience he had had. He knew that in youth just after the first world war, the *saddhu* had studied in England prior to entering the Indian Civil Service, and one night must have read Darwin and then sat in the crumbled Vedic rubble of a whole culture, a whole new unknown road opened for him

He would have liked to discuss the other phenomenon caused by Darwin, something quite apart from the quiet, logical destruction of centuries of certainty, and that was how certain Anglo-Saxon men of action had seized upon the theory and made it theirs. They had made speeches about the special civilizing mission of the Anglo-Saxon race, its supremacy over all others, and had neatly stolen so much of Darwin's theory to make it 'the survival of the fittest'; and the fittest were the Anglo-Saxons. Valuable thinking for empire-builders, and it had worked, but they could not hold onto it. Nothing lasted, no certainty remained certain and the world was continuous flux, eternal commotion of ideas, discoveries, and steady, remorseless assassinations of lesser cultures. Yes, he thought, there was a lot to be said for sitting in that cave, detached, harmless, waiting.

The Maharajah, whose father, convinced his son was a reincarnation of the King of Magadha, had called him Chandra Gupta, ate nothing but fruit on two days of the week, and kept total silence throughout another day, a day he called, smilingly, *maun*-day. There were no religious reasons for these now fixed habits. He hoped that the fruit diet might ease the arthritis in his right knee, and he used the day of silence as an excuse for isolation in his enormous library, where he drank Laprog whiskey while studying the history of the world. 'That is to say the "so called" history, or rather what has been selectively passed down to us,' as he had once said to Bingham.

Just now he was reading the works of Karl Marx in a Soviet edition given him by Bingham. 'Being Soviet,' Bingham had told him, 'certain facts are missing, naturally, such as examples of Marx's anti-Semitism and so on. But on the whole it's not bad to start with.'

'Quite touching, though,' the Maharajah responded, 'that the Soviets with their mania about the Jews should be so sensitive about their German-Jewish Moses.'

When he and Bingham discussed modern politics the Maharajah always referred to Stalin as Joey Djugashvili or 'Mrs Djugashvili's little boy', and liked to pretend he was convinced that Hitler had been a member of the Russian Communist party and had taken all his orders from Stalin. But though they joked and fantasized together, often convulsed with laughter, Bingham and the Maharajah had discovered that they both felt 'stained through and through' by what happened in Europe during and after the second world war. Europe, the Maharajah said, had attempted suicide twice, once in 1914 and again, because of 1914, in 1939. Sick now, perhaps unto death, Europe *might* recover, though it was more likely it would stumble into Communism by accident, or because of its own soul-weariness and self-disgust.

Another hobby of the Maharajah's was the cinema, and by unspoken public agreement he was allowed to go to the local cinema, which was called The Chaplin, wearing a dhoti and a cotton shirt like the other male members of the audience, and was studiously and affectionately ignored. Bingham would sometimes accompany him and if the film was an old Western the Maharajah would whisper, 'I like to think Joey Djugashvili enjoyed this one,' or, 'He's mad on Westerns, you know. God knows what dialectically materialistic undertones he saw in this one — that sheriff in the last scene, for instance, the man's obviously a wrecker, a revisionist.'

'A mad dog who will shortly receive a mighty rebuff,' Bingham might add, and, still playing with standard Soviet terminology the Maharajah, if he approved of Bingham's remarks, would reply, 'Stormy applause, Tim,' or, 'Loud and stormy applause.'

Deeper than his glooms about what the Hitler war had

done to the world was the Maharajah's sense of shock which followed the murder of the Mahatma, Gandhi, and the fact that it had been planned and committed by Brahmins was still horrifying and incomprehensible to him, even after five years. Gandhiji had asked the impossible, it was true. They all had — Buddha, Jesus, Muhammad — but thousands of millions over the generations had attempted, and would go on attempting, to live that good, harmless life, which was impossible but vital to try, or even to plan to try. But Gandhi's request to India that it turn its back on the machine-world was the most impossible of all the requests ever made by any of the great practical mystics. For Chandra Gupta, Maharajah of the hardly-known little state of Induspur, Gandhi's wish that India should reject the technology of the twentieth century, and live a simple Indian life — in fact live like the majority of the four hundred million Indians had lived for centuries, and still lived, was as noble as it was hopeless. It could not be denied that Gandhi was right, but it could not be denied either that he had asked the impossible. It was as if he had foreseen how fast the new technocratic giant would trample across the whole world, a machine that would chew up all harmless, helpless cultures, erase forests and poison oceans.

Oh, yes, the Maharajah would say, waving his hand feebly, when stopped in the middle of such a speaking vision of the world now in the making, we do know that this machine-monster *could* make a just world in which all are clothed and fed and given dignity, but Gandhi knew that the helpless millions will be more at the mercy of that machine than they ever were of hunger and sickness. There might even come a Soviet-American technocracy, both giants married at last, running a world-madhouse of twitching consumers. To have wanted an India in which people made their own simple clothes, the spinning-wheel the only tiny recognition of the giant which had plans even for outer space, was touching and hopeless, but for the Maharajah unforgettable.

Gandhi was not shot for that impractical vision, though, the Mararajah would remember to say during discussions about the murder. He was shot for asking too much forgiveness, understanding, forbearance, even affection, for the new Pakistan. Shot by Brahmins, the highest caste, representatives of the longest line of thinkers and teachers, and charlatans, in the history of the world. In a way a kind of caste killing too, for Gandhi was no Brahmin, and was shot for pressing for an end to the caste system.

The day they shot Gandhiji the Maharajah had been sitting in a deckchair, exhausted after returning from the Punjab with an ambulance unit he had formed. Even then the nightmare of the migrations of Hindus and Muslims was still in chaotic progress on the plains of the Punjab hundreds of miles from Induspur. Bewildered millions of the poor, stumbling in choking yellow dustcloud behind the screeching wooden wheels of the bullock-carts, were leaving certainties they had known for centuries, for various forms of unknown, politically proclaimed 'national goals', to form new slums on the edge of strange cities like Lahore, Karachi, Delhi. A Pandit, Doctor Durga Parshad, and Bingham had been part of the ambulance unit, and together with slightly hysterical but idealistic students, Hindu, Sikh and Muslim, all still Indians, still unwilling to separate as Pakistanis and Indians in these terrible scenes of disaster on the plains, they had done what they could in the tide of desperate people.

One scene in the Punjab he and Bingham still reminded each other of — 'You remember that poor old patriarch who gripped our hands that day?' — stayed at the front of the Mararajah's memory. In fact he had been thinking about it as he fell asleep in the deck chair that afternoon, covered with yellow dust, more stunned than tired after the scenes they had lived through in the Punjab. Dogs rootling for bodies in the shallow graves, women howling and weeping, millions of ghost-like people moving through the fog of reddish-yellow dust, towards water, towards strangerhood in new places

A very old stooped man with the powerful shoulders and big hands of an honest peasant farmer had left the ranks of the trudging mass. He came towards them, Bingham and the Maharajah, wearing a ragged turban, his white beard thick and matted, a child cradled in his left arm. Tears had appeared in his wild eyes and his huge, hard right hand had gripped Bingham's, 'not mine, the Indian's, but Bingham's, the white Sahib's,' the Maharajah would say.

'Sahib, O Sahib,' the old man, looking like Saint Joseph, Moses, had cried to Bingham in Urdu, 'Tell us what is happening to us. Why are we here like this, and to what are we going? What have we done to have lost our humble place? Tell us, Sahib. What has happened to us?'

57

Then, perhaps feeling the Indian might know the answer, he had then taken the Maharajah's hand, saying, 'Can we come back some day, Sahib? We never did any harm. Never. What has caused this madness?' as he waved his hand at the Biblical scene of fleeing millions.

Well . . . ? Jinnah? Kali, perhaps? The Prophet? The Congress Party? God? Well . . . .

The old man was a Muslim, simple, illiterate, trusting, his life of labour written in his face and body, a living artefact of a once great Islamic world, and Bingham had been tempted to try and solace him with what had once been a Muslim attitude. 'It is Fate. Fate cannot be arranged, or altered. *Lā yughni hadhar 'an qadar.*'

'What can we tell him, Tim?' the Maharajah said, low-voiced, tears in his eyes.

'Plead guilty, I suppose,' Bingham replied bitterly. It was impossible to tell even a friend as good as the Maharajah of the fury and disgust he was feeling about all this insanity, or that he meant every intelligent human being, in what had been India before it was torn apart, was guilty. But perhaps he, the representative of foreign sahibhood, was guiltiest of all. But he could not quite wear it, not for himself, yet. So they gave the old man some money, 'guilt-money' the Maharajah called it later, the palm-oil of helplessness and evasion. To answer the old man's question, the Maharajah later reflected, it would have been necessary to recite the history of the world, of the ape-angel called man.

Yes, he had fallen asleep in the deck-chair, half waking to wave away the welcoming servants with the cold drinks, and had then been startled awake again by a frightening sound, a wailing sound in the town beyond the palace where he sat, a mass of people lamenting, with fear in the sound, and it grew louder and louder. The little town had just heard the news, that the Mahatma, the beloved and gentle leader with the will of steel, had been assassinated. The unbelievable had now to be believed.

All were one at that hour in Induspur, the Marwari money-worshipper and the professional beggar, spotless Brahmin and tainted sweeper, thief and policeman, as they gathered near the palace and the Maharajah joined them, the wailing over, but tears on every face as they listened to Pandit

Nehru's low husky voice over the radio. 'A light has gone out of our lives —'

All over the sub-continent, as they heard the news, fear filled every listener. It *had* to be a Muslim who had committed this incredible sacrilege, so people whispered to each other, or to themselves, 'My God, I only hope it wasn't a Muslim who did it,' for millions of Muslims had decided to live on in India and not accept migration to the new Pakistan, all now condemned to death or banishment if it was one of theirs who had slain the Mahatma.

It was even harder to take in, though, that not only had a Hindu killed him, but a sacred Brahmin Hindu, one of the new kind of fanatics who wanted an all-Hindu India; the great bubbling Hindu soup, the stockpot of a hundred invading and melted-down foreign cultures must be skimmed off, sieved and made pure again, truly Hindustan. But they would never get that Hindustan, the Maharajah was sure, for it was India's role in history to be and stay a living museum of all thought, all men, genius or charlatan, it did not matter which. There was room for every inspiration, every idiocy.

'Tim,' the Maharajah said to Bingham, months after the murder, 'I wonder if there will ever be an Indian Shakespeare, one who will write the drama of these days. About Nehru, Panditji, the idealist and Westernized Brahmin agnostic who despised the caste system, who looked to a liberal world of East-West togetherness, but who bent his mind in order to believe in the little gnome he revered, Gandhiji, and lived to see India ripped apart and Gandhiji murdered. I can't believe I've lived through it all. Can you?'

Opening up the newly discovered coal deposits in a remote and wild area of the state took his mind off these things, and he became involved in raising capital for the venture, and trying to form a co-operative so that the profits from the coal would go to the people of the state. He knew his plans for this would not last, that all principalities great and small were doomed eventually, and that after his death some local money-lender or money-hunter would somehow seize the coal deposits. Only those who understood and loved money would make money. He would live out his life, read and think his remaining years away, a relic of the military caste which had once ridden to drums and trumpets, obedient to a hundred rituals as old as the Aryan invaders who had ridden into India with the Vedas and the worship of the mother-cow on whose stream of sacred milk the world had been suspended.

Guilt. Yes, that was his new preoccupation, and which he could only discuss with another master of the subject: Bingham. Together they would talk it over, this new awareness of how the ruling classes of Western and Eastern culture had betrayed their peoples, and themselves as well, but had not been aware of it while engaged in the betrayal. How could they have dreamed that their enemy, implacable and determined, would be the marvellous people of Russia, a slave-race who had never known freedom as Western and Asian man had known it, and who therefore had never missed it, did not know what Western man was talking about. These masses of Russia, a mass of grey unleavened dough, lovers of poetry and drink, warm and tender-hearted and brave, had been trampled upon, imprisoned and murdered by the million since 1917, and seemed to love it, to need it, and were ready to defend it all to the death, to world-annihilation if necessary. And they loved their fearful master whom it had taken another soul-engineer, Trotsky, properly to describe: Stalin, 'Genghiz Khan with a telephone.'

Would there ever be any real dialogue about the facts of living with these people under their new religion handed down to them from Moses Marx, the Maharajah wondered.

Guilt. 'Your last two wars did it, Tim,' he said to Bingham one night, and Bingham nodded agreement, guilty. Mine, he thought, my wars? Change the subject. Tonight he had something quite new to discuss with the Maharajah.

'Chan,' he said. 'What would you say to a film, a big film, being made here in Induspur, with American money?'

'Well!' Chan's eyes lit up and he put down his glass of whiskey and reached for a cigarette. 'You know me, Tim. I love films and if I thought I could act in a film, why — why I'd have to be prevented, of course. Are you serious?'

Bingham handed him a long letter he had received in the afternoon from Condy. 'It's all in there,' he said. 'See what you think.'

The Maharajah was forty-eight, a man of medium height with a handsome Rajput face, beginning to run to fat now, and Bingham watched him, amused by the avid interest in the keen hazel eyes as he swiftly read the letter, and nodded agreement again and again as he read. Suddenly he looked up and said, 'Tim, be a good chap and call Shambles Lal,' then, 'This is so damned *exciting*. Who *is* this American? *Such* an enthusiast, eh?' He went on reading as Bingham went to look for Shambles Lal. This was their private nickname for Shambu Lal, the Maharajah's *Diwan*, a sort of chief ministering amanuensis and inherited friend from older times when Chandra Gupta's father had ruled here.

'Shampers, old thing,' the Maharajah said to his *Diwan* when Bingham brought him back, 'I've a new secret to discuss with you, something to celebrate, I fear, so get a bottle of your nickname and let's drink this secret over with Tim here.' Shampers was the public nickname the Maharajah used for his *Diwan*, who seldom drank wine or spirits but when he did preferred champagne, hence his nickname. Though nearing eighty now the old man was still strong and fit, and had only recently decided he should play no more squash with the Maharajah. He always wore, in the evenings, a long black *atchkan* buttoned up to the neck and shaped to his slim and athletic figure, and loose wide white cotton *salwar* or *pajama* trousers. On his feet were pointed red velvet shoes. He was quite bald, his skin glowing brown. He always reminded Bingham of a resigned eagle.

'A curious thing, Tim,' the Maharajah said, waving the letter. 'Would you believe I had a dream about it, about a month ago? Could it have been when this American was actually writing this letter, my God —?' He picked up the envelope and examined the postmark, then the date at the head of the letter. 'No, damn it, *but* I was ahead of the letter with my dream.' He stared into Bingham's amused eyes. 'You can laugh, you cynical bugger,' he went on. 'But I did dream that a theatrical event took place here in the streets of Induspur town. I thought it was something from the *Mahabarata*, people in ancient costumes, and so on, but it's all about our own little Induspuri epic of the eighteenth century. How damn strange.' He lost himself for a while in his own thoughts, while Shambu Lal poured champagne into silver goblets, part of a set presented to the Maharajah's grandfather by the Russian tsar of that time.

'Who is this fellow Croon, and why hasn't he been to see me about this film thing?' The Maharajah took the goblet of foaming wine from the *Diwan* and raised it to the other two as they seated themselves. 'To the world of make believe!' he intoned with mock solemnity, and to the *Diwan*, 'Yes, Shampers, and this is secret for now, we have been discovered by America *and* the film business. You'd better get hold of the astrologer, the new one, what's his name? Cheers, both of you. Now, I'll just read through this again, then we'll talk.'

They drank the cold champagne and then the Maharajah read the letter again while Bingham quietly answered questions put to him by the *Diwan*.

CHAPTER 7

'There are times, Tim, when I really must follow my insticts, my intuition,' the Maharajah had once tried to explain to Bingham. He was trying to clarify what he felt about his own 'sense of mystery'. There were too many mysterious things which happened in a person's life for them to be merely accidental, or worse, what he called 'Western man's easiest and favourite temptation, coincidence'. It was simply that Western man was afraid of anything which could not somehow be worried or teased into a logical explanation. It also helped him, Western man, in his lifelong struggle against belief in any spiritual explanation for these strange happenings. 'The bugger was always waiting for Darwin and company to come along and wrap it all up for him,' the Maharajah said, and would then follow up with how Western man could at last say, with relief, 'In the beginning was the word and, of course, it was a lie.'

'What are you trying to say, Chan?' Bingham had once asked in the middle of one of these sessions.

'I've no idea — yet,' Chan replied bitterly. 'But it's very typical that I'm asked, while I'm in the middle of trying to think up an answer out loud.' Then had laughed, as usual. But the Maharajah was serious in his effort to define his feeling that this life was — somehow — all planned, but we only got brief and tantalizing glimpses of the clues, which vanished as soon as they could.

Sometimes they actually got onto 'God', and then Chan would cry out, 'That *word* — God. You see just because we are men we immediately have to give that word, God, a shape we can recognize, so for the West he became a big Daddy with a beard in the sky. That's natural, that man should try and give him a shape like that. But God isn't a being or a person or a thing, or a shape. He may be a machine without a shape, a universe in fact. What d'you say to that, Tim?'

'Those glimpses of the clues you've just mentioned,' said

Bingham. 'Those are private glimpses and cannot be conveyed to another, even partially, though people try.'

'So you've had them. You *know*.' The Maharajah was excited. 'You know what I'm talking about then.'

'I sometimes see things which I know will happen, and they happen,' Bingham then said, looking as if he regretted saying it, and still excited, the Maharajah interrupted to announce, 'I know you do. I've seen you do it. Explain *that* away.'

'Now, I'm not here to represent the West, Chan,' said Bingham with assumed severity. 'Just because I'm from the West. So don't waste any time in setting me up as your target. I'm just as puzzled as you are about this mystery of being here. And it's gone on for me a few years longer than it has for you. I'm sixty. You're forty odd. Now, you may be right about God being the universe itself. Cigarette?'

'This problem of wanting to *believe*,' Chan would often say. 'Why is it that a man wants to *believe*?' Once, having said this, he went on to add, 'Women find it easier to believe. Have you ever noticed that?' He had. It was in the conversation which followed that the Maharajah discovered that, like himself, Bingham was a widower.

They were in Bingham's house that night and were about to walk down into the town to see the new film at The Chaplin cinema, the Maharajah dressed as an ordinary town Indian in *dhoti* and cotton jacket. There was really no need any longer for this fancy dress, as he had said himself, but it was still an exciting thing to do.

They were talking about Meg Brett-Turner and how she had once said, after listening to the Maharajah and Bingham more or less accepting, or pretending to accept, the inevitable destruction of all civilization, all life, all mankind, by coming atomic warfare. 'You idiots. Life is indestructible. It will always go on, no matter what, come what may.'

How did she know that? What made her say that?

'I don't know,' she said. 'But it's just obvious. All you two are really talking about is how, with these new impossible-to-use weapons, you can still go on indulging in your favourite pastime, war. And you're depressed because you can't find the answer. So it's got to be the end of the end of the world. Which is nonsense.'

Bingham and the Maharajah had exchanged the kind of

look men are supposed to exchange when a woman says something like that.

'I suppose,' Bingham said, discussing it with the Maharajah, 'that if women didn't think like that none of us would be here anyway.'

After all, he reasoned, though careful to say it all lightly and get a few laughs here and there so as not to be thought too serious about it all, a man was in a woman's care from the first days in the womb until he tumbled into the grave. So it was not really surprising that a woman, no matter what annihilation threatened via these new weapons, should still feel certain that life would go on.

'And maybe they'll be the ones to see it will,' Bingham mused as he poured a couple of whiskies. He looked across the room at the Maharajah. 'Men will never disarm. Never,' he continued. 'But maybe international women could arrange disarmament. I don't see any other way out.'

As he took the whiskey from Bingham the Maharajah said, 'Don't you ever get lonely on your own here, Tim?' He indicated the room, the big rambling house built for the British resident in 1858 by his great-grandfather.

'I've always found loneliness, as you call it, very useful, as a matter of fact, Chan.' Bingham sat down on the Syrian camel saddle which had carried him into Jerusalem in 1917 and grinned at the Maharajah. 'Had to, of course, years ago, but once you've tasted being alone, and learnt not to feel lonely, you get to like it, you know. I hardly knew my wife. I think I got to know her better after she died. Thinking about her, remembering things I hadn't really noticed. It's amazing how much you can learn about somebody — in your memory — after they're dead.'

The Maharajah and Bingham had been friends for seven years and never until now had Bingham mentioned a wife. That was the curious thing about Bingham, the way he could hold you off without trying to. No intimacies unless he gave the signal, yet there was nobody the Maharajah had ever known so good to converse with, so stimulating to discuss even unimportant things with. It was as if Bingham had frozen off an area of himself, deliberately.

'You hardly knew her?' He must not look too eager, the Maharajah thought, so he looked around the enormous living room as if interested, as he went on, as casually as he could. 'Was she beautiful?'

'They're all beautiful,' Bingham met his look and smiled. 'Yes, I mean it. All beautiful. I say that as someone who's spent most of his life in wildernesses, with soldiers, the odd fast woman here and there, you know the kind of thing, "Ease Springs" as the infantry say.' He began to muse again. 'Yes, she was beautiful and I was handsome — perfect.' He smiled again, 'Except that I spent a total of six months with her, all staggered, odd leaves.' He took a drink of the whiskey. 'She went down on a ship between London and Bombay. Torpedoed. 1941.'

'Christ! So we both know what it's like, a wife dying far away from you.'

Bingham saw that his friend's occult area was awake again, and he smiled and nodded, saying, 'All right, I won't say it's coincidence. It all has a meaning.'

'That must have hurt, Tim. Where were you then?'

'Hurt?' Bingham sighed. He came across and took the Maharajah's glass and as he poured another drink into it, said, 'I was hurt, for her. I mean — well it's hard to describe without sounding a complete bastard — but I'd grown up quite a bit by then and had lost interest in her. I was just sorry she'd lost her life. More permanent than a divorce, and unnecessary as far as I was concerned. After all I was only twenty-six when I married her, and hardly saw her again during the next ten years. So I can hardly say I've been married. I'm a widower in the same way I was a husband, hardly at all. By the time I was thirty it was too late for me to domesticate anyway. My idea of happiness was coming across tobacco unexpectedly in some odd corner of Central Asia or Persia or whatever.' He laughed. 'True. After all my work took me to some strange places, where you borrowed a woman for a while until you moved on. No, I'm not lonely. Just uncertain.'

'You still haven't made your mind up — about what to do?'

This was an old subject between them since Bingham had retired and come to live in Induspur.

'It's just restlessness,' said Bingham. 'Time will deal with that. I miss the work. I've plenty to occupy me, though' — he made a gesture with his hand — '*Inshallah!*' He looked down into his whiskey and then jerked his head up quickly in such a way that the Maharajah knew he had made a decision. 'I'll show you something, and give you something to laugh about, Chan,' he said. Bingham rose and went down the room to an enormous Chinese wall cupboard. He opened a drawer, took out a large photograph in a gilded frame and held it up. 'I wonder if you remember this face, Chan?' he said. He came back down the room and handed the photograph to the Maharajah, then sat down on the camel saddle again and waited for reactions. He was grinning when the Maharajah looked up at him and exclaimed, 'My God, Tim, that face. Of course I do. But where was it? No, don't tell me, let me guess, let me remember.'

They often played these memory games. Bingham poured two more whiskies, humming nervously to himself, while the Maharajah made guesses to which he would say, 'No. Try again. You were made about that face when you saw it, remember? Have another look at it.' He was obviously on edge, the Maharajah noticed, for he walked the whole length of the room, still humming, then as he walked back, and the Maharajah still gazed down at the beautiful face in the photograph, he let himself go. The Maharajah was so surprised by this that he looked hard at Bingham, for he had never known him so urgent, so doubtful, so certain, so talkative even for him, and at the same time so unexpectedly pathetic.

'It's the girl in the bookshop in Delhi. Nearly a year ago I took you in there. Time you bought' — he held up his hand as the Maharajah exclaimed, 'Why yes, yes, yes. That wonderful creature — '

'The time you bought the first edition of Tod's *Rajasthan* – – yes, yes, well that's her. Proposed to me. Yes , wait, listen, it gets worse. I'm just this side of obscenity after all — a man twenty-three years older than her — yes, I'm afraid so, madly in love, I'm just on sixty don't forget — and her whole family's *for* it. Her father is one of my oldest friends, a devout but twentieth-century Muslim — I mean he likes the odd Scotch and so on — and we did a book together, the father and me, I mean, translations of eighteenth-century Muslim poetry. Tells me one night that his daughter loves me and asks me what about me? What do I feel about that? I'm free, am I not? No wife. Wouldn't matter if I had three wives, the daughter would be willing to be the fourth. Truly. You can laugh, Chan, and I suppose it is funny, but you can see my situation. I love this woman. At first I thought the father was simply trying to unload her onto me — because the girl's thirty-six, thirty-seven — taught in England and France after she graduated — never Mister Right, or Mister Wrong as Meg Brett-Turner likes to call it — but has been in love with me since I first got to know the family – six, no seven years ago. Couldn't believe it. Yet as soon as the father told me I knew, or rather I let myself know what I had never allowed myself to know, know what I mean, Chan? Always the same with the big things, isn't it, under your nose and you know it, but you don't fully let yourself know. Well, as soon as he told me his daughter loved me and wanted me to marry her I went to bits kind of thing. I mean, I had to face what I'd been able not to let myself face. That I was in love with her and despised myself for being so, I mean being my age and she hers, it seemed obscene that such a beautiful creature twenty three years younger than me should '— he stopped and pointed at the whiskey bottle, then gave a long sigh, and the Maharajah, thinking he could at last launch into his excited series of questions, was mistaken, for Bingham went on with the same urgent, staccato delivery — 'ridiculous I know. Stupid yes. Impossible I'm certain. I've been through it all a million times. Oh yes. Yes. A little bitterness too. Why didn't this happen to me twenty-five years ago, say?'

His voice raised so as to get some attention and to arrest Bingham's distracted flow, the Maharajah cried out, 'You're not in Europe now, Tim. This is India. If you were a hundred years old she's still allowed to love you if she wants to. It's still like that in this country — though it won't be for much longer I expect — but age means nothing in this matter. Let's have the bloody wedding, Tim, and I'd like first refusal of the equivalent of best man.' He joined Bingham in laughter.

'Best man at a Muslim wedding — why not, Chan?' Then, serious, Bingham said, 'She's a good Muslim, not a fanatic' — he paused now and looked grave — 'in fact if anything she's just a little *too* liberal.' Then he looked into the Maharajah's eyes. 'You hear that? Yes, Chan. I've wanted to be a Muslim for over half of my life —'

'That's well known, Tim —'

'Oh, really? You don't say?'

In a hurry to get things right now the Maharajah said, 'It's all right, Tim, nobody would care if you married an Eskimo tomorrow, or a dwarf. You're quite a legendary figure, you know, so you mustn't mind being talked about. That's the penalty for being noticeable. What's her name?'

'Razia.' It was the way he said that name, just above a whisper it seemed, that made the Maharajah feel certain Bingham did love this girl — well, woman. Thirty-six, thirty-seven . . . . Then Bingham said her name again, as if he had forgotten his friend was in the room — 'Razia.' Then he said, '*Raz O Niyaz!*' and at this play on the words for secret love the Maharajah cried out, '*Wah, wah, wah!*' and clapped his hands, laughing. Bingham grinned stupidly for a moment and turned away to pick up his drink, murmuring, 'Utterly impossible, *and* bloody ridiculous. But I'm too old a hand to feel properly ashamed, unfortunately. We're going to be late for the cinema, Chan. Let's go.'

As they got into Bingham's jeep, he said, 'I'm glad we've talked about that, Chan. It's a great worry to me. I mean, I do love Razia, but it's too late. I'm too selfish now. I've lived my own kind of life in my own way for too long, know what I mean? I'm too set in my ways. And I know what being married to Razia would be like. I've lived for a while like a member of her family and she waits on me hand and foot, as if I'm some sort of king —'

Again the Maharajah, cigarette in mouth, clapped. 'Splendid,' he shouted. 'Splendid. Tradition despite European schooling and the rest of it —'

'Oh yes, and America too. She taught there for two years. And here's another thing'; he spoke now as if seeing further into his pleasant predicament, as if looking forward to his marriage. 'Her subject is history. Couldn't be more perfect. And she's as mad as I am about lore and the rest of it. And languages, that too. And music.' He groaned and pressed harder on the accelerator. 'What the hell am I going to do?'

In reply to more questions from the Maharajah he said they wrote to each other once or twice a week, just now in Arabic, for Razia knew something of that language but wanted to improve it. A mixture of Arabic, Persian and Urdu sometimes. Long letters. Hadn't seen her for months — six or seven months. Dodging? Yes, in a way. Yes. He laughed wryly. 'Can't face up to it, that's why. Honestly, though, I feel I shouldn't do it, for *her* sake. Those twenty-three years. Yes, I suppose you're right. Doesn't matter all that much in India, and God damn it I've been here and in the Middle East most of my life now. What's the difference? But I think I know why it is. Although she doesn't need me to become a Muslim to marry her, I want to become one, but there's the one great snag. I love Islam. I love its history. I know the Koran well. I know Muslim law, all four versions of it. But I lack the one thing I really want. A belief in God, the Muslim God, any God. No, that wouldn't matter to Razia, I feel sure. But it matters to me. It's been the burden of my whole life, the lack of a faith, a belief, a trust.'

He stopped the jeep then and turned his head and looked at the Maharajah. They were in the main street of Induspur. It was swarming with people and the Petromax lamps glared down whitely on the open air bazaar ahead of them.

'Odd, isn't it?' Bingham said dryly. 'Did you ever guess that that might be my problem?'

'Often. It runs under a lot of your conversation, Tim. What's wrong with it? It's a world hobby, anyway. Only I expect you feel annoyed because you haven't been able to shake it off during all these years you've spent at it. Is that it?'

'That's it,' said Bingham, and drove on. 'I'm a religious man who has no God.' He started laughing in such a way that his mood took the Maharajah too, and they laughed all the way into the cinema, for there was no need for the Maharajah to tell Bingham that he was in the same situation, a godless believer, and in love too, but with a woman he felt sure he could not have. He could not bring himself to tell Bingham about it either. Fearing disapproval, lack of understanding? Probably. He was never sure.

In the early hours of the morning the Maharajah was still up, brooding, drinking in his study, pleased by the confidence Bingham had shown in him in telling him about this unusual love affair. He envied him too. Being loved without having to ask for it. A little maudlin now, the Maharajah looked back to five years ago when the incredible news had reached him from Egypt telling him his wife and son had been devoured by the filthiest beast of all, cholera.

Rather drunk, it was all he could manage not to go down, get into his car and drive to Megan's house, and there announce, 'I'm in love with you, as we both know. Time is passing. I want to know here and now – where do I stand?' Knowing Megan she would probably point somewhere and say, 'Why not over there? I'll stand here.'

He laughed — a little self-pityingly, he could hear it.

CHAPTER 8

Croon knew his cable to Condy, about his embarrassment over not having spoken to Bingham of his being employed by Condy, had been made pointless when he read the note from Bingham. Condy had changed his mind, so typical of him, and had written to Bingham.

Bingham's note, handed to him by a hotel servant, read, 'Dear Croon, lots of sensitivity and understanding all round. Mr. Condy had obviously regretted swearing you to silence about your "mission to Induspur": perhaps we should call it that. I appreciate you must have felt yourself to be in an awkward position, once we had met and talked. However, Condy has explained all and I must say it does sound a most interesting possibility, the filming of the story of the dancing-girl Maharani and her three officer lovers. I am going to see the Maharajah this evening and will give him Condy's letter to read. Will keep you informed.'

What a bloody good fellow this Bingham is, Croon thought as he put the note in his pocket. He was in the hotel bar, drinking gin and fresh lime juice. There was something to be said for some of these sahib types, he had to admit, gentlemanly and so on.

The hotel had found a guide for him, a very well-educated and personable young man who had arrived after breakfast and sent his card up to Croon. He read the visiting card with puzzled surprise.

'Captain Nur-ud-Din Balban.
Pandit, Guide. Mythologist and Author.'

Within the first hour of their meeting, in the hotel bar over coffee, the Guide had taken him through a most absorbing, and at times disturbing, tour of his own personality, 'in order,' Balban explained, 'to respond in full to the trust you

71

have shown in me with this dossier of your good self,' and he waved the post card Croon had handed him to read.

When he had introduced himself to the Guide and they had shaken hands, Balban had begun at once with the questions, 'You are staying here long? You are American?' Croon, prepared now after many interrogations by strangers in planes and trains in India, took a large postcard from his pocket and handed it to him. It was typed on both sides and Croon had given its preparation much thought. Now he watched the handsome young Indian read it with intense interest and obvious happiness.

The questions were typed on the card in capitals and the answers in small type. Name, Occupation, Age, Nationality, Married or Single, Children — number, sex, age, Salary and other emoluments, Reason for present visit, Length of stay, Attitude to following subjects — Reincarnation, Non-Violence, Celibacy, and so on; and as he watched the Guide turn the card over and read on absorbedly, Croon felt he had somehow matched the curious visiting card he now held in his hand.

'Coffee?' he said, as Balban finished reading and looked up, smiling, at him.

'Yes,' Balban said when they were sitting at a table in the corner of the bar, 'I will respond to your own friendly confidence in me.' He spoke excellent English with only a faint Indian accent. He was wearing U.S. army sun-tan trousers, a white silk shirt open at the neck, and spotless white tennis shoes. His black hair was thick and brushed back from his high light brown forehead and he had a fairly thick black moustache, which seemed to Croon to go well with the rank of captain.

'You were an army captain?' Croon began but Balban held up his hand, languidly, for silence.

'I was saying,' he said gently, 'that in response to this very full dossier of your personality you have let me read, I too will now place *my* confidence in you, for some meetings demand that the role one is playing be put aside. In other words I wish to tell you who and what I really am, and *was*, until I was ready for my present role.'

Christ, Croon was thinking as the waiter laid the pot of coffee and the cups before them, what have I done, what *have* I done? Yet he was fascinated as he listened. The guide was so *relaxed*.

72

'Take this captaincy to start with,' Balban picked up the visiting card from where Croon had placed it on the table and threw it down again. 'Captain of what? you ask. The answer to that is simple. Captain of my soul. There is no need for me to explain that, of course, unless I am asked. Yet that is my captaincy. I have no objection to those who read my card and wish to imagine that I have been an army captain, and therefore must be the epitome of reliability and breeding. None whatever. I *am* that epitome, as it happens, as you will discover, yet the rank of captain does help me to find customers and clients. You understand?'

'Absolutely,' Croon heard himself humouring the man.

'So much for the captaincy — a fact where it concerns my soul, a testimonial where it concerns my snobbish customers. Now the name. Nur-ud-Din — Arabic for the Light of Religion. I am not a Muslim, though. I have passed through that stage of liberation. And now, what you would call the surname, Balban. I will tell you who Balban was. He was a slave in the thirteenth century who rose to be chief minister to the king of Delhi, and since I first heard his story he has been my model, for I too was a slave. I took his name. Yes, I was Untouchable, born an Untouchable of the very lowest caste, those filthiest of creatures who handle dead bodies. A slave.'

As Balban's story continued Croon listened in a daze of wonder, calling for more coffee, and later, when he glanced cunningly at his watch and saw it was nearly midday, for gin and lime. Balban refused liquor. Perhaps it might muddle his bewildering story.

His father, having toiled as the lowest of the lowest all his life in a village far from here, and a man of intelligence well-concealed where the higher castes were concerned, had one day called his son Balban (who at that time bore the name Surkabatch) and said to him, 'My son, it is time for you to escape into the world. Once out there lie your way to freedom. Become learned, more learned than any prating Brahmin. Learn to out-Brahmin every Brahmin, then pass yourself off as a Brahmin. Be ruthless in your endeavour to achieve that ambition, for me and for the millions of shit-carriers of our caste who have lived, who live, and are to come. I order you to escape.'

'You find this story hard to believe, Mister Croon?' Balban asked.

'Everything I have seen in India has been hard to believe,' said Croon, and Balban smiled.

'A clever answer, Mister Croon,' he said with what seemed to be genuine approval. 'But I am telling you the truth, and if you find it hard to believe I shall not be offended.' Croon studied his face. Now did that mean that it was open to him to disbelieve because the story was untrue anyway? He could not decide. But the young man seemed absolutely genuine. Believe then.

'Do you know what I like to do now?' Balban was saying. 'I like to come upon a Brahmin in the street, preferably when the sun is behind me, and cast my shadow on him and keep it there. Defiling him, you see? Yes, even the *shadow* of an Untouchable can defile a Brahmin, and the Brahmin must go through a long rigmarole of baths and prayers and cleansings to follow this frightful defiling. Once I came on a Brahmin sitting in the street, talking with others outside a store. The sun was right and I stood in such a way that my whole shadow covered him. He seemed to understand what was happening, although I was dressed in a smart suit and looked like what I wanted to look like, a high-caste Indian with a BA behind my name. My taxi was waiting nearby. The Brahmin began to back away from me, and I said, "So you understand what is happening, you swine? You have guessed, have you, that I am a *chamar*, a ghastly Untouchable? My shadow has penetrated you, O Brahmin trickster, and there are more and more Untouchables like me, dressed up like rich men of high caste, travelling unknown all over India and rubbing up against Brahmins and casting our shadows upon them." He screamed and ran away, and his friends scattered too.' All this was said with quiet solemnity, Balban pouring himself more coffee, and when he finished he smiled at Croon and added, 'None of this behaviour, by the way, has anything to do with what *you* might call "having a chip on my shoulder". No, no. It is simply a game I play occasionally in memory of my father, and so as never to forget my role.'

'And how would you describe that role?' Croon asked him.

'The role of Pandit, which I am about to describe, knower of things, understander of important trivia, and master of what I believe you in the West call bullshit.' Balban picked up his visiting card and read from it — 'Pandit, Guide, Mytho-

74

logist and Author' — and then looked into Croon's entranced gaze. 'I have had many teachers, many of them British, one American, and one of them, a colonel, is still living here. This man, Colonel Bingham, is a saint for me, and if you wish to confirm my story he will bear witness for me. He sent me to be your guide here. Now — Pandit. Yes, I claim that title now —'

'Colonel Bingham sent you to be my guide?' Croon interrupted.

'Yes. He came into the hotel and told the manager that I was available if you, Croon Sahib, needed a guide to the old town and the countryside.'

'I see. Go on.'

'Thank you. Now, as I was saying — Pandit. A Pandit in this country simply means a Brahmin who has memorized and can gabble off, at the drop of a sack of rupees, several miles of religious or mythological recitations, and can define the subtler infinities of, say, how many grains of twelve grains of rice owned by a starving man are due to a Brahmin should the man die and require the Brahmin's services, or how far from the Brahmin's sacred well the polluting well of the Untouchables in the same village must be. I have memorized all the useless recitations, and when I was passing myself off as a Brahmin in various parts of India, even at the most sacred place itself, Varanasi, I could bullshit my way through the questions of any number of Brahmins. So I am a Pandit, though I only use the title if I feel like a holiday fling as a Brahmin these days.'

'May I ask a question before you go on?' Croon asked nervously.

'Certainly. Do I *hate* Brahminism? Am I still suffering from having been an Untouchable? Is that roughly the question?'

'It is, as a matter of fact.' Was India really mysterious after all?

'I would say, in answer to that, that like any truly intelligent man who has studied himself thoroughly, I hate *myself*, sometimes so deeply that it is necessary that someone else should accept some of that hatred, and who better than the smuggest of all human beings, the nearest Brahmin? It's great fun, after all, to cast your shadow on one of these proud idiots

75

and then tell him you are an Untouchable. His reactions of horror and terror are simply proof that you have every right to incite his idiocy, to be defiling him.'

'I see.' Croon, by now deep in the game, picked up Balban's visiting-card and read out the word after 'Pandit'. 'Now — "Guide". Would you care to guide me now?' He rose, and Balban rose too, laughing, saying, 'Beautifully done, Mister Croon. Beautifully done.'

'We will walk while you tell me the rest. Explain the word "Guide". I am very interested in what you're telling me.'

As Balban began to take up his tale Croon cut in, excusing himself, to say, 'And by the way, how old are you?' The fellow talked like somebody two hundred years old.

'You mean how can I have done all these things at my age?' Balban laughed. He had a soft, deep, almost artificial laugh, it seemed to Croon, and somehow sad, as if he had practised it from necessity, but the bitterness still there came through as sadness. Oh, bullshit! Croon told himself. He *must* keep a sense of proportion, which meant he must remember to keep in mind that this could be a con-artist of a new and brilliant kind. Yet —

'When I was twelve,' Balban continued, 'and not long after my father had given me my instructions, I stole six hundred rupees —'

'From a Brahmin, I trust,' said Croon lightly. Always trying for a laugh, my God, he thought. Will it ever stop?

He was pleased, though, when Balban said, 'I knew you had insight, Mister Croon, as soon as you came into the bar to meet me. I will tell you all about that later. Yes, it was from a Brahmin in the next village. He was known to have several thousand rupees hidden away. I could only find six hundred, but that was a great fortune to me. I left the district and travelled in South India, south from Madras. I bribed an old Brahmin widow to give me to a *saddhu* as his *chela* and servant, passing myself off as the orphan of Brahmin parents who had died of smallpox. Not that that really mattered. *Saddhus*, you know, give up all caste, all worldly ties, and travel naked about India, and if the *saddhu* was a Brahmin before he threw off the world he has burned his sacred thread and is casteless. Anyway half of them are liars and cheats and tricksters who travel India in search of religious widows with money, and who need what British soldiers call some mutton-bayonet practice. So I spent from the age of twelve until I was seventeen with that *saddhu*, who had been a Brahmin, and who taught me even more than he guessed he knew. I am not boasting when I tell you that I finished up as *his* master, for while he was sitting at the edge of villages with peasants adoring and feeding him, I was learning all I could of Islam, Christianity, Sikhism, Buddhism, all the forms of preparation the world uses in order to face the end, the thing they call death. And I read until my eyes closed, every afternoon and night. Then the great disaster came for me — ' He stopped.

'Yes? Go on,' said Croon. 'What disaster?' Had he murdered the old *saddhu* perhaps?

'I fell in love,' Balban said. 'Now this,' he went on, waving his arm, 'this street' — he stopped walking and Croon stopped too and looked about him at the street, — 'this street used to be called The Way Of The Rajputs, because this was where the Maharajah's Rajput ancestors rode in when they came to conquer Induspur about five hundred years ago.'

'Used to be?' said Croon. 'And what's it called now?'

'Now it's called Param Jujibhoi Road. Param Jujibhoi was a financier who bailed the Maharajah's grandfather out after he'd spent everything in the treasury. The warrior caste always ends in the hands of the moneylender. That is history. So — I fell in love.'

'Why do you call it a disaster?'

'Because I was in a state of insanity, that's why. I could not sleep. I could not read. I could not eat, shit, lie down, rest, think, I could only walk about the country like a lunatic, wondering what had happened to me. I would find myself in tears. I was a nuisance to everybody.' His voice faltered. 'We will leave that subject now,' he said very quietly, smiling to himself, sadly it seemed to Croon. 'I had better start guiding you. First we will go to the old palace and when we get there I'll tell you its story.'

By now Croon was enjoying the companionship of this unusual young man, whether he was con-man or saintly being. Just then, as they crossed the street, Balban said, 'I am twenty-nine years out of the womb, but I am much, much older than that, as you must have guessed.' He turned his head and looked into Croon's eyes, grinning affably. 'It must be hard for you to believe all I'm telling you, but there are much stranger stories to be heard in India, as you'll find the longer you stay here. India is a lunatic asylum in which the rulers are the inmates. The rest of us, about five hundred million of us, are the keepers, turning the wheel of Dharma, but all suffer from some form of insanity.'

The visiting card was produced again and Croon looked at it, saying, 'Mythologist' — thinking, Just about the right time for a look at the meaning of that, maybe — 'what's the meaning of that, "mythologist"?'

'Like any priest,' Balban said, laughing. He could produce a bright, boyish, innocent kind of laugh — a hint of self-mockery in it, Croon felt. 'I dispense necessary mythologies, for instance to the Untouchables, who used to be my people' — he pointed — 'we cross here for the road to the old palace — I've freed a few of them during my travels. But of course my main claim to the title of mythologist is my own myth, in fact all of them. I've been Christian, Brahmin, Buddhist, now a Muslim again. I recommend it to all Indians. I tell them to try it. Just rush out of your present trap and become something else, for a time, then have a change. Just face the Indian world and announce who and what you are now. You have to be brazen, though, and strong. I can tell you this. No experience in all my various lives has been as thrilling as when I hammer the Brahmins at Varanasi. I preach to great crowds — always with an escape area ready behind me, of course, for you never know in this country what a bunch of fanatics might do — I preach a new Gospel. I call it the Fifth Veda, an idea I pinched after a study of an Italian Jesuit here in the umpteenth century. He dreamed up a Fifth Veda which contained his Hindu-Christian mélange, and I dreamed mine up and preached it — in Sanskrit. You can imagine that these bloody self-opinionated maniacs, the Brahmins, who've had this country by its mental throat for thousands of years, could never dream that an Untouchable would dare pass himself off as a Brahmin, and at the sacred fount of all silliness, Varanasi, *and* do it brilliantly, in Sanskrit. If I'd laughed during one of those performances I think I could have been a dead man, and I was often on the edge of hysterical laughter while I preached. By then I was playing the *sanyassi*, beard, trident, dust-covered, rudhra-berry necklace, all the regalia, and I can assure you it was a wonderful performance. I'll be down there again next year for futher performances, and I've polished up the Fifth Veda.'

78

He then explained briefly about the Four Vedas of the Hindus, the Indo-Aryan invasion of India, and in such a way, so eloquently, that Croon thought he could see the hordes of horsemen crossing the passes into Northern India all those thousands of years ago. Balban explained how these aristocratic warrior people had invented the caste-system in order to keep the blacks, the 'Darks', that is the old inhabitants of India, out of their blood stream.

'That was the beginning of the incredible and now ancient and holy pack of lies we all live in now,' Balban went on. 'You've got to admit it's one of the best ever invented in any land, including the theory of re-birth and the rest of the mumbo-jumbo. Personally, I love it, I've got to admit it. I actually enjoy being a Brahmin who's thrown away his Brahminism and gone beyond, into the state of *sanyassi*, and what a revenge, delirious with laughter at night after a day of performing, the descendant of a million shit-carriers, polluter of the earth on which he stands, hammering the Brahmins with expert bullshit. It's worth being alive to do it. So I can claim to be truly a mythologist. I live my own myth and preach other myths. Take the Fifth Veda. It's quite simple. I've worked out how we're nearing the end of the Kali Yug at last. They love it. There's no end to the credulity widespread in this country, and it gives me a marvellous feeling when I see the mouths opening and the eyes staring so fixedly at me as I orate the spellbinding bullshit of the Fifth Veda.'

The hill was steep now and Croon suggested they stop, for, unused to walking in Indian heat, he was sweating fast. They walked into the shade of a clump of trees and sat down. Because he had noticed Balban's growing excitement as he talked about his Fifth Veda, he said quietly, 'I suppose you can get to love your own myths if you have a good audience.' But Balban's awareness surprised him again.

'Well, you see,' the young Indian said, 'I was telling you about human credulity, especially in this country, and I can assure you that I've almost convinced myself with my own bullshit. The Fifth Veda seems to make good sense.' He stopped, laughing, his sparkling dark eyes watching Croon's expression. 'Yes, I've sold myself my own myth. Why not? Anything goes here, in India. There's nothing too incredible to preach or believe.' He went on to explain his Fifth Veda.

The Kali Yug was the 'age of iron', of destruction, darkness, upheaval, chaos, and we were living in it now, and it had so far lasted many thousand years. He had put an end to all that, at least brought it all up to date and given it a final shape, a terminus. That was where the atomic bomb came in handy. Balban now spoke of 'the final Rebirth'.

'The first time I tried it out on the Brahmin crowd at Varanasi,' he said, 'and oh, by the way, one of the great thrills for me is bathing in the sacred Ganges waters surrounded by a few dozen of these twice-born unsuspecting Brahmins, the Touchables I suppose we could call them, and polluting the waters all round them, and the temptation to let them know it is very great, but I daren't risk it if I wish to live. So I can only share the ecstasy with myself —'

Fully involved now with the curious fantasy of this young-old man, Croon said, 'But you could write a book about it, under another name. Then they could all read it and wonder which one of them was the Untouchable passing himself off as a Brahmin, or a *sanyassi*.'

Balban's eyes glowed with pleasure and he said, 'Of course, of course. What a marvellous plan.' He jumped to his feet and punched his right fist into his left palm, and in a curiously old-fashioned British way exclaimed, 'By Jove, I'll do it. Damn good idea, Mister Croon. It's a wonderful continuation of my war on Brahmin idiocy. Report on the idiocy, let them read it, and carry on with my mission. They'll suspect each other. They'll never guess. Oh, thank you, you've been inspired to think of that, a book. A book. What shall I call it?' He stopped. 'No, I'm afraid it's too risky. I could only write a book once I decide I've finished with my Brahmin role, retired so to speak, you know, reminiscing.' His excitement returned and he went on excitedly, '*Then* I could do the whole thing. Tell the story about the vile Untouchable who conned them for years, polluted them by the thousand for years in their own sacred places, *and* gave them the Fifth Veda.' He became thoughtful then. 'But why don't I first write the Fifth Veda as a book?' He became greatly agitated, laughing. 'That's the best con of all, because I'll be making money out of them, another bit of revenge for the last few thousand years of shit-carrying and humiliation. Turn the Fifth Veda into a printed fact, the revelations of an inspired Brahmin, by one who has been in a coma of spiritual enlightenment so great that he has foreseen the end of the world, and how it will end, the last, 'the final Rebirth' — he burst out laughing now — 'the final Rebirth in which *everyone* will be a Brahmin and die in the holocaust, because shitting will be finished, and shit-carriers no longer necessary. Just one mighty Brahmin host as the holocaust sets fire to the world. What do you think of that? Eh?'

'I think it's excellent.' Completely convinced now that this extraordinary young man had every right to play his unusual game, Croon encouraged him. 'If, as you say, it's only one more part of the whole business of credulity in this country, then write the book about the Fifth Veda. And save your autobiographical revelations until you've had enough of living your myth, kind of thing.'

Balban sat down again, his eyes still shining, and told the Fifth Veda to Croon. Surely he must believe it, Croon thought as he studied Balban's rapt expression and heard the conviction in his voice, and he told it so well. Croon found himself listening intently, yet still fighting against the fascination of Balban's delivery. He had been warned about India. 'Anything can happen there,' he had been told. 'You can't distinguish between con and pro in India. Watch it while you're there.' Though he felt guilty in listening to these extraordinary attacks on Brahminism, for in his struggle against the emotional appeals of Communism Croon had sought to make himself tolerant about all religions, and much against his real will, he could not help enjoying the complicated fantasy of Balban's playful paranoia. Perhaps it was the entertainment of it which kept him so attentive as an audience, and eccentrics had always attracted him.

'What I've done with this Fifth Veda,' said Balban, 'is that I've wrapped up the future in it, brought the two or three thousand years of meticulously thought-out bullshit to a conclusion, *and* stroked and massaged Hindu scholastic prejudices and theories into a really satisfying solution. Now, there's hardly anybody in the world who doesn't realize that we now can, and will, end the world as we know it, with the coming of the atomic bomb — *and* the bomb has come to end not only the Kali Yug but the world as well. That is the basis of the Fifth Veda. I always start to preach slowly and quietly. I start with a description of where we Brahmins have been in thought and worship, where we are now, and where we are going — we are going, I tell them, to the final solution of all the Hindu lives that have ever been lived, which brings me to my discoveries about the meaning of rebirth.' He now sprang to his feet, walked out a few feet, turned and faced Croon, and began to declaim.

'We Brahmins,' he began, and then collapsed into laughter so unrestrained and wholehearted that Croon started laughing with him. 'I'm sorry,' said Balban, recovering, trying to be solemn, 'but at least here I can laugh, with you as my audience, which is a relief I can tell you, because you have to imagine what it's like when a piece of human dung like me has educated himself enough to bring off this kind of con and address these clowns as "We Brahmins". No, please, no more laughing. This is a serious matter.'

He composed himself and began again. 'We Brahmins are at last within sight of the long and patient journey to a total and all-embracing state of *moksh*' — in an aside he said to Croon, 'That means a state of final Hindu grace, you can be buried, because being perfect at last you're not coming back any more for one more round of living, not needing to be burned any more. The cycle is over. Now' — he started to orate to Croon again — 'a state of *moksh* which all our prayers and all our various lives through many centuries have at last brought us to, for at last there shall be one instantaneous and all-consuming funeral pyre — for all humanity at the same time all over the earth. You see, what has been revealed to me in my long state of spiritual suspension, is something never before realized, and that is that every single human being on earth, black, brown, white and yellow, were all once Hindus in other lives. The wicked did not only come back as rats or tigers or vile Untouchables, as once was thought, and thought mistakenly for some many centuries; no, they have come back in every form as human beings of every colour, and their punishment has been not even to come back as denizens of India, whether humans, animals or demons. The final weapon, which these demons out there in the other world of America and Russia think they have invented, they have only re-invented, for we all know it was invented here and was used in the destruction of armies thousands of years ago here, as our documents tell us. I here and now announce to you all the end of the journey at last, not just the end of the age of iron and terror, but the end of the long and wearying struggle of souls and of lives lived again and again.

82

Welcome then to the great engine of doom and destruction, which in one avalanche of flame will end the treadmill of those endless rebirths and give a funeral pyre, instantaneous, to every so-called human being on earth, that is to say every Hindu of every colour anywhere on earth and in every stage of the great and ancient journey to the longed-for perfection, that *moksh* so long sought by all who have lived.' Balban paused for breath. 'That is the main theme of the Fifth Veda,' he said quietly to Croon, coming to sit beside him again. 'In Sanskrit it is much more powerful.'

'And how do they react to it?'

'Ecstatically,' said Balban, letting out a peal of laughter again. ' "Master," they shout. "Master. Lighter of the brightest lamp, speak on. Speak on." '

'It's quite convincing, in a way,' said Croon quietly, for the hairs on his neck had prickled slightly during Balban's weird, comic, yet frightening messianic declamation.

'Yes,' Balban said coolly, nodding, thoughtful. 'It's pretty good, really. I like it. In fact I like it so much I believe it.' He started laughing again. 'Ah, how I wish my old slave of a father could be there to watch and to listen to me conning those vain, stupid aristocrats who have lived such lovely, comfortable lives since time began. But I suppose he would run away in terror.'

'Why have you told me all these secrets, Balban?' Croon asked him. 'Do you tell many people about these things? Isn't it a bit risky, I mean?'

'You are the only person I have ever told,' said Balban, meeting Croon's stare with steadiness.

'Why? Why me?' All his suspicions of this character were awake again now. Con, enjoyable con yes, but still con.

'It is a burden I have carried for a long time,' said Balban. 'It is something I have longed to share with somebody, and you, you have a light in your head. It shows on your forehead, and I knew I could trust you.'

'Now come *on*, Balban,' said Croon, his voice hardening. 'Am I expected to believe that you've never told this fantastic story to anybody but me? Are you serious?'

Balban looked at him, his expression solemn. 'Quite serious', he said. 'Colonel Bingham told me I was to assist you in every way while you are in Induspur, and to regard you as a friend. I don't want anything from you. I don't want money for being your guide and adviser while you are here.' His voice was becoming sharper, hinting at a temper waiting to waken. 'I have many friends in all parts of India, and what is now Pakistan, but not one to tell my secrets to. Why not share them with a stranger? I know you will never pass them on to another. That is all. Why should you wonder if I tell these things to you? It is my choice, not yours.'

'I see. And does Colonel Bingham know all these things about you? What is your relationship with the colonel, and why does he send you to me?'

He watched Balban thinking about these questions, staring at him through puffed smoke as he lit a cigarette.

'First,' Balban told him, turning to smile at him, 'I don't care whether you believe me or not. Your belief will not alter anything for me. I have told you a few of my secrets, because I needed to confide in somebody. Who better than a stranger from outside India who happens to have a light on his forehead? But I do not need your belief, do I? Your belief won't make anything more true for me than it is already, so I do not need your belief, Mister Croon. Your trust, though — that I *would* value – seeing how I have given you mine.'

'Well put,' said Croon, a little put out by this reproof, which seemed all the more powerful for having been spoken so quietly, plus the cool dismissal of his belief or disbelief. It was very convincing. But he would not apologize. Instead, he pressed on, for more information.

'Where does the colonel come into your life?' he said. 'How much does he know about this strange life of yours, for instance?'

'In his old work, before he employed anyone, as he employed me, Mister Croon,' Balban said, 'the colonel did all the researches necessary. I cannot tell you too much, but I'll tell you enough to answer your questions.' He smiled and held up his hand as if to silence any excuses about to come from Croon. 'Don't let it worry you that you think me a liar or a con-man, Mister Croon. My prey is the Brahmin world only, and that does not include yourself. Now, my connections with the Colonel Sahib.'

Smiling fondly as he reminisced now, Balban told Croon something, but only something, of some aspects of his work for the colonel. 'In the old days,' he added.

He told how, for thousands of years, even for the Moghuls,

then for the British, and now for the new government, the wandering *sanyassis* who travelled India were perfect informants to monitor the temperatures of the various Indias which made up the body of Mother India, the feelings of towns and villages, the angers and aspirations, the secret plans of the embittered or the disaffected.

'That's all I think I should tell you, Mister Croon,' he said. 'And it is another secret, of course, and a much bigger one than my role and my myths.'

'Well, thank you,' said Croon, annoyed at feeling so humbled, though not showing any of this, he thought. He was impressed, though, for this was the first time he had ever met, to his knowledge, a secret agent. 'I must say,' he went on, 'that I'm fascinated by what you've told me. And what you've told me is safe with me. I'll never mention it to anyone.'

'I knew that as soon as I met you, Mister Croon,' Balban turned his head and looked hard at Croon, somehow to Croon now, seeming like a much older and wiser man than himself. But he was not pleased when Balban went on to say, 'You are full of suspicions. That shows too, Mister Croon. There are many reasons for that. There always are. You have suffered in your life, I could guess. Suffering is a cruel teacher. Shall we go on?' Balban rose and Croon joined him on the trudge up the steep hill. They were well outside Induspur town now. As they went up the hill Balban said, 'And now my claim to be an author. You would like to hear about that?'

'Yes, tell me. I tried to be an author, without much luck, and I'll try again. But I am too busy trying to get rich in the film business.'

'You have been poor?'

That was something Croon had always found too painful to discuss, even with himself in complete honesty, except with the American, Condy, for whom it had seemed to be a testimonial of realibility. 'Yes,' he said now, though grudgingly, 'I've been poor. That can be a great help in wanting to become rich. So you've written books?'

'One book so far,' then he turned, delight in his face again, 'and next shall come "The Fifth Veda". I thank you again, Mister Croon, for that suggestion. I shall start tonight before I sleep.' He rubbed his hands, smiling. 'The book was written for the idiots in America and England, though the idiots in

America bought more copies of the book. It was called *The Seven Hells of Yogic Endeavour*. I had pains in my sides when I was writing it — laughing so much. First there was the hell called "Spasm of the Soul-Vomiting". That's when the yoga pupil performs mental exercises without sleep for three days and nights, intoning a mantra continually — that mantra, by the way, had to be bought from me by post, and cost ten dollars. I've since raised it to twenty dollars, for I was so surprised by the numbers of dollars that came to me. I had to invent personal mantras for each reader who called for one.'

'Bullshit, of course,' suggested Croon, starting to laugh, and Balban joined him in wild laughter for a while.

'Of course,' said Balban. 'Yet brilliant bullshit, I must admit that. Anyway, after three days and nights the reader would begin to feel the first spasms of the soul-vomiting. It's amazing how Westerners not only believe Indian spiritual bullshit but go on to actually feel what you tell them they're going to feel. Well, the soul has to vomit the rubbish of the student's past up, all of it, before entering the second hell. It's pretty good, isn't it? Do you like it?'

'I should think your bank manager likes it even more,' said Croon.

'Oh, yes. I've made a lot of money. Many readers have written to me and asked me to set up an *ashram*, a place where they can come and suffer and study and hear wisdom from my own lips.' He shouted with laughter again. 'But I couldn't do it. It's bad enough having to read their idiotic letters. I couldn't stand having them near me, believing all the bullshit. But remember, they need that bullshit, just as much as I need their money. I feel no regret, no shame or any of that nonsense. Anybody who's willing to go sleepless for three days and nights, and then perform a soul-vomiting, deserves to pay for it. And it makes them happy. It does amaze me, though. I really wrote the book as a joke, and to see if it would work. Now I realize that there is nothing too stupid to tell these people, and there are millions of believers out there. Millions and millions. And I had imagined once that it was only here in India that we lived these fairy stories. Wait a minute.' They stopped while Balban searched the pockets of his linen jacket. He brought out a letter and scanned its contents for a few seconds.

'Yes,' he said, and waved the letter as they started to walk on up the hill. 'This is a letter from a young man in California complaining that though he has tried for weeks he cannot perform the Seventh Hell of Yogic Endeavour, and what should he do about it.'

'What's the Seventh Hell?' Croon asked.

Before he could reply Balban went off into another shriek of laughter and ended it shaking his head, whether in despair at his correspondent's credulity or his own diabolical ingenuity, Croon could not guess.

'It took me some time to dream up the Seventh Hell,' he said. 'I invented a Zen Master of Japan who had come to India centuries ago to study yoga here. He and his Hindu master devised the seed, as I called it, of the Seventh Hell, combining Zen with yoga. In the Seventh Hell the student is by now ready for the great, final emptying of the soul and the being, so that true yoga may begin, you see. So I wrote, 'Now, at the doorway of this Seventh Hell the *chela* is about to end his heavenly endeavours, and is ready for this subtle, acrobatic choreography of the at last captured mind. Take the mind now in your hand and fling it into the air, and if it comes down again, you are still not ready, but still in the Sixth Hell. Only when the mind has been thrown into the air, and does not return, has true readiness been achieved.' His eyes serious, even a little stern, Balban turned to Croon and said. 'That is true Zen, you know. Wouldn't you agree? I mean it convinced *me*. I don't think anything could be more Zen than throwing your mind into the air and not getting it back — even catching it again could be enough, I'd say. Wouldn't you?'

Mystified, and curiously irritated in a way he could not quite define — perhaps it was this strange fellow's casual and gentle arrogance, as much as because of his crazy self-satisfaction — Croon became querulous. As he did so he wondered if it was in sheer self-defence against the lulling magic of Balban's easy and careless descriptions of how he loved to handle human credulity.

'You said earlier, Balban,' he said now, cold and businesslike, 'that you wanted to be my guide but that you wanted no money for it, so —'

Before he could finish Balban held up that steadying hand again for silence and finished the sentence for him, smiling, and nodding like a man who has waited a long time for this moment, 'So what *do* you want?' Balban now laughed in his most engaging way. 'Correct?' he went on. 'What *do* I want? Well, Mister Croon, with that light on your forehead you must already have guessed. I wish to help on this film you are planning here. As soon as the Colonel Sahib told me about that I knew why he had sent for me. I am the expert on the old story you are going to film. The Memsahib Brett-Turner has written a version of what I told her, and before her a major who lives here still, a Major Tone, he consulted me too and wrote down his version. Colonel Bingham Sahib knows that I am the one with all the facts and that is why he has sent me to you. I am taking you to the very castle in which the story began.' He stopped and pointed ahead up the hill. 'And there it is.'

Croon turned his head and looked up at the enormous red sandstone fort half a mile ahead. It was sharply outlined against the blue cloudless sky.

'It has been empty since it was cursed nearly two hundred years ago,' said Balban.

'Really?' Croon said, still staring up at the ruined fort, his querulousness forgotten, Balban's magic working again. 'Who cursed it? And why?'

'The Brahmins,' said Balban. 'They cursed it, and it has been empty ever since.'

Croon turned and met Balban's amused eyes, then grinned slowly with him.

'The Brahmins,' said Croon, shaking his head. 'Why didn't I guess it? Your favourite people.' Croon became matter-of-fact now. He took a notebook from his hip pocket and his Parker 51 started moving fast over a page of it. From time to time he snapped questions at Balban. 'The story. You gave it to who? Major Tone. Oh, Jesus, him. You gave it again to who? Mrs Brett-Turner. But they changed it, you say. Why?'

'It involved Europeans,' said Balban. 'And Europeans like the Major Tone and Mrs Brett-Turner wanted the Europans to be heroes. But none of them were heroes, Indian or European. All were after power, and money. They lied to each other and they caused each other's deaths.'

Croon closed the notebook. 'That's fine, Balban,' he said. He was about to add, 'No heroes, great, just the facts,' but he remembered there would have to be a film hero, and an American box-office hero too, so he said, 'I just want the story straight, exactly as you know it. Why are you the expert, by the way? How come?'

'So you will employ me, Mister Croon?' said Balban. It was a stipulation, a request for agreement before he told any more to Croon, and though nettled, Croon had to admire him. But still he hesitated.

'As soon as I've satisfied myself about you, Balban,' he said, 'I'll let you know if I need you. Okay?' It was not okay.

'I must know now.' The young man was firm. 'If I tell you I am your man, that I am honest, that I am worth employing, Mister Croon, that should be enough. I do not make false claims.'

'Is that so?' It was quite difficult for Croon to conceal his annoyance at such misplaced strength of character. 'Well, Balban, let me tell you this. It's all going to be done my way, see? The story end of the film, that is. And if I want to check your credentials before I employ you that's what I'm going to do. No offence meant, of course.' Just colonialism? Imperialism? Paternalism? Any fucking ism you like, baby, Croon heard himself telling himself, but you better stay on top with this character or he'll be running you and the picture. His long stay in America had left its mark, the land where you said what you meant and felt, if you wanted to stay in business, that is. But how able this strange character was. Balban was smiling, and he was shaking his head like a man being patient, long-suffering, but also a man anxious not to see this wayward foreigner make a fool of himself. A friend, in fact.

'The fact that I am here with you now is my testimonial, Mister Croon,' Balban said, with the slightest hint of heat. 'The Colonel Sahib who sent me to you is known all over northern India, *and* beyond it, as a judge of men. *He* is a hero, Mister Croon, and I have had the honour of working under his commands. *Trusted* by him.' He stopped. And waited. Croon studied him, angered by the uncertainty he felt now. So this was going to be a test of wills. But was it? Need it be? Think it over. Don't rush. Why be conned by all this Kipling-type bullshit — judge of men . . . hero . . . and trusted underlined. No.

'We'll still do it my way, Balban,' he said, trying not to smile. 'Then — if I employ you — you can do your thing your way — I mean about the story. And who knows, maybe I'll give you further work, like being my assistant. We'll see.'

But he still had to sweeten it somewhat, and was furious at the self-contempt he felt as he went on to say, 'It's not that I don't *trust* you, you understand? You've impressed me, sure. But I still want to make my own mind up in my own way. Does that make sense to you?'

Balban's smile, and his slow nodding which told of his patience and forbearance with this European waywardness and lack of understanding, only increased Croon's determination to have things his way. So they fell back on good manners.

'Certainly, Mister Croon,' Balban said. 'Shall we look at the castle now?'

'Yes, let's do that.' Pleased with himself, with the way he had stayed the course, Croon said, for the sake of something to say more than a request for information, 'Do you know how to use a still camera? I mean really well.' Christ, he thought as he heard the answer, I might have known it.

'I am an expert,' Balban replied. 'I have won two prizes in Calcutta and Bombay for my photography. I will show you them, the photographs. Why, Mister Croon?'

'I just wanted to know, but I'm glad to hear you know how to use a still camera.'

They had reached the top of the long steady approach to the fort and now stood on the level ground, the enormous red fort a few hundred yards ahead of them, Croon panting a little.

Centuries seemed to roll away for Croon as he stared at the deserted fort.

CHAPTER 9

When Brett-Turner's parents had first met Megan Jones and had discovered that she was not only Welsh but that her father owned, and *served in,* a tiny grocer's shop in a Welsh village, and then that this outlandish girl had not only made her way to Oxford by a series of scholarships but was also an agnostic (as she had informed them on their second meeting), both parents reacted with considerable passion. The Reverend Brett-Turner simulated a more dramatic heart attack than any in the past, and Mrs Brett-Turner took to her bed where she wept and sulked, the curtains drawn, until her son promised to think things over.

'I ought to have realized *then,*' Megan told a friend. 'I ought to have seen that Wally was not for me. Why did I marry him? What did I see in him? God alone knows. But I'm a born nurse, I think. I go in for casualties. On the other hand, it may just have been an exercise in will-power. I probably made him marry me so that he'd defeat his parents. I think it must have been that. And I did care for him, you know, in the way you want to give somebody a kick in the arse, *affectionately,* so they'll find themselves and so on. He had no chin either. Also there was an undertone of snobbery involved, the Welsh peasant trying to climb, one more little facet of the British class-problem that has us all by the throat.' The friend, of course, she reflected later, had to be one of her own kind, to hear that kind of treason talked, for who else could you say such things to? 'He wasn't long out of Sandhurst, Wally, and full of that embarrassing jargon his kind use — you know, everything from "jolly good show" — later "wizard show" — to "fellow's a cad", though I never heard him call anyone a "bounder", which may show a gap in his learning. Yet I was in love. I must have been. And in love nobody's responsible any more. Looking back on it I just can't believe it.'

Alone now, following Wally's departure to his rented bungalow on Buggers' Ridge, she went to bed for three days with a bottle of gin and a couple of hundred cigarettes and wrote a series of letters announcing that her 'patient', now cured, had departed in an effort to try and grow up. She felt fresh strength, increasing, as if her writing of this matter gave more and more confirmation and approval to the long-delayed separation.

To her mother she wrote, 'You were right from the start, I'm sorry to say, though I'd better admit it and get it over, it'll save you reminding me of it in your so imitable way, Mam dearest. He's not a bad man, just infuriating, stupid, and incurably dense. I think it was when I knew my nursing had cured him that I could face the fact that somebody else had better take him over. My "life of sin" after he disappeared in the Malayan fiasco had very little to do with what was wrong. It was only a nonsense that at least gave us a drama to keep us together for a few more years. I did think he had been killed, and have to admit, and so get it over, that I probably would have fallen for that American anyway. After all he was the first real man I'd ever met. For Christ's sake, Mam, don't bother moralizing in any way about that in your reply. I don't need it just now. Later perhaps you can have an orgy of recrimination, but not now. I'm feeling relieved and don't need any needling or lecturing. I've done it for myself and to myself, all I need, thank you, Mam dearest. And don't forget I'm confiding in you, so enjoy it and feel proud of it too. You needn't bother Dad with any of this, bless him, he's too thick and good for this kind of stuff. So spare him and blame Wally for everything. It's simpler. Men like things simple, and like to feel that their daughters have married the wrong men, so make your mind up to let him have and keep his illusions. What Wally needed was a brainless English rose, the type to make a *real* memsahib, the kind a chap that keeps the last bullet for when the natives finally reach the verandah and the game is up. That wasn't me.

'When I got out here that first time, and fully understood what I'd done, after meeting the other memsahibs, I felt utter despair. My God, the stuffiness, and the colour-bar, the whole bloody awful social mess, I had such a job keeping my mouth shut. To hear some little bitch from Suburbiton, ruined now by having six servants, pronouncing on the natives and their shortcomings, I can't describe what I used to feel. But all admirable, oh yes, I mean it. Perfect for the job they'd designed out here, and sometimes, off guard, you met a secret fellow being, which helped at times. But on the whole — especially when you had to listen to some little cretin describing how he'd thrown an Indian out of a first-class carriage somewhere in India — or something similar, I used to wish I'd listened harder to you. And yet I felt so deeply for them all when Indian Independence came – they *were* staunch, they *were* courageous and honest in business, usually, but I never belonged among them. And I was sorry for Wally when he had to listen to my opinions in private. He couldn't understand it at all. For people like Wally, and there were lots here like him, life was simple. We were born to rule other people, *every* other people, and surely everyone in the world knew and acknowledged that. Why not me?' Then she tore the letter up and wrote another one to her mother, short this time, and containing the facts, ending about the relief of being her own woman again and how she was going to have to learn to live for herself again. She nearly added 'until another Mr Wrong turns up and I lose my head again', but she poured another gin and sipped it, smiling to herself, pleased with the knowledge that she was learning discretion. Tell as little as possible, regret nothing, get on with the mess called living.

But why did she still feel so 'guilty' about Wally, in fact about her feelings for Wally's kind, the commissioned Peter Pans of the Empire? Stupid, but there it was, and it was probably because Wally would never grow up and because she had pushed him out of her life, being careful, though, to see that he thought he was doing it all on his own. He so needed to feel in charge, in command.

It had become a game to outrage Wally, she recalled now as she sipped her pink gin, using the coarse Americanisms she liked to use and knew he so disliked to hear from her. She had fallen for the American language as soon as she heard Joe's 'lootenant' friend say, 'Gotta go 'n' make those camphor balls dance,' going out for a pee in the club toilet. That was early 1943. It had shocked her, while it had pleased her and made her laugh. It must have been the American casual sense of realism which had attracted her first, and then the background of the war too, the unreality of it all. World War Two and a half, as Joe liked to call it. Toilet, she thought. How that one word had set the rules of the war game between Wally and herself. 'Lavatory,' he would say firmly, 'I hate that word "toilet", it's not English.' Luncheon too. Wally had always fought for 'luncheon' but she had defied him steadily and called it 'lunch'.

She heard herself laughing now as she thought about all that ridiculous human nonsense which had so maintained their few years together after the war. Write to Dolly, at least she could tell her real thoughts to Dolly. She picked up her pen and started to let her thoughts run, and listening hard to what she was telling Dolly, and herself: 'I have lied to myself long enough' — she thought as she wrote — 'because you at least cannot judge me, after your own brilliant performance as an amateur *femme fatale,* so I want to tell you that at last I am that impossible creature, a free woman. Wally has flown the coop, lives up on Buggers' Ridge — which is only a place-name now, by the way, for all buggers have moved to a more congenial area of buggery, so Wally is quite safe up there. I have been a "brave little woman" for so long that I'm almost scared of the sheer joy I feel in being absolutely alone, and to be myself, vulgar, bloody-minded, and emotionally stupid. Even the discipline of a "good education" didn't succeed in making me a sensible person. I know this because even now I find myself feeling "sorry for Wally", who is one of those very lucky people who enjoy being aggrieved, know they are absolutely right in being aggrieved, and are never mistaken in any way about such matters and so never admit to any fault which might disturb the certainty of happy self-righteousness. So that I'd find myself doing my usual stupid thing, describing my faults and opening up my personality to discussion, and letting Wally think he was being asked to play judge and jury. And when I realized the position I had put myself in I then made it into a game, for private amusement, because it was quite amazing how much Wally enjoyed his role, and I think it did help him get over the feelings of shame and personal defeat living as a coolie-prisoner of the Japanese had given him. He didn't know that, but I began to understand it. But it was my class-problem that was always the real trouble between us. You remember how I liked to stir things up by dropping odd mysterious remarks about Marxism and so on, in the club. Pathetic really, I know that now, and only a revelation, to *me* I mean, of that bloody Brit inferiority feeling borne by most of us who have risen from the feudal fuck-up that is now the British prison. Risen? You notice that word? That's what I mean. I think now that everything I did from the start of my involvement with Wally in 1940 in London was an unconscious revenge because of Wally's awful parents, and their reaction to my social impudence in ensnaring their son. I never told you of the antics of Wally's father, when he was told I was a Welsh peasant with a village grocer Dad, and that I had not only managed to get to Oxford but had done brilliantly as well. He pretended to have a heart attack in front of Wally, staggering about the room and clutching his heart, and crying out, 'You will be ruined as a regimental officer, never mind what it will do to us here.' And Wally nearly scuttled out when his mother flooded the house with tears and used to kneel down and pray for guidance, with Wally in attendance. After that I was determined to marry Wally, and know now that I did it more to crush those bloody parents of his, than because I couldn't live without Wally. Not nice to think about, but lovely for you to read about. I can see your eyes shining as you lap up this delicious stuff, because I remember how you used to say, "You never talk about it. Tell me what it's like with you and Wally. I often wonder how you stand it." Water under the bridge for me, but for you — well, lap it up, deary. And by the way, I'm still a knock-out to look at (for men, I hasten to add) and still delight to hear the creak of sharply turned male necks in the street. I know I can tell that to you because we both know you have an even better pair of tits than I have, and I say that because it will help you to bear with how much I still enjoy my own good looks. All I mean, I suppose, is that I'm wearing well at thirty-three (but rather wary about the next Mr. Wrong who is lurking out there somewhere in the world; how long will that wariness last, I wonder?) . . .'

She sipped her gin for a while and thought again about her servant, Ram Dayal. Young, in his twenties, efficient, quiet, clean. But he would have to go. She knew for sure, in her instincts, that the servant had fallen in love with her. He would have to go, yes. What a shame, for he was an almost perfect servant, but there was a way a man looked at a woman, and swiftly looked away when noticed, and she had seen it in the servant several times. Worrying, and annoying too. God but it was bloody difficult being a woman at times, well a beautiful woman to be precise. You had to keep remembering the effect you were creating, especially when you forgot you were creating it.

'Gotta go 'n' make those camphor balls dance.' Could it really be ten years? She went on with her letter to Dolly, 'It seems impossible that it's ten years since Joe came into my life, as they say in women's magazines, and nine since he was removed from it, and from everybody else's life too. And seven since I received Wally back from the Japanese. My God how I had to scheme, and quickly too, to get Wally straight out of India to London before he started hearing about how scarlet a woman his little wifie had been. Yes, I spoiled it all for the bitches here — most of whom have left, thank God — because if there was one thing they wanted to watch and stir up it was Wally finding out that the treacherous bitch who thought she'd been made a widow had had a red hot affair with a Yank — '

She stopped and went over that part of her life again, running the film she had always strictly edited for herself, but this time letting it run uncut, Wally gone and she free to be herself and so on, through her guilty mind. Yes, she was still guilty, but less each time she saw the unedited film again. She did admit now that there had been no reason to imagine herself a widow, and that she had only decided on widowhood because this man Joe had appeared and her being had been making plans for her about him. But on the other hand, a year had passed, of silence, Japanese silence, and the curious thing was that Wally's image had already faded, and she had already begun to wonder why she had married him, and knew that she hoped he *was* dead, even before that laughing, rangy American had appeared and introduced her to what she now thought of as life, well Life then. Stop cringing and stare straight at the thought-film. Face it, write it down, get it over — and slip a needle into Dolly as a balancer while doing it, a reminder.

'Perhaps I should have gone off with him, to Goa, say, like you did with yours' — she stopped writing, smiled and took another sip of gin. Yes, Dolly, you had the guts to do it properly. Came back looking as if you'd had no sleep for ten years, but never mind, none of the bitches here knew about it, while me — idiot. She wrote on — 'but I was too scared of what was happening to me. Oh yes, I'd lost my head, was

96

indiscreet, and was known to have let down not only Womanhood, but the Empire, Britain, and the Army, and Witch-Bitch Number One here, yes you've guessed, Iris Tone, saw to it that everybody in India except possibly the Viceroy knew about it. It'll tell you how much I'd lost my head when I inform you that I took that bitch head-on. It was Joe's death that did it. I was so broken up and felt so alone, that when that bitch actually had the nerve to come and *condole* with me ... Yes, an American Officer from Joe's air-unit who knew about the affair came to Induspur to look for me. He stupidly enquired for me at the club and let it out about why he had to see me, and Iris bloody Tone got hold of him, told him she was my best friend, and *brought* him here to the house. I must have been out of my mind, though, because I drove up to the Tones' house and cornered the bitch. Tone himself was away in Burma, which is probably why the Burma campaign went on for so long. I threatened Iris – told her that if she ever opened her big mouth again about my business, especially about what she'd just heard, which was of course complete confirmation about what had been the number one topic of the valley for a year, my affair with Joe, that I'd not be responsible for what I might do to her. It was a terrible scene, so terrible that it was a couple of years before I could even think about it.'

She stopped again, picked up her gin. Her hand was shaking, with the remains of what seemed to be an unchillable passion, not even ten years deadening it, but grief and hatred rising again — which just showed you how parts of you never grew up, never learned.

'I once watched you run your expert eye over Joe. You were right. He was fine, wasn't he? Thirty-one, brilliant, read everything and knew just about everything, and handsome, and tall, straight out of Woman's Monthly or something. Nothing could have stopped what happened between him and me. Life just sort of threw the switch' — she was about to write about what Joe had said to her after that first time, as the incandescence of that first experience had — she could recall the huskiness of her weak voice saying to him, 'How was it, Joe?' Imagine being able to *ask* such a thing at last, showed how far she'd travelled in no time.

Joe was about to pour iced champagne, leaning from the side of the bed. Iced champagne, my God, like an old-time film or something. She started to laugh as she recalled his reply. 'Well, we registered ten and a half on the Richter scale, lover,' he had said, smiling as he handed her the champagne. 'In fact it's dangerous, if you ask me. We could set off some kind of chain-reaction and wreck the whole goddam world.'

The B-29s were flying out of Chabua in Assam then, over China, Burma, and the murderous mountain range into China called The Hump. His plane had vanished over The Hump, one of so many heaps of aluminium in the jungle below. She always imagined him lying back dead in the pilot's seat, and for some reason with a cigarette in his lips — gave it a touch of his remembered coolness and ease of manner, she supposed.

Now, she tore up her letter to Dolly, satisfied that she did not need to confide in anybody, was learning at last to confide in herself, no cringing any more. Write the letters, yes, listen while she was writing them, and then tear them up. Growing up at last? Possibly, she thought.

Then, remembering which letter it was she had idly thought all week of writing, she opened her address book and went through the list of London publishers her mother had sent her a couple of years before.

'Dear Sir,' she wrote, 'I wonder if you will remember a novel I sent to you about eighteen months ago? It was based on a famous local eighteenth-century love affair in this part of India, which involved an Indian Maharani and her three lovers, an Irishman, a Frenchman, and an Englishman. You liked the idea but thought the novel not good enough for publication. I have just heard a rumour in the club here that an American film company is planning to film the story. Do you think this might make the novel of interest now, if I rewrote it —' She stopped writing. Go through it all again about having had four short stories published, two of them in America, worked on the novel again and — ? No. Be what she was. A secret hack. Successful. Rich. God!

She tore this letter up too, got off the bed and went to the open window. She looked out on the yellow glow of the Indian afternoon, across the valley. She could hear a peasant singing far off, her cook laughing in the kitchen nearby. Why write about the dead past? Why not a book about her brief life with that American who had liberated so much of her and, she feared often, had ruined all other men for her. None of them reminded her of him. How stupid, but perhaps she enjoyed such thoughts, a way of mourning, probably for herself more than for him. Maybe.

She had been to the club only once since Wally left. Curious that he had found the nerve to pin his Notice up on the notice-board of the club. She had written the Notice and then had skilfully got him to think he had composed it all himself, to say, after a few drinks, that he meant what he had said. It should go up on the notice-board for the world to see. Right, she remembered thinking, that's enough of these brave sentiments never followed through, so she had driven him to the club with the Notice, and sent him in to pin it up while she stayed in the car. He was sobering fast as he returned to the car, and had wanted to go back and retrieve the Notice, but she had said no, stand by your guns. Later he was very pleased with himself, as if he might know it was the first time he had ever done something which 'wasn't done', was 'bad form', or some other version of the multi-faceted Brit-class behaviour code. She did not doubt that it was that so out-of-character action of Wally's (kicked into doing it admittedly) which had made him brave enough to do what he wanted, leave her.

What a scene that was, the leaving. 'You can change your mind now,' he said, as he packed. 'It's up to you. I don't *have* to go, you know. After all a chap —'

'Wally,' she said. 'You *do* have to go.'

He looked hard at her then. Christ, how weak a face he had, really, how *right* a face it was and of its time, a sort of falsetto face masking a tiny nervous personality behind which had always stood the iron certainty of some NCO or other who was there to let him play officer. Had Wally's parents never had any money and Wally therefore had his rightful place, say a butcher's boy or an apprentice clerk, or a farm labourer, he would never have been allowed to become an officer. There was something of luxury now in the way she could feel sorry for him, or pity for him, but it was a fact that she had wasted a few years of her life on him.

'*You* want me to go, Meg,' he had faltered then, and she went on for him, 'more than *I* want to go, Meg,' and then added, 'Yes, Wally, I want you to go — just as much as you want to go. Shall we put it like that? It sounds okay to me. You?'

'I'll never understand your mind,' he complained, packing again angrily. 'But go I shall.'

Two days after he had gone up to live on Buggers' Ridge he had sent her a note containing three words, 'You were right'; and she had written on the bottom of the note, 'Good. And no more notes, thank you. Enjoy yourself.'

It was three days after Wally's departure that she had had her nightmare about the tennis match. When she woke up shaking and panting, the sweat-soaked sheet tangled round her legs, she understood that sleep at last allowed her to experience it all again, but in a shower of fragmented mirror pieces. She sat in the bed with her legs drawn up, her forehead on her knees, and this time going over the tennis match fearlessly in detail, from the beginning. She had known what was coming, known that Wally had practised himself to exhaustion with that tennis champion in Delhi, but she had never foreseen all the tragi-comic horrors of the actual match, with everyone playing their parts, all taking part in the public destruction of the little that remained of her marriage. Though really it was an execution, with Wally as his own executioner. After that ghastly evening she was frightened by how often she toyed with the idea of killing him.

Thinking about this now, she moaned aloud and wrapped her arms around her knees, and squeezed, and went on moaning.

'I know what you're going to do,' she had said to Wally as they got into the car. 'Please — don't do it.'

Without looking at her he said, while he tramped far too heavily on the clutch pedal, 'You're very fond of using the word "fuck". I've never liked it. But I'll use it just this once. They're going to see the match of the fucking century this evening. I only hope you're up to it, that's all.'

She could remember trembling as she listened to those quietly spoken words. It was like a declaration of murder announced in terms of sport. She had laughed to herself about it later, before the match, when the drinks were circulating and the Maharajah was doing the round of his guests on the white marble verandah of the palace.

She could, she knew, still get out of the match. She could

fall back on the timeless female playploy, sit down and look wan and smile bravely, so that all could silently realize something about it being that time of the month, but out loud having a terrible headache. Then Mrs Somebody or other could play Wally instead.

'What are you laughing to yourself about, Meg?' somebody said as she was rehearsing the possibilities of the playploy. It was Colonel Bingham, her favourite too-old and beyond-reach man of the world, smiling at her. 'About Wally drinking orange juice over there?'

He nodded to where Wally was standing with the Tones and two officers of the State 'army'. Yes, my God, he had a glass of orange juice in his hand. She looked at Bingham and said, 'What's it all about? The orange juice thing.' As if she didn't know.

When enough comment had been made about Wally's choice of orange juice by the others around him, and Wally was known to like his booze, he had said that he wanted to keep a clear head for the tennis. 'A bit sinister, I thought,' Bingham joked with Megan. 'I said to him, "Well, this sounds serious, Wally," and he told me we were going to see some *real* tennis later. I haven't seen Wally enthusiastic about anything up to now. He's playing you — is that right?' Bingham was amused, seemingly unaware of the iron undertones beneath all this nonsensical behaviour now slowly gathering force. But she knew him better than that. He was being polite, amusing, and worrying about the matter too, for he knew how stupidly Wally could behave at times. She would trust him with a few thoughts, she decided.

'You don't miss a thing do you, Tim?' she said, smiling. She knew she was looking good in her white silk blouse and white linen skirt which reached just below her knees. Her thick black hair was done up in a loose bun. The colonel was staring down into her large blue eyes veiled by her smoky black eyelashes. Bingham was so good-looking, and strong-looking. She was wondering when he had had his last affair with a woman, or was he having one now? Oh yes, she knew how smoothly and covertly these bloody bachelors ran that side of things out here. And what about that beautiful Indian woman she had seen him with in an out-of-the-way restaurant in Old Delhi a year ago, near the Kashmir Gate, the kind of restaurant you wouldn't have found Europeans in before Independence. But the two races were mixing now, whereas before Independence when they mixed it had been only 'officially'. Thank God the steam had gone out of all that idiocy a few months after Independence. In fact it showed how very civilized India was, in that the actual seething anger and hatred, which had poisoned the country during the freedom struggle, vanished like mist in the sun. A European could appear anywhere in India today and be welcomed, unless some of the politically indignant and indoctrinated screamed a few slogans about those bacteria-laden fleas which the Americans, according to Moscow and its satellites, had dropped from planes over Korea.

'Your mind is far away, Meg,' the colonel said. He had moved from Wally's orange juice, with swift, smooth facility after that one about not missing a thing, to how delighted he was with his new short-wave set. It was a make recommended by His Nibs — everybody's nickname for the Maharajah with those who did not know him as Chan, which was just about everybody — but Megan was obviously not listening to him. She was worrying about this bloody tennis duel coming up, he supposed, and quite right too. She looked at him.

'Well, Tim, forgive me — but I've been thinking about this story of those germ-laden fleas the Americans are supposed to have dropped on North Korea. So I *was* listening about your new radio. Do you remember how recently we all called it a wireless set? Because I listen quite a lot and they're still going on about those fleas. Do you believe the Americans did drop them, Tim?'

Serious-eyed, then grave as he went on, he said, 'Well, Meg, you know the Americans, what demons they are about these matters. And their love of experiments. You've got to think about what went into this in some training ground and laboratory in America. Each flea being taught to wear a parachute, then the practice jumps from tiny model aircraft, thousands of them' — as she started to laugh she saw the Maharajah coming to join them, and her heart seemed to quicken, Christ knew why, would she ever grow up?

The Maharajah joined the game and said, in the same serious manner as Bingham, 'Well, Comrade, we see the typical bourgeois approach here in this lady, as they call women in the West — flighty and heartless laughter while millions of starving citizens of North Korea are in the throes of diabolically induced diseases grown in the secret military installations of capitalist America. Ruling circles may try to deny . . . ' He took Megan's proffered right hand and squeezed it, smiling at her with those marvellous teeth — why was it all Africans and Asiatics had such splendid teeth? Sun, vitamin C? Bingham came back to his wonderful new radio — and Megan was thinking, 'My God, I've got to remember that I can buy a dozen of these radios now if I like.' She still had to remember all the money coming into her bank account, and all earned by her new, secret activity at the typewriter.

The enormous marble verandah on which the two dozen or so guests were talking and drinking in twos and threes was on the west side of the palace, and now, as the sun came slowly down the sky and poured onto the verandah, turbaned servants started to draw the blue silk screens. The sunlight pouring through the screens produced a sort of magical golden-blue atmosphere within, and as if reacting to this the talk grew louder, and the servants moved about and poured fresh drinks. What was special about this yearly tennis party was that nobody had to wait until sundown for liquor. It was entirely up to the guests what they drank, and now, at four o'clock, in the mysterious golden-blue haze of light on the snowy marble of the verandah, a few people started to drift out for the first tennis match. There was nothing serious about this tennis. In fact it was quite often comical how badly people played, and how seriously the watchers applauded bad play. Nobody minded if a player went on a little drunk, for instance. The Maharajah never played at these parties, explaining solemnly that as the ruler of the state he could not afford to be seen to lose publicly. He had always wanted to add 'especially losing to a European', but he knew just who among the Europeans would resent this humourlessly, and those who felt that it was a very bad show for a ruler to talk like that, even if he were only an Indian ruler of a tiny crackpot unknown statelet like this one. There was still a lot of diehardishness around, he knew, and which was easily awakened too.

He squeezed Megan's arm and said, 'I'll be back. Must circulate a little.'

When he had gone Bingham said, 'You don't really have to go on with this tennis business, do you, Megan? I mean —'

'I know what you mean, Tim. But he's been practising for

it. Imagine it, secretly practising to beat his wife at tennis.'

Bingham laughed. He patted her shoulder. 'Are you going to let him win?' he asked. Her tennis was good but it was a well known local joke that she never knew who was winning when she played. She would call out to her opponent, 'Who's winning? How do we stand?' She did not care. She just liked to play tennis. For opponents who liked to win, which was practically everybody who played tennis, this curious lack of competitiveness, and her deadly serving, could cause bad temper and quite often fury. She was such a good player, so how could she not care about who won?

'Let him win?' She was frowning now. 'No damn fear. I've thought it over. What Wally needs, I think, is to play tennis with a Japanese general and win hands down. That may be the trouble with Wally still, all this time after the war. But it's me he wants to smash, and the marriage too, and I'm willing about the marriage, but not about him winning. It's shameful, I know it. But you can all have fun watching. I mean it. I don't care. This time I'm playing to win.' She looked up into Bingham's cool, steady, amused eyes. 'You can feel the atmosphere, can't you? I can feel Wally radiating it, this far away from him.'

When their turn to play came she felt afraid about the way everybody came out of the verandah area and down onto the grassy bank to watch. It made her tremble, especially the tense silence that had fallen over the crowd. Yes, she thought, they had all discussed it, and now they wanted to see what Wally had promised her they were going to see, 'the match of the fucking century'. She knew their tennis problem was quite famous, and they all knew by now that Wally had been down in Delhi getting ready to be good enough to beat his wife, whom he had never been able to master, and not just at tennis. They were going to watch a fierce quarrel between a man and his wife in public, dressed up as a game of tennis. As she reached the court she caught the Maharajah's eye and was touched by the expression of sympathy and trepidation in his look. He smiled at her nervously. And then Wally made his announcement to the audience, as if he had been drinking a lot of whiskey, for an ordinary man would have to be somewhat drunk to say what he did.

'As most of you will know, or have guessed, or have heard,' he called out, 'this is no ordinary tennis match. My wife never knows the score when she plays. That's well known too, and it's annoyed a few people in the past, including yours very truly. I'd be glad, therefore, if someone will kindly call out the score as each point is made. That way I'll be having the first real game of tennis I've ever had with my wife.' There was some nervous tittering, then coughing, and somebody called out that he would be umpire. There was laughter, though uncertain laughter, when somebody else called out, 'Sounds like you could do with a referee as well, Wally.' Wally glowered but tried to smile. Then he looked at Megan and slammed his racquet against his left hand a few times. 'Ready?' he asked.

'Don't I have to make a little speech too now?' she called out, and the laughter was louder now, yet the atmosphere felt worse. She had annoyed Wally who stared at her uncertainly. But he was confident.

It was his serve. This was the first time, she was thinking, as she responded to his serve, that she had ever played real tennis, to win. She played with a kind of cold anger, efficiently and cruelly, sometimes meeting Wally's delivery by touching the ball so that it crawled over the net and Wally had to race to meet it, and too often failed to. The applause was loaded too, all of it for her successes, which were increasing. She won the first game, and when she served it was with all her strength, and she knew she had never played so well. It was some time too before she understood that she was not, even now, listening to the score, though she knew she was winning. Her serving was even more devastating than Wally had found it in the past. He quickly began to crumble, and to lose his temper. People began to snigger, and to call out, 'Come on, Wally? Where's all the coaching gone?' He grew flustered, his confidence dissolving.

It was when he had lost the second set that his exhibition of an almost childish fury began. He started to smash the ball with all his strength, driving it again and again past Megan's head, as if seeking to hit her with it. She watched him with icy calm.

'They're all on your side, you know?' he yelled. His face was red, his eyes wild. 'Lovely, isn't it? To be so popular, you bitch.'

He then leaned backwards as if about to throw a grenade and when he straightened up Megan was just in time to step aside so that his hurled racquet hissed past her head. There was a gasp and shouts from the crowd.

'That's quite enough,' someone shouted in a very loud, angry voice. It was the Maharajah and, tragically, Wally stared at the audience, running his fierce and puzzled eyes over them all. Then he walked quickly off the court towards his car. He drove it at great speed, but he was in such a state of emotion that he was too late to turn properly and the car crashed into the wall. He backed off and straightened the car out. Then, as Megan ran in a panic from the court towards the trees, Wally's car disappeared round the bend of the drive.

As she was running through the trees she could hear someone catching up with her, and then the Maharajah had his arms round her.

Play the cornered faun, she decided, as she looked up into his eyes. It was like a line from Saleema Begum, she thought — as the Maharajah said, smiling, 'Come on back. A drink will do you good.' Saleema Begum was writing, 'He was so masterful, so relaxed, so sure. Yes, she was his, and he knew it.'

'What happened?' she said, remembering to make it vague, and to look wildly about her. It seemed to work because he pressed her in his arms and said, 'Never mind what happened. You could do with a drink.' Damn right she could. So she let him lead her back while she went on and perfected her act, so that she did not seem to realize that she had taken part in a horrible public scene. He looked worried, she was glad to see. He comforted her too, saying softly, 'Just relax, Megan. Can I call you that, instead of Meg?' So he knew that only her real friends were allowed to call her Megan. Good.

'Of course,' she said, and adding a little vagueness, 'Why not? Yes, Maharaj Sahib, why not.'

He smiled, his arm round her shoulders now, and said, 'Thank you, Megan, and you'd better call me Chan, I think.'

There was no doubt about it now, what she had long suspected. Chan was gone about her, and why not? But she was not gone about him. She had no intention of being gone about any man, for a very long time, if she could help it that is. But you can't always help it, can you? You know not the day nor the hour when Mister Wrong will arrive, again. She was laughing, and she heard the Maharajah, his arm removed from

106

her shoulder now, saying to Bingham who had just joined them, 'She's in shock, I think, Tim.' So she stared emptily at Bingham and then smiled crookedly. Bingham, she knew, was very hard to fool, but he was fooled this time. He was all concern. He put his arm round her shoulder now, and said comfortingly, 'A good jolt of brandy will help, Meg, I'd say.' Even now, when she was in shock, he still called her Meg, and she had twice told him in the past he could call her Megan. Interesting. Didn't really like her?

All the watchers were still there, watching her. Bingham took her past them and on into the Maharajah's study. Only then, as she lowered herself into an armchair, could she exult, in silence. If she knew Wally at all he was back in the house now, staring at the wall, and wondering why he had imagined it all, that he was going to humiliate her in public by beating her six-nothing. It would have to be six-nothing to satisfy him. Nothing else would have done.

It was going to be a very long time before the bastard picked up a tennis racquet again, she thought, as she took the brandy from Bingham. He sat down on a silver stool opposite her and smiled sympathetically, even reaching out to squeeze her hand as if to reassure her. While he was doing this she worked out why she had played the startled faun and then the woman in shock, who could not remember the tennis match. She wanted sympathy. This awakened scorn for herself and she decided to, perhaps, slowly recall the tennis match, and ask for details. There was one certain thought, bigger than all others, and that was that she was finished with Wally. She enjoyed the sensation of enormous relief which flowed all over her then, and although she raised her glass of brandy to Bingham, and smiled at him, it was really raised to herself. She had won, and it was all over, at long, fucking final, wonderful last.

The tears then were just right too, though they were real, and she knew a smile through them would put the finishing touch to the short, perfect act of the woman in shock.

'Cheers, Meg,' Bingham murmured, lifting his own glass as the Maharajah joined them. 'Cheers, Tim,' she said.

I'm such a con, really, sometimes, at least, she was thinking, amused. Harmless, though. Driven to it, really, by life with Wally, though she admitted she had always been a bit of a ham in her private way. Fun, that's all. Saleema waiting all those years in the shadow of the unconscious. Result of sheer bloody spiritual loneliness, nothing else.

'Was it horrible?' she asked. The Maharajah did not seem to know how to respond to that, but trust Bingham, of course.

'Not just horrible,' he grinned. 'Revolting. But you taught him a lesson, and not just about tennis, Meg.' He and the Maharajah looked at each other and laughed, then looked fondly at her again.

'Oh!' she said, not too vague this time, and left it at that.

'A little music,' said the Maharajah, and as he went to the old-fashioned cabinet gramophone standing against the wall he looked over his shoulder at her. 'D'you care for Indian music, Megan?'

She nodded. Well, some of it, not that bloody endless cater-wauling from the Bombay film industry starlets. This was different though. A woman's voice singing hauntingly in Urdu. The voice was smoky, husky and somehow intimate, as if communicating personally with her, and the melancholy of the song moved her, and she could feel that she was growing pale. No need to act any more. 'It's beautiful,' she said. 'Who is she?'

'Malike Pukraj,' said the Maharajah. She must have fainted just then, she thought later, for she could remember the two men staring at her and then looming over her.

'She's coming to,' she heard Bingham saying. 'My God, she's — stay where you are, Meg — don't try and get up —'

She was on her feet. She felt stupidly proud of herself, of her control, for she was swaying. 'Another brandy'll do it, Tim,' she said, holding out her hand. She heard the two men laugh. She took the brandy and swigged some of it down fast, and felt stronger. This was no time to go under, a little play-acting yes, but not the real thing. She heard a little of what she was saying, and when she heard herself saying ' — managed to stop myself shooting Wally anyway', she felt panic. When she looked at the faces of Bingham and the Maharajah she saw concern in their eyes, and became firmer now.

'Tim,' she said 'Would you be a dear and drive me home?'

'I'll drive you, Megan,' said the Maharajah. 'Come on.'

'I don't want to see the others just now,' she exclaimed.

'Don't worry,' the Maharajah said. 'We'll slip out quietly

this way. Come on. Won't be long, Tim. Hold the fort for me.'

The Maharajah was holding her hand as he led her out to the car.

He drove fast. He said, 'Do you remember what happened, Megan?' and she knew her acting had been pretty good, at that moment of flight when the Maharajah had caught her in his arms, and she had thought he might kiss her. In shock and so on. She must have played it rather well.

'Not really,' she said. 'Not much. I don't want to — I — ', and waited for him to say, 'All right, don't let's talk about it,' but he actually said, 'Better forgotten anyway.' She stole a look at his profile — she was lying well back beside him. There was a grim look about his mouth, thinking about Wally's mad behaviour. She supposed any man present at that scene would want to kick Wally's arse, and quite right too.

'Are you feeling better?' His voice was tender. She saw that he was smiling, to himself. Gone about her and delighted to have her on his own for a while. And why not? All she wanted was to get into her room and close the door, sit with a large drink in her hand, and savour how it felt to be at the end of her bizarre and useless marriage, at last.

The Maharajah got out of the car, then took her hands and asked anxiously, 'Are you all right?'

She nodded and smiled. 'You are to come to the palace any time you like, Megan,' he said. 'The library is yours. The palace, the swimming pool, all of it. You understand? Yours, any time.'

'Thank you, Chan,' she said. He smiled like a boy, happily, innocently and, still smiling, he stood there until she turned on the verandah and waved to him. Honest to God but there was no understanding men, the way they stayed small boys, that is, horrible boys like Wally, or stunned with love like the Maharajah, who could do with losing just a little weight. He was so good-looking it was wrong to let himself get fat.

She got into her room, closed the door, and shaking with excitement, drank a stiff whiskey straight down, then stood there, panting, and murmuring, 'Jesus, he asked for it and he got it.' She envisaged Wally again, with those glaring eyes at the other end of the court, with all his plans to demolish her as a tennis player, person, wife, woman, everything. She giggled and poured another whiskey. She had never played better. Inspired for Christ's sake, that's what she'd been, a machine of defiance and vengeance. That was the last game of tennis she would ever play. Now come on, don't let's overdo things, dear, and she giggled again.

She woke up in the dark, chilled, the sheet on the floor beside the bed. She put on a dressing gown and went to the room she used as a study and unlocked it with the key she wore on a gold chain round her neck.

She wrote a note to Wally. 'I don't want to set eyes on you for some time, thank you. Stay out of my way. No apologies, no excuses, nothing, thank you.' She put it into an envelope. When she quietly slipped the envelope under his door she could hear him snoring. Bastard. The game was up, at last, though. Finally over.

Ram Dayal had left the Thermos flask of coffee as usual. She poured a cup of it. She went and got the bottle of brandy from the drinks cupboard and laced the coffee with it. Get plastered, might be a good idea, then sleep for twenty-four hours. The sheer relief of decision, the happiness of the made up mind, at last. And she felt impatience. Wanted to get him out of the house and out of her bloody life now, this minute. Have to play it slowly, though. Not too slowly, though. Just carefully. More coffee and brandy. She caught herself fantasizing for a moment, 'Dearest Joe, I've done it. We're free. Can you — ?' For Christ's *sake*, woman.

She got up and walked about, sipping the fragrant coffee and brandy. The brandy was helping. She could feel the excitement returning, the longing to be alone at the typewriter again, to take up where she had left off.

She had worked so hard on that serious attempt to write a real book, that book about the intrigues in eighteenth-century Induspur. Taken her a long time, that book, and all for nothing. Yet this other stuff came like a river out of nowhere into her head, sort of wrote itself really. She had not been into her study for days, since that weird spasm had overtaken her at the desk. Sheet of typing still in the machine, waiting for her. Paper with a will of its own, waiting for her.

She lit a cigarette and thought about the mystery she had stumbled on in herself, the enigma of the other woman in her who must have been waiting for years to be discovered, and now, guilt-laden, triumphant with response from out there, and with money, was itching again for notice. A bloody long way from Jane Austen, of course, but still – she did have rights, this strange other woman.

She knew that the urge to write, to go back to her desk and forget everything in the stream of mysterious trash which was making her so much money, had been growing for days, despite that strange nausea, then the vomiting, during the last spate of work. Work? Well, she could hardly call it that. Perhaps the nausea had come because it was not work at all, but pleasure, and the fact that what she wrote gave her pleasure, and a bigger surprise still, money, perhaps it was the fact of the pleasure which had induced the perplexing nausea. Also, there might be something in the horrible secret itself, shared with nobody, which had helped to bring on the frightening spasm of vomiting during the writing of the fifth chapter.

Might it not be that the writing of this trash, which she had approached so light-heartedly the first time, telling herself that she could knock off a cheap novel full of dream-rubbish in no time, to show herself and the world — and maybe make a few shekels — might it not be that it was her real vocation after all? So that the vomiting during chapter five of the latest one was simply her mind at last accepting the truth, that if she was going to be a writer then writing what she thought of as trash was her real vocation. It could be the conflict in her that had caused that weird manifestation when she had only just reached the bathroom in time, and now the conflict had been vomited up. Face it then. Say it — 'I am a bloody good writer of dream-rubbish for those millions of females out there, who, secretive about it or not, devour these rivers of titillatory-cum-heart-convulsing pulp about the real true love waiting out there for every woman.' God almighty no! No! But the money was piling up in the bank, and had been growing since she had dashed off the first one, *Rhapsody of Revenge* in five weeks,in a fever which had grown daily so that she had gone on writing into the early hours through many a night. She could not deny that it had been a wonderful experience. Face it. She had loved it. She had started out, laughing, to have some ice-cold fun at the expense of those female millions out there, and then would finish a chapter, written at speed, panting, rather like she felt after a high-pitch hour of good tennis. All in secret too.

One night Wally had come raging out of his room and asked what was going on, why was the house resounding with the thud of her typewriter? She was typing at speed when he angrily shouted the question, the floor round her desk littered with a few dozen pages of *Rhapsody of Revenge*.

'A suicide note,' she had shouted back, not even turning her head. 'A bit long, I'm afraid, but I'll try and cut it down. Go and have a few drinks or something, but leave me alone, please.'

She finished *Rhapsody of Revenge* at four o'clock one morning, worried about the excitement and happiness she felt, a woman who had been educated at one of the fountain-heads of Western culture, and here she was, trembling with happiness and hardly able to pour her celebratory gin without spilling it. She could remember the enormous moon that morning at four o'clock. She had gone to the window and stared out through the fierce moonlight at the far-off wall of the Himalayas, knowing she had almost certainly written a work of crapulous genius, in five weeks only, a tale of burning unrequited love in the India of the Mutiny in 1857. A young, handsome British officer at the siege of Mangapur, leading his loyal Indian troops, apparently for the Empire, but actually to reach and capture his lover, the beautiful young Indian princess who commanded the rebel sepoys in her castle. Then — after which — so that they — until finally — betrayed — she — in a final terrible revenge of love . . . .

She ought to have known then, staring at that huge Indian moon, that she had 'found herself'. But she was not ready to admit it. Still wasn't — hence the vomiting?

While she stared at the moon her pen-name had arrived, walked into her head, after days of choosing and rejecting. In the search for her pen-name the tension of pleasure had increased, and only after the book was published had she understood that tension. It had been caused by the act of becoming someone else, and all in secret, and it was much cheaper than going to a bloody head-shrinker. You just sat down and poured out the steaming trash onto the pages and signed it 'Saleema Begum', and got paid, instead of paying.

She had been tempted several times to confide in Colonel Bingham, for it was listening to some of his stories of the

112

Indian past that had given her the idea for her first exercise in highly saleable trash.

Rhapsody of Revenge by Saleema Begum, with its broad hints on the cover that Saleema Begum descended from a line of the warrior-aristocrats of Moghul India, sold and sold.

The shame of the joy she felt when the reviews arrived was washed away by her new bank statements. She watched with detached interest how her other new self, Saleema Begum, now began to enjoy the India of the past, for it *was* Saleema's India after all.

She wrote the next one, *Dagger of Devotion*, in fifteen days. Much tighter, neater, sharper, she noticed, the simple but riveting tale of a Kurdish youth sent from Alamut, by the Old Man of the Mountain, to assassinate a Moghul emperor in Delhi — his long and eventful journey across Persia into India, and how — once he — and saw the princess who — he forgot his — and then — ending with his betrayal of his treacherous mission and instead — she still felt a guilty bliss whenever she thought of the heights of her creative zest as she wrote the end of that story. The youth, his arm about the slender form of the princess, pursued, turning in their flight, he to fight. How he had raised the golden hilted dagger which the Chief of the *Hashishin* had given him in far off Alamut for the task of assassination, and kissed the shining Damascus steel of the blade, then handed it to her to kiss too, and then, as the screaming Moghul pursuers fell on them, he — she — until finally — he, the lover, chanting an ancient death-hymn, had . . . .

It was all very well clapping her hands across her eyes and moaning aloud in the privacy of her bedroom, 'My God, what am I *doing*?' whenever she opened her locked cupboard and looked at the row of shiny achievements, the books of Saleema Begum, but the pride of achievement was there to be faced as well. That she had betrayed her sex she never forgot, for during her education she had done her part in the eternal struggle to free herself and other women from the chains of femininity. But bullshit! What about the millions of female betrayers out there who read all these avalanches of dream-rubbish?

Certainly the climax of all these conflicting feelings had come in that eruption of vomit which had followed the extreme nausea she thought of now as 'Chapter Five'. She had not been near her desk since that curious episode. Now, face it.

She went into the room she used as a study — no need to lock it now that Wally had gone — and sat down at the desk. It was exactly as she had rushed away from it in that panic to the bathroom. Just cut out this bloody intellectual snobbery about writing down to the millions of panting females out there, and get on with her real work, writing a new kind of book, the mysterious woman from the *zenana*, the Moghul-blooded secret-teller of the *harem* reaching out to her millions of Western sisters with the other half of the cry of love which came up, eternal, out of every female heart . . . .

'You bitch!' she told herself, then lit a cigarette, and faced it. She pulled the page she had been working on out of the typewriter and began to read it. She stopped reading as she reached the words, 'with a strength of will handed down from a time of primal fortitude, when women had scornfully killed themselves as the hands of the Mongol savages reached to seize them, she —'

Distressed again, drawing harder on her cigarette, she had to admit that Saleema Begum loved her stuff, read her writing sometimes with a tremor in her throat. Suddenly it occurred to her — could the real trouble lie in the drawer here? Of course. It was probably that, not the writing of the books. The unbelievable fan letters from women in England, and lately from women in America, and most worrying of all, a few of them were now from men. She pulled open the drawer and got out the big file into which she always hurriedly jammed the letters, at times her eyes tightly shut as if it might help to erase the horrific exaltation she felt as Saleema Begum, during the reading of these heart-cries from so many strangers. Oh yes, my God, how she had to shut her mind to some of those letters . . . .

She held the file tightly, her eyes screwed up against the smoke from the cigarette in her lips, hesitating. No, read them. Face them. There was the one from a woman who had fallen in love with her, that was to say with Saleema Begum, and demanded a photograph. A touch of the butch, she had thought defensively when she had read it, but her hands were shaking, and she threw it away from her onto the desk as if it had turned suddenly into a tarantula. There was another one from some crazy man who had written, 'You are mine, mine, mine, do you know that? My hands are on your silken body, and my — ' Christ! She *could not* open the file, must not. She tore it open, then lit another cigarette. No, better still, pour herself a large slug of gin. She hurried out to the living room and sloshed gin into a tumbler, then hurried back to her desk. Have it out with yourself, this stupid — she almost added 'female' but censored it — this stupid fear of facing the real lies of life, the secret life, now made public in dreary letters, representing those of millions who craved for what probably only about one in a million human beings deserved: love. Or lurv? Bitch!

'Dear dear Saleema, first I love your name and say it to myself so often — Saleema, Saleema, Saleema. How lucky you are to have such a lovely name. Mine is Violet and I have to live with it. I am married to a monster and I live in the suburbs. If he saw your book and knew what it meant to me he would tear it to pieces, so I have it hidden away. You've opened up a new life for me, Saleema — because you know about LOVE. I — '

Oh, dear Christ. She put the letter down and drank some gin, then sat there as it hit her with its mellow fire, and let herself daydream for a while. What harm, really, to add a little honey to the river of rubbish — poor Violet in the grey rain-sodden suburbs of London peering through the fog at the magic pages of Saleema Begum whose silken body . . . . How about a bit of blind woman's buff? She put her hand at random into the pile of letters and pulled one out. Oh Christ yes, that violet ink and the jagged writing pouring out the stream of unconsciousness, 'Yes Saleema you've done it again and heres telling you baby that I am a woman been fucked by every shape and size and colour and if any woman knows it I do and that is that all men are bastards yes baby all a man wants is to fuck you and quick so he can get on with his drinking in the nearest bar and tell his dirty jokes with the other slobs who like him have to get on with training for the next war in between fucking us poor women I am an educated woman dont you forget and have had three useless husbands and have to break my ass paying lawyers to get my rightful alimony which I cannot get so I am here to tell you that when I got lost in your book I rediscovered my real self Jesus H Christ I was sobbing when the lovely Leyla hit Delhi and guess who was waiting for her there but the guy you made us all think was dead on page fourteen remember and when she saw him and you made her start to faint well Jesus the tears ran down my face and I thought of how I have been fucked until my socks fell off by nogood bastards who sold me a bill of goods with fuckall at the end of it except a heap of bills and dirty dishes and a goodbye letter because the sonofabitch has been getting it on the side some place else and now she is pregnant and I will understand you remember how you describe when Leyla makes up her mind that You Know Who has got to go I mean the guy who tried to rape her on page fifty one how do you know a womans feelings the way you do I mean the way Leyla *thinks* about that bum before she lets him have it and then watches the bastard die my god the way you describe how he slowly falls down at her feet you missed out one thing you should have made Leyla spit into his face as he fell thats what I would have done or maybe will do if I ever catch up with the last bastard who took me to the cleaners after he fucked my head off all over Central Park and we finish up with a Hamburger and French Fries which is the Big Time for him you get it yes Saleema you made my day and night and I know every one of us women is really Leyla only Leyla knew what to do how do you know all this how do you know about me because its me you write about I mean —'

Holding back tears of shame, as well as anger, she took out another letter which began, 'Oh Saleema so you too, you women of the East, you too know the same burning sorrows of the true love . . . .'

Hardly knowing what she was doing, she stuffed the letters back into the file and rammed the file into the drawer, then slammed the drawer shut with such a noise that she sat still, guilty as a child for having shattered the sleepy golden afternoon. Then she rested her arms on the typewriter and laid her head on them, deeply depressed, but surprised, even a little horrified, to find the next sentences of the new book beginning to march into her mind.

She sat up. It had to be her vocation, this rubbish; but was it rubbish? Of course it was rubbish. Get on with it and get some relief.

She wrote steadily until the dusk started, when she stopped, and saw that the ashtray was heaped up with cigarette butts again, and worse, she felt wonderful. She stood up and started to glide round the room again in one of her dances, Saleema's dances.

116

CHAPTER 10

Sweating after the climb up the hill to the deserted palace-fortress Croon looked at his watch. He was very hungry and it was now long past midday. He was about to say that it was later than he had thought and that — but again Balban had read his thoughts.

'All is arranged, Croon Sahib,' he said. 'I have got it all arranged here for you. First a cold drink.' They were approaching the enormously tall and wide gateway of the palace and Balban shouted commandingly in Hindi. Replies from within the palace were shouted back and then three elderly men wearing white turbans, long white shirts and tight rumpled cotton trousers shaped to their spindly legs appeared in the gateway. They smiled, bowed as they pressed their hands together in the gesture of *pranam*, and murmured, '*Namaste*, Sahib.'

'Do the same, Croon Sahib,' said Balban in an undertone and Croon pressed his hands together and made a fair imitation of the welcoming sounds made by the old men.

'Very good,' said Balban. 'You learn very quickly, Croon Sahib.' Croon rather liked this new form of address from Balban, instead of the Mister he had been using until now. Really like being in India, being a sahib. Balban was giving orders to the old men and then a boy appeared with a white metal tray on which was a bottle of gin, a jug of fresh lime juice, a bowl of ice, and three glasses. Another small boy appeared carrying a jug of water.

'You will notice, Croon Sahib,' Balban said, 'that the glasses are clean and shining. One of the curses of our country is slovenliness and dirt, but I will never, never put up with it. Gin?'

Croon was thirsty and all this was a splendid surprise for him. During the hour or so of the walk from the city Balban had irritated, amused, bewildered, amazed, and angered him, and now he impressed him, for as they passed through the

117

gateway into the cool shade of the towering red sandstone walls of the palace he saw what Balban had organized. This was his first experience of Indian India and he was delighted by the spread of thick cotton carpets striped in yellow, red, blue and white, which covered the ground in front of him. In the centre of the carpets a huge white cloth was spread. Cushions were heaped here and there. Far off in the corner of the enormous courtyard charcoal fires were being fanned by the old men while a small boy was packing stones about the fires.

'Sit, please,' said Balban. He waved his hand towards the cushions. 'Drink gin while I prepare the food.' Balban smiled thinly then. 'The old men are Brahmins,' he went on. 'And they will help with the food, but I will cook it. I am as clean as any Brahmin so you will not mind? No?'

Croon studied him and smiled back. 'Why should I mind, Balban?' he said.

'I have told you I descend — '

'From a long line of shit-carriers,' said Croon with affected but friendly weariness. 'Let's cut all that out, Balban. I'd like to watch you get the food ready, though, if it's Indian food.'

'Come on then. Bring your drink.' Croon followed Balban to the charcoal fires and squatted down beside him. An old man came hurrying to Balban with a big tray on which was a stone pestle and mortar and heaps of various spices, and placed it on the ground before him. Another old man brought a bowl of peeled onions and garlic and placed them on the tray beside the spices.

Croon sipped his gin and watched Balban slice and chop the onions into glistening, pungent heaps with a small sharp knife, then the garlic. A small boy swept the onions and garlic onto a plate and hurried to the fires with them.

Now Balban began to grind and pound the spices, *zeera*, *dhanya, methi, chilli*, and adding rich yellow turmeric. Croon followed him to the fire and watched the spices tipped into simmering ghee at the bottom of a big white metal pot on the glowing charcoal. He sniffed up the fragrant appetizing smell as the spices seethed in the ghee. A handful of chopped, fresh green *zeera* plant followed the spices into the pot.

Next Balban cut up the chickens and while he worked he told Croon the story of the palace, and Croon stared at the walls made of enormous slabs of red sandstone. Whenever he

118

saw ancient buildings he also saw the hordes of slaves who had toiled on them, but he no longer felt the synthetic political indignation of years ago. He had struggled hard and long not to believe that the workers' paradise of the Soviet Union had achieved an even greater form of slavery, and had had to finally admit it. Even so, he still believed that there *could be* a just form of communism. The mistake had been letting people like the Russians try it first, but as time passed he knew his hope was sentimental. Slavery, therefore, was merely a part of man's history, an ancient punishment for being captured in battle, so he let himself enjoy the results of their long and arduous labours, while Balban talked.

In the middle of the eighteenth century India was in turmoil as the long-established Moghul power, with its headquarters in Delhi, slowly crumbled and Hindu India rose against the Muslim rule. Adventurers of all kinds led rebel armies.

'Here,' Balban said, waving his knife as he crouched over the fires, 'the Maharajah of that time, the ancestor of the present Maharajah, lived only for cherry brandy, and so did his Rajput warriors. He had three wives. The youngest of the wives was a beautiful dancing girl called Zarina, a Muslim.' His voice changed. It softened, became husky, and Croon looked at him. 'She was so beautiful it is no wonder she was able to do what she liked with any man, even hard cruel soldiers — they were putty to her, all of them.' He smiled at Croon as he stirred the big metal pot of simmering curry mixture. Then he reached into his shirt and took out a leather satchel on a silver chain. From this he drew a small miniature painting done on a sheet of smooth yellow ivory and handed it to Croon, his eyes serious now, and reverent. 'Zarina,' he said. 'Look at her, Croon Sahib. Painted by the best court painter of that time, Raja Jivan Ram.'

'My, yes,' said Croon, staring hard at the exquisitely painted head and shoulders of the beautiful Muslim girl. 'She's really beautiful.' When he took the miniature back Balban looked tenderly at it, then kissed the face of the painting before putting it back into its satchel. He looked at Croon again. 'That is my love, Croon Sahib, that woman. When I discovered that she was like me, a believer in every religion, *and* before she was converted to Islam was from one of the lowest castes, I knew I had found my woman. I have seen her

119

in a vision many times. She will wait for me. You understand?'

It was too serious a business, this, Croon could see, for
anything but nods of understanding, grave facial expression,
an air of complete and sympathetic understanding. He had
already gone through several phases of doubt about Balban's
sanity during the morning. There was nothing to be done
with this character except to accept, believe, agree, understand. For instance, when he had wondered how Balban, after
his life as a *chela* of a *saddhu,* then as a *saddhu* himself, had
become so literate, so obviously educated, Balban had informed him that he had been at college for four years. A scholarship, yes, but also with help from Colonel Bingham. But of
course, Balban being Balban, the college had to be a Jesuit
college. With Balban one had to be ready for any surprise.

'She began to appear to me,' Balban was saying, 'after I
went to her tomb for the first time with flowers and prayed
there.'

'You told me earlier, Balban, that you had fallen in love and
had gone sort of mad with it. Was — '

'That is the woman,' said Balban, nodding. He pressed his
hand tenderly against his chest where the portrait was con-
cealed. 'My life was first destroyed, along with my mind, yet I
had expected it. I knew it was coming when I first began to
study the story of her life. I heard of this painting of her and
that it was last heard of in Bombay. It was in the collection of
a rich Parsee gentleman. I went to Bombay. I asked him to sell
it to me. He refused. I implored him. I begged him. I went
down on my knees to him. He would not let me have it, even
when I explained to him that Zarina had become the woman
of my life, my guiding star and my whole life. This terrible
man did not care. He sent for the police and told them I was
insane and I was told by the magistrate never to go near the
gentleman again. It took me another two years to get that
painting.' He clapped his slender golden hand against his
chest and smiled at Croon. It was an ecstatic and triumphant
smile. 'And now she is safe, mine, with me always. I talk to
her as soon as I wake in the morning, and every Friday evening, whether I am in a Muslim state of religion or not, I pray
at the mosque and then take flowers to her tomb.'

'How did you get the painting?' This character *had* to be
mad, yet Croon knew he was fascinated by him.

Balban had raised enough money to employ an expert thief, who stole the painting without fuss. It had been copied by an amused American artist living in Bombay and the copy had been placed in the Parsee's collection by the thief.

'You do not approve, Croon Sahib?'

'When you're that much in love anything goes, I suppose,' said Croon.

Balban laughed. 'Zarina did not mind,' he said. 'When she was in love she killed men, fought battles, poisoned women — nothing stopped Zarina. But if I had been there then she would not have had to do any of those things.'

The little boy had to call three times to Balban to get attention and to tell him that the rice and chicken were cooked.

'Let us eat, Croon Sahib,' Balban said. He held out the big pot of curried chicken for Croon to sniff at. Croon sniffed and felt the saliva awaken in his mouth as the fragrance and pungency of the cooked spices arose from the pot. They went and sat down at the spread tablecloth and the old men served them.

'Well, Sahib?' Balban asked him as Croon took the first mouthful of the chicken and rice and chewed it thoughtfully.

'It's absolutely wonderful, Balban. Wonderful. I've never tasted anything like it.' Balban, delighted, passed this on in Hindi to the old men and the boys and they laughed and clapped.

One night when he was drunk, and a group of dancing girls were performing a *nautch* for him and his important guests, leaders of warrior bands come to help in the war with the Moghuls, the Maharajah had lost patience with the Brahmins.

'The leader of the Brahmins, the highest of the priests, was at the gate there' — Balban pointed to the gate by which they had entered the ruins — ' and he demanded to be taken into the court where the Maharajah was enjoying himself with his guests and allies. He was refused. He sent a servant three times to the Maharajah to demand an audience. The Brahmins then were advisers to the rulers, even the Muslim rulers, for they are clever advisers.' When Croon, chewing, cocked an amused eyebrow at this, Balban said, 'Oh, yes, I am at war with the Brahmins, Croon Sahib, but it has to be said that they are very clever men, otherwise how could they have kept us lowly millions down at the bottom for so many centuries? Eh?' He shook his head slowly. 'They are as wise as serpents.'

He laughed then and slapped his chest. 'Though *I* have conned them again and again. Well, the third time he was refused an audience this Brahmin leader lost his temper, for it was a terrible insult and the news of it would be carried across the country. So the Brahmin took a dagger from a sentry and rushed into the court. The best musicians from Gwalior were playing but they stopped when the Brahmin began to shout his curses at the Maharajah. And here is what the Brahmin shouted at the Maharajah.'

Excited now, Balban got to his feet with a knife in his hand. He began to declaim. ' "O stupid and lowborn king, your house is finished now. Three times I asked entrance to advise you, for war is coming here soon, and you refuse and insult me. So I curse you and yours and I shall spill my sacred blood in your palace, so that it shall not be habitable again. I curse this place and seal the curse with my blood therefore." Then, Croon Sahib, he began to stab himself and to run among the guests and through the palace, showering his blood everywhere, and the Maharajah and the guests and the dancers all scattered in fear from him. The Brahmin then went into the hall of audience where the Maharajah held his daily audience and killed himself where the Maharajah usually sat when giving a judgement. And that was the end, for the Maharajah could not live in that palace again. Not until Zarina ruled was the palace ever lived in again. For Zarina, like me, feared no Brahmin, feared nobody in the world. That is the beginning of the story. Will you use that in your film?'

Croon nodded. He wanted more curried chicken. 'I'm eating from pure greed, Balban, not hunger,' he said. 'I can't say more than that for your cooking.' Again Balban passed this on to the old men and the little boys, and this time they cheered and then sang a song which Balban explained was a blessing song for the happy belly of the pleased guest.

'Tell me about Zarina,' said Croon and started to eat again. 'And the love affairs. And what happened to the Maharajah?'

Because he was cursed, because he was, so to speak, outlawed and made casteless, the Maharajah had to atone, had to make many forms of penance, but even so he could not live in that palace again which had been destroyed as a living place by the sacred blood his arrogance and impiety had caused to be shed there.

There had also always been unhappiness in the Maharajah's

harem, for a reason, Balban explained, which had come down in what was now an Induspuri saying. 'When a man is impotent in Induspur and cannot plant children it is said of him by the people, "That is the cherry brandy again." ' But even starved of love the three wives hated each other, Balban continued, and the two senior wives hated Zarina, the junior wife, because she was beautiful, and like the Maharajah they were cursed and were living in huts. The palace was deserted.

'Then the Maharajah was found to have leprosy and he knew he was finished,' said Balban. He pushed a plate of mangoes and grapes towards Croon. He sliced one of the mangoes and handed the slice to Croon. 'He knew what must be done but he had not the will. It was only Zarina of the three wives who had the courage to make him do what had to be done. Yes, Zarina knew how to behave. She was a queen who knew she would have to rule in that time of weakness and corruption.'

'What had to be done?' asked Croon, wiping mango juice from his chin. He knew he had surrendered fully to greed, for it was the best food he had ever eaten. 'What did she make him do?'

It was the custom then, for a leper like the Maharajah, to go to Varanasi and drown himself in the holy waters of the Ganges river. Because Zarina said it must be done the two other wives, because they hated her, opposed it. So she had them poisoned and the Maharajah went to Varanasi and drowned himself before properly appointed witnesses. 'You understand, Croon Sahib,' said Balban gravely, 'that all this happened while war was approaching Induspur. The army was rotten, useless, and Zarina had to show firmness.'

'Well, of course. What else?' Croon replied with carefully masked irony. 'The women had to go, so they went.' But this was not lost on Balban, this playfulness, and Croon remembered it was not the frst time Balban had shown how sharp he was.

'It is because you do not know India, Croon Sahib,' said Balban, 'that you make fun. At that time a man's life was not worth a single anna. You must remember that Nadir Shah, when he invaded India from Persia with his army, was annoyed one day by an incident in Delhi. He gave his orders and from early morning until afternoon his army slew the people of the city. They killed over one hundred thousand of them. That was the kind of time Zarina lived in, Croon Sahib. She knew what had to be done. With the ruler drowned and his debt paid to his family, and the two senior wives dead, Zarina began to rule. First she sent for the Brahmins' — here Croon took a swift look at Balban's face, for he knew by Balban's changed tone of voice that the Brahmins were going to get what was coming to them. It was Balban's turn to laugh, for he had not missed the expression in Croon's eyes.

'Yes, ' he said, controlling his laughter. 'You are sharp, Croon Sahib. Zarina asked the Brahmins if they would take the curse off the palace, now that their curse had made the Maharajah a leper and had caused his death, or would they prefer to die? She was able to do this because the first of the adventurers, a French colonel of engineers who had come up from Tipu Sultan's country in the south, had joined her with five thousand trained soldiers, all of them Rajputs. She gave the Brahmins one day to make up their minds. While they were discussing it among themselves she sent a message to them. One of them, she said, could be her prime minister, so that one would live. Could they guess which one she had decided upon? They guessed and she said they were right. They took the curse off the palace and she installed one of them, Parichit, as prime minister. And she let them become rich too. It was not until she was ready, when she was really powerful, that she destroyed them, for she had never forgiven them for degrading her and driving her and the others from the palace.' Balban rose from his cushions. 'Come,' he said, 'I will show you the parade ground where her troops were trained.'

As they walked Croon took out his notebook and Parker 51. He began to write at speed and Balban glanced at the notebook, then eclaimed, 'Is that shorthand you're writing, Mister Croon?' So it was Mister Croon when they were alone, and Croon Sahib when they were with non-English-speaking Indians. Interesting.

'Yes,' he said, 'it's shorthand,' and then, 'Don't tell me you won a shorthand exam somewhere, Balban.' Smiling, of course.

Balban shook his head and laughed. 'No, but will you teach me? I must learn it.'

'Certainly I'll teach you. Now, get on with the story, in fact tell it in shorthand, if you know what I mean. The bare bones of it. Characters, names, incidents. Okay?'

Balban began to compress the story now while, with the employed scriptwriter's slight sense of despair, Croon was wondering about how he was going to write this story for a film audience, an American film audience. Even if the Maharani, Zarina, had really pale skin, say golden ivory, and this guy from the U.S. Marine Corps finished up with her, how worryingly near miscegenation was that going to be? For he could already hear his Cassandra, Ted Koltz, saying, 'She's gonna have to be American, I guess. I don't know. Work it out. Or maybe the Marine captain gets killed at the end, in just the right way, okay. But stay away from problems. We don't need problems.'

CHAPTER 11

Though he found himself thinking less often about the subject these days the Maharajah could still consider suicide quite calmly from time to time. The tendency to such thoughts began, he was sure, with the death of his wife and son, and not long after that the murder of Gandhi had compounded his deep depression. Maybe it was the exploding of the atomic bomb which had first darkened what had always seemed to him a happy and worthwhile pastime, living. He had little time for such things as 'Dharma, Karma and other parlour games' as he liked to put it, and knew he was 'here' only because his father had made love with his mother (and not with some other woman on that particular occasion). Bingham agreed with him there, making him laugh by adding, 'And of course the father could easily have had a bright thought and said to the lady, "Let's be original. Let's not conceive somebody called Chandra Gupta tonight at all. Let's wait a week and conceive somebody else instead." '

He often smiled to himself over that but at the same time sensing his own feeling of awe, or wonder, at the mysteries which lay buried in the joke. There was no doubt that he was obsessed with the mystery of being, and irritated by the elusiveness of the clues which sometimes seemed so close, for a fraction of a second. Also, it was not mere depression, or spiritual aridity, which nudged him to suicide at times. On occasion he thought of committing it in sheer impatience, to start getting a look into 'the other side', the so-called next world. Boredom? Perhaps. Yet he never had enough time to pursue all his interests to the full. He resented sleep and would often struggle against it in efforts to continue reading the book he was deep in.

He could read in four languages but often envied Bingham his extraordinary linguistic gift, and sometimes recalled how, when they were walking through Kangra a few years ago, Bingham had learned enough of some extraordinary Tibetan

126

dialect from some transitory Tibetans, in three days, for them to be able to make all kinds of friends a few weeks later in the wilds of Lahaul and Ladakh. He admired, sometimes resented, and was often awed by the speed of Bingham's mind. The man actually seemed to have second sight.

Trying to pretend to listen to his *Diwan* "Shampers" just now, about the cost of the new hospital, he wondered if this new film thing would do more harm than good to Induspur. Money, yes, it would certainly bring plenty of it, but — why did he fear the new world so much these days, the modern world of brutal, practical ideas?

Shampers droned on, stopped, and then said, '*Maharaj* Sahib, you are very worried. I can feel it. What are you worrying about so badly?'

He looked into the *Diwan*'s wise, deep-sunken black eyes, wondering if he was right to have written that note to Mrs Brett-Turner, and to feel the curious excitement every time he thought about her husband having left her — 'at last'.

'Everything, *Diwan* Sahib,' he said with mock solemnity, as if discussing official business in council. 'About being alive, about having been dying since birth, but mainly about us being wise in accepting this idea of a film company being let loose in our little quiet haven here in the hills. I love the idea, I must admit. Yet — shall we have a drink?'

They decided to have brandy, and while he fussed with bottles and glasses the *Diwan*, a religious man, was firm again about the need for the Maharajah to take his soul away to some quiet corner of India for a while, and listen to what it had to say to him.

'You've guessed, have you?' said the Maharajah. He and the *Diwan* practised a special art together at times. They could discuss a delicate, personal subject without mentioning what it was, and if they felt a tendency to flounder, to stumble near the naming of the subject, withdrawal would be signalled by the Maharajah who would say, languidly, something like, 'Yes, *Diwan* Sahib, we must go into this in depth, some other time.' Finish! For now.

'Have you discussed it with the Colonel Sahib?' The *Diwan* lowered his eyes, then handed the glass of brandy to the Maharajah. They were discussing Mrs Brett-Turner.

Sighing, the Maharajah shook his head and then lay back in his armchair.

'*He* would understand,' the *Diwan* said and went on, after hesitating — most artistically really, thought the Maharajah — 'far better than I could, for — ', and then quoted from an Induspuri poet, 'for how should I, the arrow in my heart, advise on archery?' This brought laughter from the Maharajah, and, pleased, even a little smug, the *Diwan* allowed himself a fleeting sad smile. Only the Maharajah knew that the *Diwan* had been in love for years with an Englishwoman, now long dead, and who had died uninformed of this love.

Then, overdoing an air of worried contrition, and apparently sorrowful, the Maharajah said, 'The *Diwan* should really not cause the ruler to laugh about the *Diwan*'s personal sorrows,' and, nodding to himself he went on to say, 'You may be right. But — but I value his friendship so much, I — no — I simply cannot decide about it. I feel it is best not to say anything.' He frowned, seemed irritated.

'Perhaps he has guessed, *Maharaj* Sahib. How do you know?'

'I know.' The Maharajah seemed firm about that. 'I have been too careful. It all matters too much to me — even the subject of this silly discussion has never suspected.' A guilty expression entered his eyes as he stared carefully past the *Diwan*. 'I must not make myself ridiculous. Never. Though there is nothing more ridiculous than a man in — in — this state. A film is to be made. So, the masochistic victim of his own nonsensical imaginings writes a note to the subject of this discussion, remembering that that aforesaid subject' — he sighed wearily — 'you notice we're getting a bit of legal jargon into this farrago now — and how right one may be, considering the legal situation — anyway, writes a note to the aforesaid — no, *alleged* subject perhaps? — to remind said subject that said subject long ago wrote the facts of the story which is to be filmed, so that, in other words, that is to say, one therefore hopes that said subject will visit the palace — ' He lost his temper, shouted, 'Please do not allow me to go on in this idiotic manner, *Diwan* Sahib,' then sank back into the armchair, and a brooding silence.

The *Diwan* uttered a long, sympathetic sigh and came across with the brandy bottle. As he poured another brandy for the Maharajah he said in a low voice, 'I do remember all the researches the said subject made here, and the writing of the book. They were happy times, *Maharaj* Sahib.'

'And *innocent* times too, remember that!' the Maharajah said, with what seemed to the *Diwan* to be unnecessary heat, and glared at him defensively. 'Nothing was suspected of — er — the ruler's inner feelings. Nothing. But then, this is all for the film which is to be made. The story has been already written after a lot of research. Oh, blast it, *Diwan* Sahib, I'm sick of this game-playing. It's as simple as this. She's done the research and written the book. I want to see her around here again, that's all. And as far as the bloody world is concerned it's for the film. See? So why should I worry myself? Just see that I don't lose my head, that's all, while — while the lady is around here. I'm in a very curious state, I can tell you, and I need watching.'

'She is a beautiful lady,' the *Diwan* intoned as he went back and poured himself another brandy. 'A beautiful lady. Yet —'

'Yes?' the Maharajah was snarling. 'Yet? Yet? Go on.' Then he laughed and shrugged his shoulders. 'Yet she's married. And to a stupid fellow who loses his temper because his wife beats him at tennis.'

As his thoughts ceased their mad gallop the Maharajah realized he was behaving oddly, his fists clenched and trembling before his face. He had forgotten the *Diwan*'s presence. Now he smiled and tried to cover up his lapse, shaking his fists even more and exclaiming, 'My God, it's going to be wonderful to have this film made here, *Diwan* Sahib.' But the *Diwan* was not to be fooled by this stupid, face-saving action. He said, gravely, 'Are you well, *Maharaj* Sahib? You *must* go away and have a holiday somewhere —'

'My life is one long holiday!' the Maharajah said, bitterly, almost declaiming the words, and, as so often, the *Diwan* was not quite sure how much of this was the usual play-acting enjoyed by his master as cover for other thoughts. His master went on to say, in the same almost ranting tone, 'One long holiday, in my head. Yes, I know I've just been acting like a clown, *Diwan* Sahib. A slight hole appearing in the curtain, that's all. Don't let it worry you. Let's have another brandy.' He snapped his fingers, lay back and closed his eyes. Still worried, the *Diwan* stared at him, then said, gently, nervously, 'Are you sure you want more brandy, *Maharaj* Sahib?'

Without opening his eyes the Maharajah barked his answer like a military command.

'I am absolutely certain I want more brandy, *Diwan* Sahib! Pour it at once!'

In the loud silence which followed, the sound of the brandy flowing into the glass was soothing. It stopped. 'And now one for you, *Diwan* Sahib,' the Maharajah said in his normal, pleasantly modulated voice, then, comedy again – the *Diwan* felt fairly certain of that — he continued, 'You must not make me angry, *Diwan* Sahib, when I am remembering my personal inner pain, the shameful memory of a certain tennis match, and certain childish actions you have just witnessed better kept for when one is alone.' He had at least admitted several things, one of which was that he behaved *slightly* madly when alone sometimes, like clenching his fists until they shook. But it was all right, he felt as he reached for the glass of brandy, for the *Diwan* knew what he had gone through because of this love for Mrs. Brett-Turner.

'It's all so terribly ridiculous,' the Maharajah cried out now, not forgetting to make it melodramatically and self-defensively comical half-way through the sentence; 'this suffering, and for what? For the desire to commit the most tragi-comical of all the human actions.' He stopped. Let the *Diwan* work out which action that might be — suicide? The sexual act? Which one? They were the only two tragi-comical acts, surely? Though take ordinary dying . . . !

He turned his head slightly and looked at the *Diwan*'s expressionless face, and was pleased when the *Diwan*, though still playing their game, guessed right, and then sighed in the right way too. Excellent. Most praiseworthy.

'Yes, *Maharaj* Sahib, but without that tragi-comic action who would have invented brandy, and who would there be to drink it?' Then the sigh.

'You must do a poem on that, you know, *Diwan* Sahib,' he said, not quite able to keep the sardonic note out of his voice. One of the things he admired about his *Diwan* was the fact of those many years of alcoholism, and the victory over it. The *Diwan*, amazingly, could now drink *and* stop, somehing which had, a few years back, seemed impossible. Opium had done it, but just how, the *Diwan* had never revealed. It was a subject the Maharajah knew, with affection, must not be referred to again.

He wanted to talk about that tennis match. He had often wanted to talk with the *Diwan* about it, and with Bingham as well, but he wanted to hang on to his half-secret — half-secret with the *Diwan* — no one else knew — he felt sure of that — about his madness for Megan. Madness for Megan, he thought, liking the sound of it in his thoughts. He enjoyed the relief of this game-playing with the *Diwan,* hovering around the subject, Megan, Mrs. Brett-Turner, Wally's wife, 'that woman,' as Megan had been called by so many memsahibs before they got on the boat in nineteen forty-seven and sailed back to the land of rain and fog. He had been careful never to discuss that tennis match with Bingham, and now — only now . . . .

He sat up suddenly, then stood up, showing his amazement on his face, the *Diwan's* presence forgotten again. *Bingham had never mentioned it to him either,* yet they had both witnessed the tennis match along with the rest of the party present on that otherwise delightful evening. It could only mean one thing, surely — well — surely? Bingham was being his usual litmus-sensitive self. He knew, somehow, about his, Chan's passion for Megan. No. Didn't *know. Guessed.* Yes. Not guessed, no. *Knew* — with that bloody weird second sight he had?

The *Diwan* was sounding urgent again, and the Maharajah looked at him, staring at him, and then, seeing the look of alarm on the old man's face again, he smiled and raised his glass of brandy. Something head-on had to be said.

'It's all right, *Diwan* Sahib,' he said, starting to chuckle. 'I'm not going bonkers.' Not going, no. Bloody well *gone,* that's why. 'Just under strain, that's all, and a few other such-like banal sayings. You know the kind of thing. Under pressure, what?' He put on the accent so overdone by a certain type of Brit, generally the very insecure who perhaps had never got over having gone to an unknown public school. 'Jolly well got to face up to things, bite on the bullet and whatnot, eh?' This always made the *Diwan* smile, sometimes even laugh, though he never really approved because, although he liked the British as much as the Maharajah liked them he could not wholeheartedly approve of what he thought of as ridicule. The Maharajah knew this, and knew too that the *Diwan* had very little sense of humour. The old bugger didn't even know that the Brits were very good at self-ridicule — in the right company, of course. However . . . .

He sat down again. 'You remember that dreadful tennis match?' he said, not looking at the *Diwan*. He *must* talk about her, or at least the tennis match, for that was the occasion that had been some kind of excuse for Megan gradually, and cleverly too, to withdraw from him. Even though nothing had ever begun between them she had withdrawn from him. That tiny scene between them — pretended to have that breakdown — no, oh no, be fair, be fair. He did believe in that breakdown. Had to. Must. 'Ah, *Maharaj* Sahib,' the *Diwan* replied. 'Should we?'

With eyes like those of a wild animal, it seemed to the *Diwan*, he looked across at his faithful Chief Minister, just as the old man was about to say something.

'I've told you a hundred times to stop reading the rubbish-books you love so much, Ruby M. Ayres and the rest, haven't I, and to read some psychology, some real books *about* something. I am alone here' — he was playacting again now — 'desolate, desperate in my loneliness, with no one to talk with except my *Diwan* with a head full of English maidservant love-story rubbish.' He now played the *Diwan* and imitated his last words, overplayed it cruelly and knowingly, simpering and throwing out his arms, 'Ah, *Maharaj* Sahib. Should we?' He shouted the next words, 'I will not join you in this kind of shameful sentimentality, this Ruby M. Ayres slush, is that clear?'

To the *Diwan*'s horror, who half rose from his chair and then froze there for a moment, his master went on, raising the glass of brandy to his lips, 'I wouldn't mind a pinch of cyanide in this one. Jazz things up round here a little I'd say. No?' He drank the brandy down in one gulp and held the glass out again. His eyes were glazed now. Tears? Impossible. The *Diwan*, trying to overcome alarm, and out-of-date reverence, a longing to throw himself at the Maharajah's feet and clasp his ankles, rest his head in supplication on his master's feet, came quickly round the low table which separated them and took the glass from the Maharajah.

When the Maharajah had taken over the rulership — such as it was in this century — he, the *Diwan*, had performed that ancient act of reverence, and when he had risen to his feet the young Maharajah had placed his hand on his shoulder. 'That custom must go now, *Diwan* Sahib,' he had said. The *Diwan* often thought over that scene and felt the same pang. 'Because,' the Maharajah had continued, 'although my father liked it, it was of his time and his feeling. But I — I cannot let you do that for me. The time for that has gone.'

It was a deprivation still, and they both knew it, of that the *Diwan* was certain.

Covertly, pouring the brandy, the *Diwan* watched the Maharajah struggle with tears, and swallow hard, then light a cigarette with great care.

'I've changed my mind about that tennis match, *Diwan* Sahib,' he said now, taking the glass of brandy. 'There's no point in talking about it.' He raised his voice. 'I've sent a note, by the way, as you know, to Missus Brett-Turner, inviting her up for drinks. To talk about the film. She will work on the script with this fellow — '

'Mister Croon,' said the *Diwan*, laughing softly. The Maharajah smiled too, nodding, saying, 'Yes. A bloody curious name. We'll call him Crooner, shall we? Or what about Macaroon?'

'He is not quite the *pukka sahib*, Mister Macaroon,' said the *Diwan*, picking up the cue — end of talk about the 'said subject'. 'His hotel manager tells me that Macaroon Sahib is very tight with his money, about prices of everything.'

'That's the new sahib type.' the Maharajah said, smiling with what could have been real sadness. 'You don't know the new Britain, or the new Europe.' He raised his voice again. He was doing it quite often these days, these past few years actually, it seemed to the *Diwan*. 'They've ruined their Europe at last – hundreds of years of war and looting and fighting to destroy each other, and now the Russians can laugh and wait. The Russian empire is bigger than ever now. The sahibs are broke, *Diwan* Sahib.' He looked into the slightly scared eyes of the *Diwan*.

There was no doubt about it. The *Maharaj* Sahib had become bitter. He hid it, he thought, but it was there. 'Broke. And so are we. Look at this Korean war. The Russians and their new subjects, their Korean sepoys, feeling out the Americans and the Europeans. Drawing them on. Have you seen this Chinese map?'

The Maharajah rushed across the room and opened a drawer in a desk, snatched out a Chinese Communist propaganda leaflet which had been distributed in millions all over the Far East. He waved it, still shouting, then crossed the room and handed it to the shaken old man, who put his glasses on and examined it. It showed a map of the new China, and stated its claim on parts of Northern India and Burma, places which had once paid tribute to Imperial China.

'*Hindi-Chini Bhai Bhai!*' Satirical, in a tone of fury, the Maharajah shouted the new Chinese love-slogan for India, ' "Indian and Chinese — Brothers." Poor bloody old China. It had to come to them, Communism. There was nowhere else for them to go. And what about us, eh? When do *we* go? Eh?' The *Diwan* watched him calm himself, as always, swiftly. The Maharajah went back to his armchair and sat down, picked up his brandy, hunched himself over it with his elbows on his knees. He was laughing again, and to encourage him the *Diwan* laughed with him.

'You don't know what's being printed, *Diwan* Sahib — Ruby M. Ayres is dead.' Bingham, with his insatiable mania about history, as they still called it — Bingham himself called it 'a pack of cards for the academics to deal each other' — he got hold of some weird stuff all right. The new schoolbooks for East German children, and West German children, Russian stuff in English and several other languages about the Dickensian way of poverty-stricken life in modern Britain, all kinds of brilliantly contrived and sinister rubbish for the 'masses'. 'It'll give us a laugh anyway,' Bingham would say, and start reading some of it to him. Then they would begin their fantasy versions of it, both knowing it was five minutes to what might be the final midnight. The five minutes might take years to pass, but the ticking of the new clock could be heard all over the earth now, by all men and all women and all children. By all beasts and birds and by every tree and every fish in the deep. You could actually hear the world shivering, if you listened carefully enough, but what was the use of telling all that to this dear old man who was an archaeological relic of worlds beyond the time of the Moghuls? He glanced affectionately, guiltily, at the *Diwan*, and said, 'Go on, have another brandy. You know, I wish the Swiss and the Swedes had all the power over Europe. *They'd* find some way of helping the Russians discover what they've never known — freedom to *find out* — we've got to get it to them, you know, *Diwan* Sahib, somehow. They've kept out of the wars, those Swiss and Swedes.' He gave a long snarling sigh, waved his hand disgustedly. 'I'm a bloody relic myself anyway, so what am I talking about? A commissar would dearly love to put a bullet through the back of my neck, just to show The Light of the Toiling Masses, that All-Knowing Brilliant Searchlight of Marxist-Leninist thinking, Joey Djugashvili, that he, the commissar, will shoot anyone on earth if it'll keep him alive or out of the prison camps. Poor bastards. They have to get permission even to defect, even to confess to their sins before being shot themselves.' He noticed that the *Diwan*'s head was now bowed. He stood up and spoke softly, but trying for a little comedy again.

'That's all you're getting from me today, *Diwan* Sahib. I'm sorry. But I have other things to do, you know.'

Smiling tiredly the old man stood up and drained his brandy glass.

'Come.' The Maharajah opened his arms and embraced the *Diwan* when the old man reached him. Holding him tightly he said, 'I would be lost long ago without you. Remember that. Forgive me, but I have to talk about these things sometimes.'

Looking tense and alert now, and tired, the Maharajah glanced at his watch, then said, 'In two hours they'll all be here.' He looked away, his eyes vague, saying, 'What stupid creatures we are, but how necessary it all is, the merry-go-round.' He smiled and looked again at the *Diwan*. 'I'll do what you say, *Diwan* Sahib, once the film talks are over. I'll go away for a week, on my own, and if there's a soul there it can do the talking. I've nothing to say to it anyway, perhaps something polite, like "Hello".' He gripped the fat below his ribs. 'Dance some of this off, in Delhi — a few late nights at the Metropole ought to do the trick. I want you to enjoy this evening, but for God's sake don't use any of my jokes about Ruby M. Ayres with Mrs. Brett-Turner — said subject — because I stole mine from her, after all.'

He waved his hand, turned and went off for his second shower of the day. The last shower would be at midnight, the three daily showers one of his few strict habits.

As the *Diwan* watched him go he found himself wondering again if this could be the last Maharajah of Induspur, and he the last *Diwan*, after the centuries since the overcoming of the earlier Moghul rulers. All this brave and ruthless facing of 'the facts' by the Maharajah, like saying to a Minister of the Government in Delhi a couple of years ago, that if only for the

135

sake of the tourist industry the princely states should be kept alive; none of that talk really hid the Maharajah's own pride in his tribe and race, as a descendant of the Sun itself. The new Indian government had been understanding and generous to the states — they could have swept them all away with a stroke of Sardar Patel's iron pen.

The *Diwan,* a devout Hindu, and having lived so many varied lives over the millions of years, was still not tired of that wondrous treadmill which tirelessly churned the black, deep river of the ages, but he had loved and still loved the reward he had had this time around, to serve this fragment of one of the oldest Indo-European fantasies. Having discovered that this sentiment was a subject for mirth among the young, he never discussed it with anybody now, except occasionally with Colonel Bingham.

'We are all antiques, each one of us, *Diwan* Sahib,' the colonel had said to him once, with his arm tight around the *Diwan*'s shoulders as they strolled in the gardens of the palace. 'But only a few of us know that, or care. Your ancestors came down into India from the Caucasus and Persia a few thousand years ago, with your horses, and mine rode West. And here we are together, chatting in a descendant of the noblest and most sacred of all languages, our mother language.' He had murmured a few liquid lines in that language, Sanskrit, swearing by gods, musicians, men and snakes and devils — *Deva-gandharva-manusa uraga-raksasah* — that if he were to have a life again, it would be here in India. Then they had gone in for a drink with the Maharajah.

136

CHAPTER 12

After the first fitting the old tailor worked all day on the verandah with his sewing machine. In her study Megan typed steadily through chapter eighteen. She worked at great speed and in tightly controlled but rising excitement. She had promised herself a drink when she had finished with the battle scene. Now, as she typed the last words — dusk was falling on the battlefield and the wounded were crying and screaming for water — she stopped and lit a cigarette. She picked up the note from the Maharajah again. 'Dearest Megan,' it began. Dearest. He would hardly use that word unless he meant it, and certainly not with a European woman, ruler or no ruler. And what did she really feel about that? No answer. Why could she not give herself an answer to that question? Any of her female characters could have answered the question in two seconds, she knew. This man is in love with me. He is rich and fairly good-looking and he is in love with me and I could be the Maharani here. But do I want that?

It's that money piling up in the bank, she thought. It's freed me and I'm not used to the feeling. She was her own woman and needed to rely on nobody. Not only that but it had made her unable to answer the question: what did she feel about the Maharajah, now she knew what he felt about her? She sat there shaking her head, smoking. It was all very interesting, though, and there was still a thrill each time she remembered that she lived alone, no Wally, had plenty of money and seemed to be in no rush about a single thing. In fact it was the best situation she could remember ever being in. So relax and enjoy yourself.

She poured a shot of gin, squeezed a lime into it and added sugar, then water, just as the telephone rang. It was so startling after nearly three months of silence that she gasped and spilled some of the drink. The Induspur telephone system, such as it was, would usually function ten days out of a month, but this time it had broken down completely nearly

137

three months ago. Nobody missed it any more; everybody said it had become a blessing to be without it.

It was Tim Bingham. He was in the library at the club. She was coming to the palace this evening? Marvellous. All quite informal apparently. Drinks and to meet the film chap, Croon. Nice fellow. She'd like him. And oh, he was really phoning her to remind her to bring the manuscript she'd written about the Begum Zarina and company. Give it to Croon to read. Yes, he'd told Croon about it and he was keen to see it. There'd be plenty of money involved if such mundane things interested her. And how was life?

Life? Why it's lovely. Just lovely. Couldn't understand why she hadn't ended all this Wally nonsense years ago. Had no idea life alone could be so pleasant, so peaceful. This marriage thing, about how a man and a woman had to live together, otherwise — the more she thought about that bromide the more amazed she was. What she meant was that now, for the very first time in her life, she was content, peaceful, harming nobody, and able to do what she liked when she liked. She wanted to tell all women in the world about that little important discovery. Oh, he could laugh but she was serious. Wally? No idea thank you, and not the least interested. Probably drinking his head off. Definitely finished? Was he joking? Wally'd never get back in here even with a gun in his hand. No, seriously, she'd never been happier. Never. And those wasted bloody years living with him. Yes, wasted. Croon, what was he like? Nice? A big handsome fellow. Oh. How nice. And intelligent. She'd like him, but working on the film would be the thing. Yes. Okay, see you, Tim, love. Bye.

Idly she read the last few pages she had typed, sipping her gin as she went through the pages. Staggering actually to think that this stuff which just seemed to slip down her fingers through the typewriter was making her rich. And she felt so guilty about it. Why? Why not come out and announce to everybody that she was in business as Saleema Begum, and had a growing band of fans in England and America? Too educated, too snobby, too intellectually pretentious, should have been writing like Virginia Woolf? Probably. But *why*?

It would be quite impossible to give an interview in which she could be coldly snotty about the whole thing, like, 'Oh, I simply decided to sit down and instead of giving a lot of money to some bloody psychiatrist, to do my own psychiatry with the typewriter, and make money instead of spending it. I'm getting psychological release by writing this crap and the sea of readers out there are gobbling up my little problems for me, and feeding their own with my fantasies. What's wrong with that? The critics? You mean the eggheads, the real ones in the literary columns? Well, fuck them for a start. What did they know about what it could mean to some frustrated housewife in the pissing rain of some grey English suburb to be the connection with Saleema Begum via *Dagger of Devotion*, say? Why shouldn't she yearn and pine for some lean, bronzed, strong-fingered lover to give voice to her off the pages of Saleema Begum? Let the eggheads face the fact, the millions of women are out there, I'm here writing the stuff, and they are reading it. Deplore it, attack it, sneer at it, anything you like, but it's forever. Women love love and I write about it. For a man love is just a fast fuck and get on with the dinner, I have to be down at the pub to meet Jack in twenty minutes. You can read the letters I get from my fans if you like. It's all there.'

No, it wouldn't do. Stay mysterious, Saleema, and bank the money, and start facing up privately to what you want and need most now, a quick, painless divorce. Your Honour, the facts are these — and they're known to just about every grown-up person. I was young. I was walking along in the darkness carrying my little sack of rubbish on my back, a sack containing my life, brief though it had been, when I collided with another human being carrying a similar sack, but a person of the other sex. We got married for some reason or other, I mean we suddenly found that each had shot the rubbish out of the sacks into the other person's lap and we went through the other's rubbish, with sudden cries of, 'What's this? You never told me about *this*? I didn't know *that*. Who *are* you for Christ's sake?' And then, when we'd finished picking through the rubbish, that is the other person's life, we found there was nothing left to say, or do. So for Christ's sake, Your Honour, give me my ticket of freedom and I'll disappear. I'm older now and know what to look for next time, that is to say perhaps . . . .

You stand here before this court, Mrs. Brett-Turner, a woman of great beauty and obvious breeding, and make these monstrous statements about the most sacred institution of all, and then demand what you call your ticket of freedom, so that you can disappear. You have destroyed the life of a young hero from a class above you, an officer of a famous regiment who raised you up, who trusted you when he went off like millions of others to fight and die for his king and country. In his absence it was not enough for you to squander wantonly what was not yours to squander, that splendid jewel the defence of which has kept strong men sane throughout the centuries — your virtue — but you gave it not even to one of our own, but to an American, and that, let me remind you, during our finest hour. No doubt, like so many other women of your kind, for silk stockings, for chocolate, for dollars. You have had the effrontery to tell us here in this court that marriage is what you have called 'the collision of two strangers in the darkness'. You speak of sifting the rubbish of each other's lives, and having sifted it and found it wanting, you must then have your ticket of freedom, as you call it. You have made an atrocious statement and a monstrous demand before this court. Is it any wonder that the terrible bacillus of selfishness, of lust, and of hedonistic madness is beginning to affect the lower classes who have looked upwards always for instruction and guidance? Yes, a frightening madness is being let loose among the common people. We see it all about us, increasing daily, disguised by slogans such as 'fair shares for all' and 'I want my rights'. What rights, I ask? There are no rights. None. There are privileges, but there are no rights. There are no tickets to freedom, dear lady. None. We are here in this world to suffer. It is useless to deny that ancient and well-known fact. The masses of the common people are watching this case, yes, each one waiting to covet his neighbour's wife, and by permission of this court. They shall not have that permission. You shall not have what you call your ticket to freedom. Never. You shall go back to your spouse and suffer with him, so that in the fire of that noble suffering you shall be cleansed and hardened, and made fit to be worthy of the freedom and dignity which has been handed down to you by the sufferings of untold millions down the ages. Case dismissed.

She'd better not have another one. Well — a small one. Time? Two o'clock. Wasn't due at the palace until six thirty. Going to wear Punjabi dress at last, for the first time in public anyway. Lovely dark blue, and that grey gauzy scarf, the *dupatta,* flecked with gold. Letting the real and secret Saleema loose for an evening. And why not? Easy now . . . .

She poured the gin slowly. Got to take it easy. The fever, of course, the fever that always came after a good long stint at the typewriter. She picked up the last typed page again and read it slowly. Funny, she hadn't noticed it until now, how she was using pieces of her own life in this glittering crap she had just knocked off this afternoon. She sat down, read the whole chapter through, lit a cigarette and thought about her discovery. How curious. Her heroine was using her will on her husband just as she had had to use it on Wally to get him out of her life. Bullying quietly, in fact. She had to laugh as she read the lines she had given the heroine. There was no doubt about it, it was a version of her last evening with Wally, in a scene supposed to be taking place three hundred years ago in Delhi. Talk about not needing the bloody psychiatrist, but here was the proof and she had just written it. As she smoked she went over the last crazy evening with Wally, when she had poured the whiskey into him until he had drunk half a bottle.

Her memory took her back to the first time they had looked at each other and spoken after that unforgettable tennis match, for which Wally had trained so uselessly hard.

'I don't think I've much I want to say to you,' he had said, quite nastily, and brazenly looking her in the eye too. It was probably that which had decided her to make an end of this fiasco they had endured together. Do you take this stranger with his rubbish as your rubbish-sorter, to love and honour his rubbish?

'I was rather hoping for that,' she had replied to Wally's opener, but she had known he was in the mood for one of those evenings of bickering and quarrel. Why not give it to him, a real one this time, which she would stage-manage right through to the end?

It was some time later, though, after she had several times rehearsed her role, that the final evening came up.

'Memsahib!' She could hear the old tailor calling her from the verandah. He had finished the Punjabi clothes and he held them out for her, smiling, when she reached the verandah.

'Let me see you wearing them, Memsahib,' he said. 'I can still make alterations for you.'

She drew on the blue *salwar* trousers and drew the waist-cord, then knotted it, after which she lifted her arms and let the *kamis*, the long shirt of the same blue, slide down onto her body. She fastened the small silver buttons up the breast to the neck, then had a quick look into the long mirror on the inside door of her bedroom wardrobe. Then she threw on the grey, gold-flecked *dupatta*, so that it hung down in a loop just above her breasts, while the long ends of the scarf went over each shoulder and hung down her back. She stood there a long time and admired herself, especially the curious eroticism of the way the narrowed bottoms of the trousers were drawn in over her small bare feet. She slipped the feet into the small gold sandals, then said to the reflection in the mirror, 'Saleema, idiot, why have you wasted all this narcissus-time all these years? Here you are at last.'

There was no doubt about it, that with the thick black shining hair reaching to her shoulders, those smoky black-fringed blue eyes, and this divine get-up, she could have anything she wanted from any male idiot within reach, anywhere, anytime. This new woman in the mirror looked back at her with real, honest pleasure, as if delighted to have been discovered after waiting so long to be properly dressed. She could not leave the mirror, but went on enjoying herself, gazing into her eyes, so absolutely suited at last with the blue of the Punjabi dress, and shining with the happiness of this discovery. She had fallen in love with herself all over again, and after a long time too.

'Well, Saleema,' she said to the self in the mirror, 'you've written a lot of good readable crap today and now you're having your reward, recognition. We're going to launch you on the Maharajah, and you're going into the film business, or that's the general idea anyway. We're very pleased with you, both of us, and we'll get you a few more Punjabi suits. I love you, Saleema. You look like I feel, wonderful.' She blew a kiss to the person in the mirror and then went to see the tailor on the verandah. He did all the right things, exclaiming, praising — 'Ah, *bahut, bahut khubsurat hai, Memsahib*' — and then wrote down her order for six more suits, the colours for which she would choose tomorrow.

A flower in the hair, she wondered, when the tailor had gone. No, too much, at least tonight anyway, but maybe a matching necklace.

She found one of big silver beads with blue lapis lazuli

studs set in the beads, Indian and old, with its long cord of twisted silver wire which hung down her back, a red and blue tassel at its tip.

Back at the mirror she nodded approval to the new woman looking out at her. She felt so good she could drink a distillery, dance all night, enchant the most jaded of woman-hunters. She wondered if men could have such a good time for so long in front of a mirror and then, as usual during these mirror-sessions with herself, she sent out her condolences to all ugly women everywhere. It was not really fair that any woman should not be beautiful, and she often tried to imagine what it must be like to be unattractive. The world must look so different for ugly people, less welcoming, a place in which you had to struggle for notice, desire, love.

The only thing to do now, in this 'native' dress, was to go to the club and let them see it, give them something to talk about and add to the rest of the gossip about her latest doings. She felt reckless, shivery with a strange delight, silly, happy, and it all had to be given an airing, now.

For the second time she climbed into her new Hillman. She placed the manuscript on the passenger seat and then found herself driving somewhat wildly up to the club. She slowed down. Let's not quite lose control, deary, just because we're looking and feeling divine, because we're not willing to finish up through the windscreen even if we are dressed to kill, correct? Correct. It had gone to her head all right: she was singing now, she noticed, and very loudly. It was not just the discovery of this ancient Moghul self, she thought, but it was also the thing that had caused her to recognize it and get it properly dressed for an outing, just sheer bloody freedom of self at last. The human being was stupid, permanently stupid, staying on a treadmill for far too long. She would never get on another human treadmill, she promised herself.

Another curious thing was happening to her, she noticed. She felt so happy that she wanted Wally to be happy too. Have to watch that. Far too generous, as always, with this emotional goodwill to all. It had caused her much trouble in the past and it must be ruthlessly controlled, eradicated, in future.

She was driving along the edge of the ravine and through the open car-window she could hear the noise of the river below. She stopped the car and got out. She sat down on a rock and lit a cigarette. The sun was at about four o'clock, and far off the enormous high wall of the Himalayas shimmered and glowed like snowy pearl. She could see Buggers' Ridge away on her right, and Wally's house among the plane trees.

Yes, 'I don't think I've much I want to say to you,' he had said to her that first time they had allowed themselves to meet in the house after the tennis match. Yet he thought they were dropping back into their old routine, obviously, after another few days. Nagging after a few Scotches in the evening, and then rising temper as usual when she did not respond with temper but maddening him by her calm and reasonable manner, never raising her voice, never giving him satisfaction by showing hurt or resentment.

She had not known what it was she seemed to be waiting for, until one evening, after reading some English newspapers at the club, he started on a subject which had been coming more and more into his limited repertoire, the decline of Britain and the British. How Buggins, as the new working class was called by Wally and some of his friends, was taking over. She had not much time for Buggins herself but she was always willing to stand up for Buggins when he was attacked by people like Wally.

'They've forgotten how to crack the whip,' Wally had said while he poured another whiskey. 'But they're going to have to face up to it soon and take control again, or the country's finished. It doesn't worry you, of course, does it?'

She was curled up on a couch at the other side of the room studying him. He was going to look even more like a Buggins when the growing baldness had completed itself. It was his self-satisfaction in nothing at all which irritated her most of all, his quite mistaken feeling about being a member of the ruling class which had always been so hard to take.

'Me?' she said. 'Why should it worry me? The last time I was worried about this subject was when you *had* your chance to handle Buggins properly one morning in London, and failed, abysmally I think would be the right word for it. Do you remember that occasion?'

'What occasion?' He stared hard at her, worried.

'Think,' she said. 'It was the perfect occasion for a member of the ruling officer-class to put down one of the uppish serfs. I would have thought it was quite unforgettable.'

She was waiting for him one morning in a small ante-room

outside a hotel barbers' shop where he was being shaved. The door was open so that she could hear the barber lathering Wally's face while she riffled slowly through an old magazine. Wally, always ham-handed with waiters and servants, had started to snarl and complain, in a way which was already out of date.

'What the devil d'you think you're doing? D'you want to cut my ear off or something?' Silence except for the rasp of the razor, then, his voice louder, Wally said, 'Blast it, you've cut me, haven't you? You've cut me — I know you have. Have you been drinking or something?' She could hear the barber step back from his customer, and then his slow, deep, threatening voice as he warned Wally.

'Now look 'ere you. I took a lot o' that bloody impudence before the war, mate, because we 'ad to then, see? Or fuckin' out in the street to starve, right?' The voice rose, the rage still barely controlled. 'But since them days I've been around — five years in the Commandos — now then — if you fuckin' raise your voice to me once more, mate, I'll knock you round this fuckin' barber shop and then kick you into the bloody street. Now which is it? Shave or out on your arse?' Complete silence for a few seconds, and then she could hear the barber go on with the shaving. She had tiptoed out into the street and when Wally came out she said, 'Ah, there you are. Went off to get some cigarettes.' Now that was the kind of unnecessary emotional generosity she had so foolishly indulged in, yet the fact was it had been impossible to let Wally know that she had overheard that harrowing little scene. A very shiver-making little scene.

'It was in a barber's shop,' she reminded the frowning Wally. 'You were doing your patrician landlord act and the barber put you in your place, don't you remember?'

She watched the arrow sink in. After a few seconds Wally said, 'So you listened in on that, did you, pretended you — '

'Went to get cigarettes, that's right. Sensitive, you know. So don't go on about cracking the whip and bringing Buggins to heel. It's embarrassing.' He was crushed, his eyes dark with anger.

'You two-faced Welsh bitch,' he said. He stood up and started shouting, probably unable to sit still under the memory of that awful scene which for so long now he had thought to be mercifully known only to him and a barber. 'I've had enough. We've got to end this business. You're a lying cheat. I've never understood how your mind works. You're my enemy, my enemy, I know that. I've always known it.' Again he looked for a moment as if he might attack her, and as always in these moments she lay back and smoked, chanced it, and it worked again.

'Pour me a drink, please,' she said. That was another test. He poured the drink and brought it over to her.

'Now,' she said, 'sit down, and let's talk about breaking this thing up. I think you're right. It's time to finish it. You're serious, of course.'

He was not sure yet; she could see by the way he got up and went to the drinks table so that he could turn his back to her for a while.

He talked about money. She let him tell her that if she had any grand ideas about milking him for a lot of money if they did break up, then she could forget it. She wanted about another six or seven whiskies in him before she went through with her plan, so she argued as if interested in what kind of arrangement they should make when they parted. He kept coming back to her two-facedness. The revelation about the barber-shop scene had broken his careless ruling-class annoyance with the Buggins problem. After another few whiskies his voice was slurring and he shouted louder at her.

'Don't shout,' she said quietly. 'The servants. They'll think there's a man in the house.' Right over his head, she might have known.

Ready. 'People will talk,' she said, 'when we separate. You hate people talking, don't you? What about that angle? Are you ready for that?' As if on cue he responded, shouting.

'I no longer care what people think or say about us. They've had plenty to say and plenty to say it about, for years. Let them say what they like — '

'Announce it, would be better. Tell them we're separating,' she said. 'Why not?' She made it sound so reasonable that he agreed.

'Why not? Tell anybody you like, that we're finished, separated. Why not?'

'Have another drink,' she said. 'I'll be back in a minute.'

It was then she had gone into her study and composed Wally's Declaration Of Independence.

She offered it to him, saying, 'Can you read that?'

'Read it to me,' he said. He was rather far gone by now.

'It's for the gossips, really,' she told him, and then she read it aloud to him. The novelty of it appealed to him and he asked her to read it again.

'It's a smack in the face for the gossips, don't you think?' she said. She had brought a sort of terrible togetherness into the business now, and he agreed. He talked now as if he had written it himself; he liked its cosily insulting tone so much.

'Well, sign it and we'll stick it up on the club notice-board, what d'you think? A nice clean end to things and a smack in the face for the Tones and the rest of them. Perfect.'

She brought him a pen and he signed it, and then asked her to read it again. She watched his face while she read it to him, the way his mouth tightened and his nostrils dilated as he listened.

'Declaration Of Independence,' he mused. 'Yes. It's good. It'll shake them all.' He was proud of it, this Declaration.

'Come on,' she said, helping him to his feet. 'Get it up on the notice-board before the club closes.'

She drove him to the club and waited for him at the door, calm and determined, and saw to it that he saw her watching him pin it up.

When they got back to the house she poured him another large whiskey and said, 'Sit down. I've a few last words on this subject.'

She was still worried that he might sneak off to the club and take the Notice down. Another three or four whiskies should bring down his curtain, she felt.

'How long have you known this woman?' she asked quietly. 'The woman you mention in your Declaration Of Independence. Do you want to marry her? If you do, I have no objections whatever, I want you to know that.'

She watched him closely from where she was lying back on the couch. He was so unbelievably *thick*. He said, 'That's my business.'

'As you wish,' she said. There might be another woman — in Delhi for all she knew or cared — though she doubted it. But he obviously liked the idea.

'Now, one more thing,' she went on. 'This money business you've been droning on about this evening. I don't need your bloody money, do you hear me? I've got more money than you've ever handled in your life. So you can relax about that area. Are your listening?'

'I'm listening,' he said. He stared at her thoughtfully, puzzled. 'Talk about two-faced. Where'd you get this money?'

She waved her hand dismissively. 'None of your business now.' She got up and took his glass. She poured another large whiskey into it and handed it to him.

'The housekeeping money, the rent for this house, and so on, I've been paying for the last eighteen months. I've torn your cheques up, and a pleasure it's been, believe me. Now, there's a good house up on Buggers' Ridge. You can move into it as soon as you like, which is really soon as far as I'm concerned. I'll speak to the *Diwan* about it.'

'All worked out, eh?' His mind was struggling to come forward again. He was still not drunk enough not to be shaken by what she had told him. Take the key out of the car just in case he got any ideas about that Notice on the club noticeboard.

'When do you intend moving?' she asked.

He shouted again. 'When I'm ready, that's when.'

She smoked until he fell asleep in the armchair. Then she put the lights out, went out to the car, took the key and then went to bed.

She lay smoking in the dark, listening to him snore. Should have done it years ago, but then wasn't that the way with everybody everywhere, people voluntarily in traps waiting for nothing, people hammering on doors which were open, people committing murders they need not commit, because they had stayed too long.

The sun was nearing the horizon now. Megan got up from where she had been sitting on the rock and got into the Hillman again. As she drove she marvelled once more at the fact that these days were the first in her life when she had been truly her own self, free, able to choose. Nobody should be allowed to marry until they were thirty, so they could have lived a little, learned something of what it was supposed to be about. She wondered if she could dare to decide that she would never again marry anybody, just stay at peace and free as she was now. Dare to decide it and then stick to it, that is. Could she? Well, no. But why? Could it really be because a woman did need to have someone to live with and look after, and complain about and stay with? My God, if that were true .... She was driving too fast again, almost frantically. Scared, she slowed down and then stopped the car, in order to think about this small, important mystery.

She *was* feeling happy, but she could not take that step and decide to stay like this for always, free and happy. She still wanted that insurance, that emotional bonus. Extra-ordinary. She drove on, still puzzling about it.

She saw the Tones' car outside the club. Lovely.

She went into the bar and greeted the barman, Janki Nath, the lean, solemn Kashmiri. He was as impassive as always, and bowed his head to her, smiled and greeted her. She could be wearing a suit of armour and Janki Nath would show no surprise, but there was plenty of surprise from the end of the room where the Tones were playing cards with two tourists.

'Where's the fancy dress ball?' Tone called out to her.

'Why, are you looking for one to go to?' she called back, and flashed a careless smile at the four of them. She turned her head away and took a pink gin from Janki Nath. If she knew Iris Tone that card game wouldn't last much longer. Yes. She watched out of the side of her eye as the game finished and Iris got up in a hurry. Poor bloody awful Iris. Still, she was the only person in this valley who knew what a bad time Iris had had before she married the bastard she was tied to now. She was cracked enough by life before life with Tone cracked her even more. But remember, sad or not, the woman is a dangerous bitch.

'Well, well, well!' Iris began, predictably as she sat up on the stool beside her. 'So you've finally gone native, have you?'

Megan glanced down at herself and then smiled at Iris.

'Yes, it is nice, isn't it?' she said. 'I thought you'd approve. Drink?' She ordered a Scotch and soda for Iris, who said, 'You know about the film they're talking of making here? You know about it? This man with the delicious name, Roger Croon? Have you met him?'

'I've heard about the film. I wrote a book about it, as a matter of fact.'

'Oh!' Iris's voice went up and down as she said that, a kind of warning in it. 'Have you now?' It was too much to keep even for a second. She turned and called to Tone. 'Did you know Megan's written a book about your subject?'

149

Megan watched Tone's face as he turned to look at her. It tightened up, became pinched. He frowned, and then came striding up to join them.

'You've what?' he said incredulously.

Christ! Stay very cool. *His* subject?

Megan looked at Iris. 'What are you talking about, Iris,' she said, using an assumed sharpness in her tone. '*His* subject? What do you mean?'

'She means exactly what she said.' Tone was very firm, and just a little annoyed. 'I've worked on that subject for years, researched it for years first. What do you mean, you've written a book about it? What do you know about the subject? What's this all about? Is it supposed to be a joke?'

Megan looked at her watch and sighed, then looked at Tone. She had another half hour before she needed to start for the palace.

'Oh, it's just something I knocked off on the typewriter a few years ago,' Megan said, smiling, throwing it all away. 'Though I must say I didn't know it was *your* subject, that you owned it. Does anybody else know you own it? I don't *think* there's a copyright on a piece of ancient history. Though perhaps you've discovered a way, is that it?' Iris was watching them both intensely, obviously sensing the enormous potential in this new, unexpected situation.

Megan looked roguishly at Iris and smiled. 'It looks as if you're going to have to be referee here, Iris, wouldn't you say?' She looked at Tone, smiling, playful. 'Just you stop looking so angry,' she said to him. 'I'm not in the mood for tantrums. What'll you drink?'

She had thrown him on other occasions. Now his face was turning pink with the anger he was trying not to show.

'Scotch and soda, thanks,' he said coldly. 'When did you write this book? I need to know.'

'Now you know that's none of your business,' she said, roguish again, flashing her eyes at him and then at Iris, to whom she went on, 'Isn't he a dreadful bully, Iris?' She eyed Tone again. 'You really must stop trying to interrogate me like this, or I'll have to go.' She handed him his Scotch and soda. 'There,' she said, smiling. 'Cheers.'

Tone took the drink and glowered down at it, then he lifted his shaggy eyebrows and fixed his keen, sunken eyes on Megan's.

'We may as well have it out here and now,' he said, his voice determined now. 'Now this book you say you've — '

'Really. I've had enough of this,' Megan said to Iris and got off her stool. 'I'll have to go.' Janki Nath was leaning back against the shelf below the rows of bottles, watching the scene. 'Iris,' Megan went on, playing cool anger now. 'You'll really have to do something about this kind of thing. This is my club. I want to be able to come in here and not be treated like a suspect by this policeman of yours here.' She looked at Tone. 'Don't ever mention this bloody subject to me ever again or I'll put a complaint in to the club secretary about it.' She nodded to each of them and turned to leave. Tone followed her, pleading now.

'Come back and be reasonable,' he called after her. She ignored him and walked on towards the verandah steps to her car. He came on after her, pleading done with now.

'If you think you're going to sell this subject to the film company,' he shouted, 'you've got another think coming.' When she ignored him and started getting into her car he went on, still shouting, 'It's *my* subject, do you hear that? If there's any attempt to steal my research and my work you'll hear from my solicitor, and sharpish too.' He was still shouting as Megan drove away. Iris joined him

'You've made a fool of yourself again. I suppose you know that, do you?' She followed him into the club.

She sat on a stool beside him and watched him glower at the rows of bottles.

'It's the story of my life all over again,' he said to nobody in particular. 'In the army or out of it it's the same, 'Get Tone. What can we do about this fellow, Tone? Send Tone. We don't need Tone. I stole the idea from Tone actually. Take Tone's. He doesn't need it. Yes, it used to be Tone's. Here, have it. He won't miss it." He turned his head and looked malevolently at his wife's beautiful, ageing face. 'Do you wonder I'm paranoid? Do you? You don't have to worry about *me*, you know. I've told you before, haven't I? I know the whole process, everything that's going on all the time, in me, in you, in everybody around us. And I'm telling you now that that Megan bitch is out to do me. That was a declaration of war, make no mistake about that. I'm the only expert on this subject they're going to film. Years of my life went into it. Now what exactly did she say to you?' He raised a finger

151

warningly at her. 'I want the *exact* wording. Change nothing. Now — you arrived up here at the bar and you said — ?' He lifted his head as though to prick his ears, watching his wife's face. 'You said — ?'

'Are you going to get drunk tonight?' she asked. 'I need to know, because of the dinner. The phone's working again and I can phone the house and tell the cook to scrub it. Let's have the plan for the evening.'

Tone turned his head away and hung it, staring down at his face in the polished brass of the counter, the picture of long-suffering patience and near-despair.

'Tell me what she said to you about the book,' he said in a low, almost inaudible voice. 'And then I'll tell you if I'm going to stay on and get drunk.'

'I'll go and phone the cook,' Iris said, and left.

Without looking up Tone addressed Janki Nath. 'Scotch, and make it a big one,' he said.

CHAPTER 13

The *Diwan*'s office was at the south end of the palace and overlooked the huge natural swimming pool fed by an underground spring. The pool was surrounded on all sides by enormous grey rocks and boulders. The waters were dark, deep, and so cold that for years the Maharajah's father had stored his champagne in it.

The *Diwan* stared down broodily at the pool as he listened to the Maharajah's aunt, Princess Subhadra, railing at him again about his failure to 'find a bride' for the Maharajah.

'He's got to have a son if this line is to continue properly, you know that ' — and — 'it's no use me talking to him. He resents me so much, which is your doing I'm certain. He loved me when he was a boy and a youth.He's been influenced against me, but it's your duty to get him married. What are you doing about it, *Diwan* Sahib? Answer me.'

'Nothing,' said the *Diwan*, not even turning his head, but still staring down at the black pool below the wide, open window of his office.

'Nothing? What do you mean, nothing?'

Again this formidable lady had been in the town and causing trouble with the *tonga-wallahs*, who had sent a deputation to see him the evening before. She was so westernized that she had even contracted the English mental illness about animals. She would, when walking in the town, or in Delhi, any Indian city, look out for thin or mistreated *tonga*-horses and would then attack the *tonga-wallah* with her rolled umbrella. He had once seen it for himself, the cowering *tonga-wallah*, his arms shielding his head, and the Princess flailing him with her umbrella and shouting, 'You monster, if this country is ever to rise again then it must start with kindness to animals. You will at once take this poor creature and see to it that—'

'Are you listening to what I'm saying, *Diwan* Sahib?' the Princess called to him angrily.

'To every word,' he replied with quiet bitterness. 'Just as the Maharajah has listened to my every word on the subject again and again, until some months ago he warned me that if I ever brought the matter up again he would at once take a vow of celibacy and withdraw to Rishikesh. He would renounce the *gaddi*' — the *Diwan* turned and faced the Princess and continued — 'and hoped that *you* would take over and rule.' He paused. 'In so far as anyone may rule in these curious times, that is, Princess.' He smiled nastily at her. 'He is well aware of your determination to see him married again,' he went on.

'A vow of celibacy?' Subhadra was shocked. 'Is it possible? Do you mean, does that mean — has he no interest in women any more? Is that what you're saying?'

It was not at all what he was saying, yet it was a fact that two or three times the Maharajah had entered upon affairs with attractive women during the past two years, and had given up halfway.

'No woman seems to be able to replace the Maharani,' said the *Diwan*. 'He has still not recovered from her death.'

'I don't understand it.' The Princess flashed her large black eyes at him. She was famous for her skills in ju-jitsu, doing more press-ups than the decadent men she used to challenge at late-night parties, fencing and tent-pegging, pig-sticking or any other daunting skill connected with horses. That she was beautiful as well, even now at fifty, was even more of a problem for nervous men in her company.

She had once said to the *Diwan*, when she had sensed his disapproval after a feat of strength she had performed during a party, 'Yes, *Diwan* Sahib, I know you hate to see it, but I — I like to have a few insecure men around me. I like them to feel threatened in their so-called masculinity,' and had smiled her dazzling and white smile. She was so neat, so beautifully made, so springy, tense, fit, threatening, and a bloody nuisance, the *Diwan* was reflecting.

'What are you smiling about?'

The *Diwan* emerged quickly from his brief reverie, then went and sat near her, pretending gravity. He guided her away from his smile.

'I know you're right, Princess,' he told her, and shook his head slowly, the minister of state confiding his deepest worries. 'You mustn't think that the subject of his re-marriage is

154

ever far from my mind. But I can tell you this. He seems to have no real interest in women any more.' Except for the lovely, formidable lady down the road, Mrs. Brett-Turner; but that was hardly a subject he would discuss with this strange force of nature, the Princess, who was watching him with such persistent steadiness. He longed to confide in her, to ask her what she thought of the idea of the Maharajah marrying a beautiful thirty-year-old memsahib who had just got rid of a burdensome husband. Better still, he would have liked to say to the Princess, 'And what about you, Princess? When are *you* going to have a man?'

The *Diwan*'s instructions from the Maharajah were, when he was told his aunt had arrived from Delhi, 'I'm ill. Too ill to be seen. Understood? No, not ill, just asleep and exhausted, unable to be seen. Anything you like. But get rid of her. I don't want her here when we're having the meeting about the film. Those are your orders. Get rid of her. Understood?'

The Princess was saying that the Maharani had been dead for six years now and something must be done immediately to awaken her nephew's interest in his duty to the state, and the *Diwan* was thinking about the Maharajah in hiding somewhere in the palace. It had to be admitted that the Maharajah seemed more and more to be in retreat from reality nowadays, behaving in fact like a man preparing to withdraw from the world. He apparently could not even believe in his own fantasy about Mrs. Brett-Turner, and was afraid of it, behaving like an adolescent. As he thought about these things the *Diwan* watched the small, neat, striking-looking woman before him as she quietly lectured him. She was wearing a black silk sari with a design of small gold and blue flowers. Her thick black silky hair was drawn back tightly and held at her neck with a gold ribbon. Yes, he had to admit that she had a magnificent face, olive-skinned, red-lipped, large-eyed, and this face glowed with willpower and energy.

They said down in Delhi that this strange woman had had one affair in her life only, but could it be really true that that affair had been with the charming, enigmatic, playful, though just slightly forbidding Colonel Bingham? He had never been able to accept it, yet whenever Bingham's name came up in the Princess's company she would smile, somehow fondly, but then usually say, 'Oh, yes, Colonel Know-all Sahib. And how is he?' Once she had remarked, when Bingham was

155

being discussed, 'Yes, he's deep, Colonel Know-all Sahib, but he does have his vulnerable areas, you know,' and there had been just a hint of affection, ownership perhaps? in the way she said that. But it could also have meant that she knew it had been Bingham who had kept her from what she had once wanted most — a term in gaol.

It had never been discussed between the *Diwan* and the Princess, but in the early forties, when the Quit India movement had begun in earnest and the struggle to throw off British rule gathered strength, the Princess, wearing the Congress *khaddar* cloth like the rest of the disaffected, had demonstrated on the streets of various cities. Hundreds would be arrested all round her but she would be left alone, unarrested, the police and troops gone. Again and again it had happened. Hysterical in the heat, and from anger and disappointment, the Princess had eventually complained in writing to the Viceroy, about this discrimination. But Bingham, down on leave from the frontier at that time and en route to Persia, had, as an old and loyal friend of the Induspur ruling family, seen a few of his friends in high places and the Princess was allowed to continue her eccentric charade wherever she wished and was never arrested.

The *Diwan* did know that somehow Bingham had then arranged an 'accidental' meeting with the Princess and had informed her, possibly quite cynically, knowing Bingham as he did, that despite her letter to the Viceroy it was unlikely that discrimination was involved. The law of averages was a curious thing, and so on, but there were millions of other Indians left unarrested too, she must bear that in mind. The police and troops did their best but they could not promise to arrest everybody in sight during a riot or a demonstration. He had also told her that the British would certainly be leaving India after the war and that involving her family, quite unnecessarily, and for purely selfish reasons, — a longing for notoriety perhaps, or a misplaced sense of guilt about being rich and of a princely family — would not make the slightest difference to what was anyway inevitable. The *Diwan* was amused to remember all that.

He had read Bingham's long personal letter to the old Maharajah, the Princess's brother, and often recalled some of the phrases of that letter in which Bingham had tried to soothe the rage the old Maharajah had felt about his youngest sister's antics.

'This feeling of guilt,' Bingham had written, 'is merely one more small symptom, one among many, that you will find is growing throughout the Western world, in which families like your own, with ties in the west, are involved. Those who have had a good time wish to appear to be indignant about their ancestors, and to be seen to have been indignant. To have been known to have been in gaol for their convictions and whatnot. You will find them in universities in Europe as well, all guilt-laden, not realizing that if they do shed their wealth and position others will seize them and enjoy them instead. People of position and authority only lose their situations when their time is up, that is to say when they have lost their nerve, and their will. As we have both agreed in many discussions over many drinks, *Maharaj* Sahib, people like you and me, and your erring but well-meaning sister, are museum pieces and are being put on the shelf, let us hope for admiration, some day. At present, though, we must accept the roles of exploiters and tyrants. We have the same rights as any Commissar, as even Stalin himself, to let history judge the accidents and designs which cause me even to write this letter, in which I appeal to you to be patient with Subhadra. Let her work out her harmless guilt-feelings, for I have seen to it that she will never be arrested. I am fond enough of her to have her arrested myself, privately, and let her do a stretch in some comfortable private gaol, but I have not the powers to indulge her, I regret.'

Despite all that, the *Diwan* thought as he smiled and nodded while apparently absorbed in what the Princess was saying, he was still unable to accept this story about an affair between the Princess and Bingham. But only because he could not imagine Bingham in love, and that was not firm enough ground anyway, for who can imagine anybody in love?

'I beg your pardon, Princess,' he said now, somewhat startled by what he thought he had heard her say.

'You are not listening to me, *Diwan* Sahib,' the Princess told him for the second time, loudly and commandingly now. 'I said that you are so obviously convinced that, having dealt with me this morning over the matter of this marriage problem, it is therefore time I took myself off and left you alone. You are listening now, I think? Yes? I am trying to inform you, now you are listening, that I am not visiting Induspur in order to talk about my nephew's need to marry again. That is one subject.' She lifted a finger and wagged it, smiling, her eyes glittering suddenly. 'You have wonderful self-control, *Diwan* Sahib, I know, and you govern well here, but don't forget that *I* too have some power here, that I am the one who advises on finance, on investments, on markets' — her tone sharpened as she remembered past successes and victories of opinion, with and about money, and about administration as well — 'and that,' she continued, 'entitles me to be consulted about any new ventures — or should we call them adventures, I wonder — you may have in mind.' She was silent then, her eyes holding those of the *Diwan*, which were like those of an old eagle, his face expressionless as he studied her eyes.

He was delighted, barely able to stop himself from chuckling with satisfaction. He was in no hurry. He was long past the day when he would have leaned forward anxiously to enquire what it was she was talking about, or rather 'getting at'. He picked up a heavy gold cigarette box, flipped open the lid and held it out to her.

She looked at the long brown cigarettes in the box and then smiled at him as she took one in her thin, strong fingers, small diamonds glowing momentarily as a gold bangle slid down her wrist and clinked against another one.

'Well,' she said, a little lamely, conceding, 'you do keep your promises, *Diwan* Sahib,' and smiled again, just a fraction more sincerely this time, perhaps? He wondered.

'Yes,' he agreed softly as he clicked a lighter and held it to her cigarette tip. 'They arrived from Bulgaria a week ago. You were right, Princess. Your little man in Sofia still makes them. I thought you would be pleased. A thousand arrived, all packed in tins. They will be put in your car before you leave.'

She puffed on the cigarette and watched him through the Latakia fragrance of the smoke. She had always been fascinated by his shining, bony, smooth face, completely unlined, at nearly eighty too, as if each day some gifted servant damped it and then ironed it. Were he not completely bald he would look like a horrible, skeletal young man, just a little too dark-skinned for her taste. He was capable of desire too, oddly enough, because she had seen it flicker at her once or twice from his old sunken black eyes.

She knew well what a sweety-pie, loving, doting servant he was to the Maharajah, and what a cold-minded machine he could be with others when he wished. She had seen and heard him hammer a paper weight on his desk and shout to a servant, 'Remove this oaf. Get him out. He is wasting my valuable time,' and some unable schemer from a far village would be dragged from the office. He worked like a machine too. But she was well able for him, she thought.

'You must know, *Diwan* Sahib,' she said, 'what it is I am waiting for you to talk to me about.'

Delighted again, he said nothing. He knew very well what it was she was waiting to be talked to about, seeing that he had briefed that journalist in Delhi himself.

'It would be much simpler, Princess,' he said, 'if you were to tell me what it is you want me to tell you.' He smiled benignly at her, pushing an ashtray to her as her cigarette-hand began to seek for one. 'There is, so far at least, nothing heavily financial under discussion at present that need involve you.'

'So far at least.' She took that up sweetly, he thought, that dazzling smile on her face again. As the Maharajah had agreed with him the other night, they would have some problems with the Princess Subhadra, or *Subhadar Bahadur* as the Maharajah had nicknamed her with a kind of affectionate family malice, the play on her name likening her to a Moghul holder of a certain power, a *Subha*, and a *Subhadar* even now a rank in the Indian army. He did not want her involved in the film business. He dreaded it, wanted it kept secret, which was stupid and thoughtless. So the *Diwan* wanting the matter dealt with early on in the negotiations, had planted the story in a Delhi newspaper, and had already seen the headline — 'Induspur Epic To Be Filmed' — and the story the usual mass of misinformation. But it would do to bring on the Princess quickly, and here she was, getting the newspaper clipping out of her handbag and passing it to him. She did this with a quite needless air of patient triumph. He did not even take it from her, but twisted his body and head and glanced at it, then smiled at her.

'M'mm,' he murmured, as if dismissing it; 'epic indeed.'

Then he lay back in his armchair and folded his arms, staring at the ceiling, and pretended to consult her. 'It's been talked about a little,' he mused. 'What do you think of the idea, Princess? Do you think it could bring a lot of money into the state, perhaps? I must say I haven't taken it very seriously myself. And anyway it's the Maharajah's pet subject, not mine. Why don't you discuss it with him next time you come? H'mm?'

Her silence then began to discomfit him. She was waiting for him to look at her, and when he did he was surprised by the grim expression on her face, and when he heard what she had to say next he sat up, alarmed.

'If my nephew imagines for one moment that I will allow the disgraceful goings-on here in the eighteenth century to be filmed, those horrible skeletons to be dragged out of that cupboard and put on the screen for the world to look at, he is very much mistaken.'

She stood up, small, and commanding now, and as she threw the *palla* of her sari into place on her shoulder and stirred the air between them the *Diwan* caught a pleasing whiff of the scent she always used, Ma Griffe. That exquisite perfume, and her beauty, so at odds with her forceful and aggressive personality, and the fact that he had long ago lost a struggle to make his own boring wife use Ma Griffe, awakened the lifelong unhappiness of his arranged marriage, the treadmill of his life, and he lost his temper. He raised his voice as he strode to his desk, to his place of command, and stood behind it.

'My instructions come from the Maharajah — '; but she would not let him finish and shouted louder at him than she ever had before.

'What instructions? What are these instructions? How far have you both gone with this film plan? What are your instructions?'

'Any instructions at all,' he shouted. 'I obey them. The Maharajah is my master —'

'Where is he hiding? I want to see him now.'

'It is his day of silence. He will see nobody, Princess. You know that.'

'Day of silence indeed!' Her contempt for this so switchable evasive action of her nephew, which she had seen used so often before, caused her to laugh mockingly, melodramatically. 'Damned dreamers both of you, wasting your time here together, with the world going to pot all round you.' She paused and puffed on her dead cigarette, then waited. Breathing hard, his withered lips working, the *Diwan* marched back to the occasional table, picked up the lighter and, his hand quivering, lit the cigarette for her.

'Go now and tell the Maharajah that his day of silence is over — *now*. Do you hear me, *Diwan* Sahib? This is about my family, this stupid film — '

'It is about mine too, Princess.' The *Diwan's* voice was cold and hard now, under control. 'Remember that my ancestor was executed and that — '

'And so you want it on the screen for the world to see, is that what you want to tell me?'

'It is history. History.' His voice was rising again. 'What does it matter now, Princess?'

She walked closer to him, staring hard into his eyes, but he would not quail. 'You are a fool,' she told him, her voice softer now, convincing. 'My nephew is a fool too. But I am not a fool, and I don't care if they've offered you a billion dollars, I don't care if you want your ancestor executed on the screen, the film is not going to be made. Tell the Maharajah I will be waiting in my living room for him. Otherwise I will make the announcement myself to the press — '

Horrified, the *Diwan* pleaded now. 'Princess, you would not — now be reasonable, please. You will not win in this matter. The Maharajah is — '

Still calm, she beckoned for silence. 'Don't ever dare tell me again what I may or may not win. You have gone mad here, both of you, living in a fool's paradise, and now you think we're going to parade the disgusting savagery you call history for the world to gloat over — my God it's time you retired, *Diwan* Sahib. Don't you think so?'

The *Diwan* smiled slowly, his deep set eyes burning.

'I have often suggested it to the Maharajah,' he said, though not quite playfully enough for it to be insolence, so that they were merely the words of a tired old man who loved his master and would serve on, come what may, until dismissed. But an old man who knew he would go only when his master wished it, and not when this tiresome though brilliant lady decided; so he was still smiling when he said, 'Princess, there is another matter, not about history, unfortunately, or I

161

would not need or bother to raise it. But we live in more touchy circumstances in these times. Politics and so on. I am referring to your latest attack on the *tonga-wallahs* — yesterday. Princess, I must ask you to stop this well-meant crusade for the animal world or we shall have a riot in this town, and it will spread. Yes. This is no fool's paradise, Princess, these days. You do not know what is going on here, politically. I have to manage it, remember. You must not — '

'*Must not* — ?' she shouted. '*Must not* — ?'

The *Diwan* shouted so loud now that she backed away from him in what could have been an exaggerated fear of being struck. 'I said *must not* ever raise your hand to anyone in this state ever again. That is an order. I will not be responsible for your safety otherwise, Princess.' He looked fanatical, like a madman she had seen recently in a Delhi street, and then his swift change of mood to an almost silken quietude, and his smile with it, bewildered her. 'If you will kindly wait in your living room, Princess, I will inform the Maharajah of your command that he break his day of silence.' He bowed to her, then with long strides he left the office through the open door at the other end.

As he passed from the sunlit office into the darkened anteroom the *Diwan* saw the Maharajah standing ahead of him.

The Maharajah put his arm round the old man and said in a voice just above a whisper, 'You were superb. Superb. Now I'll give my performance. Come and have a drink with me in my study first.'

He walked the *Diwan* down the corridor leading to the study. 'You have talent, you know, *Diwan* Sahib. We'll put you in this bloody film. You were superb — '

'I was not acting, unfortunately,' the *Diwan* said. 'I forgot myself. But it is true, the Princess must stop these scenes with the *tonga-wallahs* in the public streets. It is degrading her.' He looked with wild eyes into those of the amused Maharajah walking beside him. ' "The Princess is a madwoman." That, *Maharaj* Sahib, was said to me by the leader of the *tonga-wallahs*' union in my office last night. As if the union is not enough to have to deal with in these days — '

'It's in the family, the madness, so not to worry, *Diwan* Sahib. Just be thankful it's not me attacking the *tonga-wallahs*.'

As they went into his study he said, 'A large Scotch for me, no soda.'

He lifted the drink to the *Diwan* in a toast. 'To talent,' he said. He drank and then looked affectionately at the *Diwan*, who had a small brandy in his hand. 'You can retire now,' he said. 'For a few hours, that is, if you want to come in and meet these film types. See how you feel.' He drained his glass, handed it to the *Diwan*. 'Do you actually believe what the astrologer said about this evening, *Diwan* Sahib? No fooling now.'

'Oh yes, *Maharaj* Sahib, of course I do. It is auspicious for you for your heart, for your lifeline. Those are his very words.'

'Really? If only I could believe in some of these things. How lucky you are. Why can I not believe? Why?' He smiled and waved his hand, then strode off into the corridor.

CHAPTER 14

A couple of years ago he and Bingham had visited a Kashmir encampment of some of the Kazakhs, who like the other millions of various communities, had been driven and hounded by Stalin. The Maharajah thought of them now as he put on the pair of light felt slippers they had given him, and reflecting again on the wonderful sense of freedom he always felt in the Himalayas he wondered if he should not simply walk out of here, disappear, instead of waiting to be disinvented, as Bingham would have put it. 'But not yet, of course. Not yet,' he said, smiling sardonically. 'Never do today what you can decide not to do tomorrow as well.'

She did not hear him approaching the entrance to what she called her 'waiting room' in this corner of the palace kept for her use. The Princess was sitting on a big hard scarlet *sindhi* cushion, her profile facing him, her arm held out from where it rested on her knee, a brown cigarette smoking in her fingers. She reminded him again of an exotic bird and once again, seeing her like this, his presence in his felt slippers unsuspected, she looked vulnerable and something even more than alone. Perhaps she was grieving about her state, her euphoria, her melancholia, and about the threats ahead in the erratic journey of her life. He loved her, detested her, feared her, and in secret cherished her. Now, watching her watch the smoke rising from her cigarette, he felt compassion, as well as an iron determination. He had learned how to deal with her. They shared many secrets, things unknown even to the *Diwan*, that proud magpie so tireless in the hoarding and sifting of all information collectable about Induspur state.

She did not hear him, as he moved silently on his felt soles, until he was about twenty feet from her. He stood quite still, enjoying the coolness of the marble floor through the thin felt of his slippers. Now he moved to his left so that when she would look up, even to her right, she would not see him. This vast room, he knew, had almost the subtle echo of the Taj at

Agra, and a low voice could appear to come from anywhere within it.

In a loud whisper he said, 'O Princess, *Nur Mahal, Muhr-un-Nisà*, Seal of Womanhood, it is I, the *Prayás Chit*, humbler of the self, defiler of past lives, come to atone to thee.' The whispered words floated, then echoed huskily in the big room, and, startled, then afraid, Subhadra looked up, her mouth open in apprehension. In his normal voice he went on, 'Well, you were both magnificent. I heard it all.' He heard her fluttering sigh, of relief. He folded his arms as she turned her head to look at him. He smiled. 'Magnificent, both of you.'

She turned her head away, then let it hang.

'Day of silence,' she said. 'So you listened.'

With her head bent he could see her gold-ivory neck. How curiously vulnerable it looked. How tender it must have made some men feel, before they received her revelation of their so sought-for insecurity. Yes, her longing to master men, unquenchable, hardly realized or understood by herself.

'Now,' he said. 'I'm going to say it again. Why don't you get in your car, drive to his house, and walk in and see him? Say, "Hello, *Bingaji*," and have a drink about old times. Break the strain. It will help you, Chuchu.' This use of her family nickname indicated that he was showing her affection.

'Don't mock.' Her head still bent, she drew on her cigarette.

'I'm not mocking.'

'You always mocked about what I called him —'

'*Bingaji*.' He laughed. 'I can't help it. It's just that I've never been able to see Tim being *Bingaji*, that's all. It sort of breaks his cover.' He laughed again.

She patted the cushion beside her, obviously placed there for him. 'Come and sit beside me.'

Sitting beside her he took her small hand, removed the cigarette from her fingers and held it out to her. She took it in her left hand. Squeezing her right hand gently in both of his, he said, 'How are you feeling?'

'They're giving me some new pills. They're not helping much. I feel afraid sometimes.'

'Stay that way. Like me. I fear nothing, but I stay afraid. It pays. Serious again. Go and see Tim, tomorrow. Do you *want* to see him? Admit it to yourself, that's all. Admit it, then do it.'

165

'You never seem to understand, Chandu,' she said. 'Never. He doesn't care a damn for me any more. You know that. I know that. How can I go and see him? Don't you know how a woman feels?'

'How a woman feels? I've forgotten.'

She squeezed his fingers, went on staring at her feet in their red-lacquered sandals. After a silence he said, matter of factly, 'If you try and interfere in this film project I'll have you certified.'

'I really do believe you'd try.' She picked up *Diwan's* gold cigarette box, threw it open, and held it out for him. 'Have one of these.' She took one herself and he lit them both.

'You'll regret what you're doing, Chandu,' she said. 'What Induspur needs is to stay sleepy, forgotten, to lie low and attract no attention, no publicity. We're tiny here. We don't matter. But if you make this film you'll bring us world attention. It'll destroy us. I'm warning you, Chandu. We should hide, be forgotten by Delhi, by government, by the world. Then it can all live on quietly. Can't you see that?' She looked into his face for the first time. 'Why don't you understand these things? This film will bring trouble, the wrong kind of change, jealousy. As to how you can let them film that awful period of our history — it's too horrible. And it'll come out anti-Indian, you'll see. It couldn't come out any other way if they film that ghastly story of two hundred years ago, and it'll wake the worst kind of memories here.' She turned her face away and bent her head again. 'Do you understand, Chandu?'

'Stay out of it,' he said, squeezing her hand again. 'Stay the financial wizard, that's your role. You've fought every idea I've ever had — the coal mine developments, the schools, the state lottery. I told you to stay out, every time. You were wrong, every time. Now. The phones are working. Go and pick one up and phone Tim.' He laughed. '*Bingaji*, that is.'

'Do you talk about me with him?'

'Never. I swear, Chuchu. We're friends. Real friends never discuss each other's private insanities of that nature, at least they never ask each other about it. If one of them wants to talk about it, to hear his insanity out loud, that's different. I think he does know I know about your affair — but I'm not sure. But he's so bloody *chalák,* so second-sighted or whatever it is, that I'm sure he knows I know. Not that it matters, Chuchu.'

'Know-all Sahib,' she mused. 'Yes, it't true. He could read my mind, but he didn't like what he read.'

'You pushed him, I suppose. Shoved him, like you shove every man you meet. Do you want to tell me about it?'

'You ask me that, from time to time. Are you keen to hear about it?'

'Not a bit.' A day might come, he feared, when he might have to have her certified. Her behaviour was well beyond eccentricity at times.

'Why didn't you have a child or something?' he said. 'That could have been the solution. Have you ever thought about that?'

'God!' She gave a sigh of exasperation. 'Sometimes you're too impossible, Chandu.'

'Just a lonely realist, that's all,' he clowned, his voice full of self-mockery. 'Running about trying to cheer up the human race.'

He stood up. He started to pace the room. He stopped and laughed. Christ, just like Tim, and for the same reason exactly. He turned to her.

'I'm in love,' he said. Yes, up came her head, open wide came her eyes, head turned sharply, red lips parted. Surprise, surprise. All woman again in one second. He came over and knelt down in front of her. 'She's a Brit. Want to meet her?'

She nodded, smiling at him. She stroked his face.

'Okay. On one condition though.'

'That I stay out of your film plans,' she said, despondent now.

'You're going to do that anyway. I'm not asking you about that. I'm telling you. Stay out.'

'Go on.'

'Be nice to her. Be nice to everybody. They're coming this evening, a kind of British-Yank called Croon, my unsuspecting beloved, and *Bingaji*.' He burst out laughting as he saw her expression, shock and trepidation at the mention of Bingham's name. He seized her hands. 'All right, I'll tell you what. You stay in your room if you like, and I'll bring the lady to see you. You can have one of those delicious feeler-meetings women love. Well?'

She was smoking silently, thoughtful. He waited. 'You realize it'll officialize it, make it more serious, if *I* meet her?' she said. 'Is that what you want?'

'*So* like you, my dear Chuchu,' he laughed. 'So you'll meet her? Eh?' She agreed, and then he came to what worried him about her even more than her antagonism to the film.

'Chuchu,' he said, a slight harshness in his voice now. 'I happen to know that you're meddling again with the landlords and the peasants, *and* our half-dozen amateur Communists — '

'I know what I'm doing,' she protested, before he could finish. 'I've spent my life here. You haven't. You leave that business to me, Chandu. I know how to work with the Communists *and* the landlords. The peasants too. I understand why Communism has an appeal for — '

'Do stop!' he said angrily. 'And listen to me carefully. My father got on well with the Congress party here, and we've got a good reputation for having seen the writing on the wall. My father *knew* and accepted years ago that Independence was inevitable. The *Diwan* knows what he's doing, and so do his council. So keep out of this problem and leave it to the *Diwan*. That's an order from *me*, Chuchu. This idea you have that you're some kind of magical bridge between the Communists' — he started laughing at the idea — 'and the peasants and so on, you don't even know anything about Marxism for a start. So I warn you — stop meddling. All the peasants want is more land, and the *Diwan*'ll see that they get it — not the Communists. I'm not worried about a few half-baked Communists. All this involves the coalfields too – they're going to be under a cooperative. Now keep out of it, Chuchu. And stay away from these Communists.'

She wanted to argue but he held up his hand. 'Enough, my dear Chuchu,' he told her sternly. Then he smiled. 'Just do what I've told you. Now, to more serious things. I'll bring Megan to see you — '

When he had left her he was still worrying about her need to matter in the running of the state, and about her lifelong habit of taking up causes after a little light reading about them, and then dropping them. Last time it had been her sudden passion for the ancient form of medicine, *Ayurvedha*, and how it could work alongside Western medicine in India which was so short of doctors. All this because she had read about the 'barefoot doctors' of the new Communist China. But this Communism bug she had picked up during the last few years was the most worrying of all. Perhaps she felt, while now knowing it, that if there was a Communist upheaval in India she might become known as 'the Red Princess', the bridge between the old patrician world and the new Marxist-Moloch. She gave the *Diwan* headaches, he knew, with her interfering in the delicate new fumblings to force the landlords to share out their land with the peasants.

He loved her but he feared her too, feared her instability and her competitiveness and aggression which went so badly with her marvellous beauty. Yes, she should have gone in for politics. She could have swayed crowds, dominated cabinets of men, and got married as well and had children. She was only a few years older than himself, and perhaps she would have been happier if she had never been a princess, been a peasant woman of some joint-family in some remote village. Then she could have used her power-drive and become the ruling family-woman, dominating the joint-family, in charge of all finances, all marriages, moves, births, every decision. Curious how, like many women, she did not like being a woman. But how right she was. He often felt gratitude for having been born a man. It was so much easier, so less complicated and painful than being a woman.

This made him think of Megan tenderly, but he wondered what she would find in him, and would she like what she found? He knew hardly anything about her, but then who knew anything about anybody? Once more the problem of identity and the enigma of being alive, then dead, arose and swept all other thoughts away again.

CHAPTER 15

The electrician worked all morning on the out-of-date loud-speakers and, when satisfied with their performance, extended the wiring up into the gallery above the spacious lounge. He then set up a small switch panel beside the old-fashioned American phonograph beside which stood the Maharajah, fretful and impatient, with a record in his hands. After another hour of trials the Maharajah was satisfied with the sound and dismissed the electrician. Three times during the afternoon of the following day the Maharajah went up into the gallery while the *Diwan* waited in the lounge below to pronounce upon the latest test.

All this for the playing of one record. Now, a quarter of an hour before Megan Brett-Turner was due to arrive, the *Diwan*, fuming, tapping his foot, waited for the record to be tested yet again. He had never seen the Maharajah in such a state of tension before. He looked up expectantly towards the gallery. He could not see the Maharajah who was hidden by the thin wall of the exquisitely fretted white marble screen through which, unseen, the Maharajah intended to watch the earliest of his visitors listen to the music he had chosen for her.

'Now, *Diwan* Sahib,' the Maharajah called down through the marble lacework of the gallery-screen, 'we know you've got a tin ear about music, but don't forget it's the sound, the quality, the tone I'm after. Understand? Now!'

After a few bars of the opening music the *Diwan* raised his hand. The music stopped.

'Well?'

'Please believe me, *Maharaj* Sahib,' the *Diwan* called up angrily. 'It is perfect. It cannot be improved.'

There was no knowing where this business was going to end. Brett-Turner's sudden and unexpected departure yesterday, the news of which had reached him this afternoon, had produced a worrying, almost boyish glee in the Maharajah when he had shown him the Englishman's letter. The letter informed the *Diwan* that he was going into partnership with another Englishman in a bar in Goa and that he therefore gave up the lease of his house. He would be obliged if the *Diwan* would make any use he wished of the furniture he had left in the house.

The Maharajah had held the letter out before him and then waltzed with it round the office. He had then stopped, read it again, and looked up smiling at the *Diwan*.

'Well, he won't last long down there in Goa, you know,' he said. 'Beach-combing territory. He'll drink with both hands down there, in his own bar too. They all do. This *could* be fate. Now, you're a great fate-man, *Diwan* Sahib, and you've got to admit that this must be fate. First the astrologer tells me this is my lucky night. And now this.' Then he had frowned, and, as he did so often when hope and happiness overcame his usual caution and doubt these days, he took refuge in light self-mockery. 'But it's got to be faced, *Diwan* Sahib, love is a form of insanity, and even now I may not be fully in charge of my mind. Don't forget that. I don't. Can't. Yet I know I'm half-insane with it already. I can see it. Strange, isn't it?' Then he had gone off, whistling.

He was whistling now as he came into the lounge and smiled at the *Diwan*. He looked at his watch.

'Ten minutes to go,' he said. 'She'll be here in ten minutes. I tell you I'm staggered by the state I'm in. It's wrong, but I can't help it. It's idiotic in fact, not just wrong.' He held his hand out in front of him and studied it. 'You see that? It's trembling. Imagine it, a man in middle age. Maybe it's all imagination, the whole thing. After all it's ages since I last saw her. I've auto-suggested myself into thinking I'm in love and that she's in love with me. That's all it is. Imagination, all of it.' He had another look at his outstretched hand. 'But it's still trembling, nevertheless. Hasn't heard what I've just said, obviously. Well, thanks, *Diwan* Sahib, you've been very patient with me today, but I'm not responsible for myself, you must see that. Oh God.'

He smiled as the *Diwan* bowed and then looked into his face with compassionate and worried eyes.

'Her company will be good for you, *Maharaj* Sahib,' he said.

It was all he could think of to say just then and as he walked

171

down the lounge on the way to his office he could hear the Maharajah ascending the steps to the gallery again, to stand by in readiness to put on the record the moment the lady arrived.

Up in the gallery the Maharajah smoked, thought about himself, wondered where he was going. Nobody knew where he was going, emotionally. 'A man chases a woman till she catches him,' Bingham had once remarked. He laughed now, remembering that. Yes, but did Megan want to catch him?

He heard her car, got to be her car, got to be, coming up the drive, then the gravelly skid and the soft jolt of braking. He let himself become keyed up, listening. Yes, unmistakable feminine steps, light and fast, coming up the wide marble steps. Weird, truly, the way the heart quickened then and experienced that throat-catching feeling of tenderness, as if the heart had fluttered up there. And to be able to study it happening, watch it while it was being experienced, and it went on happening, and now he could hear the servant gliding to meet her. He listened as her footsteps approached, entered the lounge, then, holding the sound-head of the phonograph in his trembling hand he let it down carefully onto the record. As the music began he went to the marble screen and looked down through one of the designs pierced in it.

Ah! Another fragment of fate. She was in Indian dress, the first time he had ever seen her in it, perhaps it was the first time she had ever worn it. He needed to know. Must find out.

He stared down at her, quite rapt, watching her walk slowly forward and take the drink held out for her on the silver tray by the servant. Her smile was sparkling as she thanked the servant.

Now she listened to the music as the servant left her. How delightful she looked, caught alone like this in his hidden eyes, he thought. He felt an excruciating happiness as she put her hand up to the grey flimsy *dupatta* and pulled it down a little to reveal the silver necklace. How utterly idiotic it made a man feel, to see beauty like this, and to hope to have it.

He walked towards the stairs, wondering where he was going, where he was letting himself take himself, hoping it was the right direction, a place without harm, without jealousy, pain, disappointment, hurt, anger, bewilderment. He wished he did not know that nothing lasted.

The same woman as last time was singing. She knew he

must have arranged that thoughtfully, deliberately. Malika somebody or other. She sipped her whiskey and soda, the file holding the manuscript under her arm.

'Megan,' the Maharajah called as he walked out of the shadow of the arch at the end of the lounge. 'How wonderful you look in Punjabi dress. You were made for it.'

He brushed his lips against her hand, then smiled at her.

'It goes with the music too,' she said. 'At least that's how it feels. Do you know what I mean?'

'Of course I do. Come and sit down. I'm delighted you could come.'

As he took a drink from the servant she watched him. He looked just splendid, she thought. She had only once before seen him wearing a turban, at some ceremony or other a long time ago.

As he came and sat down she looked at the yellow turban and then smiled at him. 'I love your yellow turban,' she said. 'I do hope you put it on for me. To match my Punjabi get-up kind of thing.'

'I did as a matter of fact. I must have known, must have guessed. Nice that, isn't it?'

'Very nice.' She looked round the lounge. 'I do hope I haven't made a mistake and come too early.'

'No, no,' he said. 'The others won't be here for another hour. It was deliberate cunning on my part, sheer planning, that's all. I thought we might enjoy just having a quiet drink together, before the others come. I've missed you, Megan.' He was appalled to hear himself go on to ask, 'Have *you* missed me?'

'I've brought the manuscript,' she said, holding the file up. 'For what it's worth, that is.'

He must show interest in her manuscript. Slipped up there a little about being missed, deliberately ignored too, hence the resort to the bloody manuscript. He held out his hand for it.

'Yes,' he said. 'The manuscript. Shall I have a look at it — now?' He took it from her and began to flip through the pages.

She watched him. Sulking a bit, though now he glanced up at her from his riffling of the pages, smile slightly sickly? Annoyed? Had she missed him? Well — no, actually, that is not particularly — 'Although it was unspoken between them she could feel the silent strength of his love for her, but what did she, Saleema, feel for him? Had he the quiet and effortless strength of will to awaken, to nurture, and then to master the fierce desire which has slumbered deep in the being of every woman since time began? No, she was not to be taken by brutal assault, a mere slaker of some swift and savage appetite, and then to be cast aside —'

'Are you enjoying being alone, Megan? Does it feel — any different, I mean, now he's gone — your husband — ? It was pretty quick wasn't it, overnight more or less.' He smiled. She stared at him. 'We won't have him for tennis this year. That's going to be sad. And Goa, of all places.' He waved the manuscript. 'You write so well, Megan. The film people will like it, I'm sure — '

'Goa?' She sat up in her chair and said, 'Wally? Gone to Goa?' He told her about Wally's note to the *Diwan*, pleased by the look of happiness, almost a glow, coming into her eyes. She stood up. 'At last some initiative,' she exclaimed. 'At last. And Goa — not quite far enough for me, but it'll do for a start.'

'Champagne, I think, is indicated. Yes?' Although she felt it was wrong she laughed with him. He pressed a button in the wall. She noticed how his sulkiness had vanished.

'Megan,' he said. 'There's something I have to say to you. You don't have to say anything back. Just say nothing, if you like. Let me say what I want to say and then think about it. But I've got to say it.' He turned to the servant and ordered champagne, turned back to her and went on urgently. 'It's been on my mind for a long time. I mean I spend a lot of time on my own up here — never been a lover of family gatherings, except when I have to do my duty and have them join me here — but you see, well, it's like this — you needn't feel you have to — you don't need to reply *now* — but if I don't tell you now then I — ' He stopped, a film of perspiration on his unlined light brown forehead, and as he reached for a cigarette box on the table near his chair she said, 'You're in love with me. Is that it?'

He more or less fell down into his chair, the cigarette box in his hand.

'Just throw me one,' she said.

'Throw you one?' he said in amazement.

'Cigarette,' she said impatiently. 'Just throw me a cigarette. Go on.'

He scrabbled in the box and then threw her a cigarette. She caught it neatly in mid-air, then put it in her mouth. She held up her hand as he struggled, about to reach for a lighter. 'Don't move,' she said. 'Stay where you are. Oh, here's the champagne.' As she took a lighter from her bag and lit her cigarette he dismissed the servant and opened the champagne.

'I've had eight years living with a stranger, a difficult stranger,' she said. 'He's not as bad as he became, living with me. He's a decent stupid man who needed a decent stupid wife. All would have been well for him then. Thank you, Chan.' She took the glass of champagne and lifted it. 'To Goa.' He responded, 'To Goa.'

Have to go carefully, getting much too cosy, this toasting together, conspiratorial already, racing towards togetherness.

'I'm not ready for anything like loving, or being loved, Chan. I'm out on parole, convalescent, a little mentally ill in fact. Oh, yes, you look surprised, but it's true. I wouldn't trust my own judgment as far as I could throw it, just now. But it's nice to be loved. Thank you, Chan.' She drank down the champagne and held out her glass for more. He filled it again immediately, all attention, but she could see she had slowed his ardour up somewhat. He sat down again and looked sombrely into the distance, then lay back in his chair, rejected, put off, spent.

Poor bugger, he'd been storing it up, practising, rehearsing, conning himself, for months, and now this, but she made herself fight the great enemy, hers anyway, of sentimentality.

'Chan,' she said, 'You're very nice. Thank you.' She smiled at him, not too coquettishly she felt, and raised her glass. It seemed to help a little. He smiled wearily back at her and raised his glass. Even now, in this unsteady silence, Saleema tried to assist, irritating her, this growing insidious habit — 'So it was and had always been, this primitive, elemental force, this struggle between man and woman, known instinctively by Eve and by every woman since, down the ages, the keeper of the grail itself, while Adam, like every man who followed, a mere seed-spraying machine however you viewed it —'

'Come and meet my aunt, Subhadra,' Chan was saying to her. He was on his feet and holding his hand out to her. She took it and rose. He held her hand, and then, somewhat bitchily, she thought, though he was smiling warmly at her, he added, 'I was stupid enough to tell her I was in love with you. I had to tell somebody —'

'What's stupid about it?'

He sighed, bent his head and kissed her hand, then looked into her eyes. 'She's a bit of a crackpot,' he said. 'But underneath she's a dear. We'll take the champagne along and you can get together over it.'

'I'll carry the tray,' she said. He protested and she said, 'I'm dressed for the part anyway.' She picked up the tray, and determined to make him laugh, bent her head so as to produce the picture of the old-fashioned, perfect compliant Indian wife, whispering, 'You first, Lord.' It worked, and he exploded into a roar of laughter, but which he cut off, to say intensely, 'Oh, Megan, I do love you so much.'

Hopeless, she thought, hopelessly in love with her, poor bugger, and yet she could feel she would enter the snare, could feel — could feel — 'knew that if he said it once more, was allowed to gaze into the depths of her eyes again, her secret would be discovered, and then the wild unthinking fury of her love would engulf them both —'

'This way,' he said, and, letting him take the tray from her, smiling a little awkwardly at each other, they went towards his aunt's corner of the palace.

More than anything she wanted to be alone, to think about this expected surprise, to find out what she thought about it. She could do with a little love but felt an anger which worried her when she thought about all the misunderstanding when those sacks of rubbish, their lives, would be exchanged and then ransacked, and then she wondered if she felt anything at all for him if she could even think this way. Where was the collapse of the will, the melting of the mind, the weakness at the back of the knees which she had experienced only once in her life, and that illegally, sinfully, treacherously, wrongly, unpatriotically? But maybe there was something greater to be had than this bloody love business, like friendship, being *liked,* and *liking* somebody. She liked Chan, no doubt about it. So?

'The tigress's lair,' Chan said to her, pointing at the heavy purple and gold curtains hiding the entrance to Subhadra's room. He called to Subhadra and she called back to him to enter. He looked at Megan and then, alarmed, said, 'What is it? My dear, what — ?' She was crying, soundlessly, her hands

176

gripped together. She turned away from the doorway. He, like all bloody men when faced with female tears, she noticed, went to pieces, and called for Subhadra. Then he put the tray down on the floor and put his arms round her as Subhadra, sweeping back the curtain, took in the scene and said, 'Yes, this is love all right, tears and all, everything.' To the Maharajah she said, scathingly, 'Leave her with me. Go and meet your guests. Can't you hear the car?'

When the Maharajah had left them Subhadra said, 'I'm in the middle of the menopause — or should it be called the manopause — ?'

She led Megan through her waiting room and into her living room, saying as they walked, 'I mention it because I'm getting these hot flushes and they make me twitch, so don't worry if you see me twitching suddenly, my dear. Another thing is that my mad doctor in Delhi insists that the hot flushes start from a woman's head downwards, but mine start from the feet and travel upwards. But no, that's not allowed, you see. I'm to have them in the opposite direction, he tells me.'

'Why don't you try a woman doctor?' Megan suggested, recovered now from her involuntary surge of tears. She would not have minded had the tears been self-induced, part of a performance, so that she would have been in control of the drama, but she had been overtaken by these tears and she was still feeling betrayed by them. Tears wasted in fact.

'A woman doctor? Not likely,' Subhadra said. With surprising tenderness she helped to make Megan comfortable on a divan, piling cushions behind her and tucking them in. Then she smiled down at her and said, 'Yes, you're really lovely. You can enslave him. Do that. Enslave him. Make him suffer a little when you want to. He's spoiled. What would you like, a drink, hashish, tea? Tell me. Do you smoke *hukkah*? Lift your head. That's right. Oh, divine. You're quite delicious. Why the tears? Was he nagging you? He's inclined to do that to women.'

'I didn't know he was in love with me. He's just told me, and I don't know why but it's upset me, I mean — I didn't expect it, what he said, and what I'm feeling now. I'm sorry about appearing in tears the first time I meet you.' She was still feeling upset, and angry because she was upset and could not understand why.

'We're complicated creatures, females, that's what I resent,' said Subhadra. 'I really do. These men, they just move around the world with their sexual equipment, like doctors, more or less, with the black bag, if you know what I mean. No problems. No pains every month. No hot flushes. Nothing. Just sex and boasting and shooting people and things. Have you ever thought about that?'

She put her arm round Megan and led her to a settee piled with cushions. As she settled down against a heap of cushions Megan said, 'I could do with a stiff drink. I feel very low somehow.'

Subhadra looked into Megan's puzzled face and smiled. 'Huh! Love!' she said. 'Did *he* make you cry just now?'

Megan shook her head, frowning. 'No, I don't think so,' she murmured as if to herself. 'I mean he's just mentioned it to me —'

'Mentioned it?' Subhadra cut in, turning from a side table where she was about to pour a drink. 'Mentioned what?'

'That he loved me — or was trying to —' She faltered. She was still angry about those tears, she thought, surely it could not be because of the good news that Wally had gone off to Goa. They why?

'Oh, a whiskey, please,' she called back in response to Subhadra's question. With half of her mind she was admiring the magnificent golden fabric of Subhadra's sari, the whole effect of the beauty of this small and notorious lady. It seemed impossible that this was the Princess who was known to attack *tonga-wallahs*, and who had knocked out a *góonda* one night in Delhi. She was quite formidable even in this small beautiful presence. Probably the best way to deal with her was by frontal attack, slip directly through the armour.

'Is it true, Princess,' she called to her, 'that you once knocked out a *goonda* who attacked you? It's a famous story in Delhi, you know.' Yes, that was just right, sounded as if she approved and wanted the facts.

Subhadra handed her the whiskey and described the incident.

With all the masses of Punjabi refugees around Connaught Circus in Delhi, good, honest, and unfortunate people, the city had changed a lot and *goondas*, thugs and molesters of women, were growing in numbers. One night one of these *goondas* had come out of the shadows to attack her, Subhadra

178

said. 'But I 'd worked it all out, just what I would do. I had a loaded swagger-stick tucked into the waist of my sari. I kicked the *goonda* between the legs so hard that he went down onto his knees — his screams, my dear, when he got his breath, that is — and then I gave it to him with the swagger-stick. I don't think I could manage it again, though, after the noise the swagger-stick made on his head.' She shuddered and closed her eyes. 'Quite horrible. But that was the end of non-violence for me, that incident. I was a devotee of Gandhiji, you know, at least I thought I was until the *goondas* started up in Delhi.'

She went to the table and poured herself a pink gin, then joined Megan on the settee.

'Well, my dear, and you — are you in love with Chandu?'

'Chandu? Oh, Chan, Chandu? What a lovely nickname. Do you think he'd let me call him that too, or is it too private?'

Subhadra smiled and shook her head.' I'm sure he'd love it. Well, do you want to answer the question or shall we avoid it? Tell me.'

Megan looked into her eyes, hesitant. She had never been one for womanly exchanges about these things, and now again found herself wondering why. She preferred the company of men to that of women, and often wondered about that too.

'I don't know what I feel about it,' she said. 'It's been a surprise to me. I didn't expect it.' She looked into Subhadra's shining black eyes to see if she was believed but was not able to discern an answer.

'Love is a very messy thing,' Subhadra said with what seemed an odd cheerfulness, smiling. 'Women's lives are quite messy enough without it, as we know. I've tried it. It was just a battle of wills where I was concerned, I'm afraid. The way men seem to automatically assume that they're in charge, that they're to be loved, admired, understood, you know the kind of thing, I'm sure. After all you've had a dose of it yourself, haven't you? Did you enjoy any of your marriage?'

'Oh, I'm not against marriage,' Megan said. 'Not a bit. What made you anti-men, by the way? Do you happen to know?' Now *that* was more like the approach, and asked so gently too, as if in need of information, nothing more. A slight pinkness had appeared in Subhadra's golden cheeks.

Then she lowered her eyes. Megan caught her breath as she recognized the particular kind of silence in the atmosphere that signalled she was about to be confided in, trusted, consulted now that she had so carelessly opened the way.

'Fear, I think,' Subhadra said in a strange, small voice, as if afraid of what she was hearing herself say. Her eyes were still downcast. She spoke faster now, but still in the same hushed tone. 'Men have always frightened me.' She smiled to herself then, her head still bent. 'Well, they frighten each other quite a lot, don't they, so there may be nothing odd in their frightening me too. I wonder, though. I never wanted to marry one of them. Plenty of chances, yes. Yet I was always afraid I'd weaken and marry somebody, just because I was a woman and supposed to.' She lifted her head and looked into Megan's eyes. 'I'd have been much happier if I'd been born ugly, you know. Much happier. It's a terrible thing to be attractive to men, and to fear them, to reject them. But now I'm glad. I'm over fifty.' She smiled and lifted her glass. 'Well, to you — I've forgotten your name.' More pink came into her cheeks.

Megan lifted her glass. 'Megan,' she said. 'To you too.'

They drank, and Megan could feel the thoughts racing between them. There had been one fleeting and fearful moment, so shamefully modern and Western a moment, she thought now, when she had feared Subhadra might be queer and was about to become a bore and a threat. But the poor lady was simply scared of men, the easiest creature to handle in the whole animal kingdom, even in conflict, as she had so painfully learned to know.

'Do you think you could — do you feel you might love Chandu?'

The two women studied each other's faces. Megan decided on a mysterious half-smile, still holding Subhadra's eyes. After all it was obvious that Subhadra was a mere child where this subject was concerned, still rather wide-eyed and breathless about the whole business, as long as it was about other people, and especially about Chandu.

'I'm still trying to get used to the idea,' said Megan. 'I came here this evening to discuss a film and have discovered that Chan — Chandu — is in love with me.' Subhadra's gaze was intense. This love of Chandu's was obviously very important to her. Tears then? That could kill this subject stone dead, plus apologies for disturbing her. She decided it would be too much, and she had taken a liking to Subhadra; she decided a steady firmness should be maintained. She went on, 'I've only just got rid of a man who was a well-meaning idiot, got him out of my life. It was the usual thing — young — world war two — uniforms — ' Megan waved her hand wearily and closed her eyes. 'I'm having a breather just now. Convalescent, you could say.' She heard Subhadra laugh warmly. Much better. 'So it was a bit of a shock, finding I was loved.' She opened her eyes and let their full blue force rest on Subhadra's, putting her will behind them as she smiled. 'Oh, it's lovely, yes, it's very nice being reminded you're lovable. But I need to get used to the idea.' Perfect. As if on cue Subhadra leaned forward and patted her hand, smiling, tender.

'Yes, of course,' she said, very gentle now. 'Take your time. But encourage him, if you feel you can. He needs it. He's dreadfully lonely.' She paused. 'Do you feel we could be friends, Megan? I mean do you think we get on?'

'Oh, absolutely. Don't you?'

Visibly delighted, Subhadra got up and took Megan's glass. 'Oh, I'm glad,' she said. 'Really glad. Let's have another drink, shall we?'

'Make mine a double, please. Then I must go out and join the others.'

Interesting to think that she could live here, in this beautiful palace, if she wished, and as Maharani too; and as she lay back against the cushions she let her eyes wander about Subhadra's spacious living room, all of it panellled in very old *papier-mâché* brought from Jammu a few generations ago. The panelling was covered with court scenes painted by forgotten Moghul artists: warriors and horses, hunting scenes, dancing girls and musicians.

'You like *dup*, Megan?' Subhadra called from where she was spooning ice into their drinks. 'Incense?'

'Oh, yes, I love it.' She watched Subhadra light what looked like a black wax candle and the blue incense began to drift across the room to her, Maharani Saleema Begum, considering her options — curious really, wondering if she would make small exotic Subhadra across the room there a relative or not, and of course next thought the oldest bromide — life is *so* strange. A series of accidents, yes, but sometimes you could help to arrange the accidents. To be so cool and thoughtful about it was a help too, but should I allow my life to be buggered up by emotion, because it was there all right, the emotion, waiting in the wings as it waited in the wings of everybody's life, to be called on, and now, when I'm free, and with all the money earned by Saleema? Even thinking about the possibility just opened to her by Chan — Chandu — was helping to open the snare, that oldest snare of all, which she could — would? — spring for herself. But was this the way a grown woman should feel about so elemental a matter, so casually, so detachedly? Probably yes, while it lasted.

'You will be working on this film, Megan?' Subhadra handed her the glass of whiskey and sat down beside her again.

'Yes. At least I hope so. I wrote a book about what happened here in the eighteenth century and — Chandu — thought I might be useful.'

Subhadra smiled. 'There were so many lies told about it all,' she mused. 'Only a couple of people really know what did happen.'

'Well, it doesn't really matter what did happen, Subhadra, because the film people will change it all anyway. They always do.'

'You must do all you can to make them change the woman, the dancing girl who became Maharani, Zarina,' Subhadra said, suddenly serious and firm. 'We must not allow them to show her as she was, on the cinema screen. Never.' She stood up. 'Come. I'll show you something that was not in your book, Megan. Then you will be convinced.'

As she followed Subhadra Megan said, 'So you've read my manuscript? When?'

'No, but I know what you were told. The real story is much worse. Much worse.'

They walked down a long wide corridor the walls of which were hung with old weapons, shields, swords, muskets, daggers, Moghul-style helmets with chain-mail shirts hanging below them.

Megan followed Subhadra into what must have been the old armoury. It was neglected, dusty, its walls whitewashed, weapons of all kinds from the past piled against the walls.

Subhadra stopped in front of what looked like a gigantic parrot-cage. It was about twelve feet high and was standing on an enormous block of sandstone. The ribs of the cage were burnished steel. The floor of the cage was also steel, and into it was let a trap door held by an enormous spring.

'What on earth is it?' said Megan as she stared up at the towering cage.

'It was in there that Zarina kept her last lover, an English colonel,' said Subhadra. 'She held him in it for over a year, until he confessed, until he told her where he had buried the loot of this state. The loot was enormous, a fortune even then. The colonel had been offered his old post back again by the British in Bengal — he was a renegade. He was also Zarina's lover and her commander-in-chief, and she discovered that he was leaving with his army and the loot, to rejoin the British. So she put him in there until he told her what she wanted to know.'

'My God, what a lady. And then?'

'She let him out and pensioned him. He was never allowed back to British Bengal while she lived.' Subhadra hesitated. 'That was our family fortune the colonel intended to take with him — the British used to call that kind of thing "shaking the Pagoda Tree" — making a fortune in India. They were all doing it then, Mahrattas, Moghuls, Rajputs — it must not be seen on the screen. This awful woman was my ancestor. You must be strong, Megan, and make them do the story in such a way that — it is not funny — '

Laughing, Megan said, 'Nobody'll know. The names will all be changed, the story will come out completely different. Don't worry.' Then she looked up at the huge parrot-cage again, awed, and went on, 'Though I must say if we put Zarina on the screen the way she was — they'd have to call the picture "The Black Widow" or something — '

'The *black* widow?' said Subhadra suspiciously.

'It's a poisonous spider — I mean — oh dear — no, it won't do — I — '

'Let us go back,' said Subhadra. 'And you need not tell Chandu you have seen this horrible cage — even if he shows it to you himself. He'd be angry with me. And don't mention anything about the loot and how we — how she got it back. None of the family wants that known.' Worried now, she sighed exasperatedly as they went back along the corridor to her room. 'I hope it never gets made, this film. There can only be trouble from it. But Chandu will not listen to me.'

CHAPTER 16

He was not ready for the boisterousness of the producer, Ted Koltz, as he shook hands with Croon. Koltz, somewhat over-friendly, he felt, said, 'Your Majesty, I want to tell you that I *love* your country. I'm having a ball.' The Maharajah had forgotten that Croon had telephoned earlier to say that, quite unexpectedly, the producer of the projected film had arrived and was staying with him at 'The Kipling Arms'. He had also said that Ted Koltz was in a curious state, having spent thirty-six hours in 'planes with little sleep, and he had had a few drinks, but despite this seemed determined to discuss the film with the Maharajah. 'He's a great fellow and I'm sure you'll like him,' Croon had gone on to say. 'So what do you think? Shall I bring him?'

In a good mood then, full of hope about Megan's coming arrival, he had told Croon, 'Why not? Certainly bring him. And as for having a few drinks then we'll catch him up. We'll all have a few drinks. Yes?'

Now, dispirited, uncertain after his disappointing and deflating passages with Megan, he had to fight irritation when the little bouncing American brought forward a very old and dignified Muslim and said, 'I hope you don't mind, your Majesty, but I just had to bring along this lovely old guy so you can see his marvellous magic. His name's — ' He turned to the old man in the snow-white cotton turban and loose white Punjabi dress, and said, his hand affectionately on the man's shoulder. 'What did you say your name was again?'

'Zamin Ali, *Maharaj* Sahib,' said the old man, touching heart and head in a dignified half bow. Then, apologetically in Urdu, in almost an undertone, he added, 'Forgive this intrusion into your domain, your Highness, by my humble self. It truly was not my intention to trespass in this way.'

Whatever it was that the old man had said, Croon noticed how the Maharajah's somehow sullen mood now changed, how he took the old man's hand and said in English, 'it is no intrusion at all. You are my guest.'

'I shall await your commands, *Maharaj* Sahib.' The old man bowed and withdrew to the steps of the palace where he joined his small boy assistant who sat with the paraphernalia of their magic.

Everybody sat down and drinks were brought; determined to shed his melancholy, the Maharajah became talkative, then enthusiastic as Koltz's energy and zestful talk seemed to take over the meeting.

'I'm here to tell you, your Majesty,' said Koltz, 'that in New York, Bombay, and Delhi, I've matched them dollar for dollar. This thing's airborne. We've got a project. Now, I've read the two pages of breakdown on the story Roger here has come up with. I've got a million ideas we'll kick around. But' — he beamed round at the others, one by one — 'what do you say we have a little extraordinary magic first? I tell you this lovely old guy is the greatest magician I've ever come across, and I've seen some. He does something with two little birds and a pack of cards — well, I tell you it's something else. Do we let him work or do we hold him in reserve, your Majesty?'

Amused, and already under the spell of Koltz's electric and friendly vitality, the Maharajah smiled and said, 'Let him work. Let's have a drink and see what he does.' The old man was called and as he made his way up the palace steps with his boy-assistant, Bingham arrived and was introduced to Koltz.

'I've got a stack of books for you, Colonel,' Koltz told Bingham, 'from your fan and admirer, F.X. Condy, along with a letter and — he knows you're a whiskey man — a case of Jack Daniels. You've been introduced to Mister Daniels, Colonel?'

Bingham smiled and shook his head, Koltz still pumping his hand. Such exotica from other lands was still far from general in India, for where their own national products were concerned the British had always run a very tight ship.

'Great,' said Koltz. 'Your life is really going to begin when you get wrapped round your first bottle.'

The small boy was setting up what looked like a miniature oil-rig made of bamboo strips. The old man was murmuring to two tiny brown birds perched on the palm of his right

185

hand. When the bamboo contraption was ready they could all see that a cord ran up to it from the base to a small tin bucket. At the base was a handle. The men gathered closer, all silent now, as Zamin Ali released the birds and one of them took the handle in its beak and the other flew to the top of the bamboo derrick, and waited there. Patiently the bird, contorting its body, began to turn the handle and the bucket on the cord began to descend. When it reached the carpet the other flew down and took a small pannikin in its beak and began to ladle water from a bowl into the bucket. It then stood back and watched, as the other bird slowly wound up the bucket until it reached the top of the derrick. The old man called the two birds to his hand and rewarded them with a few grains of *bajra*.

'That's only for openers,' Koltz said. 'It's the card trick — if that's what it is — it's just the greatest — I offered the old guy one, two, three, then four hundred bucks for the secret, but it seems it's kind of sacred, a family heirloom of magic, and it's going to go to the kid here, his nephew. Isn't that lovely, I mean that kind of integrity? Now watch.'

Sensing the tension from the silent group of men, Megan, who had just left Subhadra's room, came forward unnoticed, and then more or less stole into a position behind the Maharajah. Bingham watched Croon notice Megan's presence, look away for a second, his eyes again on the cards being dealt on the carpet, and then turn his head sharply to stare at her. Their eyes met in a long look, and Croon smiled at her. Bingham could see that Megan was wanting to break the mutual stare, that her eyes seemed larger suddenly, and then, an act of decision, she turned her eyes to the preparations on the carpet. Croon continued to watch her.

Zamin Ali had now dealt the cards in such a way that two lanes separated the fifty cards, which all lay face down. The old man squatted down, with the birds, one on each shoulder, staring down with what appeared to be great interest at the cards laid out on the carpet.

In his halting English Zamin Ali said, '*Maharaj* Sahib, lady, and gentlemen, I will now hide birds in this white cloth, so that can see nothing. Then, one by one, you shall each point to a card. I will let bird loose. He will point to your card.'

'Well, I've never seen this one,' the Maharajah said to Bingham, his eyes full of enthusiasm. 'Have you, Tim?'

'No, not this one, but I've been told about it.'

'First, *Maharaj* Sahib,' said Zamin Ali, the birds now hidden.

The Maharajah leaned forward and pointed to a card. Zamin Ali lifted one of the birds out of the cloth hiding them, raised it on a forefinger, and spoke to it. Bingham leaned forward, craning, to listen, the Maharajah watching him intently.

'Recognize it, Tim? I didn't.'

'Sounds like Arabic, but it's not.'

Zamin Ali lowered the bird on his finger, whispering to it now, coaxingly, then the bird stepped off his finger and faced the rows of cards.

'Now just watch that goddam bird stand and *think*. I mean actually *think*,' Koltz said in a low excited voice. 'You see that? Forget Einstein. Just get a good look at that bird thinking, *and* how about the little frown?'

The tiny bird did appear to be actually thinking, as it surveyed the rows of cards. This uncanny scene produced total silence among the now rapt watchers. Now the bird began to walk slowly down the first row between the cards. It stopped beside the card the Maharajah had pointed at. Then, to shouts, exclamations, a kind of rebel yell from Koltz, it bent forward and tapped the correct card with its beak. It then looked at its master, who made a gesture, and with a fruff of its tiny wings the bird flew to him and perched on his shoulder, where it was rewarded.

The watchers, stunned, looked at each other, their mouths open, all delighted with what they had just seen.

The Maharajah now saw Megan behind him. He stood up, his earlier mood gone. He took her by the shoulders gently and sat her down in his chair. Again Croon and she found themselves looking at each other, but, Bingham noticed, Megan always with an eye on the Maharajah.

Silence fell again as the performance was resumed, and three times one of the birds picked the card correctly, and each time the excitement of the watchers rose. Argument began. Was it all an ingenious trick, or was it actual learning on the part of the birds? And through all this Ted Koltz looked on with pride, ownership, and then announced, 'There's no way around it — he's got to come back to the States with me — we've got to get this show on the road, where it belongs.'

The final card was chosen, by Megan, and a bird was released. This time the bird wandered down the whole length of a passage between the cards, and then started down the other one. It stopped near Megan's card. Again there was complete silence and all the heads leaned forward to watch, even more closely this time, for the bird hesitated at the wrong card, appeared about to make a movement to indicate it with its beak, drew back, walked to the correct card, looked at it rather hard, then, to loud cries and gasps, seemed to really frown as it looked again at the wrong card. It was actually in what seemed to be a true dilemma. It was looking first at the wrong card and then at the right one, then back again.

'It's incredible,' Megan whispered loudly. 'It *is* thinking.'

There was a shout of relief and disbelief as the tiny bird appeared to decide, and then tapped its beak on Megan's card. Somebody started to clap and all joined in as they turned their eyes to the old man, who stood up and bowed. So moved that it appeared he might cry, Ted Koltz got to his feet and went to Zamin Ali, put his right arm round him in a brotherly and proprietary way. He looked at Croon, who was looking at Megan.

'Roger,' Koltz called to him. 'Write this wonderful guy into the movie. It's a must.' He disengaged his arm from the old man and walked forward until he was in front of Croon and had his attention.

'Now here's the scene, Roger,' said Koltz, the rest of his audience forgotten, as he began to act.

'It's a moment of decision, see? Don't ask me what — write it. Okay? So — it's the moment of decision. Dancing girls, music, and outside the battle is coming closer. Somebody's got to die, see? Something like that — anything — get it? No — I got it — somebody's got to go out there and face death — one of the two heroes — one of whom I don't have to tell you is our captain of the U.S. marine corps. The woman — the Queen, Princess, what have you' — he pointed a decisive finger at Croon — 'Got to talk to you about that — remind me — the dame's going to have to be English, French — no way she can be American I'm afraid, seeing what year it was — right — so how's the decision made? We bring in our old guy here with his birds and pack of cards. The bird picks the card picked by the guy, see? Think about what we just saw here, on screen — never been seen before — America'll go out of its goddam mind about these birds and this lovely old guy. Just that one scene'll bring them running — word of mouth, see — you've got to go see those birds, that'll be the word all over America.' He smacked his hands together in a kind of fierce glee and then raised them as clenched fists above his head, like a boxer in victory. He looked at the smiling Maharajah, who was captivated by all this. 'What do you say, your Majesty? You feel the movie taking shape, coming alive already. Right?'

Croon took this chance to draw Megan aside and ask for her manuscript. He did not need the manuscript, he needed her, and this was the quickest way to achieve it. She found her manuscript and they moved over to a settee away from the others, where Croon opened her manuscript and pretended to take an interest in it.

'I need to talk to you,' he said. 'I've got to work fast on a first draft outline, so I need to ask you a few questions, get your advice and so on. No use here. The club? Are you free?'

She wanted an even closer look at his face, and now she looked into it. From the moment their eyes had first met, she thought, that indescribable weakness had appeared in her body. Sometimes it seemed to be in her knees, at the back somewhere, and now, halfheartedly, she summoned Saleema Begum — 'it was his aura of strength, his splendid looks, his level, grey, haunting gaze, his air of confidence, mastery' — but these were real things, true feelings that she was feeling, and there was no help to be had from Saleema. Also, she felt an unexpected terror because of the sheer attraction she felt towards Croon, a terror that she was either in love with him already, or was going to be. She wanted to get away, now, immediately, and before she knew it she was on her feet, beginning to excuse herself. Sheer bloody, hopeless panic, but why, why was she losing her head this way? She knew Croon was badly smitten too, for he kept his eyes on hers, captivated, all other plans he might have had already being put aside, excused, shelved. She knew the signs and they were all there. She was used to them in other men, but this time she was looking for them, noting them, and with a mounting pleasure as she recognized the dazed, stricken look in Croon's large grey eyes. Somehow she must keep her head, stay in charge. 'I must go,' she told Croon. 'Some other time, we'll discuss the story. I — '

Chandu was now beside her. He took her arm, very gently

189

at first, but then increased the pressure, and said, with a silkiness quite new to her. 'My dear Megan, you must not feel pressured. You're here to enjoy yourself. Now come and help me with the champagne.' He smiled at Croon and took her away on his arm.

For the rest of the evening, through the champagne, the cold supper which followed, the stories afterwards over the brandies and liqueurs, Chandu kept her beside him. There was a certain undeclared but threatening air beneath his smiling attentiveness. He had watched and he had understood. Meekly she fell in with his wishes. Once or twice she looked quickly at Croon who seemed to be throwing out great waves of more than the unusual magnetism she had felt from him, his eyes fixed on her, angry, sad.

Even Ted Koltz noticed this and he once went over to Croon and spoke into his ear.

'Okay Roger, so there's nothing like a dame — but not that one. You're working, see? You want to blow your stack — call room service and make it business. But no heavy emotional stuff. I mean none. Understood?'

This was a Koltz Croon had come across only once before, in California, and for the same reason, when he had told an assistant director, 'You fall in love when this movie's in the can, not before. Get laid someplace fast, and get on with the work. But no love.'

Croon looked up at Koltz and said, 'I know what I'm doing, Ted. Not to worry.'

'You know what you're doing, *partly* that is, for now, Roger. Be careful. You could mess things up, and you on the way to your first million. Think about that — all the time. Okay?'

'Okay.'

Ted went over to talk to the Maharajah and Bingham joined Croon.

'I wanted to ask you about Balban,' he said. 'Was he — er — hallucinating — when he contacted you?'

'Hallucinating?' Croon laughed. 'So that was it. You mean —'

Bingham was scowling. 'Bloody infuriating for you. I'm sorry.'

'No, no,' said Croon. 'He was fascinating, but I knew he

was far from normal, shall I put it that way?' He laughed again. 'Is he — is he a nutcase? He said you sent him to me.'

'I did. He came to see me after he'd left you at your hotel, but I knew he was full of hashish as soon as he spoke. I mean he'd been smoking hashish on top of the opium he eats every day. He's an opium-eater but he usually makes sense, good sense. But not with hashish on top of it. I'm sorry.'

'No. He was a great help. I took a liking to him. But I've never met anybody like him before. Is all that true, about running around India defiling Brahmins, and changing his religion every few months? Or hallucinations?'

'Oh, no. It's all true, most of it anyway. I put a stop to him talking about it. It's hashish that makes him hallucinate about it, and he can be a bore. And someday he's going to boast about this playacting to the wrong people and he'll finish up dead. He said he's going to work for you. He's very reliable, but you'll have to make him swear off hashish. He's not the type for hashish, even without the opium eating. I gave him quite a bollicking when I saw the state he was in.'

'And all that stuff about his being in love with the dead Maharani. He has a painting he keeps round his neck — '

'That's what I mean. That's his hallucination area.' Bingham stopped and looked across the room to where Megan, the Maharajah and Koltz were sitting on the carpet and watching Zamin Ali doing more card tricks. 'That's who Balban's in love with,' said Bingham. He smiled at Croon. 'Meg over there. Quite harmless, though. Quite innocent. Rather touching, really. But it's all spent on a woman who died a hundred and fifty years ago.' Bingham laughed. 'Opium eaters come in all shapes and sizes. Balban's eaten opium since he was a boy. I give him a few more years. They stop eating, you know, people who *eat* opium. He said he cooked for you. Did he eat anything?'

'He ate thick milk with a little rice in it.'

Bingham nodded. 'That's it. Thick milk, buttermilk, but milk anyway. They all finish up that way, opium eaters. Poor Balban. He's brilliant, you know, but, well — flawed?' Croon joined him in laughter, and then his face darkened. He stared across at Megan. When he turned back to Bingham he said, 'Lovely, isn't she? What's her husband like?' Bingham got up then.

'You can find that out for yourself — if you're interested,' he said. He murmured something about having to empty the tank and moved off in the direction of the bathroom.

'Roger!' Koltz called across from where he was sitting with the others. 'You've got to see this. Come on.'

The Maharajah called to him too. 'Yes, Roger, you mustn't miss it. Come and have a drink with us.'

All very matey, eh? Croon whispered to himself as he walked across to join them. Smooth and matey.

Megan was unnerved by the way Croon stood over them and said, 'A wonderful evening, thank you, your Majesty,' then to her, 'Let's go, Megan, and get some work done. I want a draft of the script ready inside ten days. Okay?' She was unnerved by what must have been mockery in that 'your Majesty', and still more by the way she got up to join him and said, 'But isn't it rather late — for work, I mean?' She knew she looked concerned, just right, but after all she was working on this film now. Croon said, 'I'm one of these night people, I'm afraid.'

She wanted so much to go with him that she pretended to wish to delay, but then made the right noises, she thought. Later she could not remember just how they left. Ted Koltz followed them out to the top of the palace steps and said to Croon, 'Inside ten days huh? That's real fast, Roger.' She knew Koltz knew what was going on, or trying to go on, and she was interested in the almost clinical way she watched the two men handle the scene.

'You've seen me work, Ted,' Croon said, smiling, relaxed. 'Ten days it'll be for the story line, maybe less.' She knew Koltz was worrying about the Maharajah and what he might, must, be feeling. She could feel Koltz's need to talk about it, if only by the way he was now ignoring her, making sure he did not meet her eyes. She felt stupid, but wilful, unnerved, yet determined. She feared the excitement she was feeling, but for some reason she felt anger as well, and this helped her. She also felt certain she should turn back now, say something like, 'No, Roger, I'm too tired. I'm a day person. So what about tomorrow?' Instead she heard herself saying, 'Well, Ted, I'll do anything I can to help.' Then he looked at her. He looked hard and grim, well no, businesslike maybe. She preferred to think of it as the expression of a man used to doing deals. He said, 'Call me tomorrow after lunch, Megan, and we'll talk money. We got to pay you, after all.' But he was feeling hostile towards her, she was certain. To Roger he said, 'This is a beautiful lady, Roger,' and then to her he added, jerking his head at Croon, 'And this guy is very attractive, Megan. Right? Just see he works like he says, fast.' To Croon he said, 'And I mean on the film. Right?' He was embarrassed, though, for he smiled apologetically and spread his hands in a gesture of helplessness.

'Don't worry,' she told him, smiling. She squeezed his arm.

Then they left. Again she could have retreated, but she agreed to follow him to the club in her car. She sat in her car, worried, excited, while Croon got into his. Then she drove after him to the club.

While Koltz was outside with Croon and Megan a tense exchange began between Bingham and the Maharajah. It began with a long piercing look from the Maharajah.

'You know what's going on, of course, Tim.'

'Yes.'

'So?'

'Do something.'

'But what?'

'Depends how serious you are, Chan.'

'I'm serious.'

'You love her? Really, I mean.'

'Yes. Really. Don't tell me you're surprised, Tim.'

'I'm not.'

'You knew all the time. Yes?'

'Yes, Chan. It was obvious.'

'Not *too* obvious?'

'No. Just enough.' That was a signal for a short bitter laugh from the Maharajah, then slightly warmer laughter in which Bingham joined him. Ted Koltz came back and began to act out a part of the film for them, but it did not hide his own worries about Croon, whom he had often referred to as 'my writer'.

The Maharajah quickly lost interest in Koltz's performance, and Bingham watched him brood and smoulder and then startle Koltz with an unexpectedly firm, almost aggressive, statement.

'Ted!' he said loudly. It was a command for silence. Koltz was playing a scene in which the American marine captain was defining, apparently for all time, the essence of the military ethic, in a speech to the troops. He stopped and looked at the Maharajah, who then spoke to him with a curious hint of menace.

'Megan is very impressionable, Ted.'

'Er — you mean —'

'I intend to marry her.'

Koltz swallowed, then looked at Bingham as if for help. Bingham stared at him coldly, bouncing him off back at the Maharajah. Koltz knew he was guilty, that 'his writer' had brought threat into the Maharajah's life.

'I don't care how you do it, Ted,' the Maharajah was saying. 'But do it. Warn him. Now. Immediately. On his own. Without Megan being there. This is all between us. Megan is to know nothing. Now. Do it now.' The Maharajah stood up and began to declaim, and Bingham watched him, wondering if this was acting, game-playing.

'If this goes wrong it will wreck my life and your picture. You know that. I can see already that you know that. I will not have my life destroyed by this person who has described himself in the hotel register as a playboy by profession —'

'Your Majesty —' Koltz tried to cut in, to make some kind of plea which would become promise, but the Maharajah swept it away with his hand and went on, threateningly now.

'I will stop at nothing. Nothing. You hear that?' He looked at his watch, then at Ted. 'Find him now and warn him. Now.'

Ted looked desperately at Bingham and then back at the Maharajah. When he spoke his voice was so hoarse that he had to clear his throat. He was obviously in a state of great anxiety.

'Right away, your Majesty,' he said. 'Now, as you say. I'll call you —'

'Don't call me. Come yourself, in person. I'll be waiting here. All night.'

They heard Ted running down the steps of the palace front, heard his car start, then the car, its engine roaring and clattering, started down the hill at speed.

The Maharajah smiled at Bingham, leaned forward to pour a couple of drinks, holding up the whiskey bottle questioningly for Bingham first.

'How was I?' he said as Bingham came over to pick up his

whiskey. 'Better than him, I hope. Ted, I mean. The acting. I *was* better, wasn't I?'

'Much, much better,' said Bingham, going back to his chair.

'There's nothing I can do, really, or anybody else can do, for that matter,' the Maharajah said musingly, lying back in his armchair. 'If a woman is going to open the safe for a man, she's going to open it. That is the law. The woman has the dialling code, not the man.' He was silent for a while. Then he said, 'He's big and strong and handsome, and a playboy. But he can do nothing, unless she wills it.' He looked at Bingham and raised his eyebrows. 'You saw what was going on here tonight?' When Bingham nodded he nodded too, and went on, 'Lust at first sight, that's what it was. Well, it's up to her what happens, not him. That is the law. It's going on now, while we're talking, Act One. The Playboy enters and we know he's looking for the safe — '

'Is this going to be a farce?' Bingham asked. He knew how fond of farce his friend was, all theatre, but farce particularly, and Feydeau more particularly.

'How do we know? Megan will be directing.' He stopped and pondered, sipped his drink, then said, 'I doubt if it will be tragedy. Because I'm not sure I'm up to it. Though I do care . I do care.'

'Ted was watching it all tonight. He warned Croon off.'

The Maharajah nodded. 'Yes, I saw that. And Megan panting like a run-down gazelle. You saw that too? Don't try and spare me, Tim. We've known each other far too long. This place was like a laboratory tonight. Somebody shoved those two elements close to each other and — whatdyoucallit nearly took place — '

'Atomic? Nearly went critical, you mean?' Bingham's face was solemn.

'Yes. And there was radiation all over the place. I'm ir-radiated, I can assure you. To the marrow.' He gave a short laugh and drank some more whiskey. Bingham watched him suffer, sipped his own whiskey and thought about the last time he had suffered the rending pain and misery of a frenetic love affair. Some time ago now. Cairo. No. Alex it was. Turning up for the last time, and knowing it was the last time, and that the woman was not going to turn up this last time. Res-taurant in Stanley Bay. Night. Sea breeze cool on the cooling skin. Arak and ice in the glass. Misery of shrunken, emptied heart. *Ya qutb al-Aqtab,* you strayed from the path — that path into the Islamic faith from which, once already, he had turned back.

'What are you grinning about over there? My sorrow?'

They laughed. Bingham shook his head. 'Sorry, Chan. I didn't mean to grin. I was thinking.'

'About your own wreckage, your own life, I suppose? Yes. M'mm. I think I can manage this. I *think* I can.'

They studied each other's faces. 'I do love her, Tim. Can you believe that?'

'And you're going to sit up all night, wait for Koltz to report?'

'Why not? He can come back here and act it all out for us. He loves acting. What's your guess? She's taken Croon back to her house and now it's Act Two. She's teaching him the dialling code of the safe and he's putting on his burglar's mask — '

'And Ted bursts in on them and starts playing you, gives your speech — you will not have your life destroyed by a playboy etcetera.'

'Something like that.'

'Well, let's stop this fun for a moment, Chan. Megan may love you too. Don't you think so?'

The Maharajah appeared to consider this. After a time he looked at Bingham and said, 'Let's take my mind off my suffering for a while, and indulge in a little sado-masochism. Let's see now — how about you and Subhadra? Did you suffer there, Tim? I've always wanted to ask you about it.'

'I know you have. Yes. I suffered. Happy now?'

'Not yet. What I want to know is, what started it?'

'Kindness. That's what started it. I was kind to her over something. Then she was kind to me back. You must remember she was very beautiful. Still is, I expect.'

'Yes. She still is. Kindness, eh?' The Maharajah smiled understandingly. 'We really are in need of keepers, warders, all men, don't you think? But it wouldn't help. Kindness, eh?' He shook his head in wonder, his eyes fixed on his friend's face. 'She's so strong. So much drive, so much anger for men. It's always mystified me.'

'Mystified me too. Still does as a matter of fact.' They both laughed quietly, as if Bingham knew, the Maharajah thought, that Subhadra was in the palace and might overhear.

'If I lose Megan it's going to hurt, Tim.'

Bingham nodded. 'I thought so.'

'Let's have another drink on that,' said the Maharajah and lifted the bottle. Bingham went over with his glass.

CHAPTER 17

A disturbed, excited sahib, even though this one was only an American version and therefore not really real as a sahib, had a sort of Pavlov's dog effect on the assistant hotel manager. His head began to shake from side to side on his thin neck as Ted Koltz, for the third time, angrily demanded information. The young trainee manager, whose English was below standard anyway, could not manage to adjust his ears to this sahib's unusual accent. Panic, resentment, and anger began to show in his eyes. He wished to help but could not.

'Goddam it,' Koltz shouted. 'For the third time where is my writer, Mister Croon? Go get him. You hear me? He came here tonight? With a lady? I'm asking you.'

'Bar is open, Sahib,' the young man said for the second time. Koltz glowered at him, started to control himself. Got to play it cool or would finish up a basket-case for sure. He loved the country but certain things were getting to him, like the chaos, forget those three million beggars in Delhi, if that was possible.

'The bar's open, huh? Thanks.'

He went into the bar and ordered a treble scotch on ice. The barman started to make sense in English. He wanted Croon Sahib? That was another thing about this country. While you were screaming in the heat, and wondering when Montezuma's Revenge was going to start — or Delhi Belly as they called it here — the guy you were screaming for was standing behind you, waiting, smiling, ready to help, when you were ready, and maybe would levitate any minute now.

Croon Sahib was not in the hotel and had not been in all evening. Lady? No lady, Sahib.

'I want you to do something for me,' he said to the young alert barman. He handed him a dollar bill. 'I want you to tell that young man out there at the desk that I'm sorry. Sorry for losing my temper with him. Okay?'

Unused to such a strange request from any kind of sahib,

the barman, who knew that no sahib ever apologized about anything any time, said, 'He is not needing your sorry, Sahib, that fellow. Is wrong to give him your sorry.' He said this with such gravity that Koltz was impressed. He had been warned about getting it right in India.

'It'd be wrong, huh?'

The barman, his black eyes narrowing, jerked his head towards the door and said, 'He will be getting big head with sorry from Sahib. You know big head?' He lifted his hands and shaped a huge head round his own. 'Sahib cannot do sorry for that fellow. You are not knowing India, Sahib. Yes? No?'

Koltz considered it. Son of a bitch hated the management. Simple as that. Nothing Indian about it. Except that Sahibs are never sorry maybe. But the barman wanted a commitment. His unwinking eyes were fixed on Koltz's face.

'So Sahib not sorry. Right?' said Koltz.

The barman nodded his approval. 'Is right, Sahib.'

'Okay. Thanks.'

The barman held up the dollar bill, eyebrows raised, a mere formality he knew.

'Keep it. A consultation fee. Right. Now, I want a treble scotch on ice. Plenty of ice. You know Mister Croon? Know where I can find him?'

Out in the boondocks that's where, tangled up in the back of the car with the lady. In like Flynn. The barman was shaking his head. 'Croon Sahib drink in room. Not coming in bar now. He buy bottles outside and drink in room.' He frowned, his eyes angry now, remembering. 'He call me robber fellow. He count every anna, every pice. He make list, price-list of drinks, Delhi, Bombay, here this hotel.' A look of panic, disbelief, then scorn, appeared on the barman's face as he thought about Croon's ways. 'You know what is playboy?' He made the motions of a man dancing, throwing his head back, then tossing drinks down his throat, then, solemn again, he stared at Koltz. 'They are telling me Croon Sahib write he is playboy in hotel book. You are knowing this, what is playboy? No? Yes? How is playboy this sahib? Is not playing *here*. No. You have been his room? Knock on door? No? Yes?'

'He's not in his room.' Koltz sipped the chilled whiskey and thought about the time Croon had squeezed a coin in his fist and had then imitated an eagle screaming with pain, part of his act when anybody complained about the way Croon split everything down the middle, every tab, every expense. 'I'm saving,' Croon would say, 'but I'm making you save too.' It had become almost a religion with Croon, counting, bargaining, looking for discount, taking out the little note-book with its own pencil in its spine, and making minute calculations. 'I was a spendthrift once,' he had told Koltz. 'That was when I had nothing and whenever I made a few dollars. But since I really started saving, it works, it really works. And I'm fitter too. In New York this time I must have walked two hundred miles. Finished with cabs, the subway, the hired car.' Yes, Koltz thought, he was fanatical about everything he did, and reliable, hardworking, brainy *and*, unlike most writers, didn't mind if his stuff was torn apart, didn't think every god-dam word he wrote was solid gold for posterity. Yes, he liked Croon, but if he laid this lady seeing how the Maharajah felt about her, then this movie was dead. He looked at his watch, agitated again.

'You know where he might be, Mister Croon?' he asked the barman, hopelessly.

* * *

'Please,' Megan pleaded gently. 'We can talk tomorrow. It's very late. This one drink, then we go — then I must go — and anyway you're not a member of this club, don't forget — so . . . .'

Croon smiled and shook his head. He leaned on the table and stroked her hand. When she quickly tried to withdraw it he gripped and held it, still smiling at her.

'It's all fixed,' he said in his soft, deep, thrilling voice. 'Fixed.' He released his grip on her hand. She left it there. He stroked it slowly. 'I'm happy,' he said. 'Happy. It's the first time I've felt really happy for months. Months. That's all, my love. Just happy.' He drained his glass, smiled at her, put the glass down and then, like an old *boxwallah Koi Hai* in the Bengal Club he actually clapped his hands together a few times, and Janki Nath appeared, and smiling. Fixed.

'Same again, my love?' Croon said, in too low a voice for Janki Nath to hear from where he stood near the bar, poised to pour for the sahib who knew how to fix things.

'Well — just this one — then I —'

'Then you must go. All right, my love.' He signalled to Janki Nath, who went into the bar to pour the drinks.

'We stopped clapping hands for a servant here some time ago, by the way,' she said. 'It's — you know — *now*, I mean — '

'It's stopped for you, my love. But for me it's an imperial thrill, a colonial experience. I was a deprived child, you know, and used to read about all this, clapping hands for a servant and so on. It's thrilling. It works.' He pretended contrition, shame, appearing to shrink, and said, 'You're not going to deny me such a small pleasure after waiting most of my life, surely?' He smiled at her and stroked her hand again.

'Were you really a deprived child?' she asked, amused by his contritional charade.

'Don't get me started on that,' he said intensely, still stroking her hand. She liked the way he withdrew his hand as Janki Nath appeared with the drinks. When the servant had gone she decided to let him put his hand back on hers again. My God, she thought, I suppose it's all right. He's happy. So am I? I mean, what harm? Just this one drink and then finish. She struggled to get her breath.

'So you fixed this,' she said. 'How?'

'I have the run of this place at night,' he told her. 'That's between you and me. This marvellous library you've got here. I slipped Janki Nath there a small bundle and I come in here about midnight, or when everybody's gone, and get down to reading and research.'

'Really?' What a worker he was. And a fixer. 'You didn't take long about it, did you?' It explained his confidence when they had arrived earlier at the blacked out club, and there were the three knocks he had made on the door. She saw now that the three knocks had been arranged. Not for her, for reading and research. He was slowly squeezing her hand as he talked, and she shivered, had to draw hard to get enough breath again. Weird really being able to actually *see* the process, and feel it too, watch it happening in her, to her. She felt anger, fear, and joy as well. She must not allow herself to be played with.

'You what?' she said. 'What's that you said just now?'

His eyes were full of reverence. There was no other word for it. Reverence. His big grey, luminous eyes were looking at her with reverence.

201

'I said it's all fixed, everything. Tonight. Us.' He lifted his glass and said, solemnly, 'I name this ship "Us", and here's to Us, and all who sail in Us.'

She could not help laughing again. He was making her feel wonderful. He was such fun. Fun!

'Aren't you going to lift your glass too, my love?' he said, a hint of readiness to be hurt in his tender eyes, his glass held ready for the ridiculous toast.

'You must not call me your love, do you hear?' she said. She could hear the hopeless attempt to be firm failing in her voice. She started laughing, and lifted her glass. They drank and immediately he was serious again, tense, leaning forward, his hand on hers.

He watched her struggling slightly to get her breath again, and he said, 'That's it. I know. I've got it too. I know. It's all there, isn't it? Everything. Have another try. Deeper. That's it. That's it.' She had managed to get enough breath. She stared at him, angry again, yet touched.

'Maybe you should *direct* the film,' she said. 'Not just write it. I suppose this is your "act", is it? This is the way you carry on with all the women you meet. Yes? When was the last time you did all this? I mean the last time you were so *happy*? You've got a hell of a nerve, haven't you?' She was picking up spirit, the will to struggle. 'Who do you think you are?'

'I know who I am,' he told her, stroking her hand, smiling, quite unmoved by her challenging words. 'Have you ever been in the States? America? You're going to love it. Listen, about the story — '

'I must go.' But her curiosity was too strong. Maybe just one more drink. She looked at her glass and as she looked up again he was holding up two fingers for Janki Nath. He smiled at her. The reverent look was back in his eyes. Just an act, all of it? Just good acting? She felt afraid then, stupidly afraid. She did not want it to be just good acting, just part of the film business, part of the script for a swift screw. No, no, it could not be. He seemed to be watching her think all this. 'I don't know why you're worrying so much, my love,' he said softly. 'And what's the rush? Why be so jumpy? Just enjoy yourself. After all, we've both been waiting all our lives for this evening. Can't you see that? Why fight it, darling? Relax. Relax.'

Now that was too bloody much altogether, she knew it, yet

202

she was unable to reply, unable to think of the right thing to say back to all that impudent assumption. Anyway there was no need, for he went straight on. 'Have you weighed me up, yet, darling? I mean socially, *you* know.' He was smiling, playful. 'School, background, Mater or Mum, Pater or Dad kind of stuff. I mean do you think I'm safe to know out here, even though the empire's gone and all that? It's still vital, isn't it? *Have* you weighed me up?'

Yes, she had. She could feel heat in her face, the pink rising into it, and she saw him watching it happen, his grin genial, his hand gently kneading hers. He took it away again as Janki Nath came and placed the drinks before them. He looked at Janki Nath.

'Go and have a kip now, as usual, Janki Nath. Sleep, eh? Will you trust me to pour one more drink on my own? Okay?'

'Certainly, Sahib.' He smiled at them both, bowed, and left.

'Eating out of your hand, isn't he?' she said. She could feel the heat of the blush still in her face. She struggled with the anger and shame she felt about having been weighing him up, as he had put it. There was only one way out of it, brutally, and swiftly.

'What do you think I am?' she said tartly. 'A *pukka mem-sahib*? I don't care what you are. Why should I? You're a scriptwriter. That'll do, won't it?' But apparently not. Before she could stop herself, she said, 'Tell me about yourself.' She smiled, winningly. 'Tell me about being deprived. Were you deprived? Seriously?'

As he began to talk she knew what she had done. She had asked him to unload his sack of rubbish into her lap: his life, his mess, his collected junk of the journey of his life up to now.

*   *   *

Bingham yawned and stretched in his armchair, grinned across at the Maharajah.

'Are you going to sit on and wait, Chan, seriously?'

'What would you do if you were me, Tim? I mean if you loved Megan the way I do?'

There were plenty of times when Bingham found it difficult

to assess his friend's mood. Was he truly in love with Megan or was this just one more game?

'I'm afraid I'll lose her, Tim. Honestly. I'm afraid. She does mean a great deal to me. But — but then you can't make a woman feel for you what she doesn't feel, can you?'

'You've got it, Chan. That's right. All you can do is wait and see.' It was the best he could think of just now.

'You mean you think she'll tell me. How would it go? The words for that, I mean. Let's see.' He did a sketch of Megan saying the right words to him. ' "Well, Chan dear, it's no go, I'm afraid. Roger's walked into my life. You know the way these things happen. If you'd shown a bit more interest, a little more aggression, showed you really cared, well — it might have been different. But Roger came driving in and swept me up. Sorry, Chan." ' He looked hard at Bingham. 'Something like that, you think, Tim?'

Bingham nodded. 'If she's going to give you the news I'd say you've got it about right.'

'You don't think I've overdone it a little, perhaps, the wording?'

The Maharajah was showing a little acid, Bingham thought. 'So you're going to sit on here and wait?' he said.

'Yes.'

'Well, I'll pour this one.'

'Yes. Let's get drunk. Why not? I'm suffering, although I know you don't think I am. But I am. Bugger it. I am.'

In between laconic and sometimes melancholy statements about what each felt, and what the Maharajah feared and hoped, about Megan, the latter was reaching for thoughts about what it all might mean, living, a subject which, after a few drinks, both men would always tackle once again.

Now, as the drinks were poured the Maharajah said, 'So you think we can never know, eh? How did you put it just now? About reason?'

'Reason?' Bingham replied, settling down in his armchair again. 'Nothing world-shaking. I simply said that human reason isn't enough. It's deficient, that's all, I mean about this attempt to define God, or rather to *know* God. It's no use applying *our* human feelings to the problem. You finish up talking about Him, He. You cannot imagine the unknowable, that's all. The Muslims know that. Or rather they accept it.

204

But even they have to use He, Him, probably because they cannot dare say It. But they do know he is — there I go — he . . . ' They both laughed.

'Go on. Try again,' said the Maharajah. 'I can feel something in my mind — like a feather — like an itch — go on.'

'They do know God is beyond everything. They revere Jesus, and his mother, Mary, for them he is a prophet, and they expect him again just before the end of the world. Jesus will face and destroy the *Dajjal* — the sort of Antichrist — but — they cannot and will not accept Jesus as the son of God. To a Muslim such a thought is horrifying, blasphemous. God for them — '

'I tell you God may actually be the universe itself, with some kind of unimaginable mind powering it all, and it will never be known, never be solved, Tim. That's my latest anyway.'

'You may be right.'

'Cheers.'

'Cheers.'

'O Universe,' the Maharajah intoned quietly, solemnly. 'I am but a fragment broken off you for a time. Drinking down here with my friend, another fellow similarly bothered about what it all means. Anyway here I am, O Universe, behaving stupidly with jealousy, fear of losing somebody, and sitting up waiting for an American to come back to me with the bad news, that news always waiting in the wings to come on scene. I just thought I'd mention it, O Universe, so you might spare a thought and drop a little help to me. Her name's Megan as a matter of fact' — he started laughing and Bingham, laughing too, said, 'Give height, weight, general description, etcetera.' Then they were silent and the tick of the clock in a far corner of the enormous room became louder.

'Life!' said the Maharajah. 'This bloody life!'

'Yes. Life. A short, badly arranged holiday between two eternities,' said Bingham. 'But still — a holiday.'

'With no guide. No map. No plan.' With mocking jollity the Maharajah sat up and went on. 'And think about all those who never got here for this holiday, are never going to get here. We've been lucky.' He remembered. 'So far, sometimes, lucky. Do I sound drunk yet?'

Bingham shook his head. 'A little good news might do it.

The booze on its own won't. Not tonight anyway.'

'That fellow, Koltz, do you know what he's doing right now?'

'No. Tell me.'

'He's with them both. He's found them. I won't go into what he found them doing. I'll be merciful there. No. He's acting. He's playing me. The state I was in. What I said. I only hope he knows I mean what I said. If that writer of his is shown how to open the safe, then the film's off. And a few other things are off too.'

'Oh? Like what, Chan?'

'I haven't made my mind up yet. But I definitely feel things stirring, coming to a head. That's all I'll say for now.'

Still reclining in his deep chair, glass in hand, Bingham showed nothing of the slight sense of alarm he was feeling now. 'I hadn't guessed you felt it quite so — desperately. You've told her?'

'Yes. I've told her, and not long before Macaroon Sahib walked onto the scene tonight. Desperately? Well, yes, desperately. But is any woman on earth worth that kind of nonsensical emotion? That's the question, isn't it?'

'And what's the answer?'

'The answer's yes. Every time.' They laughed for some time about that, until the Maharajah sighed. 'I can't be bothered with the life I'm living here for much longer, Tim. It's a pain in the arse, quite frankly. I've thought it all over. If I could live here with Megan I could take an interest.'

'What did she say to you?'

'Just about nothing — wrapped up in a lot of words, though. Oh yes, she said — I'm buggered if I can remember, it was so woolly. It felt like "nothing doing" when it was added up. Something about needing time, being convalescent, getting used to being without her tennis partner, needing time.' He looked keenly at Bingham now. 'Tell me straight. You watched it. You don't miss a thing, I know that. So you saw it, didn't you? She fell for that bugger tonight like a ton of bricks. It's true, isn't it?' As if he felt Bingham was going to deny this, or prevaricate, he almost shouted the next words. 'It's true, isn't it? You saw it. Correct?'

'There's one hope,' said Bingham deftly, though without any urgency. Like a starving man before a crust the Maharajah seized the bait, the hope.

'Oh, yes? Go on. What?'

'He'll talk too much.'

Disappointed, irritated, the Maharajah poured himself another drink, keeping his eyes on Bingham and then waving the bottle. As Bingham went over to take the bottle from him the Maharajah snapped at him.

'Well, go on. Talk too much? What — ?'

'I listened to him tonight. Once he starts talking you've practically got to brandish a revolver to get a word in with him. And he's good, though he goes on too long. Far too long. He's listening to everything he's saying, too. And he loves it. There's a good chance that if he's spent an hour or two with Megan tonight, and she's let him talk, then he's probably talked himself off.'

'Talked himself off?' The Maharajah laughed sadly. 'Maybe. But of course, what I want is for Megan to come to me and tell me she cannot live without me any longer, hates Croon, she realizes that now, and there's only me in the world for her. Well, thanks, Tim, I mean for that consolation, about him talking too much. But I know that you know what happened here tonight. The fallout is all around us. Cheers.'

'Cheers.'

'What about yourself, your own diving board? Razia in Delhi. Are you going to dive or not?'

To the Maharajah's astonishment Bingham shook his head and said, 'No. I'm afraid not. I'm still European enough to feel it's not fair to her — '

'Too obscene, you mean, age and all that?' said the Maharajah sardonically.

'Yes, too obscene,' Bingham agreed, quite unprovoked. 'She's very beautiful, and too young for me. In a few years I'll probably be mumbling in a wheelchair — '

'That'll be the day. You must send me a telegram about it when it happens.' The Maharajah became scathing. He seemed outraged by his old friend's petty decision about this important matter. He pointed his finger at him. His eyes were fierce. 'I will not sit here and listen to this kind of British decency, this — this — '

'Cowardly temporizing? Geriatric evasiveness? Selfish prevarication?'

'You haven't definitely made up your mind, Tim? I don't believe it. I want to know.'

He smiled, as Bingham rose from his armchair and began to pace the room; then, unable to control it, he started laughing. Bingham did not join him this time, but went on pacing.

* * *

It was half past three now and from time to time Megan would break into Croon's steady monologue, during which he had described his early life, the slum world, his wonderful mother, his growing rage and resentment, the struggle for education, the first understanding that he had some kind of talent, the frustrations concerning this. During this talk which had fascinated her, moved, stirred, depressed, elated, harrowed, and now was beginning to irritate and bore her, her own buried social angers were awakened so that she began to vie with him about who had gone through most to get where they had got. She would cut in and exclaim, fired up by the half dozen whiskies she had drunk, 'So what? You wanted to blow up the House of Lords or something?' These brief, provocative intrusions availed her nothing, for Croon went on in the same steady, and spellbinding, way, which was what she was trying to fight, to break down. He still stroked her hand, still stared reverently into her eyes, though sometimes his eyes burned when he recalled some particular wounding or shaming moment from the early struggle.

It was his delightful physical presence, she knew, and his warm, deep, soft voice which poured all over her, into her bones, which kept her there, listening. But now there was still no sign that he might end this saga, enchanting until an hour ago, of the will to win through, the will to climb up out of the dismal disneyland of soot and brick and poverty, 'the zoo,' as he called it, 'in which the working class had waited so long for a bathtub into which to put the coal.'

She cut in again to say, 'My, what a boring Communist you could have made, eh?' No result. He went on, told her again about his target. Two million dollars, come what may. 'I don't give a bugger what they put in my way, that's the target, and it will be reached. Only in America. I love America. It's light years beyond Europe in what I happen to care about, which is mass entertainment, good cheap clothing and food, realism about living, and the crazy idea that it is possible to be comfortable here on earth without feeling guilty about it.' Finished? No chance. This time she wanted to order the drinks. He said sardonically that it was getting late. Late?

'Late nothing,' she said. 'No you listen to me for a minute. This mother of yours — '

'I've told you,' he said, pre-emptive as always. 'Yes, I've got a mother-fixation. It's a change anyway, isn't it, these days? You love your mother, don't you? Is that wrong?'

'Will you let me speak?' she said. At this, in the sudden silence which followed, they heard Janki Nath, asleep on the floor behind the bar up the room, utter a loud, strangled snore. Megan laughed. Croon went on, this time about how, with each bundle of dollars he put into the bank, his rage diminished. 'I know that's contemptible, materialistic,' he said, 'but it's better than selling the *Daily Worker* on some slum street corner and waiting for the millennium.'

'Now I *need* a drink,' she said. She got up and went to the bar, and spoke in a low cooing voice to Janki Nath. The servant got up smiling good-naturedly at her, and began to pour the drinks. Just then they heard a car careering down the road towards the club. It stopped.

'That may be Chan?' Croon suggested, smiling thinly. 'Or should I say Chandu?'

She was coming back from the bar towards him. She stopped.

'You're going to spoil it, you know, talking like that,' she said. 'Can't you hold your drink or something?'

He smiled at her. 'Listen,' he said. They heard footsteps outside, then a hammering on the front door of the club.

'Don't be scared, darling,' said Croon. 'It may be the secret police but we're both card-carrying members, in our hearts. So we're safe.' To Janki Nath he called, 'Go and see who that is, Janki Nath. We're not here. You're alone. Understand?'

Somebody was shouting through the letter-box of the club front door.

'That's Ted Koltz,' Croon said. 'And he's tied one on by the sound of him. Must have run out of booze at the palace.'

Against her will, for she felt scared, apprehensive, she did not know which or why, she admired Croon's coolness. There was a lot to be said for him, even though he had swamped her for hours with his quiet and steady oration.

'Tied one on?' she said.

'Smashed. Drunk,' he said.

209

Outside, after listening to Janki Nath's obviously lying statements through the letter box, Ted Koltz, after much fumbling, pushed a shower of dollar bills through the letter box opening. Janki Nath picked them up, counted them, and opened the door.

Ted Koltz stood in the doorway, staring into Janki Nath's cool, amused eyes. 'I like loyalty,' he said thickly. 'I like it. But not tonight. I know they're here. My friends. Right?'

Janki Nath pointed the way, then followed Koltz into the bar, disappearing in a silent glide into the library nearby, where he counted the dollars again.

From where they sat at their table Croon and Megan saw Koltz stumble across the mat in the doorway at the end of the bar, stop, then spread his arms wide as if to embrace them.

He was so relieved to see them both dressed, both out of bed, sitting there harmlessly together in the soft yellow light of the table lamp between them, that he had difficulty in finding the right words.

'My God, you kids, am I happy to see you two.' He came unsteadily down the room, smiling, his arms still spread, then stopped and beamed on them both. 'You been here all night. Right? Since you left the palace. Right?'

'Sure. Why?' said Croon. 'You want a drink?'

Annoyed, Megan managed to hold her tongue and watched the two men. She could see the relief, the joy in fact, shining behind Ted's glasses. 'Goddam it,' he said exuberantly. 'I've missed you both. I can't help it, Megan. I've got to do it.' He came forward, bent and kissed her on the cheek, then, still bent forward, smiled blearily into her face. 'You've been talking story, hey?' He straightened up and looked admiringly at Croon. 'Great, kid. Great.' Still enjoying his great sense of relief he threw his arms into the air. 'I'm so happy, my God, I'm going to do some soft-shoe.' He went into an uncertain piece of old-time vaudeville dance, causing Megan to forget her annoyance at his anxiety as to whether they had been sitting here safely all evening. She and Croon clapped when Koltz finished his little performance and Croon stood up.

'You want red-eye, pardner?' he said to Koltz.

Koltz pretended to draw two guns and then pointed the two imaginary guns at Croon, swaying, smiling. 'Yeah! Make it whiskey, kid, straight, and real fast, I gotta bank to rob before sundown, you hear me?'

'Comin' up fast. Park your ass, pardner.' Croon went to the bar and Koltz pulled up a chair and sat down near Megan. She smiled at him and he smiled back. She patted his face, and sure enough he took her hand and pressed it uncertainly against his lips. When she withdrew her hand he said, 'I haven't felt so happy since my second wife left me.' He turned his head and called to Croon. 'You hear that, Roger? I'm so happy to see you two I could sing a Jewish hymn, if I could remember one.'

'I'll write you one,' Croon called back.

'What's been worrying you, Ted?' Megan asked him in a quiet, disarming tone. 'Do you always have to know where he is?' She flashed a look towards Croon, still smiling at Koltz. It seemed to sober him up for a moment or two. He smiled back at her, his eyes suddenly shrewd.

'You've got to remember, Megan,' he said, 'that I've got no friends in this town. I know nobody. You're not mad at me, are you, for turning up like this?'

'Not a bit,' she said airily. 'Not a bit, Ted.' She patted his cheek again, forcing back the fierce urge to slap it.

She was glad he had come and stopped Croon's monologue, and she was angry with Croon for having gone on too long and so having broken his own spell. She no longer felt like having a brief, wild, secret affair with him, but she knew he could spellbind her again, after a decent interval, say a few days. A few years?

'A whiskey,' she called in reply to Croon's question. 'My last.'

'Me too,' Croon called to her. 'One more last one.'

Koltz was wondering how he could get to a telephone and call the palace. He was thinking hard about this, but smiling, laughing, as he took the glass of whiskey from Croon.

'What time did you leave the palace, Ted?' Croon sat down and put his elbows on the table. Megan watched Croon closely, wondering if he too had guessed that Koltz had been sent on an errand by the Maharajah. She wondered if she had guessed right.

'Not long after you two left,' Koltz said. 'When I couldn't find you at the hotel I waited and had a few drinks. Then somebody told me about this club — ' He faltered, feeling Megan's hostility.

'Did the Maharajah enjoy the evening, do you think?

Megan interrupted, antagonized by his evasions. 'Was he up-set that we went off to work on the story?' This caused Koltz even more discomfort and, pehaps to help him, Croon — us-ing the special voice he used for monologue, she now noticed — began to intone again.

' "The Club At The World's End." How about that for a title, eh? A man telling his life to a beautiful woman, telling of his hopes and disappointments, his plans for the world that's waiting for him out there —'

'Which consists of two million dollars,' said Megan quietly; but nothing, it seemed, could provoke Croon, or alter his ple-asure in himself. His elbows on the table, his drink in his right hand, eyes flicking from the nervous Ted to the calm-faced Megan, he went on. 'And all the time at the back of the mind the film story is taking shape. I've had some great ideas, Ted. But later, hey? I was telling Megan about my particular jour-ney — my journey to here —'

'He tell you about him and Yalta, Teheran, the war, how he nearly resigned from the war?' Koltz asked Megan, and when she looked puzzled, added, 'Yeah. I guess that was the cross-roads for Roger.' He looked at Roger. 'Tell it again, Roger. How you were in Germany and then you saw the light —'

'Yes,' Croon, without altering his soft, deep voice, took up the theme offered by Koltz, his eyes now on Megan. 'I joined the war for freedom. Like every other idiot, remember? But it was in Germany towards the end, when it was made obvious that Russia was to have, given to her, what she'd waited cen-turies to get — central Europe, including the very country the war was started to help free, Poland — that I wrote out my resignation —'

'Resignation?' She could not keep the irritation out of her voice. She sounded like a memsahib about military loyalties, but never mind.

'Yes — ' He had resigned from the war. He had written out his reasons, quite a short note, and had taken it in and handed it to the colonel in charge of his Field Security unit. A very decent fellow called McCabe who, to Croon's surprise, agreed with every word of it. 'We all knew,' said Croon, 'that American forward units were already being cheered on the outskirts of Prague, but had received sudden orders to turn round and withdraw completely. Russian was to have all Czechoslovakia — for a start. The Yanks withdrew immediately. Me? I had no further interest in the war. And my colonel agreed.' The colonel had set it all out there and then, Croon's resignation from World War Two in front of him. Croon could take his case to Eisenhower, say, but what could Ike say? He could tell Croon what Ike would say. 'No dice, son, unless you want to sign on for World War Three right now and do another ten years in uniform, and finish up maybe in the Urals someplace. I cannot accept this resignation or its implications that we start freeing central Europe from the Russians after we've just given it to them. My orders are to let them have central Europe, and that's it.' Then there was Montgomery, Croon's colonel had suggested. He could go with his resignation to Montgomery, who would explain that, given total command of every man, weapon and vehicle, every 'plane and ship, he was willing to hit Russia for six right there and then, and free not only central Europe, but Soviet Russia as well; but meanwhile Lieutenant Croon could consider himself under close arrest under section forty of the Army Act. Colonel McCabe had then sugested Croon might go to old Blood-and-Guts himself, General Patton. 'And you know what you can expect there, Croon? Patton would just slap you across the face and call you a yellow bastard and you'd finish up with the Purple Heart later.'

Ted Koltz was shaking with laughter and watching Megan, wating for her to laugh, but she would not even smile.

'So you didn't go through with your resignation?' said Megan coldly.

Croon shook his head wearily. 'I soldiered on. I — '

'It's this playboy thing, isn't it?' she said. 'We all heard about how you'd declared yourself to be a playboy in the hotel register. If you'd really felt commitment you would have gone through with your resignation and been court-martialled, for your convictions. That's what I think. What about your early sufferings, when you were eighteen and reading Marx? Even then you wouldn't commit yourself, would you? You were drawn to Communism by all the injustice round you but you held back, you didn't commit yourself. Doesn't that tell you anything?'

Would nothing pierce the thick hide of this handsome, hypnotic, smiling personality she knew she should protect herself against at all costs? For Croon was smiling at her, nodding agreement.

213

'True, true. You've put your finger on it, Megan, my darling,' he said. He looked at Koltz. 'She's got a hell of a mind, you know, Ted. Like a searchlight.' He looked at Megan again, reverence back in his gaze. 'The fact is I took no more interest in the war,' he went on. 'The Russians had won it. Once we'd got Hitler married to Eva Braun, and Eva shot him — that's my opinion, anyway. She'd wanted him to marry her for years, and when the game was up he did it, and probably, knowing his image as the Wolf from Linz had been shattered forever by the bourgeois act of marriage, he wasn't able to finish the job with his pistol.' Ted was laughing so loud that Croon had to raise his spellbinding voice slightly. Megan kept her calm, serious expression, watching Croon's face, listening hard, studying him. 'Once that was all done the war was over. Commitment? I've never had any commitment, once I'd thought it all out carefully, except to myself, just like all my masters used to have. Money, comfort, freedom, the right to personal choice. Freedom is money, but lots of it, Megan. When I was going through hell in the thirties, when they were trying to grind me down — '

'You've told me all that,' Megan said.

'Let him tell it, Megan,' Koltz said kindly, hand on her shoulder.

'I've heard it all,' she told him, still quiet. 'He's — '

'So have I, kid,' said Ted. 'It's a great story of struggle, of a guy who's determined to win and finds at last the arena he can fight and win in — America. I've heard it six times, so — '

'Six times?' she said, showing reaction now, amazement.

'Yeah. Over a period of two years, that is — and I still — '

'So why don't I want to hear it twice?' she said. Nasty. Watch it, put it right. But why? Put it right. *Now!* 'I've only just heard it, you see.' Her voice was shaky. Pretty lame, the whole thing. It was the confusion she was feeling about the deep physical attraction she felt for Croon, even now, and the disappointment and boredom his unshakeable self-satisfaction had inflicted on her. But six times? She looked at Koltz, curious. Surely he must be putting the needle into Croon by saying such an extraordinary thing, disguising it as a recommendation that she listen to Croon's story for a second time. Yes, even Croon felt something might be wrong.

'Six times, Ted?' he asked. 'Six?'

Koltz nodded. She could read nothing in his face. 'Six,

214

maybe seven times, Roger,' he said. 'It's a movie, I tell you. A story of struggle.' Then he remembered something. He sat up straight, began searching through the pockets of his suit, saying, 'I just remembered. The guy at the hotel desk gave me a letter for you, said it came in by hand, some English guy living here.' He found the letter and handed it to Croon, who, when he had opened it and read it, laid it down on the table and looked at Megan.

'It's from that — that nutcase, Tone,' he said. 'I met him a couple of times in the club here. You know him, Megan? You must do. He *is* slightly crazy, isn't he?'

'Well — he did have a bad nervous breakdown just after the war. He *is* very odd. Is it about the film?'

Koltz had risen. 'Where's the can, Roger?' he said.

'I'll show you,' Croon said. 'Come on.'

Yes. She watched them go. Two men in need of a swift, quiet talk together, while making the camphor-balls dance. When they had gone she picked up the letter Croon had left on the table, read it once quickly, and then again, more slowly this time.

'Christ,' she murmured as she put it back in the envelope, then looked at her tiny gold wrist-watch. It had been some time since Saleema had been able to make a reasonable contact with her bothered mind, but she heard her now, and let her speak. That hidden, age-old, all-knowing spirit which lives in every woman's heart, and which but waits for consultation, whispered to her now. She could hear it plainly, warning her. 'Be apprehensive, yes. Strange things are trying to happen. Control them. Be firm. The burning love you have sought so long — is it that which now looms over you? Take care.' For it may be Mister Wrong at last, and is Miss Wrong ready for him?

Not very funny really, she thought miserably, her mind running over Tone's strange letter again, but Croon kept coming in, stepping across her thoughts. She was imagining him talking to other women, talking even his mesmerizing, and finally numbing, autobiographical set-pieces, and was worried again to find she felt jealousy, pain even. Truly humiliating, and barely credible, yet there it was, a fact. It had to be passion, that convulsion of what had until recently been called the soul, a raging fever of the senses — still on a leash though — oh yes, well under control — so far. It had to be

215

passion which was trying to distort her determined will to stay herself.

Saleema talking again? Couldn't say, could barely breathe.

CHAPTER 18

It was only after he had written and had had delivered what he thought of as his 'two masterpieces', one of them a letter to Croon and the other to the Maharajah, that Tone told his wife about them. They were at breakfast on the verandah of the house which had been in the possession of Iris's family, the Woodberrys, since the days of Colonel Woodberry.

About to spoon up the last of the reddish-orange pulp of her slice of papaya, Iris closed her eyes and dropped her spoon. She pressed her hands over her eyes and murmured, 'Oh, my God! My God!'

She got up from the table and wandered about, her hands still pressed to her eyes, then stopped, and in a choking, barely audible voice said, 'Oh, Freddy, Freddy, you're such a dreadful man. Are you mad — or just wicked? Wicked.'

Tone, his breakfast finished, had just lit a cheroot. He impatiently waved the cloud of smoke away from in front of his eyes and said, 'Just as I expected. Drama, drama. Always drama. Sit down, Iris, there's a good girl.' He used the same understanding parental manner when dealing with what he called her waywardness as she used towards him and his endless struggle to achieve what he called 'common, ordinary, human justice'. On one occasion he had defined his quietly megalomaniac determination to achieve 'recognition', 'recompense', 'a hearing at least', as 'understandably paranoid'. He knew he was paranoid and could explain just why, could chart the journey of failures and, at great length, would sometimes clarify for Iris the workings of the fascinating mechanism of the 'test to destruction'.

Being tested to destruction was how Tone now saw, and saw clearly, what Life was trying to do to him. It would never succeed. Never. He would survive, and would win, he would not go so far as to say 'undamaged', but undestroyed. Life would not win this strange, you might almost say 'occult', series of battles, spread over many years and made up of a series of curious misfortunes and disasters, and with never a stroke of fortune, never a victory. Even Iris had had to admit it seemed mysterious, his steady and unremitting bad luck, but she would never agree to see it as he had begun to see it, as part of an almost satanic plan by something or other — 'out there' — to wreck and eventually destroy him. He had spend many years proving to her and to many others, but mainly (it now seemed to her and these others) to himself, that there was no God, no divine plan and so on; so, she wondered, how could there now be anything 'out there', with this evil plan to destroy him? It could only mean that, at last, he was ceasing to be merely eccentric, and was approaching madness. Yet he could sit there at the breakfast table, calm, smoking his cheroot, while she sat with her hands over her eyes, and feared to ask about what he had said in his letters to Mr Croon and to the Maharajah, though she knew the subject was certainly the Woodberry manuscript. He could sit there and, as always, try and change the subject, this time by a commentary on the phenomenon, increasingly reported in the press and on the radio, of these Unidentified Flying Objects. As she half-listened to him she saw that he was again, though tentatively and carefully, throwing out hints that they might be tied up in some way with the mysterious 'force' which seemed to lie behind the series of disasters which had made up his life since the end of the war.

' — an accumulated force of sheer evil, maybe,' he was saying now, 'sent up from billions of human beings over the millennia, thoughts, acts, everything filthy and mean you can think of, and now at last manifesting themselves in these apparitions in the sky. To hell with creatures and flying machines from outer space. Nothing of the sort. Simply the piling up of millions of years of sheer bloody-mindedness down here and at last taking shape in the sky. And — acting upon my life. You understand, Iris? I'm supersensitive to them — and there must be many others like me — being driven up shit-creek year after year by this force of evil which cannot be otherwise explained. *That* could be the thing "out there", whatever the force may be behind it, which is trying to destroy me. The testing is over as far as I'm concerned, and I've survived it, survived destruction. You've admitted yourself that the horrible bad luck I've been having for about eight years now is far more than bad luck. It's a plan. Nothing else.

A plan to bring me down and end me up in a bloody strait-jacket.' He laughed. It was a short, gay laugh, that of a man who has seen and overcome all that has been brought against him. 'Yes, Iris. There had to be an effect, of course, and that's paranoia. Quite understandable, and with time, eradicable. But that's all. They've tried to drive me insane, they've thrown everything at me they could think of, but I haven't broken, my nerve has not failed me, and I can still see straight.' He paused. 'What are you looking at me like that for?'

'Like what, Freddy?'

'Like a bloody madwoman.'

'Tell me, first, the letter to the Maharajah, what you said in it. Don't dodge anything, *please*. Tell me.'

'You know damn well what I've said in it. We've talked about if often enough lately —'

'*You've* talked about it, Freddy. You. What did you say in the letter to the Maharajah?'

'I've called for a meeting, first with this bloody self-confessed playboy, Croon. About the film, and the *real* story of what went on here in your great-great-grandfather's time.' He grinned genially at her, and as usual when her ancestor Colonel Woodberry was mentioned, said, 'That very able and virile old boy who lived in a time when men were really men. Yes, Iris, the time has come, as I told you the other morning, to kill several birds with one stone. That is, get it all out in the open, publish the colonel's book with the true story in it, make some money, and get in on this film caper. I've put it to Croon, and I've laid it all out for the Maharajah.' His cheroot clenched in his teeth, he rubbed his hands together in satisfaction. 'I've put it to the bugger straight — let's end one and a half centuries of hypocritical, bloody nonsense. In other words I've told him we're going to publish, and that the real story of events here at the end of the eighteenth century can then be used in the film. After all, who cares now who screwed who, or hanged or mutilated who a hundred and fifty years ago? And —'

'I care. I care.' She shouted the words, something she seldom did these days. Interested, he watched her eyes as he puffed on his cheroot.

'That's understandable — once, Iris. But there's nobody around now who gives a damn that you've got a touch of the tar-brush. That you're related to the Maharajah. In fact that gives it a touch of glamour — for some people these days — you know what I mean. The British have gone. You've even got this bugger Bingham in Indian dress now, so why can't *you* wear a sari if you want to? You have a right to do so, in fact. I could get used to it quite quickly, I imagine, as long as the book makes money at last. *I* need the money. You don't. I cannot go on living off your money any longer. I'm soaked in research on that period since you gave me the Woodberry manuscript and — '

'I did *not* give it to you. I loaned it to you to read, and you stole it from me.' There were tears in her eyes. 'I should never have let you see it. But you never stopped until I gave it to you to read — '; overcome by tears of remorse and anger she rose and hurried from the verandah.

Tone sat on, smoking. Bloody women, Christ it was impossible to have any kind of rational conversation with them, about anything. He wondered how the Maharajah would take his letter. Lot of work gone into that letter. About twenty bloody drafts during the last two days. But it was just about perfect, the final draft. Real meaning nicely veiled, almost buried under the bullshit about historical document, contribution to the story of the eighteenth-century turmoil of India, ancient customs now forgotten, picture of a forgotten age, exotic, passionate, stark. And — perfect film! Everything. Love, tenderness, sadism, cavalry, bravery to point of unbelievability, magnificence of Indian dress of the period, clash of cultures, and that incredible princess. And below it all, swimming under it like a grey shark, but hinted at in that sentence he had written and rewritten so many times, and ending ' — as you know, my wife, being the last of the Woodberry line, and now bearing another surname, my own, the fact that you, your Highness, and your family, are related to her, will never be apparent to the reader of the book, when it is published,' below it all, the threat. There had been great temptation to go on and add, 'the fact that Colonel Woodberry, the forgotten military hero of this state, was the father, through Princess Zarina, of the Maharajah from whom both yourself and my wife, therefore, descend, can be of no interest to the world at large in these days, even if it were to be deduced, which is impossible now.' Yes, Maharajah Chandra Gupta Woodberry. Knocked quite a hole in the Rajput warrior facade, put like that, come to think of it. But *did* the Maharajah know about that interesting link in the genealogical chain? Iris was absolutely certain he did not, could not know. So just that fleeting hint about the common descent of Iris and the Maharajah could be enough to get the noble cheque-book out and resume the pension which stupid, idealistic, young Iris had so impulsively cancelled by her letter to the Maharajah's father just before World War Two. He had weighed it all up from every possible angle, before writing and sending off his final draft. He was certain the Maharajah would pay not to have the Woodberry manuscript published.

Tone was so excited as he thought over what he had at last found the courage to do, the gamble was so considerable, that he felt the need of a large Scotch. He was pleased too that Iris had fallen for the stuff about publishing the manuscript and getting in on the film caper with the real story contained in the manuscript. Main thing was that the Maharajah get the message quickly, resume paying the rightful pension — for continued silence — in fact a resumption of common, ordinary, human justice.

His mind fondled and inspected each stage of his letter to the Maharajah again, searching obsessively for any blatancy, any distinct threat of blackmail, but no, no, it was a masterpiece in every way. All that was evident in it was his, Tone's, care for history, his wish for the film people to know the real facts of the story they wished to film, and, thoughtful, casual, and sensitive, his officerly and gentlemanly assurance that the blood relationship between Iris and the Maharajah would never be deduced from the manuscript, when published.

He lit another cheroot and then went over to the side table and poured himself a large whiskey. He had had to make up his mind about one important decision, before he had written down that long pondered sentence about the common ancestry of Iris and the Maharajah. Whatever the Maharajah's reaction he would never allow the Maharajah to see the manuscript. If the Maharajah dismissed the matter, which was very unlikely indeed, and said 'go ahead and publish', he would do so, but only after a more strongly worded warning to him about what was in the manuscript. He frowned and thought it all over again swiftly. Was it clear enough, the implication, that the bugger's real name was Chandra Gupta Woodberry? It was, and he thought it was, the book would never be published, but the pension would be resumed. But . . . . His mind felt exhausted. He tried to go over it all again, but he was not up to it. He sat down at the breakfast table again and drank some whiskey.

He was so deep in tired vacancy he did not notice Iris's return until he saw her sitting opposite him at the table again.

Tear-stained face. Pink eyes. Accusing look. Grim. Christ, why couldn't she show some character, some determination, some loyalty to him now that the decision had been taken? He had told her a hundred times, once he had got over the shock, which had taken some months after reading the bloody manuscript, that he could not care less about her touch of the tar-brush, for after all it was not as if she descended from some British Tommy's cast-off sweeper woman. No. She was descended from a beautiful Muslim woman who had become a legend for her —

'Is it too late to get the letters back?' Iris spoke quietly, resignedly, almost wanly, hopelessly.

'I don't want them back,' he said. 'Even if I could get them back.'

The fear and apprehension she felt showed in her eyes as she looked accusingly at him.

'Self-destruction,' she said, almost dreamily. 'Test to self-destruction,' and tears appeared in her eyes again.

Startled, Tone said, 'You what?'

'Test to self-destruction,' she repeated in the same way, as if talking in her sleep. 'That's all your life has been, Freddy, all of it. Don't you know that? And now you've done it. We'll lose this house. I gave up the pension, yes, but the old Maharajah assured me I could keep this house forever. He was a good old gentleman.' She sobbed now, still looking at him. 'Oh, you are a terrible man, Freddy, a terrible man.'

Christ. Woman crying. Face all twisted up, mouth working, and trying to — trying to — The unease he had been feeling as he searched the letter over and over in his mind, time after time, since despatching it, now became uncertainty and a vague fear.

Of course Iris knew everything that was in that manuscript, but had he been pretending to himself that her fear of its publication had always been connected with that most dreadful and besmirching inheritance during British times in India, a touch of the tar-brush? No. But she was certainly scared, and

222

it was not just about the possibility of losing this house, which had been lived in by a Woodberry from the time of the eighteenth-century colonel.

'Exactly what is it that's worrying you, Iris?' he said. 'You know the manuscript should be published. You know the film people will love — '

'Stop telling lies to yourself, if that's what you're doing,' she said. Her tears had stopped. She gathered strength. 'Tell me exactly what you wrote in that letter. Don't lie to me.' But Iris was only looking for confirmation. She knew the gist of the letter from the times when he went on and on about the pension she had renounced, snarling, sometimes saying when he referred to the Maharajah and his relatives, 'After all, they're family, for Christ's sake. They're Woodberrys. They don't want it known, so you deserve the pension, you bloody idiot. What possessed you to give it up?'

He did not reply to her question. She spoke what she suspected, feared. 'Was it in any way a blackmail letter, Freddy? Answer me. Now.'

He smiled at her. God, how ugly he was becoming as he got older. As ugly as herself. What a horrible couple they were, had become. Hot tears came to her eyes again, when he said, still smiling, 'I wouldn't call it blackmail. A slight suggestion of greymail, possibly, but all above board. The letter's a masterpiece. Do you want to see the copy?'

Did she? She shook her head slowly, then bowed it, covered her face with her hands and shook with quiet weeping. Ever alert during such scenes between them, Tone saw the servant approaching the verandah from the kitchen, and called to him to go back. Come and clear up later. Plenty of time. The servant acknowledged the order, turned and went back to the kitchen. Bastards. Like shitehawks for family gossip, they were, couldn't even change your razorblade but it was all over the bloody country that the sahib was about to cut his throat or something. No privacy of any kind anywhere, anytime in this country.

'I'm going to my study,' he said. He felt done up, quite buggered in fact, what with the work on that letter, and the — the — well, the worry now it was delivered — Iris's craven bloody fears and tears. Even so it was diary-time. Not the usual few thousand words today, but a few lines would do. The habit, the daily diary entry. Not to worry. Had taken a firm line, and would keep to it, stick to it through thick and bloody thin. But as he walked to his study he wondered again about the letter, tried to imagine the Maharajah reading it, and getting the message — the message, the message. It's all right. Nothing to worry about. Message buried, but there in the letter. Forget it.

As he wrote some cryptic diary notes he heard the sound of Iris's car starting, heard it drive away. He dropped his pen, wondered where she had gone, her tearful face, her state of mind, her — she could not possibly have — gone to the palace? No. Didn't have that kind of nerve, and she was too clever to lose her head and do something as stupid as that. Yet — he went out and poured himself another whiskey. He felt so nervous now, so shaky. Ought he to have sent the letters, well the one to the Maharajah anyway? The answer was trying to be no; he fought it, and failed. On the other hand if the Maharajah took it the wrong way (the right way) and — and — took some kind of hostile action, then he could deny it, could make the Maharajah see reason. He simply wanted to publish the manuscript for history's sake. So what are you afraid of, *Maharaj* Sahib? I don't understand.

Often, when Iris was out of the house, Tone would sit in his study, lulled in the silence into one more wandering journey back through the past few years of his life. It was like a silent film show, the main scenes flickering, then hardening for clearer viewing in the very private projection-room in his head. If he could only view these scenes patiently, he was sure, he might discover the key to the enigma of 'the test to destruction' he had been undergoing since the court-martial just after the war's end. Superstition was now involved, he knew, and accepted. After all, the unconscious, collective or otherwise, could be allowed to give whispered voice on this mystery of steady failure, when all else had failed. For it was not just a matter of mistakes made one after the other, and which had involved the loss of all his money, his self-respect ('your incredible vanity, Freddy,' as Iris had put it), his aggressive readiness to take on Life and all it could throw at him; no, it was something so extraordinary, the beating he had taken, that he was actually beginning to believe in a 'force of evil' focussed by something 'out there' on him, Freddy Tone. Imagine it, to have come to this, well — to have been forced to consider it.

Then, like light suddenly switched on in the quiet theatre of his head, he heard Iris's voice again — 'test to *self*-destruction'. The film show was over, before he could get back to the court-martial. Iris again. Yes, Iris again. Dear Iris who was so determined not to understand him, and then, *flash*, came the other picture which always came when he thought of her unwillingness to understand him: the wise-cracking Yank officer at the table next to his in the Grand Hotel in Calcutta, 1944, trying out a new line, stroking the face of the beautiful Eurasian girl dining with him, and saying, 'I'm unhappy, baby. My wife back home understands me.' Sinister really, the way that joke scene always arrived, nudging him, trying to manoeuvre him into accepting that Iris knew him, too well. She did not, and never would. No. Never. He felt alone, splendidly alone, fighting his battle unaided against these — against this — this strange force 'out there'. The letter to the Maharajah was trying to push its way again into his mind, along with those haunting words, 'test to *self*-destruction'. He must not surrender to doubts, to the new thought trying to dog him, that his letter to Chandra Gupta Woodberry might after all be the end of that long test — he fought off the words 'self-destruction', but back they came.

Often she had asked him to give her the full story of the military offence which had caused his court-martial. He had always talked all round it, never explained, but then how could he, he had been so bloody drunk in the middle of the last nightmare days of the Burma campaign, before his arrest. Tempting, yes, always tempting, to see himself as a loser marked by that court-martial, a loser who could never get anything right again, taking wrong decisions due to failed nerve and morale. But it never stood up, that easy explanation. He was marked down by something 'out there', and now, despondent and afraid, he was giving in to doubt and panic, could have overdone it with that brilliant letter to the Maharajah. Iris had poured her poisonous fears into his works.

He got up from his desk and went across the room to look at a snapshot of himself in filthy jungle battle dress, Willy Coggin beside him, arms on each other's shoulders — near the smashed, stinking ruins of Kangyo village, that was — he could smell the heaped Japanese corpses again and hear the shattering sound of the corps artillery registering, thundering, switching — eight tons of high explosive a minute — to the new suicide targets of the running Japanese masses in their rags, switching again, and the noise of the diving planes with their chattering cannon, after they had dropped their bombs in blinding flashes. The blinding sheet of the heavy rain, the flooded paddy fields, the stinking forests, the scratching misery of ringworm and prickly heat in the thick steam-laundry heat.

The mud-smeared war pictures came one after the other, and were suddenly interrupted by the idea that he should take the Woodberry manuscript out of the drawer of his desk, go out into the garden with a box of matches, set fire to it, see it in smoking ashes, and then send a note to the Maharajah to say he had destroyed it. Placatory, defeatist, realist, craven, but calling loudly to be done at once. Get a grip on yourself, for Christ's sake. What's the matter with you? Another Scotch might help. No. Clear mind needed until this new development he had caused had shown results, the right and only results, an urbane and Rajput-Woodberry agreement to resume the pension. He started to write the Maharajah's reply in his head: — 'Dear Tone, in reply to your most interesting letter, etc., etc. I feel, taking the long view, that despite your admirable sentiments regarding the need to document every aspect of Indian history in every way we can, the time is not yet ripe for publication. Incidentally, I have never understood your wife's decision to cancel the pension which, I am informed by my advisers here, she did after approaching my father, and therefore I have decided that the payment of this pension, agreed so very long ago, should be resumed . . . '

Where could Iris have gone, in that distraught state? One more Scotch. As he poured the whiskey, his mind fingered the letter he had written from the Maharajah, the obvious reply to his.

More war pictures as he went back to the framed snapshot on his study wall. Willy Coggin. Mystery of slain friends, vanished voices, why him and not me? Why the enemy sniper looked that way and not this way, the oldest dice game in the world.

The discovery of the captured British booze in that destroyed village — oh, oh, anguish again of that memory: he closed his eyes tightly, against that searing memory, to which there clung a letter lying in a drawer over there, and which he must have read a hundred times, in sorrow, in fury, remorse, self-defensive counter-argument — all of it useless, useless. Another Scotch? No. No. Enough, enough, cool head needed. He went over and wrenched open the drawer, took out the letter, so tired and limp now from so many readings, which that vindictive bastard, Coggin's 'best friend', that snotty little captain, Delfield, had written him after the court-martial. He always read the last line first, he noticed once again: 'Having read this I dare you to sue me, how about for defamation of character? What character? Yours contemptuously . . . .' Another thing he did, he noticed again, after that ritual of reading the last line of the letter, was to slump down in the chair at his desk and start reading the letter right through. He knew he did all this after a few drinks, if he once opened the inner cinema and started that old silent film. How many had he had this time? Four Scotches? Five? He had to read the letter.

' — and damn lucky you were to get away with being cashiered only, when you and I, and the rest in the know, knew that was less than what you really deserve, ten years' hard labour in a military prison as well. Your smart-Alec defending officer was a lawyer in peacetime they say, and probably therefore was well used to getting crooks off the hook. Only you know what really happened and the time will come when you will need to tell it all —'

'But I don't even know exactly what happened myself, for Christ's sake!' This shouted at the wall beyond the desk, another thing that happened when he read this letter, took part in this Scotch-directed ritual. What next? To the files, of course. He was inebriately amused, when he opened another drawer and got out the big manuscript of his life story, that he was able to throw open the huge typescript at exactly the right place, where he had put down in sequence all he could remember of what had happened on that terrible, bomb-happy, drunken afternoon in the Burmese monsoon of nineteen forty-five.

Next, again as usual, he found himself topping up the Scotch again with not too much water, then back to the desk with the brimming glass in his hand.

Before he sat down he called out, melodramatically — a little fun could always help — the Japanese commander's orders to his troops, the order, as it turned out, for their massacre: 'Cross the Sittang, or die!' Interesting, hearing that bat-tle-order, so Japanese and as always obeyed; and now he was in an agony of mind about the letter he had sent to the Mahar-ajah, and maybe was turning to the older disaster for some kind of relief — which had set him on course for all the un-canny failures which had followed? 'You may be walking under the wrong star. Try another star, maybe.' Who said that? Who? Bingham? Yes, Bingham naturally, after he had put the case to him one night in the club, the case about his continuous misfortune. The 'wrong star', for Christ's sake! Naturally it had to be one of Bingham's Arab solutions to such problems, Bingham the eighth pillar of wisdom. Yet it appealed, the idea of walking under the wrong star, had some-thing sort of tragic and doomed about it, as if he had been picked out by Fate for dooming.

Concentrate. He re-read the page of his life story. The cine-ma opened again and he saw the vastness of wild plains and forests, rain-swollen rivers carrying hundreds of speeding Japanese bodies, broken Burmese huts, and other groups of the ragged enemy masses swarmed onto the river's edges under the flails of shell and machine-gun fire. Twelve thousand, at least, killed in six days. Too late, that was why. 'Twenty-Eighth Japanese Army will attempt to break out and cross the Sittang river into Siam on the eighteenth of . . . ' Corps HQ had announced, and this warning had crept up through forests via sputtering radios until it had reached Cog-gin and himself by barely legible pencilled note, probably from that little bastard Delfield himself, if he knew anything. The days had gone by, eighteenth, nineteenth . . . twenty-seventh . . . thirtieth: weeks of delay, but no Japanese break-out; and by then the killing machine was in position, despite mud, blinding monsoon rain, despite everything which that wild terrain could invent.

Snapshots glowing one after the other in his head. Smashed village, Burmese all gone. Recce. Sepoy came back with steel helmet full of eggs. *Bahut achcha*! Found them in a hut, and boiled quickly in mess tins, and wonder of wonders still eat-able. Lying down under the trees, listening to the raving artil-lery to the right of them. Then, making everybody sit up, the sharp crack — grenade? — of an explosion from the direction of the village. Recce — tiptoe and eyes flickering on stalks, Lovely Japanese scene in centre of village clearing; who else for Christ's sake, in any world's army in any century, could have produced such cold artistry? Four ragged, ringwormed, starved, monsoon and shell-happy Japanese, their steel helmets placed beside them where they had knelt in a tight circle for their final Samurai sacrament, flung onto their backs by the explosion of the grenade they had obviously held tightly in their circle of pressed foreheads, their last grenade, and so, fairly shared, to headlessness.

Shudder again, remembering such murderous, calculated, spendthrift contempt for life. Another Scotch, bugger it. But he sat on, empty glass in hand, continuing the journey through the cinema to when they had found the booze in that hardly damaged village. Japanese too shagged to carry it further? Probably, or were drunk enough anyway to stagger into the artillery fire on their way to the Sittang, so wide, so swollen, each Japanese carrying a long slender bamboo raft slung on his back, rifle and rusted bayonet at the high port.

'Scotch, gin, and bloody beer, my God!' Coggin shouting and then the mad rush to see this treasure glistening in the hammering grey sheets of rain. The guns had stopped. Sometimes the rain came like an enormous grey, glistening roller, threatening to sweep them all away.

The runner had arrived when they were halfway down the first bottle of Scotch —beer for that bloody English sergeant, sullen and glowering because the two members of the officer-class had stuck by the rules, beer for the other ranks, hard liquor for the officers. A runner with a message for Major Tone. Important. Really? Remembered Coggin tittering with him. Important? Probably some bullshit about a new issue of green blanco for webbing, or a request for an arms and ammunition return by 1600 hours. Stuffed it into the breast-pocket of his battle-dress blouse. Yes, he remembered that clearly. One of these fatal moves, mistaken moves you make when you start walking under the wrong star. 'Bollicks to you, Bingham!' he could hear himself shout, as he went back to the table for another Scotch. Wrong star, my arse. Was pissed as a coot, that's why, that day, he had forgotten the letter from HQ miles back, Staff types snug in a big teak house hidden in the jungle. Fatal though. Probably one of the strangest letters ever written in the history of warfare, come to think of it all over again, once more for the millionth time round. Yes indeedy, as that Nisei chap from the U.S. Interrogation corps used to say. Yes infuckingdeedy, as that moaning English sergeant would have put it. Managed to get that favourite word into the strangest places like 'roll on refuckinpatriation', and even referring to the combination-tool for the Bren as the combifuckination-tool. Bastard sergeant, but still, give him his cunning due, he had played the old soldier, nicely puzzled and forgetful, when he gave evidence for-against him at the court-martial, despite his dark resentment about not being able to get as drunk as him on the hard liquor for 'officers only Didn't help though.

Gap commences here in film show. Never to be filled with accuracy, but obvious enough what happened — with bodies to show for it, including one British lieutenant. One Japanese officer, three Japanese privates, *and* one British lieutenant. Yellow hair. That's right. Rain splashing off his empty, dead, blue eyes. Lying on his back sprayed by a magazine of Bren, like the Japanese tumbled with him.

Could remember standing, stumbling, standing again, with Coggin, a careful, watchful even though drunken, half hour later, over the bodies, triumphant and glowing, until they saw the yellow-haired British lieutenant lying with them. Could remember vaguely Coggin, as amazed as himself, thickly Scotch-tongued, saying something about having made mishtake 'n' knocked off Brish prishoner. But how bloody come prishoner wearing pishtol in holshter doshn't make bloody shenshe, Freddy. Run the film again from when the sepoy sentry called quietly, 'Major Sahib, Japanese coming.' That's right. Sergeant out on patrol with the rest of the sepoys and only himself and Coggin, bottle of Scotch finished, gin about to be opened, then rush to the Bren. Could remember vaguely, mistily, arguing about who should be number one on the Bren, and who number two, giggling, shoving. Five Japanese in the rain, not a care in the bloody world apparently, rifles slung, tramping into the Bren sights. Two long bursts. 'I swear Coggin fired the Bren,' he had told his defending officer weeks later, before the court-martial. But who knows now, even now? Coggin was in his Burmese grave, where that sniper had put him just before sundown that horrible day, and there was only the sepoy, who had vanished into the milling hordes gone back to India after VJ-Day, Bomb-Day, Doomsday, Goodbye-Old-World Day.

Wished he had that ignored letter he'd stuffed into his

breast-pocket to read now; yes, strangest bloody letter ever received and unread until too late by soldier in any war in bloody history. Drunk? Six Scotches, he made it. He made his way back to the table in the dining room and inspected, with over-careful solemnity, the bottle of Scotch. Nearly finished the bloody bottle, my Christ. How? Try to remember the wording of that letter from the Staff bugger back in cover out of the rain and carnage.

Woken up with hangover and sodden through with monsoon, to find bloody sergeant totally pissed beside empty gin bottle under the trees at edge of village. Correct. Left the bugger there. Gone back to his own corner of village, and then discovered forgotten letter. Read it then. Read it about a dozen unbelieving times — about a new bomb exploded on Japanese city — fucking fairy-tale bomb with power of twenty-two thousand tons of TNT. Japanese expected to surrender — or make all-out maniacal Banzai attack — much more like it. URGENT AND IMPORTANT. Could remember that. After the bullshit about the impossible bomb — biggest bomb known in the war was the ten tonner and could only be carried by Halifax or Sterling bomber, not even by Yank B-29s — came the orders. Standing Patrols Only. No firing unless fired at. Now he remembered how the guns had stopped, remembered that clearly even though smashed on the Scotch with Coggin, laughing and telling jokes, only sound the hissing, pissing rain of monsoon afternoon.

He and Coggin had wiped out a Japanese parley-party, one of several which had responded to feelers following the first atomic bomb on Japan. There were about twenty thousand Japanese still dug in behind the British forward troops, and the British wanted the Japanese in front of them to order these dug-in Japanese to surrender, following the atomic bomb, which they knew had all but made the Japanese command realize that Japan was defeated. That Japanese party, its officer having refused to conform to British suggestions about surrender, had been escorted back by a British lieutenant: 'You will watch out for this party, having instructed all troops in your vicinity to do the same, and will not open fire unless attacked.'

Wrong star? Walking under the wrong Scotch, more like it — poor bloody Coggin, rolled him into a deserted slit-trench and heeled in the earth on top of him, forgot even to take off the grey bit of his identity discs, still too drunk to know what year it was even, Coggin didn't know he was hit, never mind what hit him.

'Freddy.' Iris took hold of his arm and shook it. He lay with his head on his hands, his arms on the desk, half-snoring, his life story open on the desk in front of him, a letter in his hand. She leaned over and tried to take the letter out of his hand so she could read it, but even drunk, his protective mechanism still worked, his secretive mania still watching out for him, so that he came to and stood up, staring at her blearily, folding up the letter. He said, as he straightened himself and assumed that over-sober correctness of manner so familiar to her, 'So you're back. But from where? From where?'

'You'd better go and lie down, Freddy,' she said, with a quietness close to hopelessness. 'Go on, Freddy. Go and lie down.'

She had seen the bottle out there and how little whiskey was left in it, she knew he knew that, but fuddled though he was he said, 'After you.' She might have known it, for she had seen him farther gone than this and he still remembered to lock his study, as he locked it now. Not that she had any plans to explore it, not really, for she was afraid of what she might discover among those masses of paper and files. There were times, yes, when she burned, if angered, to know what secrets he guarded so carefully in that study, but it never lasted long with her. But she must soon know where he kept that Woodberry manuscript. Not now. When he was sober again. Tonight: it could not wait longer.

CHAPTER 19

Bingham opened his eyes and, staring up at the strange ceiling, realized that the soft music he could hear was not part of the dream which was already escaping his attempt to seize and examine it. He could never remember his dreams, though sometimes he could retain fragments of the end of one, but now, his mind gathering speed after deep sleep, he listened to the marvellous sound of Lahorewalla singing to God in Urdu. He knew too that he was lying on his back on a settee in the living room of the palace, and then he heard the *Diwan* say, 'I remember you liked this record, Colonel Sahib.' He rose on his left elbow and looked across to where the *Diwan* was smiling at him from the armchair Chan had been sitting in during their all-night talkative vigil.

'*Diwan* Sahib,' he said, smiling back at the old man. 'What a thoughtful way to wake me. Where is — ?'

'I have a note for you from His Highness,' the *Diwan* said. He came over to the settee and handed Bingham a letter, then sat down at the foot of the settee, adding, 'He has gone up to the bungalow at Kadanwali. He is very upset, very erratic. You must make him take a holiday away from here, Colonel Sahib. He will not listen to me.'

As he opened the letter Bingham looked at the *Diwan* and said, 'When we are in love a holiday is not the best answer, *Diwan* Sahib.' He knew from the Maharajah that the *Diwan* was 'the only other person' who knew what he was 'going through'. The *Diwan* smiled sadly and shook his head. 'Yes, I know he is in love, but I think there is something more.'

It was obvious to Bingham that the old man wished to discuss this 'something more', perhaps felt they could enlighten each other, for he had taken the trouble to wake him with a piece of his favourite music, and was sitting there watching him intently with worried eyes.

'Something more? What's happened, *Diwan* Sahib?' Surely

233

all must be well. Ted Koltz had telephoned from the club at about half past five that morning to say he had spent the evening with Croon and Megan at the club, in other words the unspoken message that 'the safe' had not been broken into, as Chan had preferred to put it after putting down the telephone. Then they had both gone to sleep, both fairly drunk.

'Colonel Sahib, you are his best friend. I know that, otherwise I would not suggest that we confide in each other. All I can tell you is that Major Tone's servant arrived two hours ago and insisted upon delivering a letter personally to His Highness. He said those were his Sahib's instructions. I found this very annoying indeed, as you can imagine. I sent a servant with the Major's messenger and the letter was given in person to His Highness, who then came to me in my office. I have never seen him in such a state of temper. Never. He would tell me nothing. Instead, he wanted to know where I had stored the personal papers of Bapu Sahib — '

'Bapu Sahib?' Bingham exclaimed, his mind exclaiming: Tone. Iris. Woodberry. Colonel Woodberry. Bapu Sahib. Bapu Sahib, the first reconstituted ruler of the state, great-great-great-grandfather of the Maharajah, after the fall of Colonel Woodberry, died 1810. Bingham, immediately cautious, and very relaxed still, went on, 'Oh, that'll be about this film project. Bapu Sahib will be a key figure in the film. So what is the problem, *Diwan* Sahib?' He knew what the problem was, all right, or was trying to be. Years ago, after hearing various rumours from one or two officials 'in the know' about the state's history, he had looked up certain records in Delhi. He knew too about the Woodberry manuscript, and that great efforts had been made by the now long dead Bapu Sahib to obtain it from the Woodberrys of the period, that a pension had been set up, that the Woodberrys had held on to the manuscript, and that a mystery had been buried by that pension.

'Possibly. Possibly,' the *Diwan* was saying, and then, 'Your letter, Colonel Sahib. Perhaps His Highness — '

'Oh, yes.' Bingham read the letter quickly. ' "Dear Tim, please stand by, if you will be so kind. The *Diwan* will inform you of my whereabouts. I may need your sage advice. I only hope your hangover is even worse than mine. Thanks again for helping me drink through my travail, but now I have something tricky to think about. By the way, you have a most unusual and interesting snore. Remind me to give you my rendering of it. Be in touch soon. Chan." '

Looking up at the *Diwan* Bingham smiled and said, 'He sounds in good form. This film thing is doing him the world of good.' But he could see that the *Diwan* was not taken in — not quite taken in. Going to talk about Tone? What else?

'The letter from Major Tone, Colonel Sahib,' said the *Diwan*. 'It has upset His Highness. It can only be about this film they are planning to make. The Princess is terribly worried about this film. You do know that the subject of the film, the history they plan to use for it — is, well, it is a most painful subject, and is always has been — for the family. You understand me, Colonel Sahib?'

Bingham nodded, waited, holding his tongue. He could see that the old man was full of words he hesitated to pour forth, and that he wished he, Bingham, would say them for him, guessing rightly that they were both feeling around a subject which might better stay buried. He let the *Diwan* try another tack.

'This Major Tone, I have only talked to him twice in all the time he has lived here. The house he lives in — you know, of course, that it has always belonged to his wife's family.' He stopped, and Bingham, careful not to show his great interest, watched the *Diwan*'s black, deep set eyes flick away from him while he considered how much more to say. An almost maniacally private person himself, even in some ways with his friend the Maharajah, Bingham was amused but touched, and decided to help.

'Are you a breakfast person, *Diwan* Sahib?' he asked. He looked at his wrist-watch and, surprised to see it was nearly midday, 'I mean a light-lunch person? Say, an omelette?' He knew that the old man, although nothing would induce him even to *look* at a piece of beef, had lost most of the other taboos of the Hindu world, and would be willing to sit with him and talk, over a meal. 'I think it might help if we talked about what we know. I too, *Diwan* Sahib, feel just a little apprehensive about this letter from Major Tone.'

The *Diwan*'s nod of understanding and agreement was immediate, and he rose at once from the settee.

'Excellent, Colonel Sahib,' he said with what was obviously immense relief. 'I need your advice about this — this — I don't know what to call it. We both know, I think, that there

235

is' — again he stopped and Bingham knew he would have to take the *Diwan*'s hesitancy by assault, by direct reference to the Woodberry manuscript, by finding out just how much they both knew of this ancient secret.

'An omelette, Colonel Sahib.' The *Diwan* smiled and put his arm round Bingham's shoulder as he rose from the settee. 'I will see to it, and we will talk. Yes.' He gave a deep sigh of satisfaction. They walked together to the stairs leading up to the gallery, and while the *Diwan* went up to switch off the gramophone, Bingham went on to the small private dining room in which the *Diwan* and the Maharajah sometimes talked and dined together.

Bingham found he did not need to break into the fortress of the *Diwan*'s life-long guardianship of certain secrets. Both of them had seemingly come to the same conclusion, that it was a time for directness, for an exchange of clues.

'Is it hot enough for you?' The *Diwan* was sitting opposite Bingham at the dining table and Bingham had taken his first mouthful of the omelette.

'Perfect, *Diwan* Sahib. Plenty of fresh green chillies.'

'The cook did say he knows how the colonel sahib likes his omelette. Good. Now, it is this Woodberry manuscript we both have in our minds, I think. Wouldn't you say that that is what Major Tone may have written to His Highness about? So that this film plan is already causing the problems which the Princess herself is so worried about? You know too that Mrs Tone has inherited this manuscript?' Eating hungrily, and nodding after each of the *Diwan*'s questions, Bingham felt he must not let the old man assume too much. He interrupted the *Diwan* gently.

'I ought to tell you, *Diwan* Sahib, that I have never heard of the Woodberry manuscript officially, and by that I mean when I served the British government in India. I wish to make that quite clear. I have twice in my life heard of this curious manuscript, and only then from the old Maharajah, once, and again from a Brahmin long dead, and they didn't know why this manuscript was such a very secret matter.' He laughed. 'In other words, *Diwan* Sahib, the world has long forgotten what the hell the manuscript is about, even if anyone in the world now happens to know of its existence.' But the *Diwan* was not relieved by these words. If anything, thought Bingham, he looked even graver than usual, and made exactly the right reply.

'Except Major and Mrs Tone.'

They eyed each other now, wary, but friendly, and then, as if both appreciated and were pleased by the trust they felt in each other, they smiled and nodded to each other.

'Is it true' — Bingham caught himself up quickly and corrected himself — 'well, of course it *must* be true, the old Maharajah told me so himself, that a considerable pension was paid to the Woodberry family — for generations in fact — but that the present Woodberry representative, Iris Tone, cancelled the pension? The old Maharajah sang her praises for that — not that he begrudged the money. He felt Mrs Tone — she was not Mrs Tone then, lucky lady had she only known it' (his first hint to the *Diwan* to speak his mind about what he thought or knew about Tone) '— he felt she had shown a great sense of honour, and some pride too. But he did say he would give a lot to know what was in that manuscript. What do you think *is* in it, *Diwan* Sahib?'

The *Diwan* began to drum his long, pointed brown fingers on the table like a *tabla* player, his eyes fixed on Bingham's.

'I may even be wrong when I said just now that only Major and Mrs Tone know what is in it. I would like to think that only Mrs Tone knows what is in it. Because, I ask you, is it likely that that lady, no matter what her mental problems, and I think we can both agree we know she once had some, is it likely that she would tell . . . .' A pause: did he want him, Bingham, to take the ball here? Did he not wish to be the first to criticize Major Tone? Best to assume so, anyway. Push the boat out and get it done with.

'You mean, tell that garrulous, idiotic bugger the secret, whatever it is, even though he is her husband? We are confiding in each other, *Diwan* Sahib, so let us speak out. I am worried about this letter from Tone. We may be wrong to worry. We may be worrying about the wrong thing.'

The *Diwan* shook his head, still drumming his fingers on the table. 'I think we are worrying about the right things, Colonel Sahib. Let me tell you exactly what happened here this morning after the Maharajah read this letter from Major Tone.'

Tone's servant had been told to wait, after he had delivered his master's letter to the Maharajah. The next thing the *Diwan* heard, sitting at his desk in his office, was the hurried approach of the Maharajah in the corridor leading to his office, and the Maharajah shouting, to himself, 'You want to play games with me, you bastard, do you? Well, let's play, Major Tone, but to the bloody finish, I warn you. I warn you.'

He seemed to have calmed down a little when he entered the *Diwan*'s office, but his eyes were burning, and he paced about, stopped at the window and stared down into the black pool in the rocks below, and then turned and smiled at the *Diwan*.

'It was a very strange kind of smile, Colonel Sahib. Forced — you know? I was quite worried, especially by his eyes. He looked a little mad, I must say it. Yes, a little mad. I have been worried about him for some time. I mean the strain he is under. He has not really got over the death of the Maharani and the boy, not even now.

' "You remember that rather pretentious parchment-type paper my father used to have for his official letters, *Diwan* Sahib?" the Maharajah said. Yes, there was still some stored in one of the drawers over there.

' "Get a sheet now and in your best Victorian copper-plate handwriting, *Diwan* Sahib, take a letter. It will be short, and by God, full of wog wiliness, Asiatic cunning, Oriental devil-ry, you know the kind of thing this kind of tiny bastard like Major Tone expects from niggers like us, *Diwan* Sahib? Of course you do. It was tiny bastards like Major Tone who wrecked their empire for the British, was it not? Jumped up from their little suburbs and given ten Indian servants to shout at . . . . " '

In great fear and anxious haste the *Diwan* had searched a drawer until he found a sheet of the stiff yellow parchment-paper, and had then sat at his desk, waiting. But the Maharajah had not finished with his fierce, cold railing yet.

'His next instructions, Colonel Sahib, before he dictated the letter to Major Tone, were very odd indeed.'

The Maharajah had said he wanted the letter delivered to Tone as it would have been delivered in his grandfather's time, and he then described the manner of it. When he heard, amazed, what this meant, the *Diwan*, though not sure himself about the details of the custom, the *dastur*, knew it was intended to overawe, and even scare, Major Tone.

As he described what the Maharajah had instructed him to do about the delivery of the reply to Tone the *Diwan* was quite surprised by the hilarity it caused Bingham, and he had then smiled uncertainly himself as Bingham's head bent and he shook with laughter. It occurred again to Bingham that the *Diwan* had never understood the sardonically humorous side of his master, and probably never would.

It had taken nearly an hour to load the boxes of ancient documents, from the time of Bapu Sahib and the two Maharajahs who had descended from him, into the Maharajah's station wagon, and then he had read the final draft of the short letter he had dictated for Tone. 'That's fine,' he had told the *Diwan*. 'Now, write that out in your finest copper-plate while I'm having a quick drink and then I'll sign it.' It was to be delivered to Tone at midnight tonight, and with the full traditional ceremonial of the past. 'Get the clothes and the badges and the rest out of the museum room. It want it solemn, you understand? I want it pompous but solemn. It'll be bright moonlight at midnight. Put it about, if it's necessary, that it's a rehearsal for a part of the film we're going to make.'

'At midnight?' said Bingham. The *Diwan* nodded. 'He wants to give Major Tone a shock, he said.' He sighed again, then looked at his watch. 'I have to rehearse the message-party this afternoon.' Tears came into his eyes. 'It was being in the museum room that upset me,' he said, his voice husky now, the tears still filming his eyes. 'Seeing the magnificence of our past again, all those wonderful clothes and uniforms.' He stopped and Bingham reached over and patted his hand understandingly. The *Diwan* peered into Bingham's serious gaze, blinking against his tears. 'I saw everthing clearly when I was in the museum room, Colonel Sahib,' he said mourning in his quiet voice now. 'I saw that I am only a caretaker for the new government in Delhi, and that the world of the past has stopped forever. The ruling family I and mine have served has not been cruel or greedy for over a hundred years. The people of the state do not want the past to disappear — and what is India without its past, its traditions? But it's too late now. I will have to see to it that I do not show my tears when

I see the message-party this afternoon, dressed in the beautiful clothes and turbans of the past, on horseback with swords.' As if to assure Bingham that he was still in charge of the deep emotion now shaking him, he smiled. 'So,' he almost whispered the words, 'we, you and me, Colonel Sahib,, do not know what it is in that letter from Major Tone which has so upset His Highness, and we don't know what it is in this manuscript which required a pension paid for over a hundred years to the Woodberrys.' His dark, haggard, bony face slowly hardened now. 'Although the Woodberry family have had the use of that house since the pension began, it is still the property of this palace, of this state. You know what I am meaning, Colonel Sahib?'

'You could dismiss Major Tone from the state, send him away and take back the house, you mean?'

'It has occurred to me, yes.' He wanted to hear Bingham's opinion.

Bingham shook his head. 'You want my opinion, *Diwan* Sahib?'

'I think I know your opinion. This thing is between the major and His Highness. Whatever it is about only they know. So I should stand well back and do nothing, just carry out whatever instructions His Highness gives me. That is your opinion, I think.'

'That's my opinion, *Diwan* Sahib.' He paused. 'Do you want to tell me the Maharajah's reply to the major's letter?'

'Oh, yes,' said the *Diwan*, remembering. 'Yes.' He closed his eyes for a couple of seconds, then recited the words of the reply. ' "To Major Frederick Tone, Temporary Officer, Royal Indian Ordnance Corps (Cashiered) — " '

'Good God!' Bingham exclaimed.

'Yes, in brackets, "Cashiered",' said the *Diwan*. 'Yes, I must say I was surprised. Not about the major having been cashiered. I'd heard about that vaguely, you know. But putting the fact like that in an official letter. Of course, His Highness knows that the major will never run about in the club, or anywhere else, complaining about having that written to him in a letter. Oh no, I shouldn't think so. Then the letter itself. Quite short, but very puzzling, to my mind: "I am in receipt of your most interesting letter. I am also, as you will know, profoundly moved to learn of your interest, not only in Indian history, but in the history of this ancient state, and of your

wish to add to its documentation by publishing what you re-
fer to as the 'Woodberry manuscript'. I note also your decision that you will act as 'adviser' on the film to be based on
the period of the 'Woodberry manuscript', and that you
would appreciate my 'reactions' to your proposals. These I
shall arrange for you to have, quite soon. Meanwhile, patience
should be the watchword, and prudence your guide, about
any action at all regarding publication prior to further discussion. I am at present staying up at Kadanwali, whence you
will shortly hear further from me." '

Watching Bingham starting to laugh halfway through his
recital of the letter caused the *Diwan* to frown with
annoyance.

'I find it all very worrying, Colonel Sahib,' he said with
some severity. 'What is so amusing about it for you?'

'Just thinking about Major Tone reading it, that's all.' He
knew it was no use trying to tell the old man how much his
Maharajah had enjoyed devising that reply to the crass and
overbearing Major Tone. The *Diwan* now asked about Tone,
about his cashiering from the army. Was it for dishonesty, the
usual thing about bad cheques, hand in the regimental till and
so on?

'No. It's all very sad, really,' Bingham told him, his eyes
staring off into the past of the war period. He told how Tone
was in charge, in Burma, of some of the huge dumps being
piled up for the two years of fighting to come, across Asia to
Japan. The Japanese in Burma were finished, nearly two hundred thousand of them killed in battle from Assam to the bor-
ders of Siam. Dumps which were mountains of web-equip-
ment for the infantry, uniforms, helmets, boots, rations,
ammunition, petrol, oil and lubricants, medicines, for the new
armies coming from shattered Europe for the final assault
against Japan. On the killing-ground near the great river
separating Burma from Siam, Tone, like every other officer
they could sweep up for the final drive against the remains of
the Japanese Twenty-Eighth Army, had been thrown in with
a scratched-together group of spare Indian soldiers.

'He got drunk, apparently, and shot the wrong group of
Japanese. There was a British officer with them, taking them
back to the Japanese lines after a failed surrender conference.'
Bingham started laughing again, but against his will, as he
went on, 'Tone probably thought he would get the Military

241

Cross for what he had done, when he sobered up and was told what he had done. Anyway he was chucked out of the army and nothing's gone right for him since.'

'I have never liked him,' said the *Diwan* firmly. 'I've only talked to him on the odd occasion, and on one of those occasions he gave me a very insulting lecture about what he called, if you please, "the corrupting effect of the Indian world on the European character, and how it had finally destroyed the British empire".'

'That's Tone,' said Bingham. 'The soul of sensitivity always.'

'Mrs Tone shut him up, I'm happy to remember. She was very angry with him, poor lady, and apologized to me. It is no wonder she has had these mental problems at times. I sent her to a very good German doctor in Delhi.'

'I remember,' Bingham said. 'Well, Tone's going to find himself in deep waters by the sound of that letter you're sending him.' He got up from the table, excusing himself. 'Will the message-party be passing by the club tonight? I wouldn't mind seeing the pageant.' He started laughing again.

'Yes, it will pass by the club. It would do no harm if you put it round that it's part of a rehearsal for the film, would it?'

CHAPTER 20

The Maharajah slowed the station wagon about fifty yards from the old red sandstone building still called Sabziserai, for here in the old days, before petrol-driven transport, the farmers and peasants bringing vegetables and fruit in for the public markets in their bullock-carts had stopped for rest and refreshment. Nowadays it was lived in by a few agreed retainers from the days of his father and grandfather, but he had given the best living quarters to Balban along with charge of the building and its upkeep.

Once it had held nearly a dozen of the old palace servants with their families. Those who were still living here, three old men, two of them with wives, were all that were left of the intriguing, gossiping clutter he had known in boyhood in the palace. His father had inherited a liking for the mess and chaos of the past, the palace and its courtyards full of squatting, arguing, quarrelling petitioners, holy men, distant relatives from the countryside, spies, musicians, dance troupes, travelling actors and jugglers. Three months after his father's death he had cleared them all out, paid them off, and ever since held them at bay, especially the relatives. Twice a year, apart from religious festivals, though he had cut these down too to an essential and inescapable half-dozen or so, he allowed a couple of days of the old clutter in the palace for a swarm of relatives. They had stopped resenting his aloofness long ago, especially since the death of his wife and son, for it was accepted throughout the state that this tragedy had rocked his mind and personality, had made him even more of a kind of public recluse.

He got out of the station wagon and strolled towards the Sabziserai, thinking over again the instructions he wishes to give to Balban. As he neared the entrance to Balban's quarters and thought of the age of this sprawling fortress-like building before him, built by a female ancestor in the struggle against one more wave of Muslim invaders, he marvelled again sadly at the tenacity of killer-man and his still unshed habit of continuous war. He hated the bloody past as much as he revered it. Escape, escape, go, wander away; an inner voice had been whispering to him for years. He now listened calmly to it again, and knew it spoke now because of the angry nausea he felt for the world, for the stupid and inept vileness of people like Major Tone, who had lived, lived now, and would always live, in every corner of the earth. The major wanted attention, to matter more than he did at present, to cause uneasiness and distress, and then to be pensioned off, silenced by money. But he chuckled again as he thought of Tone receiving the reply he had written to his creepy and so carefully threatening letter, a letter written from a kneeling position, quite the wrong position from which to issue a sugared threat wrapped in a spurious love for Indian history. He was aware too that his present grief over his need to mean something to Megan meant that the major had chosen a particularly inopportune moment to cast his poisonous dart, for it had provoked rage instead of an anxiety to placate and silence. So he must keep cool and play a slow, steady game, giving himself time to think out each move, and finally act in such a way that the unfortunate and bothered Mrs Tone should not suffer too much. He must retain his sense of fun at all costs, terrible fun though it promised to become. His longing to read the Woodberry manuscript was so strong that it felt like a horse straining to bolt with him, but even this still amused him, he was pleased to notice. Now, he must brief Balban and place him on the new chessboard set up by the failed and hamhanded major.

As he entered the tall, arched gateway into the *serai* and walked across the grey, barefoot-polished stone flags, he could hear Balban's voice calling out a sort of sermon in Hindi. He often envied Balban his extraordinary sense of freedom, his irresponsible arrogance towards Indian society, a mish-mash but still an ordered mish-mash, carefully layered and seemingly unchangeable no matter what the alien cultural shocks it must continue to absorb.

'Communism?' Balban had once replied to a question about India's future. 'Why not? It'll end with Lenin's statue in the temples, a red star on his forehead, and flowers heaped about him. Another one for the pantheon. Why not, *Maharaj Sahib*? India is tolerant in the end.' Where did he get these mad ideas, this lowborn, handsome, so intelligent, casteless young man? From his wandering life, his insatiable appetite for reading, his varied and feverish bouts of education, and his almost lifelong love of acting, acting the *saddhu*, the guide, the cracked philosopher, the clown performing before the shadowy *Atman*, that never to be known and forever shapeless spirit of the universe itself, the unmanifestable soul of the so long sought-for 'reality'? Yes, that could be the way to live, as Balban lived, playing out the role of a happy madman in a mystery-play with no beginning and no end. Which reminded him, he had never yet asked Balban for his views on Darwinism. If not already infected, Balban might do wonders with it, wind it into the comical, but oddly disturbing, plot of his mystery-play.

He stood now and listened to Balban declaiming to his audiece. Friendly megalomania was in the voice, surely the hallmark of every religious idiot, atheistical or otherwise. He laughed quietly as he listened to what Balban was saying: Balban in a temporary Buddhist role and, as always, hypnotic but comical. Surely the gentle lord Buddha himself would have smiled approvingly on this sincere though unsteady apostle just now giving Buddhism another six months' run, even though next would come a stretch of Catholicism, then Brahminism, Islam . . . .

'I see some of you smiling,' Balban was saying to his audience, probably hardworking peasants in need of a little entertainment, the odd student and petty merchant, craftsmen on the way to the town with their basketwork, copperwork, handwoven cloth and pottery. 'But let it be the smile of pleasure, not of malice or contempt, for why should we not enjoy ourselves for half an hour together? Consider me mad if you wish. I shall not object. But consider carefully what I have just said to you, that for today I am the voice of the converted Emperor Asoka who ruled India two thousand and three hundred years ago. He called himself Devanampiya Piyadasi, yes, "the beloved of the gods", and he left his inscriptions in all corners of India for us to read, and to forget. He called on men to be good, to kill no more, to make and not to destroy, to dig wells, plant trees, and all this because he had seen one of his own battleships covered with dead and dying men. But this beloved of the gods did not step down from his throne to find his own peace, after he had understood the message of the lord Buddha, to dig a well and plant a tree. No, he went on ruling, and left us inscriptions, and these are all he is remembered by. It is better to be forgotten but to have understood, to have obeyed the right teaching and then to die and be forgotten. I wish I could tell you that the Emperor Asoka heard his own message, understood, left the throne, dug a well, and then vanished from history. How good it would be to know where that well was, to travel to it, draw water from it, and remember the goodness of the self-deposed emperor, and how sweet that water would taste, how brotherly to him one would feel drawing up that water from such a splendid, humble monument to teacher and pupil. But he did not leave us even one well from his own hands, only his proud, vain, useless inscriptions for the quarrelling historians to date, and redate. I hope you have understood my useless message — to remember Asoka and to do better, to dig the wells and plant the trees, and enjoy it while awaiting the inevitable annihilation, whether in the old-fashioned personal way, or as they promise us now, like a swarm of ants in a grass fire. So remember the uselessness of the Emperor Asoka, who meant well, lived well, inscribed well, but left us nothing but his name and his inscriptions, and a sentimental affection for the idea of a reformed egoist. I hope I have entertained you with these useless statements. I will go further, will suggest something even more ridiculous than the emperor's inscriptions. I suggest that you dig the well, but dig it secretly on your neighbour's land, and then let him wonder who did this for him, and never let him know. Who knows but that the even more impossible might then occur — you might find a well dug on your own land by another unknown, by another madman.' The Maharajah, leaning against the sunwarmed sandstone, drew on his cigarette and listened intently to the burst of laughter from the audience, which then stopped and was replaced by what he felt certain was a very uneasy silence, like his own. A voice shouted, 'And you? When will you come onto my land and secretly dig a well for me?' More laughter, some of it harsher now, and the voice called out again, 'For it must be done by a madman, so you say, and who better than yourself, an acknowledged madman?' A great deal of laughter followed this, kindlier now, and shouts of, 'Answer that. Answer.'

'I can give you your answer,' Balban shouted loudly now.

'We are living in a new India, they tell us. Everything can be tried now. Hands up, those of you who will join me in digging wells and planting trees, for no wages except a bowl of grain or rice a day.'

Silence as the Maharajah listened to Balban waiting. 'Not a single hand raised,' Balban shouted. 'Not one. So you have understood my message today, that preaching, recommending, seeking to convert, telling people what is right to do, these are simply acts of vanity, performances of the ego. I have preached uselessly to you, and I have proved that. I hope we have all enjoyed ourselves.'

There was some clapping, the sound of a crowd moving off. Then the voice of an old man was raised across the sounds of sandalled feet crunching on the shale of the *serai* courtyard.

'You will, someday, beat together the hands of grief, young man, and you will weep the tears of a bitter remorse, for these mockeries. But even so, in this world of increasing evil, even the voice of the fool must be allowed its turn. *Jai Shiv! Jai Shiv!*' There was some scattered clapping for this, and more shouts of '*Jai Shiv!*', for it was lord Shiva who was worshipped in these hills, and the disappearing audience celebrated his name in shouts from the oldest voice of India. Yes, the Maharajah mused, treading out his cigarette-butt, the India before and after Buddha, whose mission had seemed to win for a while, but then had been swallowed and digested in the eternal soup of Hinduism.

Standing in the great stone doorway, staring out at the yellow heat of the afternoon, the Maharajah felt again the deep, warning pull of uncertainty, stronger now since listening to the laughable inanities of Balban, so like his own of these last few years. Inane but deadly, because undeniable, though forgettable for a time in laughter, drink, women, music, sensation. His heart was no longer in the game he had planned to play. He had come with a set of instructions for Balban, to give him his role in the cast of the play which Major Tone had started to write, and which he, the Maharajah, had started to direct. He was already rewriting Balban's role, because of a feeling of increased uncertainty, anger, nausea, and all because he had heard this comic sermon and the serious answers of an India which no longer needed him, or other Maharajahs, anyway. Shiva was permanent, Vishnu too; nothing else. He called a small boy about to pass by and told him to call Balban, tell him that there was a messenger from the palace awaiting him. That the little boy looked impressed did not impress his Maharajah, nor the anxious speed with which the boy ran off to deliver the message from what had once been on high, the palace of the rulers.

He had intended that Balban should play a major role in the message-party to Major Tone, dressed in ancient costume and wearing the great silver sun-badge on his breast, and then report on the state of shock and dismay this amazing reponse to his letter had caused the major. But what point was there in being royally preposterous in response to sheer, greedy, bloody-minded wickedness? Speed, seizure of that manuscript was the proper response. While listening to Balban preaching he had compared his own tiny princely goings-on in this matter with those of the Emperor Asoka and his useless inscriptions. Yes, his present position as an out-of-date prince, an ancient Indian artifact awaiting a museum label, and — he laughed when he thought of the still secret outrageousness of it — entitled, it seemed, to the surname Woodberry as well. His present position was becoming impossible. History was ready to sweep him away, and he was awaiting it. Why? How stupid it made the tragi-comic efforts of his grandfather to get a couple more guns into his entitled salute from the British, for having helped put down the sepoy mutiny of 1857. He must get that Woodberry manuscript into his hands, and soon.

He was impatient, restless, but noticed again the strong, springy stride of Balban as he came towards him across the cool stone flags of the wide corridor. Balban looked rather splendid and convincing in a saffron dhoti, nothing else, his golden-brown body lithe and muscular, his health and happiness evident in every movement. How free he was. Could he still be eating opium and look so wide awake, so fresh and ready? He could, and had done so for years. How could it be that this charming, intelligent lunatic could be so reliable, so likeable, and so honest? Was he perhaps some as yet unknown kind of modern saint? It was too ridiculous even to consider, but — he must not start laughing now, remembering the disturbing sermon. He must be firm with Balban, kind as always, but no badinage, no speculative chatter about the meaning of unmeaning. He needed Balban to act with speed, reliability, and absolute obedience. No fun and games with

248

Major Tone. He did not smile as Balban reached him, and Balban obeyed this silent instruction with his usual understanding. He stopped, his face grave, about to make his greeting, his hands rising together in *pranam*, but he showed no surprise when the Maharajah, still silent, pointed quickly, commandingly, to his own feet. Balban knelt immediately and placed his forehead on the Maharajah's shoes while lightly gripping the heels of the shoes with his strong slender hands.

So it was to be a secret, sensitive mission he was about to be given, one which called for discretion, but most of all for silence. On the two other occasions he had been signalled so curtly and silently to 'take the dust' like this, something the Maharajah never allowed to others of the old days and customs, he had been given a mission and had been well rewarded for his endeavours.

He rose to his feet and the Maharajah was amused to see the glow of intensity in his eyes now, the excitement of the lover of intrigue, and he was pleased by the signs of this readiness and understanding. No need for that demeaning preamble, 'now remember, nobody must know about what I am about to . . . .' But why was it that he sometimes felt a swift sadistic wish to knock Balban down, see him cringe at his feet? A surge of atavistic caste-fury? Fear of the brotherliness he sensed in himself for this lunatic so obviously devoted to him? And thinking of that he spoke at a tangent now, out of anxiety, out of the trying to adjust to the genealogical shock Tone had ᵯudged into his life-long image of himself.

'Tell me,' he said, very curtly, 'is Colonel Woodberry still remembered among the people, the villagers? Do they remember him still?' Oh, yes, he was still remembered in the distant villages. They still, the old men especially, would say on occasion, 'Whether penis or sword, wield it like Woodberry.' God almighty! Yet — wait . . . .

He stared into Balban's steady eyes, his temper ablaze. He shouted, 'I've never heard that saying in my life. Are you making this up, Balban?' He must not make a fool of himself, descendant as he was of Rajputs — (and of Woodberry?, for this Woodberry mania now slowly seizing him could sense the toothless grin of the old men behind that startling saying Balban had just imparted to him).

Balban was quite cool, absolutely unmoved by this display

249

of princely temper, and in fact annoyed him further by saying, 'But, *Maharaj* Sahib, I can bring you old people now who will tell you —'

'Enough! Enough!' Then, friendly now, 'So he is remembered for the sword, for courage, is that it?'

'Oh, yes, *Maharaj* Sahib. The people in the town, since they have heard about the film to be made, are saying, "Ah, the story of when Rajput and Sahib were truly men, when life and death were fourteen annas to the rupee. Woodberry with his cavalry, and Bapu Sahib and his mother, Zarina, will rise from their graves to see this film."'

Bapu Sahib, son of Zarina, ancestor of himself, and, the Maharajah thought, still searching Balban's unflickering eyes, son of Colonel Woodberry. A longing to strangle Major Tone now.

'And Bapu Sahib was a hero,' he said, still watching Balban. How suspicious, how nervous, that letter from Tone had made him, but Balban nodded. 'Yes, *Maharaj* Sahib. He was a hero and is remembered as one, to this day.' What skill, behind the screens of the *zenana*, Zarina and her women must have used to hide the true facts, to weave in that time of savage tumult the convincing lies that had come down as history. But such public, lying tapestries had been woven then all over India, all over the Middle East, even in flea-bitten, ambitious Europe, in every court in the world, great and petty. So nobody suspected what had to be in that long-hidden, accursed manuscript. He must have it, soon, now.

One more test. This time to discover the steadiness, and the reliability, of Balban's honesty and loyalty, so unfaltering — up to now. He knew something of what had been going on during the last couple of days, the secret hurrying comings and goings in the palace.

'Now there is something else, Balban.' He stopped there, half smiling, his eyes still holding Balban's, and waited. It was sweet relief to hear the young man's immediate and unworried response, and to see what concern appeared in his face.

'You had gone from the palace, *Maharaj* Sahib. I tried to find you, so I could tell you. The Tone memsahib had been to see the Princess Subhadra, secretly. The Princess sent for me, secretly, asked me to swear loyalty and to work for her, to find out what Major Tone is doing with you, and why. To prevent this film being made. She threatened to have me

250

beaten because I would not obey her. I ran away and came back here.' Tears were in his eyes now and his voice was shaking, delighting the Maharajah despite the curious affection and rage he felt for his constantly tinkering, interfering, meddling, intriguing aunt. 'The Princess knows there was a letter written to you by Major Tone, and this letter has put the Tone memsahib in tears, and she is afraid of what you will do, *Maharaj* Sahib.' Balban stopped. His chest was heaving slowly from the emotion he was feeling. His eyes looked wildly at his master's. The Maharajah's face was expressionless now, but he nodded, satisfied.

'You did well, Balban,' he said, and there was a threat in the way he said it, especially when he added, 'Didn't you? You could so easily have been weak and made a mistake.' Too tiresome to go on about running with the hare and the hounds, and probably having to explain it so it could be added to Balban's mountainous store of unforgettable information.

'Never, *Maharaj* Sahib,' Balban said, standing to attention like some old-time sepoy, proudly, barely hinting at resentment of such an implication. 'Never.'

'First you will deliver a letter from me to the *Diwan*, cancelling the nonsense I had planned for tonight, the message-party. Then you will rejoin me in my car. Come.'

Balban walked beside him towards the station-wagon. 'I think you will enjoy what you are going to do, Balban,' he said. He named an old retired police officer, 'another good secret-keeper'. Before driving off, with Balban in the passenger seat, he lit a cigarette. He never offered Balban a cigarette or a drink, or shared anything of such a nature with him and this, he thought now, he would one day alter. As they drove off he began to tell Balban what it was he wanted him and the retired police officer to do.

'The Tone memsahib, Balban,' he said, 'is a woman of some honour, and she has proved that in the past, though you must be careful with her. Her mind is unsteady. But her husband, the major, why, there was a time once — long ago in the past, of course — when I would have hung him up in the sun, or had him chained to an elephant's foot and dragged for fifty miles until he died.' He clicked his tongue in disgust at these thoughts, while admiring the power of good manners, tradition, custom, in the way Balban not only restrained what

251

must have been almost unbearable curiosity, to know what it was that made Tone worthy of these out-of-date thoughts, but showed not a sign in his face at all of that curiosity. A very formidable fellow, this Balban, but he felt secure in the fear he knew the young man had for him as his ruling master, no matter how anti-progressive the rest of the world might consider it. He must never *quite* trust such a clever and amiable lunatic, but he knew Balban knew this. These days, with the press in India athirst for any story which could defame or ridicule people like himself, even the pettiest prince must be certain of a neeed loyalty, even from a likeable lunatic.

He drove in silence for a while, once again thinking about how he seemed to be at the centre of a growing cloud of unusual happenings, and all of them to do with his vulnerability and his need to decide what he must do with his life. There could be no doubt any longer that the machinery of fate, in the guise of a plan to make a film, was speeding faster every moment. He was still having quiet fun in response to the shock Tone's letter had given him. He had even enjoyed, at his leisure, sifting through a heap of musty family documents, part of the mass he had taken with him to the bungalow, though well aware that he was resisting urgency, fighting a sense of panic. For it was no longer what was he going to do with his life, but now it was also, Who am I? Am I now somebody else because of the hint in this poisonous letter? How can that be when I am still the person I thought I was, until I read it?

'Balban.'

'*Maharaj* Sahib.'

'Do you know a newspaper called "Flash"?'

'I've seen a copy, *Maharaj* Sahib. But I — '

'They've sent a reporter up here, from Delhi. He's sneaking about here, asking about this film of ours. I've refused to see him so far. Look out for him. Avoid him. Answer no questions. Nothing, say nothing. Understand?'

It was one of these new magazines and newspapers which had started up since the departure of the British, slick, scandalous, brash, daring, readable, nauseating, fascinating, hateful, and frightening. Normally he would have met the fellow and shot him a smooth line of patter, but now, now, following Tone's letter he could see all kinds of horrors ahead. *Flash* was a tabloid, its motto printed in red across the top of the front page — 'Faith, Hope and Clarity'. It had done things so far which no paper in India, even some of its new and sleazier rivals, had dared to do, and it had a special, cheerfully malevolent interest in the lives of the Indian princes, the once private sins of politicians, and it sought to offend all forms of what could be called Hindu religious vanity. Its huge photograph, in a recent issue, of a starving skeletal cow with a balloon caption coming from its mouth saying, 'I'm willing if you are,' had caused a national uproar among the cow-worshippers of the most traditional Hindu groups. The inference that it would be better to be served up and eaten as hamburger rather than live as a starving scavenger, opened up many old spiritual wounds. *Flash* also liked to report on which politicians had gone down to Goa for a drink, now that the anti-drink forces were closing bars all over India.

'Is that you, your Highness?' the voice on the telephone had been soft, Oxbridge, insinuatory yet worryingly friendly, 'I'm Sonny Sodawallah, reporting for *Flash*, you know. It's about this marvellous film you're making here. Now I don't want to write a lot of garbled, half-baked misinformation, so I'm wondering when you can — '

Sonny Sodawallah. Names like Sonny, Bobby, Robin, Dizzy, were still in use and smacked safely of an upper-class, moneyed, Oxbridge background. Sodawallah, a name put into use a hundred years ago by a Parsi merchant who had cornered the British Army mess contract for soda water to go with the Scotch, indicated that Sonny was not really doing it for the money. Normally he would have welcomed Sonny Sodawallah, but now he feared this reporter being led to Major Tone. Action, speed, urgency.

'Not scared are you, Balban?' He was himself scared, having noticed at what wild speed he was driving. Balban just smiled, lay back, revealed nothing.

It was going to take more than a note to the *Diwan* to set up all his new urgencies, he decided. And should he or should he not corner his aunt and shout at her, cow her, threaten her?

He had called Bingham from the bungalow, forgetting it had been three in the morning until he heard Bingham's startled sleepy voice saying, 'Chan? This is no time to commit suicide. I forbid it.' He needed Bingham's advice, needed to hear himself out as he talked his worries — some of them, that is — out loud to his old friend. Bingham would now be waiting for him at the bungalow. There was so much happening, and trying to happen. It must all be worked out, meticulously. Nothing must go wrong. Now this bloody reporter —

'Here we are,' he said, and stopped the car on the edge of Papra village. 'Give old Ganga Ram his instructions as I told you. And *don't discuss things* — '

'*Maharaj* Sahib, *please* trust me.' He looked into Balban's eyes, smiled, patted his shoulder. 'Of course, Balban. Absolutely.'

There was an answer of delight in the way Balban turned and strode off into the little village in search of the old retired police inspector, Ganga Ram, one of the old Rajput school, devoted, dogged, and as cunning and silent as a hunting-leopard.

'He's delighted, *Maharaj* Sahib,' said Balban, half an hour later, the station wagon speeding across the plain towards the city. 'When I told him he was to take orders from me he said, "If they are the orders of His Highness I would take them even from the lowest sweeper's mouth." '

Balban laughed shrilly and the Maharajah, grimly amused by this unconscious irony from the old police inspector, said, 'Never mind, Balban. You are the brainiest of Brahmins for me, and tonight be that for Ganga Ram too.' Now, with neurotic, feverish intensity, he began going over the plan again, scared something might be forgotten, overlooked. 'It's got to be tonight and no failure,' he said. 'It must not fail. Tonight.' But by the time he braked the station wagon at the palace he was again all uncertainty, unreasonable anger, and strangely fearful. Balban sat in silence beside him, waiting, not springing from the car to open the door on the Maharajah's side and then wait for him to descend. He knew. The bastard knew, had picked it up with that radar of his that his master had changed his mind.

'Well, Balban?' he said testily.

'The letter for the *Diwan* Sahib — ' Balban hesitated, waited.

'I've changed my mind. Tell Ganga Ram when he joins you. Nothing is to be done tonight. Nothing. You understand? You will wait for new orders from me. Sleep tonight in my library. Keep away from the Princess. But you will deliver a note from me to Major Tone, you personally. And watch out for this Parsi fellow from the press. Keep out of his way.

If he stops you then just tell him any lies you like. I'll tell you what — tell him the film is about the time the lord Buddha came to Induspur — '

'Of course, *Maharaj* Sahib,' Balban was immediately at one with the idea, enthusiasm in his voice. 'But the lord Buddha — he never did come here, did he, *Maharaj* Sahib? I've never — '

'He'll have been here once you've told the story. Don't forget that. We have Indian rights at least.' He started to laugh. 'That's it. The film is to be called *Brahmana-Bhojana* — how the Buddha came to the eating-festival of the Brahmins and preached the virtues of hunger, and how he was intrigued against — you know, you'll love it, Balban, knocking the Brahmins and so on. Come on.'

They got out of the station wagon and Balban followed him into the palace.

Outside the *Diwan*'s office the Maharajah pointed to the carpeted floor of the corridor, and Balban sat down with his back against the wall and waited.

The *Diwan* was sitting at his desk, a mass of documents concerning the new land surveys of the state in front of him. Year after year a government department in Delhi swallowed up, like a great maw, mountains of information with which it redrew the shape of what had been British India and 'The States'.

The Maharajah sat down in an armchair and smiled at the old man.

'This bastard from *Flash*,' he said, and raised his eyebrows. The *Diwan* smiled malevolently and nodded with satisfaction.

'A smooth gentleman,' he said. 'But dangerous, from that filthy magazine in particular. Polished and well-educated too. I had him in here — '

'Oh?' There was alarm in the Maharajah's voice, but the old man raised his hand and patted the air in reassurance.

'Oh, yes, *Maharaj* Sahib. We must not put a foot wrong there, with that dirty rag of a magazine. No. I poured a lot of drink into him.' The *Diwan* smiled to himself again in obvious satisfaction. 'Give me the drinking journalist who drinks right through the interview. I had water from a gin bottle, of course.' He tittered, rubbed his hands together. 'I was really *so* friendly, praising *Flash*, read it every issue, you

255

know, anxious to help, give the fellow a good story.' He looked archly at the Maharajah, very pleased with himself. 'I'd already telephoned Mister Croon and Mister Koltz at their hotel, warned them, told them what we preferred this newspaper brute should hear, and what he should not hear. I told them to answer no questions about palace life or doings, even their opinions, or their negotiations with you, *Maharaj* Sahib, about this film.' The *Diwan* sat back in his chair, smiling again. 'They hate newspaper people too, Mister Croon and Mister Koltz, or as Mister Koltz put it to me, "until I have them in my pocket". He had drunk quite a lot of whiskey by the time I sent him off to meet Mister Croon and Mister Koltz.'

'Is it only this film he wants to write about?'

'So he said.' The *Diwan*'s eyes met the Maharajah's, who nodded.

'Yes. So he said. You kept him away from the Princess?'

The *Diwan* frowned, then became agitated, rose from his desk, sat down again and began to pull at his fingers until the knuckles cracked. 'So far, *Maharaj* Sahib,' he said. 'So far'; though seemingly not too confident about maintaining this position, and unable to voice his real feelings about the Princess. His sunken eyes were glittering with secret thoughts now.

'I'm sorry we had to call off the message-party,' the Maharajah said. 'It would have been so delightful, really, but it was what I believe they call in the theatre "too much", "over the top", you know. I've got to do this right, get it absolutely right. You understand me?'

There was a silence and the *Diwan* turned his head and stared out of the window at the distant dusty hills, saying, '*Maharaj* Sahib, is it not possible to enlighten me a little more? To tell me something of what it is that is worrying you so much?'

'Oh? Do I look worried?'

'The Princess has been at me.' The strain of suppressed rage in the *Diwan*'s voice caused the Maharajah to start laughing but, quite accustomed to this, the *Diwan* continued. 'She is insistent, demanding, wanting to know what *I* know.' He looked pleadingly now at the Maharajah. 'Can you not enlighten me just a little, *Maharaj* Sahib, please? Surely, after all my service — '

256

'Out of the question,' the Maharajah snapped at him. 'It is a matter between myself and this nasty little excrescence Tone, that's all.' The *Diwan* was amazed to see the contortion of his master's handsome face, the bared teeth, the hands clenching and unclenching. 'Maybe I'll give this bastard from the news-paper, Flasher Sodawallah, a story after all — when I'm finished with Tone, that is. I'll give him a smell of Tone's court-martial and set him on Tone.' He became excited at this thought, his voice rising. He stood up. 'Yes, by God, that's what I'll do.' Now he put his hands on the *Diwan*'s desk and leaned forward, looking into the *Diwan*'s eyes. He said, '*Diwan* Sahib, have you enjoyed your life?' They were silent for a few seconds while they stared at each other. The Maharajah was smiling again, his sudden anger apparently forgotten.

'I have, *Maharaj* Sahib,' the *Diwan* said solemnly. 'So much that I am ready for the next one, whenever it wishes to begin.' Another silence. I'm getting him ready to retire, that's what it is, the Maharajah was thinking. But why? Why?

'The next one? Your next life?' he said.

The *Diwan* nodded. 'In my last life I suffered much,' he said in a low voice. 'That was clear to me when I was still a young man, working for your grandfather in his last years. Yes, I knew that, because of my happiness in this one, in my work, that is.' He looked a little frightened now, the Maharajah thought.

'Only in your work you were happy?'

'I am still happy in that work, *Maharaj* Sahib,' the *Diwan* reminded him, alert again.

The Maharajah was shaking his head, affectionate wonder in his eyes. 'So you believe all that? How lucky you are. How lucky. Though I wonder. I wonder. To have to come back and pay for your happiness in this life. Is that what you be-lieve?'

The *Diwan* smiled to himself now. 'Believe?' he said thoughtfully. 'Believe?' He looked at the Maharajah again. 'No, I would not say "believe", *Maharaj* Sahib, It is not like that. A Christian, or a Muslim, *believes*, or he may lose his faith, then he *dis*believes.' He shook his head, laughing softly to himself. 'No, no. It is nothing like that. I live my lives as they are given to me.' He stopped, thinking; and the Maharajah waited, thinking, he is talking to me as to a man who knows and understands nothing of these things.

The *Diwan* now pressed his thin hands together, as though in *pranam*, but actually in respectful, almost prayerful, request, for he said, 'You are very troubled, my son. If only I could help you. I am the *Diwan* and you are my prince, but I know I am not helping you.' For the Maharajah the ensuing silence seemed very long. He felt isolation too, utter detachment, and yet somehow it comforted him, he felt love, loved, wonder. Again, as if on the very knife-edge of understanding, he experienced, strangely, an instantaneous vision of his sitation, of a player troubled about his part in this endless play. The player opposite him, old, experienced, could not convey to him that experience so much greater than mere knowledge which can be voiced, and explained.

'Yes, I am troubled,' he said, more to himself than to his listener. 'But I've always been troubled, and against my will, against my wishes. Troubled about the point, the meaning, the meaninglessness, the waste of not knowing. And now I'm troubled about who I am. I'm still who I've always thought I was, yet I may not *be* who I've always thought I was. I may be somebody else instead. But then we only know who we are because we've been told from childhood, called some name or other, and we become that, believe that, act upon that. But we're nobody at all, really, only what and who we're called. There's no such thing as an inch, or a yard, or a mile. They're simply called that, for convenience, and have become that. But they're not that at all, really. Like I'm not who I'm called. Do you get the hang of any of this, *Diwan* Sahib?'

He felt the old man was watching him with simulated calmness, pretended acceptance, but secretly wondering if his ruler's mind was collapsing in front of him. To help, to break the silence, he went on to ask, 'Do you know anything about Zen, *Diwan* Sahib?'

The *Diwan* shook his head. 'No, *Maharaj* Sahib?'

The Maharajah tried again, to explain to himself while listening carefully. 'You see, *Diwan* Sahib, you only have to think for a moment of the millions of billions of human beings who have lived and died, vanished, unknown, leaving not a clue behind them, not even names, not even the names they were given so they would think they knew who they were. Then you have to think about all the prayers they said in a thousand languages, all they suffered, went through, feared and hoped until they vanished like those who went before them. Don't you think it would be a piece of impudence — well, let's say a pointless assumption on my part, to think I've come to some conclusion, found a meaning to the mystery? After all those millions of billions who knew nothing either, who prayed, burned offerings, tormented themselves, then vanished, so that they need not have been here at all for all they mattered. Now if some giant dictatorial government ever saw things that way, don't you think it would be quite entitled to wipe out the human race altogether, as some kind of answer, some kind of ending to what's been an endless and unanswerable dilemma? That may come, you know. It can be done now, at last. Can it be that that's what all the work through the centuries has been about, reaching this situation we're in now?'

To his surprise the *Diwan* nodded, as if agreeing with him, and he then opened a drawer in his desk and searched in it for a few seconds. He brought a sheet of paper out.

'Colonel Bingham gave me what he called "the score so far" only a few weeks ago, after I'd asked him what he thought about the international situation. That American general, you remember, the Korean War general, and the cold war, wanting to drop the atomic bomb on China. We were discussing all that and I asked him if he thought the human race was in danger of being destroyed.'

'What did he say?'

'He said it's not quite ready yet. He said there's not enough terror yet. He said it needs time to get all the weapons lined up, and he wrote "the score so far" down for me.' The *Diwan* read from the paper in his hands.

' "U.S. atom bomb 1945. Soviet atom bomb 1949. British atom bomb 1952. U.S. hydrogen bomb, five million tons of T.N.T. equivalent, 1952. Work continuing on both sides, for bigger and better bombs." ' The *Diwan* looked up. 'It is Colonel Bingham's opinion that human beings can not live without some form of war, some form of turmoil as he calls it, some kind of fear of each other, and that it is impossible for man to disarm. He believes that when it is all ready the planet will be devastated.'

'I agree,' said the Maharajah. 'Do you, *Diwan* Sahib? Does it worry you?'

259

'It does not worry me at all, *Maharaj* Sahib. After all, what is the world for me? It is me. When I am gone the world is ended, so the world ending doesn't worry me.'

'But what about your next life?'

'I know nothing about my next life, *Maharaj* Sahib. I must await all that. Perhaps the end of all the cycles is now coming and it is all finished and done with.'

As he walked to the window the Maharajah said, again as if to himself, 'I love learning. I've loved learning everything I've learned, so I don't mind being what I've become. I'm an amateur Indian and an amateur world-person. I don't really belong anywhere any more. Yet I feel I've lost my innocence. I've lost what may be the most valuable thing a man can have, a lack of understanding. I've lost that. I care now. I want to hear and read the bloody news, want to know what's happening out there. I'm going to stop that. I'll give my radio away for a start.' He stood at the window. 'I envy the thick, the stupid, the illiterate, who can look up to the others, the so-called learned, and wait to be told what's what —'

'It's not going to be like that for much longer, *Maharaj* Sahib,' the *Diwan* said with surprising asperity. 'Innocence? Truth? There was a time in the villages when a man would not dare to lie. They would scratch the river Jumna and the Ganges out on the earth, then stand him between those two holy rivers and question him. And he would not lie, even if telling the truth meant his death. Not now. They would lie now to the gods themselves. It's finished, *Maharaj* Sahib, the world I knew as a boy. Finished. There is so much evil in the world now that the birds themselves can hardly fly through it. Yes, there is the end coming, because it has to, and I know that it is only the Western side of me that regrets it, and wishes men would be good to each other.'

'Quite. Quite,' said the Maharajah abruptly, ending the spell they had wrought on each other. 'Now, I want a sheet of notepaper. I'm going to write a curt, clever little note to this bastard Tone.'

The *Diwan* rose and the Maharajah sat down in the offered chair and wrote the note to Tone. He looked up when he had finished it and said, smiling, 'It's interesting, isn't it, after all I've just said? You see I'm still caring, still trying to get things right, to get things organized *my* way. Maybe it's that in man which will save the world, the care about trivia and the devotion to things that mean actually nothing, which will ensure the safety of the planet so we can go on with the habit of being alive, then dying.' His short explosion of laughter made the old man uncomfortable.

He got up from the desk and stretched his arms, moaning with pleasure, and then looked at the *Diwan*. 'And there's my new guilt, *Diwan* Sahib,' he said. 'My sociological guilt, my parasitical situation now as a caretaker of this little museum of ours here. My guilt as a useless mouth, a leech on the body of society, that is according to the politicians of what we might call "the new indignation". I pretend my guilt, of course. I'm pretty good at it now. I was thinking I might give this Flasher Sodawallah an interview. Tell him about my guilt, how I've seen the light, come to understand how it's the Communist leaders' turn to live in this palace and suck the people's blood for a while. The happiest people in the world today are the Communist bosses in Russia, with their private, secret warehouses full of food and drink and Western goodies of all kinds, and they deserve it. After all they've done what the tsars wanted, expanded the Russian empire, and will expand it further now. I think I'll tell Flasher all that, nicely, of course, gently, realistically. Praising the Communists for their loyalty to the great Russian expansion, and appearing to mean it. From what you've seen of the man, do you think he'll lap it up — if I give a good, solemn performance, I mean?'

'Oh, *Maharaj* Sahib,' the *Diwan* was fearful, his hands clasped. 'Please be careful. He's quite a clever man, educated. In fact I wonder how he can work for that filthy paper.'

'He works for it because they want to shock the human race, spit in its face. That's because they're so tired of the dreary remains of the Victorian world we have here. After all we're very far behind, *Diwan* Sahib, very old-world in many ways. The Flashers of this world want to see anger, outrage, denial, explanation, remorse and all that kind of nonsense. What better than to tell Flasher that if I had enough money I'd join the Communist party tomorrow, but that I can't afford it, not yet anyway? I could come out of the interview as an eccentric, a semi-mystic, an acceptant and gallantly repentant half-baked intellectual on the way to an understanding of the real world in which we live. They love that expression, you know. The *real* world.' He went to the door, turned. 'Now, tell the Princess that you've seen me and that I'm in a state of frightening rage. Warn her to stay in her room and out of the way. Tell her that I said to be careful. I don't quite know what I mean by that, but perform, *Diwan* Sahib. Be stern. I'll telephone you tomorrow.'

CHAPTER 21

'Please.'

'No.' A pause. 'No. I can't. I — '

'Megan, *please*.'

'I said no. No. I can't.'

'Well — how about no, Roger. Just say my name, at least, Roger. Please, Megan.'

Lying on the other bed in Croon's hotel room Ted Koltz called to him, 'Tell her you're on your knees.'

'I'm on my knees, Megan. Please,' Croon pleaded.

'Christ, no, no,' Koltz shouted at the ceiling. 'I was kidding.'

But Croon was winning, or so it seemed. Koltz leaned on his elbow and poured another whiskey into his glass, watching Croon with amused blue eyes, shaking his head as Croon turned, still holding the phone to his ear, and grinned at him.

'How did you know I was here at the palace?' Megan asked, nodding to Subhadra who was standing by the drinks table, holding up a bottle of gin, her eyebrows raised. Megan put her hand over the mouthpiece and said to Subhadra, nodding towards the quietly weeping Iris Tone slumped on the couch, 'A brandy mightn't do *her* any harm. H'mn?' Then angrily into the mouthpiece she snapped at Croon, 'Oh, do shut up. Do stop whining. Where's all that boring arrogance gone, that manic monologue of yours?' She looked up, took the drink from Subhadra and caught her eye, meaningly, as she said into the mouthpiece, 'I'll tell you what — Roger' — God, it came so unwillingly, his name, interesting, really — 'I *will* have a drink with you at the club, on one condition.' She listened to him for a moment, then went on. 'That letter you got from Major Tone, at the club. Yes. Bring it with you, and tell me about it. I'll tell you why when I see you. No, not now. When I see you.' She smiled up at Subhadra who was smiling, nodding an almost frantic approval, and then even bent over and kissed Megan on the forehead. She took a bran-

263

dy to Iris and sat beside her. Iris looked wrecked, racked, pale, wet-faced from silent weeping, and cowed and shocked after the shouted, bullying tirade from Subhadra, just before Croon's telephone call. But she had kept her secret, had held her tongue even when almost unbearably provoked by the domineering, insulting treatment she had been receiving from the amazing little Princess. This was her first meeting with Subhadra in years. At one point in Subhadra's pitiless attack on her weakness, her two-facedness, her determined evasiveness, she had tried to escape from the room. But the Princess had raced to the door ahead of her, placed her back against it, pointed imperiously at the couch, and shouted, 'SIT DOWN, YOU SILLY BLOODY BITCH.'

Iris had clasped her hands together, tears flowing, and had turned her anguished eyes on Megan, pleading, imploring silently.

'Better sit down, Iris,' Megan had said quietly. 'After all, *you* came to the Princess for advice, help, whatever the hell it was, didn't you? Come now, sit down and try and calm yourself.'

'All women together,' said Subhadra with a kind of smiling, sardonic satisfaction. 'Just us three. It's lovely. *So* lovely, don't you think, Megan? We mustn't trust each other *too* much, I suppose.' Then the bright, gay, snapped-off laugh as she sat down and sipped her drink, watching Iris across the rim of her glass with the eyes of a bird of prey.

'All right, Megan,' she said. 'I'm listening. Tell all.'

'He's in love with me. D'you want to hear more?'

'No, thank you. Just about this letter from Major Tone.'

She kept darting arrow-like glances at Iris, as if wishing her gone, yet fearful that she might escape before her tormenting secrets were wrung from her. It was the sheer, almost bovine, sullen stubbornness of this strange woman which so infuriated her.

'I see,' said Subhadra in response to Megan's reply. 'So you saw him get this letter from Major Tone, you say it was given to him by this American in the club. Now I know what was happening here, believe me, Megan. The two men here, Chandu and Colonel Know-all Sahib getting drunk and waiting for news of you after you ran off with this man with the stupid name.' She raised her small, beautiful golden hand. 'No excuses, please. I don't want to hear them. So the American found you in the club with this man. Those were his orders from Chandu, you know. Find Megan and see what she's doing and tell her to stop doing it. Oh, you didn't know that? *Well!*' She now picked up Megan's urgent eye-signals for silence in front of Iris. Subhadra looked at Iris, who was holding her forgotten brandy, staring down at her feet, her mind apparently very far from this scene she was slumped in. Waiting for another tirade, for orders, possibly.

'I don't think we need let that worry us, do you?' She jerked her head at Iris and smiled at Megan.

'Did you get a chance to read the letter?'

Megan began to blush and her eyes became evasive, and her realization of this increased the heat of the blush. The Princess smiled scornfully, affectionately at her.

'So you got a look at it. Good. I knew you weren't a complete fool. Go on.'

Megan let out a long quivering sigh and, head back, drained her glass of gin and tonic, then looked at Subhadra. 'What a splendid interrogator you'd make, in some dictatorship or other, Subhadra,' she said, smiling. Subhadra smiled back at her.

'I know,' she said. 'And who knows, my chance may come, the way things are going these days.' She turned to Iris and gave her an order, like a head hospital matron with a tiresome geriatric patient. 'Come along now, Iris. Get on with your brandy. I'll be back to you in a minute. Come on now, down with it.' Without a glance at Subhadra, but still sullen, glumly determined, Iris drank some brandy and then stared bleakly at the wall.

'Go on, Megan. The letter. What did it say?' But Megan felt too ashamed of having allowed Subhadra to bully Iris Tone without protest to be able to ignore the results any longer, and kept her eye on Iris. She looked not merely tragic, but ridiculous as well, and that seemed worse, much more humiliating. But she knew that was not the real reason for trying to ignore Subhadra's eager questioning about the letter to Croon. After all, Iris Tone had caused her much pain by her gossip in the past, so why should she be squeamish now about seeing Iris getting a tongue-battering for a change? No, it was that she could not make up her mind to tell Subhadra what

265

she had read in Tone's letter to Croon, at least not while Iris was in the room. Now Iris looked at her. It was a look of desperate appeal, but for what?

'Now, Iris,' she said harshly. 'Just what is it you came here to say to the Princess? And why can't you say it? Why? Tell us.'

'Yes,' Subhadra shouted, turning on Iris again, the Croon letter forgotten, and again Megan shivered. She did not know why, but seeing this version of Subhadra had frightened her. She had never seen such wilfulness, such vehement authority demanding obedience, and Iris Tone's almost comic, yet immovable stubbornness in response was very surprising.

'Answer, Iris. Answer,' Subhadra yelled at her. 'What did you come here to say, and why won't you say it?'

'I can't,' Iris muttered, as if to herself, looking down at the Bokkhara carpet. 'It's about the letter my husband wrote to the Maharajah. I told you that. I haven't read it, but I — ;' as she hesitated Subhadra shouted at her, louder than before.

'Yes, yes, yes, we know all that, and that he wrote the letter about this manuscript you've been paid money to keep secret all these years. We know all that. What is it in this damned manuscript we'd all forgotten about until your husband got hold of it? And what has he said to the Maharajah?' Subhadra was panting and Megan saw, with shock, that her small hands were clenching and unclenching, as if she was about to seize Iris Tone by the throat. But Iris could not talk. She rose to her feet and said to Megan, 'My family have lived five generations in India. I have never been treated like this before in my life.' This statement seemed to give her courage, for now she eyed Subhadra with cold, sad eyes, and said to her, 'I came here because I want to prevent trouble, that's all. But I cannot — I don't know — it's not possible to say what I want to say.' She frowned, puzzled by the intricacy of her dilemma, and now tried to describe it, to excuse her maddening refusal to say what she so wanted to say. 'If I say it, it will cause great trouble, but if I *don't* say it and the Maharajah never does see the manuscript, then I was right not to say it. I see that now. But if I do say it and the Maharajah never sees the manuscript anyway, then I will have been wrong, I mean — '

'Oh, shut up,' Subhadra shouted.

'I wish to go,' said Iris.

'Do let her go now, Subhadra,' Megan said.

'Go!' Subhadra pointed dramatically to the door.

Iris was almost whimpering. 'You must try and understand —'

'GO! NOW!' Subhadra rushed to the door and opened it, then walked to the drinks table and stood with her back to the other two.

Iris smiled in a curious, sad, sly way at Megan, saying in a low voice as the passed her, 'It's wonderful the way you keep your looks in this climate. Your skin, I mean. As for mine . . . .' She dragged her fingers down both her sallow cheeks and passed out through the doorway.

Her back still turned to Megan, Subhadra said in a cold, menacing tone, 'Don't think for a moment that I've forgotten about the letter to this Croon gentleman. You read it. We both know that. Now — tell me what was in it.'

'Major Tone wants a job on the film, that's what it's about.' Megan spoke in a clipped, mechanical manner, like a young officer reporting after his first patrol. 'Threat about something. He'll publish this manuscript which will blow everything sky high and stop the film. He's more or less told this to the Maharajah. So what does Croon think? Then more about his, Tone's, expert knowledge, how useful he'll be as adviser on the film.'

'I knew it. I knew. I knew it.' Subhadra addressed her melodramatic cries to the ceiling, her back still turned. 'I said it. I warned Chandu. I warned him. I don't know what it's all about, but I do know the family have always been afraid about that manuscript.' She turned and looked at Megan, her black eyes shining. 'Chandu's up in his bungalow with the family archives. Do you know that? He's been behaving as if he's lost his mind.' Now she mimed a woman whose burden had become too much. She clutched her hands against her breast, rolled her eyes up towards the ceiling, said, 'It's all too much. Too much,' then made her way to the settee and lay back on it. An amateur actress herself, with much experience alone before her bedroom mirror, Megan felt offended by the crudeness of Subhadra's performance. 'A brandy is indicated, I think, Subhadra,' she said, drawling the words so as to convey just a hint of the boredom she felt, but it was lost on Subhadra, who said, 'Yes, Megan. A brandy would help just now.'

Megan sat beside her as Subhadra sipped the brandy. She

said, 'May I offer a little advice, Subhadra?'

Subhadra looked at her, considering it, then she smiled and patted Megan's hand. 'Go on,' she said.

'Leave it all alone, Subhadra. Don't interfere. Let Chandu handle it himself. Don't you agree?'

'You're already talking like his wife. Do you know that? H'mm.' She patted her hand again. 'You upset him, you know. Running off like that with Broom — '

'Croon.'

'Don't you care, Megan? About upsetting him. Don't you love him?'

Megan got up, disturbed again, went to the window and stared out at the distant Himalaya range. 'I'd better go,' she said. 'I haven't been any help, I'm afraid.'

'I asked you to come because I'm afraid for Chandu,' said Subhadra bitterly. 'Can't you understand? He's so stupid and wilful, once he starts something. Go to him and tell him to stop this film.' As if suddenly inspired now, she leapt up from the settee. 'Yes,' her voice was strong again. 'Go to him and stop this film, otherwise I shall go to this monstrous creature myself and demand this manuscript. This dreadful thing must be finished, now, once and for all. Tell Chandu that. That you love him. That *I* love him. To stop the film and I will get that manuscript.'

Megan could not help laughing as she studied Subhadra's face, the black eyes now somehow beady, burning with curiosity, with longing to know what was in that manuscript. She had to explain. 'Get that manuscript *and* read it,' Megan said. This did not annoy Subhadra. Instead she smiled, tenderly, at Megan, and said, 'Well, of course, darling. We've only *heard* about this bloody manuscript, as some kind of threat, so of course I want to read it. Now, you drive up to Chandu and get him to see sense.'

'Don't go to Major Tone, Subhadra.'

'Tell Chandu I'm thinking of doing just that,' Subhadra put her arm about Megan's shoulder and walked her to the door.

'Nobody must know I read that letter from Major Tone to Mister Croon, Subhadra. Please.'

'You do what I want and I'll do what you want.' She laughed, then embraced Megan warmly, adding, 'This film is not going to be made.'

CHAPTER 22

'Iris,' said Bingham coldly, set upon defending himself, 'it'll have to be some other time, I'm afraid. I'm late for an appointment and I have to go.' If anything she was in a far worse state, by the look of her wet eyes, than the last time she had come to his house a year ago 'for help, for advice'. A year ago now?

He was half-way down the stairs of the club on the way to his jeep when Iris Tone got out of her car and called to him. He was shocked by the hysteria, the desperate pleading in her voice. He must not get involved, though he knew it must be about this bloody tiresome Woodberry saga. Better to go straight to Tone perhaps and bully him into an explanation? No, though — no! He was on his way to stay with Chan up at the bungalow, get dragged further into this probably quite unnecessary mess Tone had started, and he was late, having had to go through the club accounts with Janki Nath, with a sandwich and a beer for lunch.

When he reached his jeep Iris Tone gripped his arm and said, 'Tim, please. I know you've never liked me. I'm sorry, so sorry. But I've no one to turn to, and I'm so frightened —'

'Frightened?' He turned and looked at her. How good-looking she still was, wasted, neglected, the thick black hair greying now, the dark eyes splendid still despite the messy bleared effect of the unshed tears. Even so she reminded him of a crow, a bedraggled crow, wings broken by years with Tone. 'Frightened of what?' He sighed exasperatedly. He looked at his wrist-watch. 'Come on. Tell me about it. But quickly.' He ran up the stairs of the club, turned on her, 'For Christ's sake, Iris, get yourself together. Come on.' She was still standing, looking pitiful by her car, staring up at him in appeal.

'Don't *swear* at me, Tim,' she called up to him, her face starting to distort with the threat of tears. 'I'm in such trouble.'

Trouble? This bitch had caused more trouble in the past with her gossip, her anonymous writings, her — but he knew why, was sorry for her, and feared her talent for meddling, for the mess she could cause because other people's private lives had always been her only hobby. He could not control his temper.

'Get up here, quickly, come on, Iris.' Then, sorry for that almost military command, said as if to a child, 'Come on now, and tell me what the trouble is. Hurry.'

He took her into Janki Nath's office. The Pandit looked up from his desk. Bingham jerked his thumb, winking at him. 'Come back in ten minutes, Janki Nath.' The Pandit picked up the book he was reading, Kabir's poetry in Urdu, and glided out of the office. Bingham closed the door. 'No, I won't sit down, Iris. I'm very late. Now come to the point. I don't want a scene like the last time. No tears. You're frightened, you say. Frightened of what?'

Perhaps it was only her grudging, cantankerous, brooding affection and admiration for him which gave her spirit then, hearing his almost snarling tone with her.

'I'm not frightened of *you*, you know,' she said defiantly. 'Stop shouting at me, Tim.' Tim. Christ!

'What's all this Tim business, suddenly?' he demanded, defending himself again.

'You've always been Tim to me,' she said, very thoughtfully. 'We can't all help our feelings, I suppose.' She smiled at him. The smile trembled on her lips. 'Yes, I have feelings. Strange, isn't it?'

You can say that again, thought Bingham. It was an expression used by Ted Koltz which had amused him, pleased him. For some time now he had been fighting his curiosity about this bloody Woodberry mystery, dreading the dangers of finding himself in the forests of other people's private lives, private agonies. Had his own to defend anyway, like everyone else; which reminded him about the jokers who sent their friend a telegram — 'All is discovered. Leave immediately.' Fellow took the next train, never seen again.

'Look, Iris,' he said, with menacing quiet, revealing his strained patience, his need to leave. 'Tell me what's the matter. What do you want me to do? Now come to the point, *please*.' He was pretty certain there was a blackmail job involved somewhere in this business. Bugger it, get to the point, brutally. 'What's Freddy up to now?' he said.

'So you know, do you?'

She was going to do it again, like last time. A year ago? Demanding help, advice, and then winding long skeins of maddening talk about everything else except what she had come to talk about, unable to say what it was she needed to say, frightened of herself.

'I said what's Freddy up to now?' he shouted at her. 'If that's what this is about then either speak up now, or I'm off. I've got to go, do you hear me?'

'Freddy's been bouncing cheques,' she cried, her voice breaking. 'He's being sued. He won't tell me anything.' Her breathing began to quicken. She closed her eyes and said, 'I'm going to divorce him.'

'Anything else?'

She opened her eyes and glared at him. 'What bastards men are really, all of you,' she said in a low, vehement voice. 'What fools women are. "Anything else?" Is that all you can say?'

'That's not what you came to me to say, is it? Now, for Christ's sake, Iris, get it over. Is there anything else?'

'I want you to come and talk to him. He's frightened of you.'

'Don't talk bloody nonsense, frightened of me. Christ give me strength. What do you want me to say to him?' Bugger it, why not? 'Come on,' he said. He took her by the arm, led her out of the office, winked at Janki Nath.

He could feel what he always thought of as 'a dirty mood' growing in him, something he usually fought off by shutting himself up in his study and sitting down, one more time, to try and learn Hungarian. It was a form of masochistic self-help, and he often remembered congratulating a Greek barman in Beirut years ago, whom he had heard speak five languages perfectly, and the barman saying 'Yes, Monsieur, and I can even speak Hungarian.'

'Jeeps frighten me,' Iris wailed, sitting beside him as he fiercely rammed the gear lever into third. 'Don't go fast, please. You know how jeeps turn over so easily, Tim. I remember —'

'I know,' he shouted. 'I know. You've told it in the club a hundred times — you saw so many jeeps turn over and kill everybody during the war when you were in Bangalore. Hand me a cigarette out of the case. It's in front of you.'

She handed him the cigarette. 'Now get on with it. What's this about a letter sent by — by' — he so wanted to shout 'by this bastard, Tone'; couldn't even use his name, Freddy — 'by your husband? What's going on?'

'All you have to do is — you're the Maharajah's friend and that's important — so if you — '; she covered her face with her hands and cried, 'Oh, my God —'

'Jesus Christ allregimentalmighty,' Bingham growled. He shouted at her again. 'Where is this bloody manuscript? The Woodberry thing. Where is it? That's the problem, isn't it. Come on. Answer. Speak up. Where is it, and what's the problem?'

'Ask *him*. Him.' She began to declaim. 'Him. Him. Him.'

He turned his head slightly and said, acidly, 'You mean I should ask *him*, I gather. Lighter!'

'What?'

'LIGHTER! It's in front of you.' She handed him the lighter. 'I want to see him alone. Understand?'

She nodded, kept on nodding, almost eagerly, like a child.

He could almost feel her eagerness, her wish to have him dominate, humiliate, this half-baked character she had used up so much of her life on. Because she enjoyed the suffering, the need to feel resentment? I've been dragged in to this. Right. Very well.

'Now, Iris,' he lowered the shout in his voice a little. They were nearing the Tone house. 'Who owns the house? You?' He knew she owned it, but he wanted room for a little rhetoric.

'Yes. It was given to my ancestor and we've had it ever since.'

'And you're inviting me in today? Correct?'

'But what's that got to do — ?'

He shouted again, louder now. 'Are you inviting me in to the house now, today? Yes?'

'Well, yes. You *are* going to talk to Freddy, aren't you?' Her voice was loaded with disappointment, accusation, that readiness to be let down, misunderstood.

'And you own the house, not him. Good.'

He was in such a dirty mood that when he rammed his foot down on the brake the jeep slewed for a few yards on the red, crunching gravel in front of the house.

Instantly Tone came out on to the verandah. 'So you decided to come back, did you?' he yelled at Iris. 'I was wondering. I wondered if you'd sailed for *home* or something.' He barked, laughing, pleased by the sledge-hammer subtlety of this old British-Indian sneer at the country-born who spoke of 'home', England, as if they had been there.

'So you're still drunk, are you?' Iris said as she went slowly up the steps.

'Not quite. But working at it.' He looked at Bingham coming up the steps. 'What's *he* doing here?' He turned to Iris. 'What's going on?' He was very animated, eyes bloodshot and staring, but breaking into barks of laughter when he said, 'I've just received a royal command, Bingham, from your pal — yes, the bloody Maharajah himself. Amazing, eh? Me, the outcast, the only bloody sahib never allowed inside that palace, and now I'm invited. Well, as you can see for yourself, I'm so bloody delighted I'm just about off my head. And now *you're* here, right after I get the royal command —'

'Come inside, Tim,' Iris said.

'So you're Tim as well now? This is a big day for me, Bingham. Come in.' He swept his arm in an overdone pantomime, bending forward as he did so, towards the entrance to the living room, darkening Bingham's already 'dirty mood'.

Tone sat down at the head of the enormous Victorian family table on which were heaps of books, sheets of manuscript and one or two old maps of the State. Bingham sat in an armchair. Iris, querulous now, stood in the doorway and interrogated Tone.

'What are you talking about, the Maharajah? Have you heard from him? You're drunk, still drunk, aren't you?'

Tone took an envelope from his pocket and waved it at her. 'You were wrong,' he said, aggressive, but quieter now. 'He got the message, read between the bloody lines, like I said he would.' He took a letter from the envelope and read it to her. ' "Dear Tone, I have read your interesting letter. I think it is splendid that you have decided to publish the Woodberry manuscript. I will expect you for drinks this evening at seven when we will discuss your plans for this long delayed project." Well?' He asked the question with an air of triumph, a man who had obviously endured much scepticism and had now proved how right he had been. 'You ran out of here like a lunatic, didn't you? Terrified, craven in fact. You wouldn't listen to me, would you?' Old rancour began to surface again.

'You've never listened to me. This should have been done years ago. Years ago.' He glared at her, waiting.

'Well — I'm glad, Freddy.' Iris smiled at him tiredly. 'So glad.' She swallowed with difficulty, seemingly close to tears. She looked at Bingham.

'Would you like a drink, Tim?'

'Thank you. A whiskey'd go down well. Nothing with it, please, just water.'

When she had gone Tone eyed Bingham with hostility. 'How much has she told you, Bingham? She's been out all day, gassing her head off as usual, of course. What d'you want here? Or should I say, "To what do I owe this great honour?" The Maharajah's talked to you, is that it?'

Lying back in the armchair, relaxing himself as much as possible because of the antagonism he felt for Tone, Bingham said, 'Whatever it is you're up to this time, Tone, I hope Iris is wrong to be scared. She *is* scared, and badly. I didn't want to come here. She begged me to come, and to talk to you. Try and make you "see sense", as she puts it.' He laughed. 'I needn't tell you that that's the last thing I'll try to do. I'm here because of a very pressing invitation from Iris, that's all. And I'll be off as soon as I finish my drink. That clear?'

'So you didn't want to come here at all, is that what you're saying?' Tone's manner was surprisingly restrained, Bingham thought, for he had certainly been drinking heavily by the look of him.

'That's about it, yes.'

'What is it you've always had against me, Bingham? All of you, that is. When they were here, those who went home, you were all against me. Right? Now we've got this bloody Maharajah, who has pretended I don't exist, coming to heel with this letter.' He tapped the letter which lay on the table before him. 'I don't need to take any notice of this bloody invitation. I don't need to go and visit this bugger. *He* needs me, though — '

'So you'll go. Now, you be very careful, Tone. I mean for Iris's sake. This is her house. Whatever you're up to, she's very scared about it. If you're playing games with the Maharajah be very careful.'

Iris interrupted what was almost certainly going to be a heated response from Tone. She seemed in an oddly gay mood now, and after laying the drinks tray on the table she did what seemed to Bingham a startling thing. There was a thick, rolled magazine on the tray which was secured with elastic bands. She now picked this up and playfully struck Tone across the head with it, not too hard, but enough to make him lift his hands to protect himself. It was obviously something she had done before, and which Tone was used to, for he laughed as she hit him again and he again sought to protect himself.

'You wicked boy, Freddy,' she cried, gaiety in her voice, striking him lightly about the head, and then the blows became just a little harder. Then she fetched him one under the jaw so hard that it almost caused him to fall from the chair, and as she did this Bingham looked at her face and quailed. The white glistening smile was there, of the wife playing this strange game with her husband, but as Bingham looked at her eyes, worried and embarrassed as he was, and saw the expression in them he stood up, anxious to leave. Although he could not let himself define it he saw that these two shared an as yet uncommitted murder.

'Not to worry, Tim,' she called to Bingham, smiling, the ferocious expression gone from her dark eyes now. She threw the magazine onto the sofa nearby. 'He can be so wicked, you know.' She looked with an almost motherly expression down at Tone. 'You always convince me, don't you, Freddy?' She handed Bingham his drink, then pushed the jug of water to him.

She leaned on the table, as if the better to look into Bingham's eyes, and he tried to stare back into hers, afraid they might reveal the shiftiness he sensed she was seeking in them.

'Do you know anything about the strength of the weak man, Tim?' she asked. Bingham heard Tone's savage guffaw while he tried to hold his own against Iris's black, hypnotic stare, heard Tone call out, 'And his tenacity, his unbreakable rubber will. All mine by the way, Bingham, stolen by her from me, my own statements about myself.' Another guffaw.

'Yes,' said Iris, her gaze still locked in Bingham's, 'his own words. "Weakness is strength," he said, after I told him he was weak. You know it's true, do you, Tim? That the weak man uses everybody and everything around him? That he can destroy the strong? So I'm asking you to be firm with him. Firm.' She raised her clenched fist above the table but before she could bring it down Bingham said, raising his voice slowly as if to a child, 'No-o-o, Iris. Put it down quietly now.' Iris unclenched her hand and laid it on the table again, and went on, 'He stole the manuscript from me — '

'Borrowed,' shouted Tone. 'On loan.'

'And now he's going to publish it, unless the Maharajah resumes the family pension which I cancelled years ago. I'll lose this house if he does that — '

'That's not her real worry,' Tone shouted. 'Tell him your real worry. Go on. Tell him.'

'I really must go, Iris,' Bingham started to rise from the chair but Iris pushed him down into the chair again, saying frantically, 'No. No, Tim. I will not let *you* be weak. No.'

'Get the idea now, Bingham?' Tone called out. 'Why I get pissed at the club, when I can? Which reminds me.' Tone, blocked from Bingham's view by Iris until now, got up from the table and went to pour himself another drink, laughing to himself.

Iris stayed in front of Bingham, her hands on the table again, her voice softer now, in appeal. 'I'm leaving you with him, Tim. I'll be in the next room. I won't listen, I promise. But I'm asking you to be strong, to stop him, to — '

'That's enough, for Christ's sake,' Tone shouted impatiently. 'He's got the message. Be *firm*. Well, give the bugger a chance, Iris. Let him have a go. Now shove off and let him do his stuff. I'll call you when he's finished.'

'I'm relying on you, Tim.' It was almost a whisper, and Iris smiled at him. It was a smile so sickly, so false, so tremulous, yet so pathetic, that Bingham lowered his eyes and said, 'Do go. Do leave us alone for a while, Iris. Now. Please.'

When the door closed behind her Tone came back to the table with his drink and sat down. He grinned feebly at Bingham.

'For years she's tried to break herself against me. Tried to smash herself against me, and smash me as well,' he said, still grinning, raising his glass as if to her splendid efforts through rubber, and bounce off, there's a certain amount of frustration builds up. Inevitable, right? You can not control a bundle of rubber, any more than you can smash it. Right? Now, I watched you taking in that little domestic scene' — he flicked a finger towards the rolled up magazine on the sofa — 'where she pretends lovingly to knock me about with that thing. I could see it shook you up a bit. Eh?' He grinned again. 'And why not? You could see how it might become a length of lead piping, say, right? Oh, I know what's going on, Bingham. All the time. Everywhere.' He looked at his wrist watch. 'Almost time for the old army routine, a shit, shave and shower. M'mm.' Suddenly bright-eyed, cheery, he smiled at Bingham and said, 'Right. You've got to be *firm* with me, don't forget. So get on with it. Be firm.'

'Why don't you give Iris back this bloody manuscript, Tone, and save everyone a lot of trouble?' Bingham said.

'Ah! Are those your instructions from His Nibs?'

'You're a stupid, maddening bugger, Tone, aren't you?' He said this in what he meant to be a friendly, headshaking tone, a kind of tribute to incorrigibility.

'I'm gambling for high stakes, Bingham.' Tone was businesslike now, grave and decisive. 'I need the money. After all it's only a bloody pension which was allowed to lapse. Nothing more than that. I simply want the pension to be paid again. Now here's an idea for you. You have a lot of pull at the palace, we all know that. You could swing this thing in two minutes, *and* take your cut from the pension. See? On the other hand if you feel taking a cut is far below your sense of honour and all that bullshit, then you can do it to save everybody a lot of trouble, as you put it. Talk to His Nibs. And don't forget this is history we're talking about, not merely money. I need the money and the world needs the history. Right? So how about it?'

'Tone.'

'Yes?'

'Seeing you're talking about cuts and so on, may I ask you what happened to your cut, your three million rupees you and the others fiddled in nineteen forty-four? I mean the time you sold the million pairs of condemned army boots twice over, and nothing could be proved?' Bingham was amazed by Tone's calm and cool reaction to this reminder of a little-known scandal, one of many on the long, tortuous, multi-million rupee supply line of the war.

'After the court of enquiry — which cleared me, don't forget — I was kicked into Burma. I never got my cut in the end. How much do you know about the case, by the way?'

In nineteen forty-eight, when the last British troops were

ceremonially marching out of India, a military voice had been heard to shout, though unheard by the troops, 'AB-O-U-T TURN!'

An incensed, and highly placed, member of the Congress Party, standing with Bingham above the crowd watching the ceremony, had gone to some trouble in an effort to find the owner of that commanding voice. He was never found, though Bingham's suspicions that it was Tone were later confirmed by another officer, an he had then been shown extracts from Tone's military record, in which was the unproven case of the tiny scandal of the million pairs of condemned army boots.

'It hardly matters now, I think,' Bingham said. 'So you're broke and you want the Maharajah to pay up. I don't think he will.'

'He will. I know he will. I've read the manuscript, you see, and you haven't. Neither has he. So what do you say? Talk the Maharajah into seeing sense and take your cut, or do it for high-minded reasons and what have you? Don't forget I'm well beyond any sentimental or honour-of-the-regiment kind of bullshit. I've got to be a realist. I'm right up shit creek with a broken paddle, and what's more I'm due for some bloody justice. I'm not asking for charity. Just for a resumption of the pension, and the manuscript then stays on ice.' He got up from the table. 'And there's one other thing you'd better bear in mind. This meeting never took place. Nothing I've said to you here has ever been said. So don't waste your time reporting any of it to His Nibs.'

Bingham sighed, stood up. 'Call Iris,' he said.

'No bloody fear.' Tone grinned at him. 'You call her.'

'You'll finish up in clink, Tone. You know that?' Bingham said. He was impressed by this Tone he had never met before. Not the Tone of the clubs, arguing, quarrelling, proving, or staying last in the bar in these latter years, waiting for everyone to go so that nobody would discuss him behind his back. Iris had complained of this to Bingham during her last demented, frustrating effort to confide in Bingham over a year ago, confirming for him this newly developed aspect of Tone's increasing paranoia.

'Could well be,' Tone said cheerily. 'But I did say I'm playing for high stakes, don't forget.' He turned and called for Iris.

'Your knight-errant is off, my love,' he shouted. To Bingham he said, 'You'll be there tonight, I suppose? Think it over, my offer. Your pension won't be worth four annas to the rupee in a few years from now, don't forget. Funny you reminding me of that boots job. Bastards. Yes, the other two got the money. I got here.' He laughed softly, then turned to Iris as she came into the room.

'Well?' she said to Bingham.

'He wants the money, Iris,' he replied, and turned to go, but Iris said, 'Wait. I want you to witness something before you leave.'

'Please, Iris,' Bingham begged, turning.

'Either you give me that manuscript now, in front of Tim, Freddy,' she said. 'Or I leave you. Which is it to be?'

'You leave me.'

'That's your last word?' she asked.

'There's no such bloody thing as a last word, Iris,' Tone said angrily. 'Now start getting ready. This may be your last night out with me.' He laughed. 'And then again, it mightn't.'

'You heard all that, Tim?' Iris was grim now, her face pale.

Bingham threw his hands up in the air and said, 'See you later, I suppose. 'Bye.'

As he got into the jeep Iris came into the verandah.

'He's certifiable, you know it, don't you? Don't be taken in by that quiet manner, Tim. Tell the Maharajah, please. Tell him that Freddy's out of his mind. That's all. Just tell him that.'

Without looking at her, Bingham waved his hand and drove off.

Having decided to go straight to the Maharajah's bungalow, which was about twenty miles from the palace, Bingham weakened as he was about to drive past the club. He wanted very much to be quite alone for a while. He felt so depressed now that he was even tempted to drive home and telephone some excuse to Chan. He went into the club by the side door so as to find Janki Nath in his office.

The Pandit, reading as usual when off duty, stood up and bowed to him.

'I'd like a large, a very large whiskey, Panditji,' said Bingham. 'In the library, please.'

'Right away, Colonel Sahib.'

When the Pandit had gone Bingham walked into the library

and sat down in his favourite chair at the end of the room, between the high bookshelving. Had there been a deep cave to enter, he realized, he would have preferred it even more; it was as if he needed complete isolation from all other human beings. Sitting down he now understood the reasons for his increasing sense of trepidation. An uneasiness in what he thought must be his subconscious had emerged, in a form of premonition, during Iris Tone's sinister little scene with Tone, and now something was urging him to prevent something. In the press, in the new books about the body, the mind, he had picked up the new key-phrases, 'distress signals', 'cry for help', and others about what used to be called suicide. Yet Iris had said she was leaving Tone. Would she? Then there could be no murder, no suicide? But he knew couples like the Tones needed to be together in order to postpone, through aggression and quarrel, any real meeting with themselves. Perhaps Iris was leaving rather than do what she did not really know it was time for her to do, murder Tone. The thought seemed so bizarre that Bingham laughed, while all the time he felt he should be at the telephone warning somebody not to do something. The Maharajah not to go any further with this game he was playing with Tone? The Tones to leave immediately for a holiday in Mussoorie? Or Razia to come and collect him, take him over, make the decision to move on together to the next stage awaiting them both?

He went on with the inner examination of these disturbing thoughts while hardly aware that he had taken a drink from Janki Nath and thanked him for it. In fact he was halfway through the strong whiskey before he understood that the most disturbed person around these days was himself. This revelation walked in on his mind seemingly out of nowhere, a voice saying, 'Your life has been a long rehearsal, but for what? You've joined the audience instead. What is is you are waiting for? Age, sickness, death?'

Yes, he had to leave Induspur, had to move on, find something to pretend to do again, like work, service, devotion to some duty or other. He was dying slowly of boredom. Surely the greatest of sins? He was lazing his life away in this sun-baked dreamland, like so many imperial servants after the deaths of many other long imperial performances, whether it be here, Capri, Narbonnensis, Lima, or one of the islands off Greece three thousand years ago. An artefact, he must leave this museum. He could almost hear Chan laughing – another artefact. He now wished he had not thought of and voiced that understanding of their archaeological situation. And now, again, he experienced the shiver of premonition, a sensation almost of certainty that he was seeing the immediate future unrolling in his head, as had happened half a dozen times before in his life.

The first time had seemed to last an hour inside of two seconds, when, aged twenty-one, a subaltern with the Tenth Irish Division at Suvla Bay, he had instantaneously foreseen that he was about to be grievously wounded, and woken up days later, between life and death, in a hospital tent in Lemnos.

He tried to shake off that now 'historic', ancient war period, as he usually did, but this time it stayed, the voice within saying, 'No, look at it all. Consider this mysterious thing you have, which people call "second sight". Have a good look at it. Is it true?'

Like many who had been tiny working parts of the enormous war machines, who had served, uninformed and dwarfed by great landscapes, mysterious plans, he had read many books about the first world war in an effort to find out what he had been doing. After recovering from his wounds the rest of his war experience had been so unlikely that he had never risked telling it for a second time. In fact his whole life, come to think of it, was so unlikely that he still had difficulty in telling it to himself. Whole areas of it had been locked off by agreement with himself, but now, sitting alone in the silent library, awake to this new manifestation of 'second sight', he saw he must eventually examine it all and try and see what it meant.

He looked at the empty glass in his hand and, knowing he had drunk a glass of whiskey, he sensed the strength of the mood of melancholy meditation struggling to seize his whole mind. The glazed look of hatred for Tone in Iris's eyes he had caught for a second: was it that which had drenched him with this pessimistic flood of clamouring thoughts damned up by a so long-frozen nausea?

The letter from that curious bugger in America came up again for an instant. F.X. Condy. He laughed with a kind of tired affection. F.X. Francis Xavier. A name which dated any Irish-American possessing it. Practically knew which year the

281

ancestor had sailed from Queenstown, in a time of iron piety and sullen hunger. Christ, whenever that letter from Condy sneaked into his mind, and reminded him that Condy had done research into his life — all that impudent stuff about how he, Bingham, was an Irishman, when actually he had been without a nationality since nineteen fourteen — but wait! Wait! Amazed suddenly, he saw now that it was that letter from Condy which had forced open the archive in which he had sealed up older and deeper wounds than those inflicted at the Dardanelles thirty-eight years ago. And now another flash of understanding. Nationality, identity. Was that why he had for so long identified himself, privately, with Islam all these years? No, surely not. Too simple. Too easy, handy, glib, pat-psychological? Not really, no. Don't think. Let the thoughts occur, listen. Hear.

'Telephone call for you, Colonel Sahib,' Janki Nath called to him for the third time. He looked at Janki Nath now, puzzled, unwilling to be dragged from this series of remarkable revelations.

'I'm not here,' he called back testily. 'I'm — tell them I've gone. I'm —'

'It's the Maharajah, Colonel Sahib,' Janki Nath said urgently.

The Maharajah on the telephone. Where are you, Tim? You're late. Another chance not to listen or hear, to seal up the archive again, to decide to forget again? Start chatting and laughing with Chan again, re-enter the role of retired colonel with sealed archive within, get involved in the Tone manuscript mystery, and start living day by day again? Friendship left him no choice.

'Thanks, Janki Nath,' he said, and went to the telephone, but even on the way to it the unsuspected secrets kept appearing from the unsealed archive, ' — can that be why I wanted to be a Muslim so long ago, because I needed a new nationality, because Ireland didn't want us when we came back from "the war to save the small nations", as the Great War had been called. Save all the small nations except one, Ireland.' Christ, he didn't want all this old rubble from an old life coming up again. 'Hello, Chan. Where are you? Oh, yes, the bungalow. Well I'm in the club library as a matter of fact.'

'You sound a little edgy, Tim. What's up?'

The Maharajah was not feeling as breezy as he was trying to

282

sound, thought Bingham. Must remember to think about another new discovery now sliding into his mind's vision — the *two*, not one, the *two* occasions in his early life in which he had found himself to be suddenly somebody else, had been disinvented, classified as wanting and uncomfortable to know, once by his family, once by his people. Good God, yes, yes. 'What's that, Chan?' he said. Must pay attention. 'Me sounding edgy?' he said into the telephone. 'Come on, Chan. *You've* been on edge for days. Do you want to tell me what it's about? I'll tell you why I ask — and as you know, I never ask.' He told of how he had been 'shanghai-ed' by Iris Tone, had been faced with Tone, then all that had happened in the Tone house. When he had finished he knew by the silence at the other end that it had had a strong effect. A few more seconds passed in silence and then the Maharajah said, 'Good. That means Tone is really shaken, that he's going to come to heel, the bastard. You've guessed, haven't you, Tim, that he's got a hold over me, as they say?'

'Is that what it is?' said Bingham. Much better than saying, 'Of course, it's obvious.'

'More or less. Yes.'

Good Christ. Another inspired revelation made him forget he was supposed to be listening on the telephone. That glazed look of hatred, just the second's glimpse of it he had had, he now knew he had seen once before in a woman's eye, his mother's during one of the quarrels his parents had had over his, Bingham's, 'escape' from the seminary. 'Your son has absconded from the college,' the letter from the seminary had told her. The scalding pain of such long-repressed memories caused him to cry out aloud, well not *too* loud he hoped, as flustered, he heard the Maharajah saying, 'What the hell *is* the matter with you, Tim? Are you ill or something?'

'Yes,' he said, feeling almost faint now. 'Yes. Ill. I suppose that's it, really. Yes. Though not physically ill, you understand, Chan?' He laughed, frantic for a moment. 'It may be I've been dodging so much for so long — myself? My objectives? My daily round doing nothing? Maybe all that. I don't know. But I've got to make up my mind, I've got to come to some kind of decision about what I think I'm doing.' He laughed again, then said, in a different tone of voice, 'I haven't told you all I saw when I was with the Tones an hour ago. You'd better go carefully there, Chan. It's quite volcanic, the atmosphere those two have achieved.' He laughed. 'Christ, who needs scientific mystery, problems of physics, when you've got human beings, especially two of them trying to understand each other? Eh?' He uttered a long, growling sigh and said, 'Go easy there. I don't know or care what your secret is in that direction, but don't play with it too long — '

'I'm not playing with anything,' the Maharajah said curtly. 'Tone's playing, not me. Come on up soon and have a drink with me. I need your ear, badly.' Yes, he was quite nervous.

'All right. See you soon.' He put down the telephone, thinking, Weak again. Get involved, give advice, talk and talk. But it's myself I've got to sort out. He felt haunted by his many selves, knowing again that he had been wasting his life during the last few years. Take all this nonsense about becoming a Muslim. What were the facts, really. Never mind that. Now now, not now. First, why was it that the sight of that hatred-in-playfulness of Iris Tone's had broken down a well inside him, drenched him with a feeling of despair and reminded him all over again of the pointlessness of being alive? — no matter how much point he had always given it, and still could, oh yes, yes, still could.

Christ. He called for another whiskey, sat down again, collapsed into the chair really, burdened with this extraordinary feeling of depression. *Taqiyya,* he thought. Amazed again by a new revelation emerging, he whispered the Arab word again, *Taqiyya,* something he had practised for most of his life: dissimulation, equivocation, concealment. *Taqiyya* was practised by Muslims when living amongst enemies of the faith; it was a careful willingness to appear to be like the others while staying the secret self, but he knew now that his practice of this ancient art had been against an enemy within himself, a self he had created, against an enemy self so wounded that he had tried to drop him at the roadside over thirty years ago. The fact was that he had nowhere to go, except everywhere, no sense of 'home', place to return to, longed for, to die in. To have broken with all ties, family, home, had never seemed menacing until now, but perhaps it loomed now because he wished to move on, could not accept 'retirement', but to move on to where? He tried for comfort in the thought that this harassment he was allowing himself to inflict upon himself was purely mood, a temporary depression. Loneliness? Something he had never suffered from. Couldn't be that. But probably was. The disgust and nausea he had experienced at the sight of Iris Tone with that rolled-up magazine — was he letting too much unconsciously acquired Freudian claptrap into his reaction, seeing enraged sexual frustration in what was merely rightly earned human hatred? He laughed as he took the whiskey from Janki Nath. It looked as if he was going to have to sit down tonight, stare hard into himself, and reveal his true autobiography to himself, develop the psycho-negative and study the true print. His life of continuous adventure had ended a few years ago, or rather his many lives, and all he had to show for it was a tall, distinguished-looking, healthy, somewhat learned man, who seemed to have come from nowhere, and had nowhere to go. It had been so long arriving, this confrontation with his pointlessness, that he knew an exhilaration would shortly arise, and that he would once more sit down and attempt to write that book again. My God, yes, because if anyone was the blueprint of the culture-chasm, which was the theme of the memoirs he wished to write, it was himself. He had never been able to fool himself in any of the bewildered worlds he had lived in, Hindu, Muslim, the rest; in fact, he had become part of the whole reeling Afro-Asian set of doomed cultures, had studied daily the results of the collision of the West with these obedient masses under their various forms of despotism, despotisms which would have remained, probably forever, but for the intrusion of what had now become the restless culture of the world, 'the West'. What a stream of stuttering thoughts and realizations had come to him last year when he had been cornered by one of the newly inspired Africans, member of a delegation to India, a pathetic puppet of the new 'negritude', armed with a slick, chic instant-Marxism, trying hard to hate 'the West' while wearing a Rolex a friend had to remind him to wind, and with secret dreams of the big car, the mansion, and all the other symbols of the only worthwhile product of the whole journey of 'the West', the bourgeoisie.

'I must inform you,' he had said quietly, deadpan, to the excited African, who had just accused him, a complete stranger, but white, of course, of representing all the evils of something or other, 'that I have no guilt for you to work on. None of any kind. I'm sorry, that's the way things are. But you'll find plenty of guilty performers if you look around.' It was true, they were all over the place, pouring out of the woodwork, these breast-beaters, longing to apologize for, say, Copernicus, for every thinker from Plato on, and these new, severe Afro-Asian lecturers reprimanded and castigated 'the West', while belonging to it and demanding ever more and more of 'the goodies' the West was producing in growing floods.

He had started the book several times. Had he the will to try once more? In this unusual depression weighing on him now it seemed unlikely.

He could hear a woman's voice raised in indignation. He got up and walked to the door of the library, listened. He could hear Megan saying, 'It's nothing to do with your personality. Nothing to do with it. You're obsessed with yourself. You're the vainest creature I've ever met. Can't you imagine that I just don't happen to want to marry, not just you, but anybody else either? I don't need it. I don't need anybody in marriage. I'm on holiday from all that stuff.'

Bingham could hear a laugh he recognized, then Ted Koltz saying, 'So there you have it, Roger. Now let's get on with some business. Where's your script?' Then he heard Croon saying, 'So now we know what you don't want, Megan. But what about what *I* want? Am I all that repulsive to you? Tell me.'

Go on, tell him, Bingham urged her silently, grimly. God almighty, yes, this same dialogue would be going on in another million years — and then he remembered to remember the new codicil to all such thoughts — providing, of course, that they don't drop the ———— , which they most certainly would.

286

CHAPTER 23

The Parsee community of Western India had never been encumbered by the multi-deitied accretions of thousands of years of Hinduism, had never been a part of its ancient, trudging caravan of castes and allotted cycles of rewards and punishment called lives. When Arab Islamic armies took Persia in the eighth century, and gave that Indo-European people the new religion, and a lasting schizophrenia thereby, the Zoroastrian ancestors of the Indian Parsees fled to Bombay and stayed Zoroastrians.

The Maharajah was thinking about this as he watched Sonny Sodawallah get out of his small dusty car and then look up at the bungalow. He was unable to see the Maharajah, who was watching him from a curtained window of the study.

Curious. He recognized the tall, slim Parsee, had seen him with Subhadra and her friends in Delhi once or twice a year or so ago. He watched Sodawallah take a short gold cigarette-holder from his pocket, slip a cigarette into it, light it, and then, with his hands on his hips, puff on the cigarette while he slowly surveyed the bungalow. 'Pricing it, no doubt,' the Maharajah thought, 'and getting it wrong, seeing he's a journalist.'

Sodawallah had rung twice that morning, seeking an interview, and the Maharajah had taken pleasure in delaying games, but when it had occurred to him, in his state of tension and anxiety, that Sodawallah might seek an interview with Tone, about the film, he had telephoned him at the Kipling Arms Hotel and agreed to an interview. An admirer of the Parsee community, of their philanthropy, their swiftness to seize new ideas — they were always first with anything new and useful from Europe or America — and of their honesty and drive in business, he already looked on Sodawallah as a failure, for being a journalist and especially for writing for the sensational *Flash*. He looked a gentleman too, which made it worse. A gentleman yes, but cocky, just a little too self-confident, perhaps slick would be the word, slick in order to write the smart-Alec, nudgingly-knowing, iconoclastic *Flash*-type articles which so outraged the old and the religious of Bombay and Delhi. Cocky because of the way he was strolling up to the bungalow entrance, cigarette-holder clenched in his teeth, hands in his trouser pockets, lanky, handsome, looking so well dressed in his light grey tropical suit and an open-neck light blue silk shirt.

The Maharajah turned and looked at Balban who, in his new role as butler-in-training, was standing with his hands behind his back like a soldier at ease, quite splendid-looking really in his starched white high-necked tunic and sharply creased trousers.

'Now, Balban,' the Maharajah said. 'You know what a shit is, of course? Yes?' He raised his eyebrows and Balban nodded, waiting.

'A shit is a journalist who writes gossip for trashy newspapers, and there's one out there now, come to dig around in, my life.' He smiled. 'So when I press the button for drinks, don't forget that the drinks are for the guest — and *not for you*. Is that clear?'

'It is clear, *Maharaj* Sahib.'

'Good. I want your mind clear and steady for what you've got to do tonight. No drinking. No opium. No *hashish*.' Harshly he added, 'Or you'll regret it, Balban.'

'I promise, *Maharaj* Sahib.'

'Good. Bring that shit in.'

The Maharajah strolled to a far window so that his back would be to Sodawallah on the other's entrance. He would be lost in thought, staring out of the far window, and would then turn slowly and stare coolly at this intruder who made his living out of rooting about in his betters' lives and doings, after which he would invent and weave a lying tale of scandalous doings. Bastard. But likeable, so at ease as they shook hands, Sodawallah having offered his first and with a charming friendly smile, nothing of the cunning secret-seeker in it at all. About thirty-something, say thirty-seven, dark blue-green shave on the olive-gold jaw, and piercing, hooded green eyes. It took a few minutes, after they sat down with words about the journey from Delhi, state of the roads these days etcetera, for the Maharajah to realize that Sodawallah had taken charge. Well, no, perhaps in his present state of anxiety, though anguish might be a better word, his mind full of Tone and threat, that Sodawallah had put him at ease would be a better description of the relief he began to feel. He resisted the wish to clear up the connection with Subhadra too fast, yes he remembered now, a dance at the Imperial Hotel over a year ago. He had dropped in for a drink at Subhadra's table and his fellow was there with the crowd of a dozen or so, and being amusing, he now recalled.

Sodwallah had a grave, serious manner, a soft deep voice, and perhaps it was a trick the way he kept this voice low so that the listener had to lean mentally forward, as it were, and listen harder. He had the Maharajah's concentration quickly, especially when, stretching his legs and lying back almost languidly as he said the startling sentence, 'I know, Maharajah Sahib, that a visit from a carrion-crow working for *Flash*' — and again the slow, beguiling smile — 'must have conjured up visions of God knows what "sensational revelations" to come for *Flash* readers, but the fact is that I'll toss off a thousand words or so about this film thing, and that's not why I'm here. I can't say too much about my real work, you understand, but it is in the area of security.' There was only the lightest underlining of that word, security.

Christ almighty! 'Well, well, now how fascinating,' said the Maharajah. 'You mean you're up here on security work, that you use *Flash* as your — your sort of — '

'Cover?' Sodawallah smiled again. 'Well, no, perhaps that word would exalt my status as a — er — government agent, though I do, of course, enjoy the spy novels.' Then he seemed to think about it for a moment or two, and said, 'Though I suppose you're right, yes, but I'm rather a fanatic about honesty, in my way, and while I would prefer the word "cover" I'm afraid I must use the word "deception" instead.' He folded his arms now and stared hard at the Maharajah. 'All this I'm telling you, *Maharaj* Sahib, is highly secret, and between us both, in confidence. Yes?'

'Obviously.' The Maharajah hoped his amazement was not showing, that his facial expression had not in any way revealed any immature or unsophisticated reaction to this unexpected shock he had just received. He nodded, sagely, he hoped, and said, 'So let's get on with it. You're here on some kind of mission for the government, is that it?' Immediately he was annoyed with himself, 'cover' and now 'mission', and yes, Sodawallah smiled again.

'First I'll clear the decks as the British used to say,' Sodawallah said. 'May I smoke?' He waved his gold cigarette-holder. The Maharajah nodded and accepted a cigarette from the heavy gold case Sodawallah held out to him. 'I specialize in the princely states,' he said, puffing at his cigarette. 'In more ways than one, that is. I write this bloody bazaar-gup for *Flash* — that's my "cover", my act of public deception; but my real work is keeping an eye on subversive movements, conspiracies, in the states allotted to me, one of which is your own, *Maharaj* Sahib.'

'So that's why you were — that's how you come to know my aunt, Princess Subhadra, down in Delhi?' This fellow could do with just a little jolting, he was just a little too much at his ease. Conning Subhadra in some way? But Sodawallah smiled and shook his head.

'There is no way I can discuss this matter without, I am afraid, *sounding* offensive, *Maharaj* Sahib,' he said. He paused, waiting, and the Maharajah replied, 'I understand. Go on.'

'Would you say that the Princess Subhadra is not — is — er — not in her right mind?' He stopped, considered, and then went on, 'Sometimes? Occasionally?'

Christ almighty! Without intending it, the Maharajah was on his feet. He walked to the far window and looked out of it, and, remembering now that he had forgotten to do this as planned, on Sodawallah's entrance, he turned and stood with his hands in his trouser pockets, swayed up and down on his toes and heels, and head slightly back, haughty, contemptuous, yet friendly. He was feeling offended, exhilarated, intrigued, and afraid, mostly afraid, and he knew he was still off balance after hearing that this visitor was far from being the fun he had intended him to be. He had, instead, official rights to peer, to examine, and to pronounce upon what he found, and what was worse, he was likeable, charming. He was smiling now, but watching steadily, as he said almost too quietly to hear, 'Please do understand, *Maharaj* Sahib, that I regret very much to have to disturb you with this unpleasant subject.'

What was the word for this fellow, the word that he was

trying to find to describe his charm — insidious? Yes. Insidious. But it did seem genuine, and the bastard *was* actually likeable. Even so . . . .

'You'd better tell me what you're here to say, Sodawallah,' the Maharajah said with an effort at chilliness. 'Trot it out. All of it.' Then he felt, having heard himself, that he was fighting off friendliness, good nature and goodwill. Nevertheless he must go on trying to remember to be suspicious, watchful, self-protective, blackmailable, one of those playboy-maharajahs who made news, always the wrong kind of news, the kind of news the public had been trained to want.

It was important to keep an edge on his sword, a glitter in his suspicion, so he said, 'For instance, you come in here and start hinting that the Princess may be bonkers — oh, sorry, yes, you *did* say "not in her right mind" — but you know her personally, don't you? I've seen you with her in a party. Remember?' Now it was his turn to smile, but Sodawallah smiled too, agreeing, quite unembarrassed by this attempt at a hard line. Limp, relaxed, quietly affable, he stood up.

'I've met her, yes, but I don't *know* her,' and now, so casually, only a yawn missing from the tiredness he seemed to be feeling with this suddenly hostile host, he said, and smiling, sadly, with it, 'Oh, well, never mind, *Maharaj* Sahib. I apologize for upsetting you. I'm the last for any kind of scene, you know, and you're obviously under strain. But then who isn't these days?' His quiet voice became even quieter, so that the Maharajah came forward a couple of paces, intent, listening hard, and visibly shaken. 'All the princes I meet are the same, and it's understandable, but even so . . . ' His voice trailed off now, and his smile seemed tired. He made a gesture with his hands, understanding, hopelessness, capitulation to temper and aristocratic haughtiness or stupidity in it. He was pulling out, withdrawing . . . . The Maharajah was staring at him in uncertainty, confusion, anger with himself.

'What's she done?' he asked. Now, it was clear the bastard was going to punish him, play hard to get back onto the line again, but no, not at all. He put his finely shaped head back and considered his host, those dark green eyes hooded, an expression of almost saintly gentleness in them, and said, 'Before I answer that question I'd like to think things over. I don't need this particular assignment, and as for your hostility, arrogance, that kind of caper, I always retreat from it as soon as I meet it. I came here as a man of honour, and because I have an affection and respect for the Princess, having met her a couple of times socially in Delhi. The speed with which you like to take offence doesn't suit me, it so happens — '

'Offence?' The Maharajah's voice stumbled. His eyes were burning. There was a desperate expression in his face. His mouth moved, seeking for words, while he sought to control what was plainly an oncoming fury. He was consumed with curiosity and anxiety, and at the same time anxious to placate, to understand and be understood, while not really wishing to hear what it was that had excited his curiosity and anxiety. Nor was he sure of how to handle this mysterious and like-able, yet infuriating personality with the gentle manner and voice. 'Can't you — don't you understand,' he said to Soda-wallah, 'that all this is a bit of a shock, you know. I mean you come in here and ask me if I think Princess Subhadra is — what did you call it — ? What did you *say* about her —?' Christ almighty. The Maharajah walked to a settee and sat down on it. Cracking up? He took a quick look downward at his wrist-watch. Tone here in an hour.

'I merely asked you, and I regret it, and apologize for it, if you thought the Princess might not be in her right mind,' the smooth, velvety voice was saying. The Maharajah looked up at him. The Parsee was very relaxedly slipping another cigarette into his gold holder, but he looked severe, for him, that is. 'You take offence. I understand.'

'I *am* under a certain amount of strain,' the Maharajah said lamely, coughing a little after saying this, striving to control the lava of rage still convulsing near the surface.

'So I noticed.' So the bastard noticed. Indeed.

'I felt somehow that you might have unusual powers of observation,' said the Maharajah, knowing it was no good, that it was hopeless against this surprising, *and* likeable — that was the ironic angle here, that this bastard was so very likeable. He had better put things right, now, at once.

'Do sit down, please,' he said. 'I'm sorry if I have offended you. Yes, my aunt, the Princess — ' He started hesitating again, and Sodawallah sat down and watched him intently, though gradually lying back, as if uncoiling into languor again, in the deep armchair. 'The Princess *can* be — unpre-dictable.' Now a silence followed, and he waited, sensing ris-ing rage again but forcing it down. He was very conscious of

292

being in the presence of a complete stranger, and a stranger who had information he wanted to have and wished he did not have to have. Christ alone knew what it was going to mean, what Subhadra had been up to now. He looked at the stranger now and then heard that voice again, urging, in the deep corridors of his being, 'Leave. Vanish. Go. It's over anyway.' Yes. The stranger was lying back and actually examining his gold cigarette-holder, his air almost that of a man alone in his own bungalow, and who knew, might be doing what he had just threatened to do — thinking it over. Yes, by God, what were the words he had used? 'Before I answer that question I'd like to think things over.'

'I'm sure I don't know how to help you, *Maharaj* Sahib,' Sodawallah said, utterly at ease as he spoke, and somehow, weary of it all anyway. Punishment? Possibly.

Just have to take the punishment I suppose, the Maharajah thought, resigned now. He had slept very little these last two nights, and just now, God only knew for what reason, he had remembered that he was supposed to be in love with Megan. That seemed centuries ago. He watched Sodawallah and said nothing.

'Would you like a drink?'

Sodawallah seemed not to hear the question, but mused on aloud. 'All right,' he said. 'We'll put aside the question of her state of mind and simply deal with the facts as I know them.' He turned his head and smiled at his host, who smiled back with an effort at affability, and wondering if this odd character could see the fear he was feeling, in his eyes.

'And what are the facts?' he asked, not meaning to add in that acid tone, 'if facts they be.' Terrified that Sodawallah would show weariness again and stand up, he hastily made a joke of it, reaching for Zen, anything for a laugh. 'As a Hindu, don't forget, I have a right to wonder what a fact is?' He had to do the laughing himself.

'What would it be, *Maharaj* Sahib, that would cause the Princess not only to become a member of the Communist Party, but to work against your plans for making a cooperative of those coal mines?' Sodawallah offered him a cigarette from the gold case, but the Maharajah did not notice this. He was staring at Sodawallah, his mouth open and his eyes quite empty of expression.

'You knew nothing of this, *Maharaj* Sahib?' Sodawallah asked.

The Maharajah, his mouth still hanging open, shook his head, and went on shaking it.

'Would you like a drink?' he asked Sodawallah.

'Thank you, yes, I would rather.'

The Maharajah got up from the settee and stood, looking down at the Parsee government-agent who stood up as well and lit their cigarettes.

'It's unbelievable. You do know that?'

Sodwallah nodded. 'I expect it is,' he said.

'She *is* mad. I've never wanted to face that,' the Maharajah said. He seemed now to be braced by what he had heard, Sodawallah noticed, puzzled by it.

Sodawallah was even more puzzled by the brutal, careless tone the Maharajah now adopted as he went towards the door leading to the rear of the bungalow.

'Not that I give a damn who joins the Communist Party anyway. You might be one yourself for all I know, or anyone else knows. Eh?'

He turned at the door and looked at Sodawallah, who was smiling, nodding agreement.

'True. True. You never know, do you? The thrill of conspiracy and belonging?' Sodawallah was saying, still smiling. 'Look at those English types who went off to Moscow — '

'Yes,' said the Maharajah. 'It makes you wonder when the royal family are joining as well — '

My mind is just about made up, I'd say, the Maharajah was thinking as he said, gaily, 'What'll you drink?'

'Scotch, if you have any — '

Curious really, a Maharajah going out of the room to get drinks. All very democratic.

In the kitchen the Maharajah gave Balban his new orders.

'The visitor is not a shit, Balban,' he said. 'So it's whiskey, and brandy for me. Bring the bottles in and the rest of it and leave them on the table. Then wait here.'

Balban nodded and started to glide around the kitchen in that snakelike way he had — glasses, soda.

'Balban.'

Balban looked at him. 'Yes, *Maharaj* Sahib?' He could sense that the Maharajah had important things to say to him, and he became solemn, attentive, expectant.

'Later. Later,' said the Maharajah uncertainly.

'Yes, *Maharaj* Sahib.' Balban began to move about again,

thinking, He has been given news that has upset him. He is not himself. But he has not been himself for a very long time.

As he rapidly broke the seals on the bottles of brandy and whiskey he watched the Maharajah with devoted eyes, wishing, hoping he could help.

'Are your nerves steady for tonight, Balban?' the Maharajah, at the door now, asked him.

Balban held up his hands before his face and looked between them, grinning, at his master. They both watched the hands for a tremor.

'Steady as rocks,' said the Maharajah. 'See they stay that way.' He went back to join his visitor.

Feeling exhausted now he made an effort to be bright. He knew he was creeping along towards the end of what they called his 'tether', rather a frightening thought that. He would never have believed that a note from a lowdown cashiered blackmailer would have produced the strange mental effects he had been experiencing since the reading of that note. It just went to show you — or something. Sodawallah seemed to be trying to help. He was chatting, actually chatting, saying, 'What do you think about the state of India these days, *Maharaj* Sahib?'

'Do you mean have I that famous thing, a solution?'

For the first time Sodawallah laughed, actually laughed.

'All right,' he said, shrugging his slender shoulders. 'I just thought I'd let you get over the unhappy news I've given you. I'm very sorry. I feel a terrible cad really.'

The Maharajah stared at him, unbelievingly. He had not heard this kind of stuff — man of honour, and now cad — since he had been at that imitation English public school 'in the hills' as they used to say, and which had been so much more over-compensatorily English public school than even Greyfriars at its faggiest.

'You want my solution to India's problems, Sodawallah?' he said. 'I'll tell you. Fifty million more Sikhs for a start, and all of them to farm the whole of Northern India, all of it as far as Bengal. And, about five million more of your own kind, the Parsees, in charge of all Indian business. Then the rest of us, the Hindus, could eat and get on with our treadmill. That's what I call it. The treadmill. It's a big wheel, you know, call it what you like, *dharma, karma*.' He sighed. Balban came in with the drinks and, at a signal from the Mahara-

295

jah, laid the tray on the table and left. 'Nothing much happened here in India, you know,' he continued. 'Nothing much changed under the British, except perhaps a few hundred million more people added to the population, all of us entangled in our various stages of *karma*. But at least fifty million more Sikh farmers, joke about the *Sardarji* as we may, would mean India would be at least fed.'

Hardly listening, his head bent, Sodawallah said, 'Does your *Diwan* keep you fairly well informed, *Maharaj* Sahib?'

'I don't allow him to.' Sodawallah looked at him. The Maharajah seemed to be hesitating again. 'No, I don't allow him to tell me much. And why should I? It's all over, the princely stuff. We have to be swept away, quite soon, I'd say. Wouldn't you?'

'Yes,' said Sodawallah. 'I think you're right. It seems inevitable.' He took the glass of whiskey from his host and held it while he poured soda into it, saying, 'I'd better tell you about this Communist thing, *Maharaj* Sahib. Yes?'

'I have guests coming soon, so if you don't mind, make it short, for now, that is. We can talk more some other time — perhaps.'

It seemed to Sodawallah odd, that 'perhaps', the way the word was ... thrown away. He could feel that his host had had enough of him, and not just because he was expecting other guests. He started to tell the story of the conspiracy in which the Princess was involved, how the *Talukdars*, the landowners who had once collected the taxes in the time of tyranny, *zulm*, generations ago, were now taking legal action in Delhi in an effort to retain possession of the coal discoveries, how Subhadra was leading Communists from under cover to —

'Ah, to hell with it,' the Maharajah said in the middle of Sodawallah's delivery. 'I don't want to hear any more.' He looked at his guest. He had at last upset him, which he had not intended to do.

'I *beg* your pardon,' Sodawallah said with what was intended to be freezing politeness.

'Try and understand something, Sodawallah,' said the Maharajah. 'I'm over the shock you've given me. Got it? Over it completely. So the Princess is a Commie. Well, I don't give a damn any more, not even if she married Stalin. You see I'm beyond all that bullshit.'

Again this brutal manner, thought Sodawallah, his mouth open now as he listened with great interest, and wondering if this fellow might not be bonkers as well as the Princess.

'I've never wanted to rule this place, or to rule anybody or anything as a matter of fact. Interesting that, isn't it, when I'm supposed to be hanging on to my princely rights and wanting to be loved and all that? Bullshit. Now what do you want to do, arrest the Princess? Tonight?'

'Good Lord, no.' Sodawallah stepped back a little, he was so surprised by what seemed to be the Maharajah's eagerness for the suggested arrest. 'It's not a crime to be a Communist, *Maharaj* Sahib, at least not yet it isn't, not in India anyway.'

'True,' said the Maharajah, sneering to himself as he said it. 'Too true it isn't. But try getting up on a soapbox in Moscow and preaching anti-Communism.' He laughed to himself, waved his hand dismissively. 'Anyway, thanks for your news, Sodawallah, and good luck with your — your cover story, I hope, for *Flash*. Write anything you like.'

'Thank you.' Sodawallah's manner had become cold now. He put his glass down on the table. The Maharajah looked at it and clicked his tongue.

'Dear me,' he said. 'You're offended again. You're not going to finish your drink?' He looked at Sodawallah. 'Come on now, where's that smile? Give us a smile.'

Only a slight dilation of Sodawallah's nostrils indicated the anger the Maharajah thought, hoped, he must be feeling.

'I came here to discuss a serious matter — '

'Serious for *you*, as it happens,' said the Maharajah. 'But not for me.' He laughed. 'All you've told me is that my aunt is a Commie. What's wrong with that? She's got as much right as you or me to be a Commie if she wants to. And they want the loot, the coalmines, these dreary bloody *Talukdars*. Are you surprised? Am I? But what about the people? The masses? Is that what you're going to say in reply? The masses.' He grinned. 'That's the word you use for the people in *Flash*, isn't it? The masses. Hundreds of millions on the treadmill of their *karma*. It's in the blood now, after all these thousands of years. *Karma. You're* not coming back for another life, are you? You're a Parsee. What about me, a Hindu? I'll probably have to come back for another go, probably as a reporter on *Flash* — '

'May I go now?'

297

'Go? Of course you can go. I want you to go, you cad.' The Maharajah began playacting in what seemed to be a threatening way now. 'You've probably been conning me anyway. Secret agent?' He gave these words all of what seemed to be his contempt. 'Just a bloody hack from *Flash* and you think I believe you're a government agent? Bullshit.'

Sodawallah, his eyes fierce now, turned and strode to the door. When he reached it he turned. 'There's trouble coming in this state,' he said, his voice shaking. 'Most likely bloodshed. You're living in a dreamworld, all of you — '

'That's my job as a prince, to live in a dreamworld. You've said so in *Flash*. I read the series on the southern states. Now it's the turn of the north. Fine. Get on with it.'

'You must be drunk. Are you drunk?'

'Drunk with power. Don't forget that. Write that.' The Maharajah began to quote an opening to the article, ' "There he stood, this monument to tyranny and oppression, and though laid low by the mighty democratic surge of this new, vibrant, revolutionary Congress millionaires' India, he was still drunk with the power he no longer possessed" ' — but Sodawallah had left and the Maharajah followed him out and watched him walking towards his car, calling after him. 'And don't bother sending me a copy of your article, Sodawallah. Don't forget — write anything you like.'

Sodawallah turned and looked at him contemptuously. It was nearly dusk.

'I came here to try and help,' he said. 'That's all.'

'So did I. But I was too late. Like you.' He walked back into the bungalow for another drink, his mind beginning to touch and feel the Tone problem again, while trying to fight off the useless rage he felt about this news he had had about Subhadra. Forget it. It's nearly over, if nothing goes wrong tonight.

He was looking at his hand to see if it was steady, his whiskey glass in his left hand, and looked up to see Balban in the doorway to the kitchen, watching him. He smiled, and with this permission, Balban smiled too.

'Your hand is steady, *Maharaj* Sahib,' he said.

'Yes,' he said, thinking, Even though I feel so scared. Nothing must go wrong. This was the night of decision. Would he take the decision though?

His hand might be steady, but was his resolve? For instance, why let himself seethe in this way about the capers of the little aunt he loved so much, who had caused so many commotions in the family in the past? Already he regretted his treatment of Sodawallah, whom he suspected had had a great deal to drink. It was that silken, impudent friendliness of Sodawallah's which had upset him, the chummy intimacy with which he had mentioned Subhadra's mental instability. He, Chan, would never understand her, though he loved her, felt compassion and protectiveness for her. She was a chronic and entertaining liar, though 'storyteller' would be the kinder word. Even so, many of the tales she told turned out to be true, confusing her friends, infuriating himself because he had doubted her.

He was sitting near the telephone, tempted to pick it up and bully Subhadra, insist upon hearing the truth about this latest caper about being a Communist. Several times during the last couple of years she had provoked him to outbursts of temper with the form of grave prattle she could assume about international politics, about 'American imperialism', 'the Soviet experiment', and once about how they would 'have to give Communism a try. Look at China'. He found her particularly provocative because it was his secret belief that a communist revolution in India was inevitable. The museum, the caretakers of which for a thousand years had been Muslim, Afghan or British, would smoulder for a time, erupt here and there, and then would explode in a spontaneous combustion of the clanking contraption which had lasted so long, too long: the religio-social treadmill worked by hundreds of millions of hungry, landless peasants. There were times when he made himself believe that the new native government would be able to make the time in which to do the almost impossible, actually change India, feed, clothe and educate it, and by educate he meant convince every peasant that he was never coming back to live yet another life. But did he know enough about India, he would ask himself, to hold such convictions? He of the 'lost innocence' — as he sometimes jokingly thought of himself (and sometimes of the 'lost ignorance') — he could never be sure which. 'Lost innocence', yes, whenever he thought of good, well-meaning, pious souls like the *Diwan*, like even the unfathomable Balban out there in the kitchen listening to his thoughts. India, free, made him wish he had been allowed to stay an acceptant Hindu, one who had not been vulnerable to the fever bacillus of the Western way. Sheer bloody misplaced sentimentality? Probably — possibly — no, probably.

He simply could not face up to the coming destruction, the destruction speeding faster now with freedom, of the oldest form of stoicism, hope, acceptance, willingness to believe, left on earth: the Hindu way. He knew it would have to go, but he wanted it saved. His education had alienated him, but he had loved that education, that discovery of endless problems, and solutions to come. Since the infection he could never have enough information about each new revelation, and when he read about new scientific discoveries he would forget, for a time, the pessimism the most challenging of the discoveries had left him with. He did not believe man could survive himself, now he held that fearsome and final weapon. End of long exciting journey? Yes. Reason for an increasing sense of isolation, detachment? Not really.

No, he was displaced. He was a displaced person, a social and racial oddity. He drew in his breath sharply. Chandra Gupta Woodberry *as well*. Its very absurdity, its dismissal of an identity he had been shedding for some time anyway, gave him a feeling almost of exaltation because now he truly did not know who he was. He looked at his watch. Time the Tones were here. Tonight was going to be very important. His heart was beating faster. Interesting, Yes, he felt impatient for the trial he must give himself tonight.

The telephone was ringing. He got up and backed away from the telephone. Balban came in. 'Answer it,' said the Maharajah. 'See who it is.' He did not want any kind of bad news.

'It's the Colonel Sahib,' said Balban. He handed the telephone to the Maharajah, who pointed at the whiskey. Balban poured a large whiskey slowly, eyes on his master, eyebrows raised, until a nod told him 'enough'. The Maharajah pointed to the soda and Balban poured until the nod. He handed the drink to his master and went back to the kitchen.

'You don't say. Why? What's it about?'

Bingham had been in the club library, he said, where he had overheard a row starting up between Megan and Croon, and had gone in so as to announce his presence as an unwilling eavesdropper. He had finished as a referee. He was making this call to say that Megan wanted to see him.

'Bring her up here. Why not? She could, if she wanted to,

change everything.' The Maharajah became silent then, mumbled something, and went on, 'Though I'm not quite sure about that. I think my mind's made up, once I've got one or two things straight. So — bring her up. I'm in a drinking mood. You sound in better form than you did earlier.'

'Somebody else's problems can always help.'

'Cynical bugger. Well, come and share some of mine. I'm thinking of opening up a bottle of Cloud 29. Remember last time?' He started laughing. So did Bingham, who said, 'Splendid. Why not try it on Tone? Now *that* could be interesting.'

'That's the whole idea' — he heard Bingham calling something to somebody, yes, to Megan.

'I've got to go back and referee again, Chan. See you soon.'

The Maharajah got up and strolled slowly round, stopping at portraits or enlarged photographs of family members, stopping longest in front of the portrait of his grandfather, the one who had, for quite the wrong reasons, like so many other Indians of his kind, tried to come to terms with the British way of living and thinking, that was to say — with the increasing pressure of the cultural shock from the West. Following the savage clash of 1857, known as the Sepoy Mutiny by the British, a new direct British rule, shrill with religious evangelism and a quite new and simmering race-feeling, had caused a surge of shame and self-consciousness among many upper-class Indians. They started to try and reform Hinduism, to 'clean it up' — it had been attacked and sneered at so much in so much British print, and then, heatedly, uncertainly, in Indian print as well. How could one identify as an Indian with these hundreds of millions of primitive, illiterate idolaters who had a god even for smallpox? They were mired in, sunk in, a bog of superstitions, all of it administered by their Brahmin supercaste, and for thousands of years. The Victorian puritanism — you could even find aspidistras in red pots painted over doubtful frescoes — had seeped into the thinking of people like his grandfather, and the answer to the regiments of Hindu gods seemed to be a neat, precise, manageable monotheism.

His grandfather had become a member of the *Brahmo Samaj*, a reformed Hinduism, though he was without the brains and talents of many of the upper-class Indians who joined it. For people like his grandfather, a traditional Indian making a real effort to understand and value Western think-

301

ing, this departure from 'primitive polytheism' was often a barely conscious public declaration of shame disguised as a new enlightenment, or as a living proof that age-old Hinduism could renew itself again and again. Various forms of the new touchy, defensive 'Hinduism' seemed not to know, at first, that they were a declaration of something new: nationality, self-conscious and striving Indian nationality, pavers of the way to the Indian National Congress Party which some day would start the struggle to free India from foreign rule.

Poor old Grandpa. His longest and most disappointing struggle in life had been with the Viceroys, trying to get a couple more guns into the salute allowed him.

The Maharajah laughed affectionately as he stared into the handsome, arrogant face of his grandfather. (Could he have suspected that he was a Woodberry? Or had he paid that pension like others so as not to find out?)

'They're on their way to me tonight, Grandpa,' he whispered to the portrait of the handsome man in the blue turban. 'I'm bringing an end to something tonight. Think about it. Pity we can't have a quiet chat about Darwin Sahib, the same chap *I* keep trying to understand. He did for your religious efforts, I know. He hasn't done for mine, though. My God is the universe, the huge machine we totter about in declaring our love, cursing our luck, getting drunk, reading millions of books written by other people, strangers we'll never meet sending out their thoughts about why they think we're here and who they think we are. Cheers, Grandpa.'

He lifted his glass to the portrait and finished the whiskey.

He listened for a car grinding up the hill in the dark-blue starlit night. He hurried out into the verandah and listened. Nothing, only a couple of drums thudding in a far off village, and in another direction the mad sexual yells of jackals.

'Come on you bastard, Tone,' he said. 'Get up here and let me sort you out. And I'll sort myself out too. Come on and let's see if you've got the nerve to name your price.'

Rubbing his hands he went back for another drink.

CHAPTER 24

It was against his usually cooler judgment that Bingham wondered if some occult force was at work: this time the power of a malevolent unhappiness released by Tone? He had not only written some kind of threatening letter to Chan, but one to Croon as well, and, forgetfully, Megan had revealed to Croon that she had read the letter.

The sneaking visits of precognition he had experienced over the years, were like whispers and nudges from some personal *jinn*, or perhaps from the *Shaitan* himself, and they always made him think again about his acceptance of his own pointless transience. Thank — thank — well, God — for the persistence of the irrational, which always made way for fresh illusions. Without illusions — and they crept up on one always without warning, demanding to be lived and enjoyed, then if possible eradicated — without them, what would be the use of living? It was surely irrational to believe that he and the five or six people now drawn together by this plan to make a film, a film that was not needed but would probably be made, and might then be discovered to be needed, to believe that it all had a deeper meaning now being worked out. But that was what he believed. He knew that this small scene he had been cast up on, was beginning to shift and that this lull in his life was coming to an end. And the happenings, the parts of this now assembling kaleidoscope of what he knew to be one more chunk of destiny — though God alone knew why — seemed all to have been expected, by that *jinn* which had appeared again within him. Even so he searched it, angrily and coldly examined it, ransacked it for error, for the eternal human longing for the irrational, the occult, the impossible, but he could not fault it.

He sat back and let Megan have her almost hysterical row with Croon, occasionally exchanging an amused glance with Koltz, who was smoking a cigar and, in brief bursts of concentration, reading parts of Croon's film script.

303

Having accidentally revealed that she had, unknown to Croon, read Tone's letter to him when he had left it on the table during that long afternoon of Croon's monologue in the club, Megan took refuge in a shouting, blustering attack on Croon's suspicious, anti-feminine, lower-class, petty little under-cultivated mind. Out of all that Croon seized the only barb which had pierced his cool, smiling, goading self-confidence.

'Lower-class?' He was snarling, forgetting to use the advantage she had given him about the letter. He sat there scowling at her, but visibly trying to control himself, to dam the tide of words struggling behind his working lips. He managed a slow but trembling smile of careless defiance. Quite admirable, really, that effort, Bingham was thinking, watching the fury die down in Croon's eyes. Croon went on to say, 'So you really fell for this bloody Raj stuff you used to live here, eh, Megan? The beautiful Welsh Celt, an aristocrat if anyone ever saw one, crawling up the Viceroy's leg and feeling *accepted*. Right?' He watched her closely, and Bingham watched Megan working this one over, could understand her thrill in being so praised by Croon, and yet so downed as well by what had come with it.

'I'm off,' said Megan. She picked up her glass and threw the whiskey in it into Croon's face. He smiled at her again and said, 'Now *that* — you're going to feel silly about that. Later, of course, much later, when you think about it, you silly bitch. I'm surprised at you, pinching a hammy piece out of a million B-movies like that.'

Bingham could see that Croon was done with her, and that was expected too. He had a feeling that Megan should now throw the glass at Croon, while screaming something or other, though he was not sure. No — not the glass. She leaned over and tried to smack his face instead, but Croon caught her by the wrist and held her struggling arm. Ted Koltz threw the script down and stood up. He seemed angry at last.

'Either get into the fucking sack, you two,' he said, 'or cut this goddam boring scene out. Okay?' He looked at Bingham, 'What do you think, Colonel? Enough?'

Bingham shrugged. He looked at Megan, smiling. 'Shall we go now, Megan?' He had told her he would drive her up to the Maharajah's bungalow. Megan wrenched her arm free, her fierce eyes on Croon.

'Now don't start crying, kid,' Koltz said to Megan. 'Or you're going to wreck a beautiful scene.' He gave a forced laugh and slapped Croon on the shoulder. It was then the *jinn* told Bingham that this film would never be made. 'Roger,' Koltz was saying. 'How about we go to work on this?' He shook the script in front of Croon's face.

'All right, Tim. Let's go.' Megan took his arm but she was staring at Croon. There were tears in his eyes.

'I'm disappointed in you, Megan,' he said to her. He stood up and walked out of the room.

'He's like this with all the women,' Ted said, grinning. 'He does a big heavy snowjob, *and* means it all, but he goes on and on. Now I'll tell you about a guy I knew in the business years ago. Great salesman, superb talk-artist. He'd go into the guy's office, right? Snappy dresser. Good looking. And he'd *sell*. See? He'd really sell. He'd throw his spiel there and the guy behind the desk is sold. The guy can't wait to sign. He gets his pen in his hand and he reaches for the contract, but the salesman won't give it to him. Yet. No, this goddam talk-machine doesn't know when to stop. He goes on with the spiel. And the guy behind the desk puts down the pen and gets up. It's over. But this snowman is still talking, still selling, while he's being pushed out of the office — '

'I knew he was a womaniser,' Megan cut in. 'I guessed that right away.' It was an accusation, but Koltz laughed.

'Now, Megan,' he told her. 'Every man alive is a womaniser, if he can make it. You find a man calls another one a womaniser, you know that guy can never make it. He's jealous, see?'

'You believe that, Ted?' she looked at Bingham. 'You don't believe that, do you, Tim? That every man is a womaniser?'

'Of course he is, Megan. Unless he's ill — '

'Or a fruit maybe,' Koltz added.

She looked at them both, her eyes mysterious for a moment, then amused. 'Bloody men,' she said. 'Womanisers.' She seemed to forget them both for a while, her eyes fixed in a stare beyond them.

'When do you start the film, Ted?' Bingham finished his drink, lifted the glass and raised his eyebrows enquiringly. Koltz shook his head. 'Thanks, no, Colonel. The movie — well, Roger's come up with a few good ideas.' He waved the script. 'The money here's fallen through, though. India's

305

made of foam rubber when it comes to negotiating. They don't want us here, the money boys. Fine. So we'll shoot it on the back-lot back home.'

'In America?' said Megan.

Koltz nodded. 'We can get a second unit, shoot some stuff here, and do the rest in California. It's all there, the plaster and the art department. No trouble. And this country — I love it, but as far as making movies goes, forget it. I can see the chaos coming — a twelve-week schedule here means twenty-two weeks, maybe ten years. Don't need it. And they don't need us.'

'They make hundreds of pictures here every year, Ted,' said Megan defensively, scornfully. 'Did you know that?'

'Sure.' He grinned. 'And I've seen a few of them. Great for this part of the world. They can make one in six weeks, a month. And all the same movie, with different faces. But that'll change some day.'

'How very superior, Ted,' she began.

'Yankee imperialist you mean, Megan? Forget it. Just facts, that's all. Only reason we came here, we were assured the other half of the money is here. It is. Only these guys love to negotiate. The bureaucracy here — they've got four guys saying maybe when one could say it, and maybe say it faster. And I mean *maybe*. I'm not against that, so long as I'm not working here. No. We do the movie fast in California. You want to come over, Megan?' He smiled at her.

To Bingham's amazement she walked to Koltz, as Koltz opened his arms for her, and in the next second, the *jinn* nudging him, Bingham watched the two embrace, and then Koltz placed his lips against Megan's mouth. They stayed in the embrace for a few seconds, drew apart, and Koltz looked across Megan's shoulder at Bingham and smiled.

'What about me, Colonel? You think I'm not surprised too?' Koltz looked at Megan. 'We want a line here, Megan,' he said. 'Like — ' He began snapping his fingers.

'The line here would be, "As if in a dream they suddenly found themselves in each other's arms",' Megan said, looking up into Koltz's puzzled eyes. ' "Without warning, both of them unsuspecting, the world had changed for them both." ' She was smiling up at Koltz, whose eyes, wary now, were looking down at her, searching her face. He smiled nervously.

'That's strange,' he said. 'Really strange.' He was afraid.

His eyes were still searching her face, her smile. Bingham watched Koltz's fear showing, how he wanted to believe what was happening to him, and feared to believe it. And those words, that line Megan had supplied at Koltz's request — what was the spectator supposed to make of that, never mind what Koltz was trying to make of it?

Bingham coughed, cleared his throat loudly. Megan turned her head to look at him, smiling. Christ, it was unbelievable. Her eyes had that marvellous, secret-looking expression, tender and triumphant, he had never fully examined in a woman's eyes before, and the banality, as well as the vulnerability of it, came fully home to him. He laughed. And Megan laughed too. As if he felt he ought to, Koltz laughed as well.

'Are you both very surprised?' asked Bingham, more to remind them he was there, and fighting embarrassment, than needing any reply.

'Now it's happened I'm not surprised,' Megan said to Koltz, her arms still round him.

'Megan, I don't know what to say,' Koltz told her. He seemed now to be overcome by what had happened. Bingham tried again.

'Shall I wait for you in the car, Megan?' he said.

'No. Let's keep to the obvious,' said Megan, turning her head to smile at him again. Her eyes still had that dark, strange expression in them, a sort of quiet glow. 'Let's get a bottle of champagne opened.' Christ, thought Bingham, she's going to make this real. It probably is real, for her, and will become real for Koltz, once he got over the joy he was still obviously afraid to feel. About fifty-odd, fifty-six, say, quite fit, likeable; and he did not seem able to believe in his luck.

As Bingham turned to go and order the champagne he saw Koltz and Megan sit down at the table, gripping each other's hands, looking into each other's eyes. He felt pleasure for them, and nausea, irritation, and a kind of angry amusement he could not understand. He also felt a kind of shame for feeling all this, and a deeper, guilty shame when his *jinn* whispered, '*Can* any bloody man ever really say he understands women, or knows what they are going to do?' He had fought that kind of obvious bullshit all his life, mysterious womanhood and so on, but what about the line Megan had supplied to Koltz? What could that mean?

Janki Nath gave him a quick hard stare as he snapped,

'Let's have a bottle of champagne. We're in a hurry.' He stood there, watching Janki Nath gliding towards the icebox, and thinking, I suppose that's my cue to plight my troth with Razia, if only I knew it. Christ, is there any end to the possibilities of the banal? And yet — I was touched. I *was* touched. I *am* touched. There. I love women and the way they do things, sometimes. Quite often, actually. Yes. She didn't know what she was going to do, when she walked over like that and embraced Koltz. No. He was going to believe that. He believed it. It was too real not to be believable, and because it was banal it was true, real. Yes. But Jesus Christ, why was he not as surprised as he should be? It was obvious now that Megan was going to have to solve something, and she had solved it, and —

'Good, Janki Nath. Three glasses, that's it. Bring it in.'

He followed the Kashmiri into the room where Koltz and Megan were laughing together, and he heard Megan say, 'Ted, I've never felt so happy. Really. I mean it. I didn't expect this at all, and yet I'm not surprised.' She looked brightly at Bingham as Koltz took the bottle of champagne and Janki Nath left. 'I suppose I ought to cry or something, Tim, don't you think? That's what women are supposed to do in this kind of situation, overcome and everything. I will after the champagne, probably. Oh God, I feel — I feel . . . . ' She got up and came to Bingham. She embraced him, and as if she could feel the resistance of his hidden *jinn*, said, 'Do you wish us well, Tim?'

Yes. He smiled down at her, his arms sliding round her. Hell of a body, tight-skinned, smooth, the womaniser's grail. Yes, she knew he wanted to wish them well and wondered if he could in truth. She could read a man like a book, was reading even him, and he could feel himself being read as she smiled up at him, and he said, 'I'm delighted for you both. Let's drink to it.' He looked at his watch, and without even waiting she nodded, slightly annoyed, saying, 'Yes, yes, yes, Tim. We've got to go.' She frowned, looking straight up into his eyes, and said, 'Especially now I've got something to say to Chan. I'll have to get my lines ready, won't I?'

'You'll manage, Megan,' Bingham said, and they exchanged a knowing look, joking, serious, probing. 'Wait and see.'

'You bastard,' she whispered, smiling again. 'Tell me, Tim. Have you ever *belonged* to a woman? I've always wanted to ask you that.' Her eyes were roving over his face quickly, and he could feel the intensity of her curiosity, and could see the sincerity of her goodwill for him. He saw the desert of his life, all of it.

'Several times nearly,' he said. He listened carefully to what he was saying next. 'But I've never really had enough time to commit myself. Though this time — ' The champagne exploded open and the cork flew past them.

'Tell me in the car,' she said.

So like a bloody man, she thought as she turned to Ted Koltz. So like all of them — 'never really had time to commit myself' — to *commit* themselves, for God's sake, take time off from their work, their 'real' work, to screw the woman, lie to her, remember to love her. And their work. Even Joe, she had had to make herself admit, had showed that too. They screw you for about a year or so and then they have their work again, or another woman. But I'm *interesting*, she told herself, fascinating, in fact, let's fact it, and I've got *my* work too. Will Ted last? That's a good title. 'Will Ted Last?' Bless him. She touched his hand as he handed her the champagne. She remembered how Iris Tone had once said to her, 'I *hate* being a woman. Yes, I do. I don't know why. The bastard I'm married to, I suppose, though I've always been a bit of a tomboy at heart.' Defensive. Like Subhadra, another screwball. Yes, I've got my work too, she thought. Safe. Mine. My secret work, my real me. I'll never belong to any bloody man ever again, I expect. I love Ted, though. Funny, that. Get things straight tomorrow with him. No questions, no exchanging the sacks of rubbish called lives. No bloody fear. None of that. Lie your head off rather than any of that nonsense, but strange how she was already wondering how many wives Ted had had. Enough. None of that.

'Well,' said Ted, lifting his glass. 'As a dedicated moral coward all my life I ought to tell you, Megan, darling, that I'm glad *you're* going up with the Colonel to see you know who before I do. So you can give it to him straight. I don't know if he's going to believe you. But then is Roger going to believe *me*? So we're carrying this burden together. Right? We're going to run into a certain amount of flak. But tell me this, Megan. Is this really happening?' He looked at her intently, grinning, but anxiety in his eyes.

Just a simple little nod and a smile would do it, she thought.

Yes. 'To us, darling Ted,' she said, raising her glass. 'I'll tell you know who. He's married to a dead woman anyway, for life.'

'Can I look at my watch again, Megan?' Bingham said, raising his glass.

'I hate leaving Ted here,' she said to Bingham.

'Drink up,' he replied.

'I'll be okay, Megan,' Ted said to her. 'I've got a lot to think about, and try and believe.' He laughed. 'Come back here and we'll get tanked up. What do you say, Megan? Maybe Roger can be best man? Think he'll play along?'

They drank, then were silent, thinking about Croon. Then Bingham's thoughts passed to Megan: curious how she seemed to know Chan well enough to make that matter-of-fact statement about him. Married to a dead woman. Now he had heard it he knew it was true.

'Funny, I come to India to make a movie, then I'm not going to make the movie, but I've come here to meet you instead, Megan,' Koltz said. 'I wasn't going to come at all.'

Bingham sighed, audibly. Here we go again, he thought.

Megan said, 'All right, Tim. All right. Let's go.'

CHAPTER 25

'Get up!' Iris commanded. During the last hour she had sensed this coming, his collapse of will.

'I see we're in the foetal position,' she said acidly, and sat down at the foot of his bed. How she had learned to hate that expression 'foetal position', and his long explanations about its meaning. That was during his Freud mania, when it had been psychology and psy-God knows what all day for months on end. Again he had discovered his 'real bent' for a time — how he ought to have been a psychologist, a psychoanalyst. She had sent off for all the books and had then endured the most harrowing and shaming harangues, interpretations, diagnoses of her character, her mental condition, his own suppressions, tensions, most of them caused by her abberations. The mania had slowly burned down, flickered out.

His breathing seemed fast. She pulled back the sheet and saw that his face was shining with sweat. The 'cold weather' was ending but the heat had never bothered him. She got up and leaned over him. His eyes were closed. At least the sweat was real, the rest, the breathing and the curled-up foetal position could be just another of his performances. In his long struggle to dominate her she had learned to recognize a 'performance', but could never be absolutely sure. It had taken years for her to know that he was never sure himself. She knew that the aggression she felt for him, which could never quite become hatred, was part of her love for him, her possession of him as well. The contempt she could feel for him still caused her deep pain at times, and until recently he had still been able to work her up to join him in some new enthusiasm, some new path to failure — failure which he now discussed as his 'way of life', sneering and joking about it. Now, looking down at him, looking for a flaw in what might be a performance, and on the edge of an outburst, she said, 'What's the matter?'

311

He kept his eyes closed. He spoke in a low voice, like he talked in his sleep sometimes, but it was also the voice he could use during long, lying, self-deceiving soliloquies at night, after a row, she in one of the twin beds, he in the other. He could fascinate her with these exploratory journeys, talk her to sleep, wake her with a shout, and go on, about their inability to understand each other, about his absorbing study of his relationship with some new assumed self. He had genius, he sometimes told her, but for what? Would he ever discover what was waiting in him to flower? And then he would voice one of her hidden thoughts, like the astounding occasion when, discussing his awareness of this elusive genius, he had said, 'Have you ever considered, Iris, that I might have been a great criminal, that I'm simply a suppressed criminal genius?'

'My God. What makes you say that?' was all she had been able to think of to say in her shock.

'You've passed on your thoughts to me, that's all,' he had said, 'and they're probably right too.' She had denied any such thoughts, went on heatedly denying them while he smiled. He was always one step ahead of her in intuition, she had learned to accept that, but he was many steps behind her in will and determination, and she knew *he* knew that. But he could always spellbind her if her will was ever forgetful. He was trying it now, she suspected, when he said, still in the horrible foetal position, eyes closed, 'It's India that's done for me, Iris. I saw it all this afternoon, after you told me you were leaving me.'

Panic and rage arose in her at once, the will to fight against giving any more understanding, any more surrender to his clever, insinuatory megalomania.

'There's no time now for your philosophy stuff,' she exclaimed, desperately. She drew back from the bed.

He ignored her warning tone, the hint of frantic shouting to come. 'You know what I'll do if you do leave me, Iris,' he said. 'The question is — do you want it done? And again, why are you doing it? Because you want it done?'

It was an interesting question and she started to think about it. She sat down at the end of the bed again, afraid, elated, and unable to focus her mind on the several questions all wrapped in what he had just said.

312

'Well? What's the answer? Don't pretend to yourself. It's not the time for that. Now. Do you want me to put the questions again, or have you understood?'

Inspired, she said, 'Where are the keys to your desk?' A feeling of faintness came over her when he said, still unmoving from his position, 'They're over there on the dressing table.'

She had never been able to find them before. In the two years of hide and seek, never discussed, since she had so mistakenly given in to his insistent, determined wish to read the Woodberry manuscript, and held on to it, she had never even seen the keys to his desk.

'Ah,' she said. 'So that's it.' She understood. 'You're not coming with me to see the Maharajah. Is that right?' She went over to the dressing table and snatched up the keys. 'Do you still want an answer to your question?' she asked.

'Well — now you've got the keys we both know the answer, don't we? The one you'd give. I don't have the guts. That's the answer, isn't it?'

'You amaze me,' she said. 'Get up and come and face the Maharajah with him. Apologize to him. At least do that. For my sake.'

He stirred in the bed for the first time, turned over on his back and smiled at her. His manner was contrite, convincing.

'Yes. When it comes to the point, after all my efforts, I find I don't even believe in it.' He clenched his fists and shook them, still convincing her as he cried out, 'Why? Why, Iris? Because I haven't the guts? Or because you said you're leaving me.' But he spoiled it by looking at her, lowering his fists and saying, 'You're not leaving me, are you? What's the use? What's the point? I can't help being me. You can't help being you. Let's make the best of it. You've got your way. You've won this round. And I let you. What more do you want me to do?'

Playing with the keys, tossing them in her hand, she sat down at the foot of the bed and looked at him. He closed his eyes and turned on his side again.

'I was looking at a photograph of myself this afternoon, while I was packing,' she said. 'Taken in Bangalore during your leave — '

'June forty-four,' he murmured. 'During the Imphal show,

313

before I took the convoy of ammunition to Shillong. Remember that? Promised my captaincy — again. What a bloody hope. Yes. I remember.'

'I'm talking about my photograph,' she yelled. 'Not your captaincy or anything else either. Just my photograph. Do I make myself clear, Freddy?'

'All right, all right,' he said. 'Don't shout. Not now. I'm on the edge of a breakdown. I'm certain of it. Don't start crying. I'm listening. The photograph. Go on. Tell me about the photograph.'

'What do you mean, you're having a breakdown?' she asked.

'It can wait,' he said with a quiet bitterness. 'One can always put off a breakdown when there's a photograph involved, especially a photograph about the past. I know the photograph. That's your favourite one, isn't it?'

'I was beautiful, wasn't I? I was surprised today, looking at it again. What a life it is for a woman. All about looks. Now I'm becoming a riddled, wrinkled bag. God. God.'

'It's the mind that's important,' he said. 'The mind. The body's just a bloody nuisance. Listen, Iris, here's a question came into my mind this afternoon. Have you ever *liked* me, I mean anything about me? I don't mean my looks. Bugger all that. I mean the personality. Have you ever *liked* me?'

'You've never asked me *that* before.' She was frightened.

'Playing for time again. Playing for time. Answer the question.'

The most frightening thing he had ever said to her was an occasion about five years ago. Yes, no, six years ago because that was the year . . . .

'Answer. Answer.'

That was when he had said, in that grim, thin-faced, thoughtful way he had, 'It's just occurred to me, recently, that the human sexual act is so comical, degrading, ridiculous, I don't know what the right word is for it yet, that it's probably the reason some simple anchorite soul in some desert in the Middle East, some time before the Bible was written, invented the devil. You see, it would have to be the devil that invented such a — well, such an *unnecessarily* monstrous set of contortions for human beings to have to go through — while in public he's such a hypocritical, intellectual, dreaming aspirer to true greatness, with dreams so at odds with this private reminder of his animal degradation that only a devil could have thought it up for fun.' Something like that. She had found it running through her mind at least once a day, afraid of it, convinced by it, resentful of it, and had never slept with him since. And he had never asked her to since, either. But they both *knew*, she knew that, and never mentioned it. Even now six years later the thought of it could still crush her spirit. That was why she could never like him again.

She found herself in the living room, the keys in her hands, Freddy calling after her, 'You'll have to answer the question. You know that. I like you anyway. There. I don't know why either.'

'You'll never get round me again, you bastard,' she shouted, breaking into sobbing, and ran to his study.

'It's in the bottom right-hand drawer,' he shouted.

It was when she had the heavy red, leather-bound manuscript in her hands that she feared he might find the guts to do what she had always feared he might do if his luck didn't change, if some mania or other didn't make money for him. She hurried back to the bedroom and stood in the doorway.

'What do you mean — India's done for you?' she asked. 'You were nothing until you came here, and you were nothing until you joined the army in the war, a fifth-rate clerk in Calcutta. So what's India done to you?'

'The climate, everything. We'll have a talk when you come back.' He sat up and smiled at her. 'Eh?'

'Maybe *I* did for you, Freddy,' she said. 'Is that what you want to say?'

'You look quite scared, Iris.' He pointed and said, 'Light me a cigarette, will you?'

It was an intimate act he sometimes asked her to perform, and she usually performed it, knowing how a wifely wife should do it, sitting back with the match in her hand while the man puffed at the cigarette, pleased with this intimacy.

'I'm finished,' he said. 'Finished. I won't commit suicide. No. But I'm finished.' He lay down on his back and pulled the sheet up over his thin chest.

'All right. Then I won't leave.' Then she lit the cigarette and as she was handing it to him he said, 'That's up to you.'

Even now the bastard could not show his weakness, had to perform. And worse, wanting to say, 'Very well, then I'm leaving. Now,' she could not say it. Why? Why?

315

'You once said to me you could have been a great criminal. Do you remember saying that?' Hammer it in, go on, but don't shout, don't lose your temper. Do it the way he does it. 'And now you're frightened to see the Maharajah, after all your threats and all your talk, and after humiliating me — with your letter to him — '

'Don't forget the letter to that bugger Croon, as well. Get your facts together. So — and what's the result of all this talk, all these threats as you call them? I don't have it in me even to be a petty blackmailer. That's the way to put it. You never get it right. Never. *I* have to do it for you. Yes, I'm finished. And now I'm waiting for a nervous breakdown. Anything else?'

'I'll never understand you. Never.' The whole day exploded in her and she heard her screams. 'NEVER! NEVER! NEVER!'

'Remember when the servants used to come running when you screamed like that, Iris? Those days are gone. Bloody cynics, sitting in the kitchen and laughing.' He went into an Anglo-Indian cheechee accent, saying, 'Memsahib doing nut in bedroom again. Werry werry bad, my Gahd, and non-wiolent Tone Sahib following Gandhiji teachings in hope of getting just rewards some day — '

Laughing hysterically, though still in a nervous commotion, she hurried away from his cunning performance, for he knew what made her laugh, thinking, 'I'm stronger after all. *I'll* never have a nervous breakdown. Never. I've got my job to do as a poor bloody woman. Stick it out. But why? Why?'

The car was outside the bedroom window, and as she opened its door Tone looked out of the open window.

'I *might* come up myself. Now I'll tell you something. If I know His Nibs he's going to be very disappointed not to find Tone Sahib there tonight. I know the Indian mind, don't forget, how it works etcetera. And he's getting the manuscript free, after all. So if you think things look chummy enough then tell him I need transport. And I'll come up and do my stuff, whatever that might happen to be. What do you say, Iris?' He smoked while she thought about that. She was so bloody slow, had to grind everything over in her mind, seeing pitfalls everywhere, and always fearful, always anxious not to offend the great, her betters. He watched her trying to understand this new turn. She had quite a good mind, but ponderous, like her ponderous granite will, and she could be

316

as thick as a five-inch plank, once that mind was made up. It amused him to see her say now, 'But — but I thought you were afraid to see him — I mean how can you — '

'No, Iris. *You* said I was afraid to see him. I didn't. But when you say something you think everyone else said it instead. I'm simply saying that if things look chummy up there then organize the transport and I'll come up. There might be a piss-up, once he's got his hands on that manuscript. I'm just saying that I'm willing to join the party, if there's going to be one. Remember I've been treated like a pariah dog by that bugger, up to now. So feel out the ground. This could be the start of a new social life for me, my rehabilitation. Don't bother saying, "I'll never understand you, Freddy." You won't. Feel out the ground, that's all.'

She had often tried to humiliate him during these subliminal sexual angers, which she felt to lie beneath their long struggle, and now she tried again, telling herself that it was still possible to reform his character. Perhaps it was because she felt herself humiliated again by his smiling, insulting assumptions. Also, the love she had for him, diseased now though it was, demanded that she force him to 'be a man' and face the Maharajah with her.

He was about to increase the smoke-screen of talk he always used when in the deeper throes of his self-hatred, and she had come to accept it, pretend, ignore, but always loathing how it had destroyed her self-deception about him, her right not to understand too much. But he knew even that, she felt sure. And now it was her calmness which was worrying him, and it was speeding up his smiling, playful talk.

'Stop being a worm for a minute, Freddy,' she said, and he stopped talking, and was about to assume another style of his never-ending self-defence, poor devil, and she could not stand it, not just now anyway. 'Shut up for a minute and listen,' she went on, still calm. Must, must remain calm for this important delivery. 'Now, you've got two minutes to put your clothes on and join me in this car, Freddy, *and*' — she pointed her finger towards his face, extending her arm to do it, immediately recognizing its vulnerability as melodrama, for his banter, but he was still too surprised to bring on a new performance — 'any copies you may have made of any of this manuscript, bring that too. You've got two minutes, Freddy. TWO.'

He opened his mouth, just long enough to say, smiling again (and she thought, My God, of course, he's like an eel. His mind is like an eel). 'Or what'll you do, Iris?'

'I'll leave now and never come back. I'll have you thrown out of this house by the *Diwan*, and you can go your way. You can find some other woman to charm, lie to, fight, be weak with' — hearing her voice beginning to shake, which meant tears on the way, and shouting possibly, she finished quickly, managing rather well, she felt — 'I hate us both, Freddy. I didn't once. But you've trained me well, haven't you? I *mean* what I've just said. I want you to be a man and face the Maharajah. You're a mess, but you've made me one too. So we've got that in common. Yes, I hate us both, my God, my God. Now go and do what you know must be done. Or this is the last you'll see of me.' She saw the eel sliding about in his eyes, and when he said, feeling her for a little fun again, a little more time to think, 'Iris, don't you understand what you're trying to do? You want to be proud of me, that's all. Proud of me as a bloody man in front of His Nibs. *And* I suppose you want *me* to hand him the manuscript and apologize?' Again he was smiling. Another inspiration came to her, as she saw through one more piece of his ingenious mechanism, understood for the first time how many times he had *let* her dominate him while appearing to be amused by it. Her determination began to fall apart again as her mind stumbled about in the effort of this unwanted recognition. How could it be that he never seemed to care how much he revealed to her of the depths of his talent for self-abasement? Good God almighty, could it be love, trust, intimacy; his way of showing all that?

'No! No!' She moaned the words aloud, and at the same moment saw new hope in his eyes as she voiced this searing thought. She could never, never handle him, no, never. Oh, God. Not knowing what she was doing, tears rising, she turned and opened the car door, then heard him call, 'It's a deal, Iris. Two minutes — from now!' Let him make a comedy of it, then, she thought as she watched him hurry away from the window, shouting, in this new performance, 'One — two — three — four . . . .'

She got into the driving seat of the car, feeling spent, sickened with victory, but as always, conscious of her lack of that feminine subtlety women were supposed to have, that gift she

318

believed in and was born too cold-natured to possess? Could that be true? Or was it part of the mixed mind Freddy had left her with during his non-stop daily sermons during his Freud period? No, she knew it was something in her genes. Born beautiful but unable to have a conversation, preferring an argument instead, and she was unable for argument with this eel-minded man she thought she must love against her will. The will. Had she too much will perhaps?

He was staggering to the car with his burden of many hundreds of days of scribbling. Good God, and this was only a part, she knew, of the years of scribblings. The compassion she felt for him as he dumped the load of paper, it was nearly a foot high, into the back seat of the car, caught her unawares. She turned her head and looked through the windscreen at the stark beauty of the moonlit landscape, that Indian night she loved and which would always be alien for Freddy, for people like Freddy who had come to this land to take their tiny part in an already dying imperial pantomime. A fifth-rate boxwallah who had never been allowed to enter the sacred Bengal Club, until he got the temporary right once he was dressed up as a lieutenant during the war. Could it have been then when she had had her first worries about him, about the speed with which he had rushed into that club and signed his name in the book, then told her about it; so much more artless he had been then. She had refused to go in with him, to proud to let some little counter-jumping Englishman — who might know — whisper to another one, 'I say, wouldn't you say that woman's got a touch of the tar-brush?' Swine!

'Are you listening to me?' Freddy was demanding, sitting beside her now.

'Have I ever done anything else, Freddy?' she said as she started the engine, still looking through the windscreen. The words had come out lovingly. She was so surprised that she began to laugh, and even her laugh surprised her, it sounded so happy and carefree.

Before he could ask her what she was laughing about, and she could see the wonder from the side of her eye, she said, 'I was thinking how good you can be when you do that cheechee Babu accent. You have such a good ear, haven't you?' Then, taking up her battle-position again, added, 'Which often makes me wonder why it is you've never been able to learn an Indian language properly.'

319

He put his head in hands after that. She glanced at him as she put the engine into top gear. Well, he had quite a bit to think about, hadn't he? With the jolly British throwaway chill — so important to her once, she recalled, with other Brits from 'home' when 'putting things right' — she said, 'That's right, Freddy, dear. You think about what you must say to the Maharajah,' then, 'Courtesy costs nothing, after all.' Very clipped, authoritative, and *right*.

He was silent all the way to the Maharajah's bungalow, though he did sit back and fold his arms, which pleased her. As she cut the engine in front of the brightly-lit bungalow they heard loud laughter from within, male and female, and the laughter sounded drunken, quite wild and unrestrained. It drew them together for a moment, as if they were in the club, and they looked at each other questioningly. But she maintained her authority, mastering her wish to discuss their common nervousness as the laughter erupted again.

'You know what to do,' she said. 'Nothing must be said about this dirty mess you've made, Freddy, in front of whoever's there. We'll get the Maharajah alone. So leave the papers and the rest of it in the car, until you've spoken to the Maharajah. It's got to be done properly, and quickly too. I think they're a little drunk.'

'Anything else, Sar'nt Major?' he asked waspishly.

'Come on,' she answered. 'And let's see you give a performance. Do it right. Like a gentleman would do it.'

She was out of the car now and he followed her, complaining, as if he had lost his form. They eyed each other in the moonlight, his eyes angry, hers sparkling with false gaiety. A woman going into battle for her man, he thought.

The Maharajah was out on the verandah now, and so *jolly*, so welcoming, Iris felt as she smiled up at him. The threatening tears were gone. Her heartbeat quickened as the Maharajah called down to her. He did not *look* drunk.

'Well, Mrs Tone, you do look lovely. I hope you're in the mood for the finest punch you'll ever drink in the length and breadth of this ancient sub-continent.' He ignored Tone.

CHAPTER 26

During the drive to the bungalow Megan talked non-stop about what had happened to Ted Koltz and herself in the club, repeating every few sentences, 'I don't know what to make of it,' or, 'What am I do make of it?'

'I mean there we were, practically total strangers, and it was before I knew what I was doing I was in his arms kissing him. I feel so insanely happy, my God. What do you make of it, Tim? Don't answer. I don't want to hear anything negative, because I *know*. I can't explain it. I can't understand it. Very well, I've had a few drinks, but you know I can hold my booze, Tim. Right? Nothing to do with the booze. God I love him so much and I knew it all the time and didn't know it as well. What am I to make of that? Of course I was madly attracted to that gramophone record, Croon, any woman is attracted by a man who looks like that. And I was about due for a fling but thank God I woke up in time or I'd have lost Ted I expect. I wonder though. Am I behaving like a kid of seventeen? Impossible. But how can it be I'd never thought of Ted that way, then there I am in his arms, happy? It doesn't make sense does it? I don't want your opinion, Tim. I need to talk, that's all. I'm not worried. No. It's not that. Nothing like that. But after all I'm a grown and experienced woman with a brain and now this has happened. I'm so happy I'm frightened. But why? What of? I can't see any reason why it's there before your eyes and you don't see it and then suddenly there it is. Bang! Well that's what's happened. You saw it, Tim. We threw ourselves at each other and you could see he was just as shaken as I am. Poor darling he's probably sitting there in the club now and writing me a letter about am I sure I know what I'm doing — oh God, no, I don't want that. No letter. We should have brought him with us, Tim, but no then there's Chan to consider and it's going to be bad enough telling him without Ted being there as well. And Ted's scrapped the film here. I'll get the blame for that, you see. Yes, Chan'll blame me. The woman always gets the blame Christ what am I *saying*.' She laughed. 'Ignore that, Tim, though there may be something in it but then I've never been one of these bloody females who write to Woman's Monthly about their love problems. I can write Woman's Monthly with my left hand, d'you know that? Where was I? Oh yes, Ted and me in the club. I'm shocked by it in a funny way and at the same time I don't care what anyone thinks about it. I mean it couldn't be explained, could it? Now how'm I going to tell it to Chan? He said he loves me but I've never really believed it somehow. Chan's not quite real somehow. I don't know what I mean by that. He doesn't *need* anybody. That's how he feels to me. I'm worried about Ted on his own there in the club. I shouldn't have left him there. D'you think I ought to go back to the club and scrub this visit to Chan? No I won't do that. Can't do that. The cards have to be put on the table but if Chan wants an explanation what am I going to say? What would he make of it if I told him? I'm not really worried, Tim, it's not that. It's only that if I dared to write a story about what's just happened to Ted and me who'd believe it? Even in Woman's Monthly. I'll tell you a secret now. Only for you, Tim. Understood? I've always had this plan in case something like tonight happened with a man I knew I loved. I don't want to know anything about his past women. Nothing. Absolutely nothing. No questions. I mean I don't know how many wives Ted's had, do I? And I don't care. I'm never going to find out. And if he starts telling me I'll tell him the new rules. We start at scratch — AS OF NOW. No questions, no probings, no jealousies then. Just us starting off together and never looking back. Never . . . oh God.' She had just heard Saleema making a few suggestions, saying, ' "Looking only forward together, hand in hand, each made anew by this burning benediction . . . ." A-a-a-h! Tim! Tim! Stop the car please.'

He stopped the car and she wrenched at the door-handle, saying, 'I'm going to be sick, Tim. Please don't listen will you? Oh! Oh my God!'

She got the door open, Bingham saying, 'Have a good puke and don't worry about it.' He heard her stumble away in the moonlight, heard her wailing and then the sound of a despairing retching.

322

When she returned she lay back in her seat, her face white and sprinkled with perspiration.

'You're so kind, dear Tim,' she murmured, gripping his hand. He smiled at her, offered her a cigarette. As he lit the cigarettes she said, 'Seriously, what'll I say to Chan? How'll he take the news?'

'Play it by ear,' he said. 'He's had a few drinks by now. Have a few yourself. No man can advise a woman about this kind of caper, Megan, except a psychiatrist maybe. That's why they become psychiatrists, so they can get the chance to advise women about what no woman would listen to for five minutes from a man outside the consulting room. A man knows less about women than even women do — '

She fired up on hearing this and he drove on and listened again.

'That's all invented by men, that nonsense, Tim. Mysterious womanhood. It's rubbish. I've heard you, men, talking this rubbish, *you* know — about "who knows what a woman's going to do next?" and the story about "my wife likes tea and I like coffee so we compromise. We have tea". I can't stand that kind of male rubbish, Tim. Oh I know what you're going to say — "then what about tonight with Ted? Explain that one". But Ted did it too. We both did it. I swear we were moved by some force outside ourselves. And it was all so innocent wasn't it? So lovely and good and right. Oh God.' She moaned.

'Want to be sick again?' Bingham asked helpfully.

'I'm all right,' she said, fighting nausea. She was silent for the rest of the way.

As Bingham and Megan went up the steps onto the bungalow verandah, Balban appeared. He was naked except for a snow white *dhoti* which billowed over his shins as he greeted them.

In Hindi he said to Bingham, his black eyes glowing with happiness, 'Revelation has come, Colonel Sahib. The rain of wisdom has fallen on the garden of his mind. We are to go forth to eternal pilgrimage, wearers of ash, carriers of the trident, beggars for bread, wanderers of the eternal way. It is decided, and was decided before the drinking of the nectar which awaits you both.'

'You've come in time,' the Maharajah said as they entered

the living room. In his right hand was a half-full bottle of Cloud 29. He eyed them both, smiling his delight in seeing them. Balban brought two glasses and the Maharajah poured the heavy yellow liquor into them. Megan sniffed hers. It smelled of fruit and flowers and there was a faint scent of sourness, like that of *sake*. She tasted it thoughtfully, then said, 'My, it's delicious. What is it?'

The Maharajah told her it was made from a secret recipe, crushed fruit and alcohol with *charas*, the best of the hashish, simmered in the sun in huge glass jars for days and then stored in cool darkness. He seemed to be extraordinarily happy, calm but brimming with goodwill and serenity.

'Don't be afraid, Megan,' he coaxed her. 'You are a happy person and the *thandai* will only raise your mind and give you wonderful peace. For me this is the last drinking I shall do.'

'So you got it, did you, Chan?' said Bingham, pointing to the red leather-bound Woodberry manuscript which lay alongside a mass of other manuscript. 'Is that the famous Woodberry book?'

'It is indeed,' the Maharajah said. 'An now they are building its funeral pyre. An act of expiation you might call it. That wonderful woman, Iris Tone. She forced him to come here and to surrender the manuscript along with his own drivel about it. She dragged him here with his guilt, that worm, and I trod on him. He cried you know. Yes, he cried. That was the Cloud 29 I threw into him. He sobbed like a wicked child and asked for forgiveness, so I put him to building the funeral pyre.'

'Funeral pyre?' Megan said, frowning. She had finished the delicious drink and held out her glass for more.

'Who's driving?' the Maharajah asked her.

'I am,' said Bingham.

As he poured the *thandai* into Megan's glass the Maharajah said, 'How I have longed to read that accursed manuscript, and now I have it I have overcome the longing. I am about to cremate it unread. It is the biggest victory I have ever won, the conquest of curiosity.'

'And you've got the Tones out there building the pyre for it?' Bingham smiled and tapped his glass. 'How much of this stuff have you all drunk, Chan?'

'Enough. The cremation is symbolic, naturally. A burning up of my past, of my world.' The telephone was ringing. 'Let it ring.' He flicked his hand dismissively and went on, 'Tonight, quite soon, I vanish from your life, dear friend, and from yours too, beloved Megan.' The telephone stopped ringing and just then, from outside the house, came what sounded like the roar of a wild beast. The Maharajah, shaking with laughter, led them to the open window at the end of the living room, and as they looked out they saw, and heard, Iris Tone smack her husband across the face so hard that he went staggering away beyond the heaped pyre of branches.

'You fool,' she yelled at him as Tone came stumbling back to her. When he reached her she stroked his face and they heard her say softly to him, 'You have no strength, no will, my dear.' They went on heaping up the wood on the pyre, Tone hardly able for it.

'He thinks he is a tiger,' the Maharajah said. 'I've never seen that effect before. Whereas I am merely a little more my usual benign and tormented self.' He began to shout orders to Tone. 'Hey, you, tiger-boy. Come here.' Tone came running, giggling. He did not seem to recognize Bingham or Megan. Instead his goggling mad eyes were fixed on the Maharajah. He had drunk a whole tumbler of the *thandai* and did not know who he was any more.

In a mockery of barrack Hindustani the Maharajah snapped orders at Tone. 'Getting book and papers fast. *Jildi*. Putting on firewood. *Ek dum*.' He laughed to himself as Tone ran off to obey.

They all went out and stood round the pyre while Tone went to and fro until he had piled all the documents with the big red Woodberry volume on the pyre.

'Thank you, Iris — may I call you Iris now?' said the Maharajah as he lit the pyre. 'Thank you for all you've done for me.' It was her signal to leave. She came up to where the Maharajah stood. They stared at the leaping flames together. Tone knelt down before the fire.

'How could you do it, *Maharaj* Sahib?' she said in quiet wonder. He put his arm round her shoulder and whispered into her ear.

'Take a bottle of *thandai* with you. Balban will give it to you. Drink it tomorrow with your tiger. Train him with it.

Goodbye.' They shook hands and Iris called for Tone. They all watched him follow her to the car. They listened to the car departing.

'Tim, can I have a word with you?' The Maharajah beckoned to Bingham and they drew aside. Megan was singing softly as she stared at the blazing pyre. She was experiencing a bright, tremulous hallucination and she slowly backed away from the flames which had become, in her increasing feeling of ecstasy, so incandescent that she feared she would be blinded. She went into the house, still singing to herself.

'Anything you want or would like of mine, Tim, take it. Have it. The *Diwan* will see to it.'

They heard the phone start ringing again. 'Let me answer that bloody thing for you, Chan,' said Bingham. He sounded exasperated.

It was the *Diwan*, sounding almost frantic. What was going on? Why would nobody answer the telephone when he had what could be grave news for His Highness? Bingham let him carry on with his angry complaints for a while and then said, 'All right, *Diwan* Sahib. Tell me. What's the message?'

There had been an outbreak of violence in the countryside. Ten miles away. The Princess was involved. Two villagers had arrived on a motor-cycle with the news. There had been an angry meeting of the peasants who were threatening to kill the landlords. They wanted a share-out of the land. It had been promised them. The Princess had gone there with a member of the local Communist party, and believe it or not, had called the landlords to the meeting. Here the *Diwan*'s voice broke down, for he was close to tears now. The Princess had made a speech to the peasants, and the *goondas*, the hired thugs of the landlords, had attacked. The Princess was one of the badly injured. An ambulance and police had hurried to the area. He was awaiting further news.

Balban came into the room with the Maharajah. They were wearing old shawls round their shoulders and each carried a heavy linenwork bag slung on his shoulder.

Megan had climbed onto the sofa and had pulled a quilt up over her. She was humming softly.

Bingham made his decision. He put the telephone back on its old fashioned hook and shut off the plaintive grieving voice of the old *Diwan*. Pity the phone hadn't rung after Chan had departed, but still, a white lie here and there —

'Wrong number,' he said. 'So it's not the *thandai* talking, Chan. You're really on your way?'

The Maharajah smiled and shook his head. 'No. Not the *thandai*. I'm disappearing. I've practised disappearing in small ways during my life, but this is the real one. I'll have no name, no identity, nothing. Natural selection will be operating, of course, and I may emerge as a fully equipped and able nobody. That's the target anyway. And you?'

'Me? Oh, I'll have a few more drinks and who knows, Razia may kidnap me. It's the only way I can see us getting together.' He seemed to be quite serious about this.

Balban came and knelt at Bingham's feet, swiftly 'took the dust' and then rose again. He seemed to expect an instruction.

'Look after each other,' Bingham told him, a command. Bingham and the Maharajah embraced, slapping each other's backs in the country style, then drew apart. The Maharajah looked across at the sleeping Megan, then at Bingham.

'I should kiss her, do you think?' he said. Bingham shook his head.

'Just vanish,' he said. He watched his friend take a look round the pictures of his ancestors, then beckon to Balba Bingham followed them out into the moonlight, down i the garden. Balban was trying to subdue his excitement, li hound which had awaited this particular outing.

The two men moved off. They both turned and raise right hands.

'*Jai Shiv!*' Bingham called, raising his own right heard them laugh. They turned away again and b them disappear into the darkness.

Megan was so fast asleep, so relaxed by the *thandai* that he had to carry her to the car.

He managed to wake her as the car neared th she had had a most wonderful dream in whi understood all about herself, everything, remember any of it.

'I know,' said Bingham sympatheticall hashish. Sheer brilliance until you la much better.'

Ted Koltz came running out of Megan. Bingham nodded underst quietly.

He drove to the palace where h

near collapse. He was at his desk, the only light that from his desk lamp, but Bingham could make out the figure of Soda-wallah sitting in an armchair, a police inspector in khaki uni-form, and a man he had never seen before. From the accusa-tory harangue he was delivering, the *Diwan* quickly made it clear that this stranger was a member of the local Communist party. He pointed imperiously to a chair and Bingham sat down on it. The *Diwan* went on with his hysterical outburst.

The Princess was dead, along with several peasants and one of the landlords. A team of the *Rashtriya Sevak Sangh*, athle-tic young men of the far right-wing, had come down from the hills and cleared the area, being of great assistance to the police inspector, and had then gone back to their camp.

'And you,' the *Diwan* shouted, pointing at the Commun-ist, 'you dare claim again that the Princess was one of you, as you put it, and I will not be able to control myself. I'm warn-ing you.' He stood up in a passion, threatening with his clen-ched fist, completely out of control. 'You will never have our sacred country. I'm telling you. I will kill you myself if you ever dare claim the Princess as one of you, you son of a whore — ' His voice broke and he strained his thin neck, swallowing hard, while the police inspector whispered, 'Please, *Diwan* Sahib. Calm yourself, please.'

The old man sat down and covered his face with his hands.

While the inspector crossed the room to comfort the *Diwan* Bingham left them. As he drove home he wondered why his *jinn*, who had clearly indicated a disaster, had not steered his apprehension towards Subhadra. Dutifully he mourned her, regretting again the bouts of irritation he had vented upon her, able to smile now when he remembered her anging up a large portrait of Stalin and standing back to atch its effect upon him when he had entered her room. An air? Well, hardly. There had been one savage assault upon h other and then he had left. The rest had been politics of a which to think of even now aroused him to hopeless fury shame. She had tied his mind up in knots, played all kinds addening practical jokes on him, had once stealthily set his newspaper while he was reading it in a hotel lounge, another occasion had told his friends he had finally ted her to Communism. In the end he had run away, as no other description for it. He had sneaked off and

328

near collapse. He was at his desk, the only light that from his desk lamp, but Bingham could make out the figure of Soda-wallah sitting in an armchair, a police inspector in khaki uniform, and a man he had never seen before. From the accusatory harangue he was delivering, the *Diwan* quickly made it clear that this stranger was a member of the local Communist party. He pointed imperiously to a chair and Bingham sat down on it. The *Diwan* went on with his hysterical outburst.

The Princess was dead, along with several peasants and one of the landlords. A team of the *Rashtriya Sevak Sangh*, athletic young men of the far right-wing, had come down from the hills and cleared the area, being of great assistance to the police inspector, and had then gone back to their camp.

'And you,' the *Diwan* shouted, pointing at the Communist, 'you dare claim again that the Princess was one of you, as you put it, and I will not be able to control myself. I'm warning you.' He stood up in a passion, threatening with his clenched fist, completely out of control. 'You will never have our sacred country. I'm telling you. I will kill you myself if you ever dare claim the Princess as one of you, you son of a whore — ' His voice broke and he strained his thin neck, swallowing hard, while the police inspector whispered, 'Please, *Diwan* Sahib. Calm yourself, please.'

The old man sat down and covered his face with his hands.

While the inspector crossed the room to comfort the *Diwan* Bingham left them. As he drove home he wondered why his *jinn*, who had clearly indicated a disaster, had not steered his apprehension towards Subhadra. Dutifully he mourned her, regretting again the bouts of irritation he had vented upon her, able to smile now when he remembered her hanging up a large portrait of Stalin and standing back to watch its effect upon him when he had entered her room. An affair? Well, hardly. There had been one savage assault upon each other and then he had left. The rest had been politics of a sort which to think of even now aroused him to hopeless fury and shame. She had tied his mind up in knots, played all kinds of maddening practical jokes on him, had once stealthily set fire to his newspaper while he was reading it in a hotel lounge, an on another occasion had told his friends he had finally converted her to Communism. In the end he had run away, there was no other description for it. He had sneaked off and

'Wrong number,' he said. 'So it's not the *thandai* talking, Chan. You're really on your way?'

The Maharajah smiled and shook his head. 'No. Not the *thandai*. I'm disappearing. I've practised disappearing in small ways during my life, but this is the real one. I'll have no name, no identity, nothing. Natural selection will be operating, of course, and I may emerge as a fully equipped and able nobody. That's the target anyway. And you?'

'Me? Oh, I'll have a few more drinks and who knows, Razia may kidnap me. It's the only way I can see us getting together.' He seemed to be quite serious about this.

Balban came and knelt at Bingham's feet, swiftly 'took the dust' and then rose again. He seemed to expect an instruction.

'Look after each other,' Bingham told him, a command. Bingham and the Maharajah embraced, slapping each other's backs in the country style, then drew apart. The Maharajah looked across at the sleeping Megan, then at Bingham.

'I should kiss her, do you think?' he said. Bingham shook his head.

'Just vanish,' he said. He watched his friend take a look round the pictures of his ancestors, then beckon to Balban. Bingham followed them out into the moonlight, down into the garden. Balban was trying to subdue his excitement, like a hound which had awaited this particular outing.

The two men moved off. They both turned and raised their right hands.

'*Jai Shiv!*' Bingham called, raising his own right hand. He heard them laugh. They turned away again and he watched them disappear into the darkness.

Megan was so fast asleep, so relaxed by the *charas* in the *thandai* that he had to carry her to the car.

He managed to wake her as the car neared the club. She said she had had a most wonderful dream in which she had at last understood all about herself, everything, and she could not remember any of it.

'I know,' said Bingham sympathetically. 'I'm the same with hashish. Sheer brilliance until you land again. Whiskey's much better.'

Ted Koltz came running out of the club and embraced Megan. Bingham nodded understandingly to him and left quietly.

He drove to the palace where he found the *Diwan* in a state

327

hidden himself in the house of a friend in Agra. Yes, she had broken him, no doubt about it. He laughed as he stopped the car, sat there and thought over his stupidities, his complete inability to cope with what he had so thoughtlessly started. But he had had much more than a nodding acquaintance with death in his life and he bade her farewell as he entered his living room and reached for the whiskey.

Though he had come in silently so as not to wake his servant, Hafizullah appeared in the doorway and saluted him.

Bingham gestured and Hafizullah came forward and squatted down before him.

He said that the Light of the Existence, the *Masjid Ababil*, the sweet swallow which nested in the mosque, had telephoned earlier in the evening. Unusual for a servant who had served a bachelor for years, Hafizullah not only admired Razia, he wanted Bingham married to her as well. Perhaps in this way he would be brought to make that longed-for submission and enter Islam.

'She is coming up from Delhi. She is bringing her father with her. So — you see, Colonel Sahib . . . . ' He left it there with all its implications, as much as to say, 'Well, when the father comes it is to plan the when and the how of it.'

'When?'

'She did not say. She asks that you telephone her, at any hour, it does not matter.'

'Thank you, Hafizullah. Sleep now.'

Hafizullah withdrew and Bingham poured another whiskey. His hand went out to the telephone as he prepared himself for the long slow-burning, provoking effort of making a call to Delhi. But he withdrew his hand again, sipped his whiskey and wondered: should he do it to Razia, inflict himself upon her? He snatched up the telephone and before he could hesitate again he wound the handle at great speed. He was through to Delhi in two minutes. Another occult occasion?

When he heard her voice he gathered up his whole life and threw it away, with all doubts, all havering and equivocation. It would be now or never.

'Razia,' he said tenderly. 'I have something important to say to you, but it is for you and me alone to share just now, and is not for the lanes and byways yet. I am about to make

329

my declaration. It is for you.'

'I am ready to listen, my king,' she said in Arabic. So perhaps she had guessed.

So he began the declaration of faith, belief, which he had nearly made when with the *Sanusiyya* at an oasis in southern Libya during a military operation in nineteen sixteen. He was amazed at the relief he was feeling as he intoned in Arabic — '*Ashhadu an la lilaha ill-Allahu wahdahu la sharika lahu wa ashhadu anna Muhammadan 'abduhu we rasouluh.*'

'Oh, my king, you have come through the doorway to me.'

He had just borne witness that there was no god but Allah, who was without partner, and that Muhammad was the servant and apostle of Allah. It was done. He was home.

'Wake Hafizullah and let him bless you as your brother, my king,' she said. 'Do it now. Now. He has prayed for you.'

He put down the telephone and called Hafizullah. He told him the news and his servant opened his arms and shouted, '*Allahu Akbar Allahu Akbar!*' They embraced and then Hafizullah had to go away so that he could weep somewhere alone, declaiming God's greatness as he went.

'Well, that's done too,' Bingham said into the telephone. 'Now I've got to have a name. Start thinking about it. What about "slave of Razia"? Abd-al Razia.'

'Blasphemer. We will find you a name, my king.' There was the familiar click as the line was disconnected and he was cut off.

As he waited for the telephone to ring he hesitated, for the first time in his life, as his hand reached for the whiskey bottle.

Blasphemously, he made the ritual of the most godless of men, the *beduin*. He poured some whiskey on to the carpet, whispering, 'One for the *Shaitan*, devil of torment, and one for me, the weak of spirit.' But he could not bring himself to finish the act and pour the whiskey. He put down the bottle and began to pace the room, reciting the ninety-nine names of God. There was something familiar in this situation and he laughed as he realized he was back. He was back with temptation again and with the war against it, after a lifetime.

He felt hope, fear, elation, but there seemed to be a true lightening of heart, a sense of belonging, like a link in a long chain of a will to reverence.

A will to reverence. But for what? The world. Not enough.

The universe? Too much, too vast, that geographic eternity which it seemed certain, judging by what was going on among the scientists, would soon be travelled in. They would, one day, be actually able to travel through what had been a religious word called eternity. It would become geography, examinable, mappable, writeable about, and the World, this tiny football, could be handed over to a travel agency for those who stayed.

All very well, these thoughts, but he knew they were part of a call to examination of what he had just done, that telephonic declaration of submission. Could it have been the very first telephonic declaration of surrender to a culture he loved so much, Islam? And was that enough, a surrender to the culture, a culture which he knew was already deep in schizophrenia, rent by a longing for everything the West had to offer, yes, even its trash, and a new will to purify itself, punish itself, strip itself, so as to return to that fabled, clean, trim, sure and vital world the Prophet had known and propagated? He had joined it at last because he felt all this, this love and compassion for a religio-culture never understood, and probably never to be understood, by the West?

He suddenly felt the tension in his pacing. He regretted what he had done. No he didn't. No, it was . . . . He went on to the verandah and called for Hafizullah, heard his sleepy answer, then went back to his pacing in the living room. When he heard Hafizullah approaching he quickly sat down on the thick grey Kashmiri felt covering the floor, crossed his legs and relaxed his arms across his knees, the hands hanging down. He did not wish Hafizullah to sense his crisis. Without a word between them Hafizullah understood, and sat down on the carpet opposite Bingham.

Bingham was silent, and let it gather strength, until Hafizullah said, 'You are troubled, brother. What is it? What can I do for you?' The sincere concern for him in Hafizullah's steady, unwinking black eyes, and the reliability in the dark, craggy face which hid so much experience they had shared in other times, seemed more intimate now, as if they were at last two Muslims, one of them about to voice a problem about the most important thing on earth, to a Muslim, belief, faith. He was fairly sure that Hafizullah knew he was already experiencing a visit from the Slinking Whisperer, the devil of doubt.

'Hafizullah, my brother,' said Bingham. 'You have had your troubles, and I have shared them with you.'

'Again and again,' Hafizullah said gravely. 'And again,' he added, smiling.

It would take a month to say why he had made that telephone call with all its even now unknown meanings, and about another six months to say why he wished he had never made it, and then a few years to explain why he was glad he made it if only he could believe in it and live up to it. So how to begin? He began a quiet attack, compressing all the thoughts he had been growing in his head with the years; 'and they are not about religion, Hafizullah,' he said. 'Understand — they are not about religion. They are about what I have been doing all my life, and about what I have just done. I have joined you, so now I can speak my mind, which is also *your* mind. Are you ready? We have spoken of it all before, but in a way that — '

'We have spoken guardedly, carefully.' Hafizullah's black, solemn eyes were now amused. 'Yes. Now we can speak. Brother — may *I* speak first? May I help you? Let us exchange our doubts, yours about God, and mine about the world?'

Bingham, relieved, nodded. 'Let us smoke while we talk,' he said, but as Hafizullah made a movement to rise Bingham raised a finger and said, 'Let it be my turn to serve? Yes?' He smiled and Hafizullah laughed and when Bingham had brought the cigarettes and lit them, Hafizullah began to unleash a cataract of the kind of thoughts which had beset Bingham for so long, a welter of words about dying Islam, how it must stay alive, how it must adapt itself to the shocks of Western discoveries, buy them, steal them, but somehow get them and share them, and most of all the education . . . .

Bingham stopped him by raising a finger. 'And still stay Muslim,' he said. 'Yes, I know.'

They had had a tentatively jokey conversation not long ago about Mossadeg in Persia, who had challenged the West about the price of oil. But it was about more than oil. Even so he ought to take this opportunity and say his so long-hidden piece, about the whole erupting cultural war, which had begun, in Egypt, in Persia, in India.

'The Qur'an,' he said. 'It was a fortress. For over a

thousand years it was the fortress of the Muslims. And now
—'; he stopped, worried, his eyes searching Hafizullah's.

'Say it, brother,' Hafizullah ordered. 'Say it.'

'And now it is a prison. It is a prison? You — we — cannot
hide in it and at the same time want all the things the West has
discovered, science, medicine, physics, games, everything
Islam is trying to afford to buy, from the Atlantic to the farth-
est Muslim village in Asia — and then decry the West as
materialistic, atheistic, lost, doomed.'

Alarmed as well as stirred, Hafizullah got to his feet and
stood back. Bingham looked up at him.

'I have said your thoughts,' he said. 'And the thoughts of
millions of — us Muslims.' He paused, and Hafizullah said,
despondently, 'It is all true. It is said among us everywhere.
We hate and want the West — '

'And believe and disbelieve in the God of the Qur'an.'

Too much too early in this brotherhood, for Hafizullah?
'Can I think, brother?' he said. 'Can I put my thoughts
together and show them to you? I love God. I wish to be
filled with the goodness of God. You know that, my master
for so long, and now my brother as well as my master. There
is so much I want to say.' His face was full of perplexity and
suffering. 'There must be a way. I have spoken of this with
Muslims when we were in Egypt, in the Yemen, in Persia —
but only secretly.' He sneered to himself. He was lost, and
Bingham tried to help. He rose to his feet.

'I have declared, brother,' he said. 'I too long for God. But
have I done right? I have told you I have no faith — '

'Leave it to the Light of Existence, to Razia,' Hafizullah's
voice rose in a kind of hyperbolic declamation. 'She will help
you. That is her task. That is why God put you in each
other's way.' He covered his face with his hands and spoke
through his fingers. 'If we cannot put the world to rights then
may we not put our lives right, and say nothing?'

Bingham had known for years that Hafizullah had been
tempted to join this sect, that *tariqa*, this heresy, or any
teacher of some new version of the long expected messiah, but
that he prayed regularly, and never missed one of the five
daily prayers.

'We will talk again, Hafizullah. You and me. We will exchange our most secret secrets.'

Hafizullah dropped his hands and laughed delightedly, like a child. 'Yes,' he agreed. 'We will help each other. While I help you to gain faith I will strengthen my own. That may be the meaning of our long association. The road has narrowed.'

Bingham said, 'Sleep now.'

When he had gone Bingham sat down again near the telephone. Nothing had changed. Perhaps all he had done had been to step noiselessly into the culture he felt so much for, and which he would take refuge in from the storm. But that storm was in his own being, he accepted that. It was about the bearing of eternity. Nothing more.

Short-listed for the
Booker Prize

SOUR SWEET
Timothy Mo

An intriguing and finely written novel of the enclosed Chinese community living at the centre of 60s London.
'Brilliant . . . classic comic scenes . . . an excellent book.'
Sunday Times
'Uncovers a vivid, densely populated city within the city, whose inhabitants have an individuality and energy that makes the surrounding English look very grey. More than a touch of early Dickens . . . has a flavour all of its own.' *Observer*
'In SOUR SWEET Timothy Mo has brilliantly combined the comic with the frightening.' *Daily Telegraph*
'The characters and atmosphere in SOUR SWEET are enthralling, and Mo has a deliciously gingery sense of humour.'
The Listener

FICTION   0 349 12392 6   £2.95

Also available from ABACUS

FICTION

SILVER'S CITY	Maurice Leitch	£2.50 ☐
SUNDAY BEST	Bernice Rubens	£2.50 ☐
THE TRIAL OF FATHER DILLINGHAM	John Broderick	£2.50 ☐
SOUR SWEET	Timothy Mo	£2.95 ☐
THE SIDMOUTH LETTERS	Jane Gardam	£1.75 ☐
GOOD BEHAVIOUR	Molly Keane	£2.95 ☐
CUSTOMS	Lisa Zeidner	£2.95 ☐
WHEN THE EMPEROR DIES	Mason McCann Smith	£3.95 ☐

NON-FICTION

PHYSICS AS METAPHOR	Dr. Roger Jones	£3.50 ☐
THE DRAGON AND THE BEAR	Philip Short	£4.95 ☐
THE SECOND STAGE	Betty Friedan	£2.95 ☐
MEDIATIONS	Martin Esslin	£2.95 ☐
THE BAD BOHEMIAN	Sir Cecil Parrott	£2.95 ☐
SMALL IS BEAUTIFUL	E. F. Schumacher	£2.50 ☐
GANDHI – A MEMOIR	William L. Shirer	£1.75 ☐
FROM BAUHAUS TO OUR HOUSE	Tom Wolfe	£2.95 ☐

All Abacus books are available at your local bookshop or newsagent, or can be ordered direct from the publisher. Just tick the titles you want and fill in the form below.

Name _____

Address _____

Write to Abacus Books, Cash Sales Department, P.O. Box 11, Falmouth, Cornwall TR10 9EN

Please enclose cheque or postal order to the value of the cover price plus:

UK: 45p for the first book plus 20p for the second book and 14p for each additional book ordered to a maximum charge of £1.63.

OVERSEAS: 75p for the first book plus 21p per copy for each additional book.

BFPO & EIRE: 45p for the first book, 20p for the second book plus 14p per copy for the next 7 books, thereafter 8p per book.

Abacus Books reserve the right to show new retail prices on covers which may differ from those previously advertised in the text or elsewhere, and to increase postal rates in accordance with the PO.